GRAVITY

A Mageri Series Novel
Book 4

DANNIKA DARK

Also By Dannika Dark:

THE MAGERI SERIES
Sterling
Twist
Impulse
Gravity
Shine

NOVELLAS
Closer

THE SEVEN SERIES
Seven Years
Six Months

ACKNOWLEDGMENTS:

This book is for every reader who has taken the long journey with me down an uncertain path. I have created this world, and you have brought it to life. Each turn of the page is a heartbeat, keeping the story alive.

Sacrifice only means something when you're willing
to give up everything for a greater purpose.
—*Twist, by Dannika Dark*

CHAPTER 1

"I can't believe I'm letting you do this," I said as Logan's hands cradled the back of my head and pushed it down.

"Hush, Little Raven. I'm an experienced male who knows what he's doing. Stay still and you won't get hurt."

"How long is it?"

He chuckled darkly. "Didn't anyone ever tell you that size doesn't matter?"

My chin pressed tightly against my chest as I listened to the *snip snip* sounds from the scissors behind me. Sadly, I'd been neglecting my hair over the course of the past year since my transformation as a Mage. Christian, my guard, had accused me of growing a new breed of cat on my head. He said if I didn't do something about it, he was going to put it down. Justus would have footed the bill for a hairdresser, but frivolous things had remained low on my priority list.

After I'd made a remark about it, Logan had taken my hand and led me into the bathroom. He offered to cut it, and I thought he was kidding until he lifted a pair of scissors from the drawer.

The last lock of hair fell on top of my foot. I stared in dread at the pile of black hair on the floor. The towel snapped away and Logan gave it a hard shake.

I lifted my eyes like one of those sad puppies at the pound, and Logan held a fist in front of his mouth, suppressing a smile.

Logan wasn't built like most men. His tall, V-shaped physique and sinewy muscle tone proved it. Not large muscles, just defined. Although it did seem like since I'd met him he'd filled in a little more. Broad shoulders, a confident gaze, and a unique face—masculine and predatory all at once. Especially with his deep-set eyes framed by a prominent brow. Yet when he smiled, it was nothing less than spectacular and I melted like butter in the hot sun.

His golden eyes lavished me with affection. The same savage eyes that could make the toughest man tremble in terror. Logan's fierce expression contrasted with his polite mannerisms. Those characteristics are what had made me fear him when we first met. A Chitah ran on instinct, and I could never underestimate for a moment how dangerous he was.

"Someday I'd like to see you with short hair," he said, tugging at the ends that fell just below my shoulders.

I turned to look in the mirror, unable to·erase my smile as I shook my glossy black hair. Logan had given me an angled cut with layers that suited my oval-shaped face.

"I think not," I murmured, brushing the tiny hairs from my arms. "Short hair isn't for me."

He watched my reflection in the mirror from behind, leaning in close to pull in my scent. I shuddered and spun around, pushing myself up on the sink. "How did you learn to cut hair like that?"

Logan stepped forward and set the scissors down. "In a family of males who are not mated and don't visit the barber?" He chuckled softly. "It's a role I took on for lack of options."

"Why not one of your brothers?"

"After Levi shaved our heads many years ago, we decided not to rotate the responsibility."

I softly stroked his jaw and wondered if Logan had done this for his mate long ago. He leaned into my touch as he often did when I initiated physical affection.

"You should quit your day job and cut hair. Sure beats a killer for hire."

Logan eased between my legs, sensually running his hands up and down my thighs. He smelled like a thunderstorm when he nuzzled my cheek, and I loved the smooth feel of his freshly shaven jaw. My hand caressed the nape of his neck, exploring all the soft spots. When I stroked his Adam's apple with my thumb, it stimulated an immediate reaction.

He began to purr.

Damn, I loved it when that man purred. It was intense and deep, like distant thunder or a well-tuned motor. That primal, seductive sound gave me goose bumps and made me want to curl up against him.

I reached around and stroked his long blond hair, tied at the nape of his neck.

"Speaking of haircuts," I said, giving it a tug. "This is getting a little long, isn't it?"

"Oh no," he said defensively and stepped back. When Logan folded his arms, he meant business. "That stays."

Logan's beautiful golden hair rivaled the length of my own. If it were a little bit longer, he'd be able to wear it in a braid.

"Care to explain? Who are you? *Samson?*"

Logan shrugged lightly and his arms fell to his sides. Chitahs were notorious for their piercing gaze, but I no longer felt afraid when I looked into his eyes. All I felt was a desire for him to say sweet words and make me blush. And he could still do that—turn butterflies into pterodactyls within my stomach. Within the black rims of his eyes that encircled the bright amber hue, I saw a man with a secret.

"Not a good enough answer, Logan. You promised we wouldn't keep anything from each other."

He traced his long finger across my bare knee and looked down thoughtfully. "It's part of the courting."

My head jerked back. "Huh? You never told me this."

He blinked slowly and lifted his eyes to mine. Logan's demeanor altered, and he spoke with honor and a hint of bashfulness—something I *rarely* saw in him.

"When courting a kindred spirit, Silver, the male does not cut his hair. To cut his hair is to cut his chances. Once the female accepts him as her mate, only then should it be trimmed."

"Is that symbolic, or do you believe it's true?"

"Do you think I want to find out?" His brows angled over his serious eyes.

"If this goes on for years, you're going to look like…" I tapped my finger against my chin, trying to remember that fairytale.

"Rapunzel?"

"Yeah, that's it. Or maybe the Winkle guy." I bit my bottom lip as Logan put his hands on the counter on either side of me and bumped his nose against mine playfully. I ran my fingers through his hair while he whispered something unintelligible against my neck.

"If you ever get locked up, Logan, just throw down your tresses and I'll save you."

He twirled a lock of my dark hair between his fingers, bringing the soft tendril to his nose as he drew in a deep breath.

"Do I still smell like lemon cake?" I asked. My fingers wandered along the tight muscles on his arms, sliding underneath the sleeves of his light grey T-shirt.

He suddenly crouched low and ran his nose along the length of my body—close and inviting. God, I loved it when he did that.

Smelled me.

What a strange thing to love about a man. The gesture felt erotic and the tiny hairs on my arms would stand up. With each inhale, his soft purr rumbled and I pulled his face close to mine, planting a soft kiss on his warm cheek. He caged me with arms that had once climbed a thirty-foot tree with blinding speed to rescue me—his agile body leaping from branch to branch as he held me tightly to him.

"Put your mouth on mine, Little Raven. I'm ready for a taste of lemon cake," he said in a deep and tumbling voice.

"Maybe I'm not so sweet," I whispered, wetting my lower lip with a sweep of my tongue.

Logan's eyes followed every movement, and he licked his lips in response. "I want your mouth… on *my* mouth. Do it, or I'll have to find something *else* to kiss."

His gaze wandered down the length of my body to where his hands were stroking my hips. A five-alarm fire heated up my cheeks and he burst out laughing, leaning in to give me a smoldering kiss. I nibbled his lip defiantly and he moaned as if he were sampling something delicious.

"Do you have more information on the labs?" he asked, switching gears.

The secret labs conducting experiments, attempting to create a mutant Breed. My Creator, Samil, had been involved. After his death, we searched his home and uncovered a list of names of children born from Breed experiments, including mine. Simon had done a little research and found that some of those children were still alive, but had been adopted out to humans when the scientists discovered nothing unique about them.

Samil, on the other hand, saw potential.

We were uncertain how many people were involved and what advances in science had occurred in the years since my conception. What if there had been a genetic leap with those human children as they aged?

"Simon's tracking down Grady, the man who seduced my mother into this whole thing," I said with irritation. "He might know if the experiments are still going on. Then again, he might not."

"You still refer to her as your mother."

I sighed and wiped a few stray hairs off the sink. "I know; it's a habit. Maybe she *was* afraid of Grady finding her someday, but she could have loved me. She could have tried."

He brushed his knuckles along my cheek and lifted the anguished scent from my emotions. "Sometimes love comes from those we least expect."

I played with the ends of his T-shirt, thinking how right he was.

"HALO is working on a special case by request of the Mageri, so Justus hasn't had the time to pursue this any further. I'm meeting with Novis later tonight. Maybe he has some good news." I rested my head against his chest.

"As much as I'd love to ravage my beautiful Little Raven, I must go. Leo is waiting for me at the Red Door and I suspect it's more than just a social visit." He kissed the top of my head.

I looked up and smiled. "Come here, Rapunzel, and give me a kiss that counts."

"All my kisses count," he said in heavy words, watching my lips.

Very slowly, I locked my legs around his thighs and a low vibration emanated from deep within his chest. Logan's tongue glided across my lips as he curved his hand around the nape of my neck, massaging ever so slightly.

He kissed me slow and hard. I caramelized in his arms, sweetening to his taste as he consumed me.

It counted.

"Well, this is an interesting change of scenery," I remarked, admiring the fifties décor within the diner where Novis chose to have our meeting.

A silver border trimmed the edge of our cherry-red table. Two juicy burgers rested on our plates, buns smothered in sesame seeds and exploding with pickles. Instead of fries, we opted for homemade onion rings. Novis insisted on old-fashioned milkshakes with real ice cream served in tall glasses, guaranteed to make my throat freeze. I removed the cherry and placed it on a napkin. Novis reached over and dropped it into his glass, pushing it down to the bottom with his red straw. The building looked like an oversized trailer from the outside, and the cook wore a large, greasy smock and a huge smile on his face. He was stout and round and looked like he enjoyed a good cigar. Rumor had it he made the best burgers in town.

"You changed your hair," Novis said politely. "It's quite lovely."

I touched it and smiled generously. "You noticed."

"If there's one thing I've learned in my extended lifetime, Silver, it's that you should *always* notice a woman's hair and compliment her when it changes."

"Now I'm not so sure if you really like my hair or if you're just trying to be polite," I said, eyeing him skeptically.

Novis laughed and his shoulders lifted in rhythm. He took a hungry bite out of his cheeseburger and a pickle fell on the plate.

With a mouthful of food, he said, "The office gets stuffy. I like to get out and brush shoulders with civilization once in a while." An onion slipped out and he frowned, deciding how to assemble his burger again. "Things change but stay the same. This hamburger doesn't taste like the one I had in 1950, and it sure doesn't taste like the one that I had in 1922."

"Better, or worse?" I asked.

He shrugged. "Different."

"We should do this more often."

The vanilla milkshake was killer and I savored several long sips. I started to dip my onion ring in ketchup, but dunked it into the shake instead. After a bite, I decided it wasn't good, so I stuck with the ketchup. Sometimes odd combinations worked together, so I always kept an open mind. Novis watched observantly and dipped one in his chocolate shake. Then he tried it with mine to compare.

"I should have gotten vanilla," he remarked.

"I guess no one ever told you about double-dipping." I glanced out the window at the street. "Look at the snow coming down," I said in awe. "I've never seen this much snow before. Justus said last winter was a mild one for Cognito. I can't believe it's come so early! Everything looks so… clean. And bright! Look how the lamps illuminate the street." I tapped my finger on the glass.

Novis stared, but not out the window.

"What?"

He gave a sideways smile. "Sometimes I forget. It's nice to be reminded of the simple things. I've seen a million snowfalls, and when you're as old as I am, the newness wears off. Seeing life through a Learner's eyes is as close as I'll come to recapturing that feeling of youth, but few are as enthusiastic as you. Now I know why humans choose to have children."

Which was an odd statement. Novis revealed he once had a family. Did men in those times only have children to pass on their names and assets? Perhaps children were a necessity for labor. Some subjects are too personal to broach over cheap burgers.

Novis shook out of his blue jacket. His face was fresh and young with piercing blue eyes framed by dark, angled brows. He had a strong nose like a Greek sculpture, and his face wore chiseled characteristics that had been filtered out of the generations over time. I once asked him how old he was and he said he couldn't remember. Maybe after a thousand years he stopped counting.

"We found Grady," he announced, combing his fingers through his spiked black hair.

My onion ring went down the wrong pipe and I began coughing.

Novis stepped out of his seat and slapped me on the back. Based on his technique, I had doubts he'd ever taken a CPR class. *As if* I could die from an onion ring. Nevertheless, I gasped for oxygen and washed it down with a few long sips of my milkshake.

"What? You found who?"

Novis slid back in his red vinyl seat. "Grady was the only name we were given, so we checked the Mageri records and found three candidates."

"Who's we?"

"Simon and yours truly, as I am the record keeper. One has been deceased for two hundred years, and the second is of African descent. That left us with the third, and he fits the profile of the man who handed your mother over to the lab that created you."

Well, that was one way to put it.

Created.

Not conceived the way normal people were. Yep, that's me: mutant extraordinaire. "Where does he live? Was he taken into custody? Did he admit anything? Where did you find him?"

"Whoa, that's a lot of questions, Silver," he said, holding up his right hand. "Allow me to savor my meal before you begin the Spanish Inquisition." He slowly chomped on a pickle and wiped his fingers on a paper napkin. "Grady resides on the East Coast. We haven't questioned him yet."

"He could have gone anywhere in the world, but he's here in America?"

Novis sniffed out a short laugh. "In the days of the early settlers, we stuck together because it was a dangerous time with humans. Over the centuries, society became more… civilized. We began spreading out and establishing territories. A Mage who no longer desires to maintain property will sell it directly to the Mageri, who pays more than the market price, to say the least. Life is long, so it's better to secure a number of homes. Eventually, everyone migrates back here. It's attractive," he said, waving a hand as if stating the obvious. "Despite our differences, we naturally congregate where our numbers are higher. The cities along the coastline have maintained steady numbers, but many who refuse to follow the laws of their elders have tried to create settlements in less Breed-populated cities. Territorial disputes still occur, especially among Shifters who have just been able to acquire land in the past century or so."

"Okay, thanks for the history lesson. What about Grady?" I sat on my hands, ignoring the food on the table.

"The point I was making is that while we have the world to travel, you can't keep a flame from a moth. Christian will assist in questioning the Mage. He's the only Vampire I trust and will be compensated for his services. Before you put the thought in your head, Silver, you won't be going. We don't know if Grady is still involved with the experiments, so I don't want him to know who you are. I've asked you here tonight because it's in your best interest to know about our plans, as they will directly affect you."

"In what way?" I rubbed my arms, too nervous to bother correcting him about the moth comment.

"For two nights, you'll be without a guard. This is a sensitive matter and is not Mageri protocol." He ran his finger across his lip contemplatively. "They like doing things by the book, and yes, sometimes we must conduct investigations that don't follow our own laws. It's imperative that every Mage believes in our system, but there are times when a delicate situation must be handled in an efficient manner. We don't always have time to gather all the facts in a… legal way. As my apprentice, I'm placing my trust in you for confidentiality. This would directly affect my standing on the Council if they found out what we're up to," he warned. "I didn't want you inadvertently finding out the truth and letting the cat in the bag."

"You mean *out* of the bag."

Novis averted his eyes to watch snowflakes piling up on the ledge of the window. The large wet ones stuck to the glass, showing off their unique designs.

"Christian was reluctant to take on this request because he is in your service." Novis scrunched his face and I knew Christian had given him hell. "We've secured his trust by ensuring that you will remain locked in your quarters on high security."

"Wait a minute. I didn't have a guard before I took on this job.

Why is there a need now? I'm not the Queen." I dropped my arms on the table with a heavy sigh and pushed my plate away. While there had been a few times I could have used a guard, the overwhelming majority of my days were uneventful.

"No, but being my apprentice puts you in a vulnerable position. I have trustworthy guards, but I can't afford to spare one or it might compromise the security of my people. It's a long process to acquire a replacement. In any case, a Mage couldn't offer the same protection as a Vampire."

"But a Chitah can," I pointed out.

He dipped his finger in his chocolate shake and lowered his voice. "Chitahs are excellent trackers, but guards they are not. There was an unfortunate incident some years ago when a Mage hired one as a guard. The Chitah flipped his switch and turned on the very man he was hired to protect. If you're about to offer up Logan, then remember that his feelings for you can be just as blinding. He would be no match against Tarek, for example."

Three puncture marks on the right side of my neck burned at the mention of Tarek's name. By no less than a miracle, I'd survived a Chitah bite, but the scar had never healed. Even after ingesting Vampire blood and receiving healing light from Justus, nothing would erase the evidence of that attack.

"A Vampire is not as fast as a Chitah," I reminded him.

He shoved an entire onion ring into his mouth, licking his thumb as he smiled politely at the pretty waitress who left us the bill. Novis dusted a few crumbs from his fingers. "Have you ever played the childhood game *Rock, Paper, Scissors?*"

"Uh huh."

"Same concept," he said. "A rock may tear a hole in paper, but paper always wins. There's a logic you follow with the Breed. We could also employ a Gemini since they have strength beyond even a Vampire, but Geminis don't work as guards and avoid complicated situations. Emotions trigger violent tendencies that could put the person that they're hired to guard in harm's way. And you *do not* want to be around a Gemini when they're angry." He waved his finger.

"Hulk syndrome?"

His brow furrowed, not understanding the comic book reference. "If you look at a basic fight without weapons, a Vampire can absorb our energy and it has no effect on them. They're strong, and therefore most avoid getting too close to one. A Chitah bite has no effect on a Vampire, nor can one track a Vampire by scent. Their energy is not detectable to a Mage, although there are exceptions to that rule. Christian has been doing what he does since we found him, and he does it better than anyone. His track record is impeccable, and he's saved countless lives. Is anyone perfect? No. But he's as close as it comes. When you are dealing with so many different situations and Breeds, there is always risk. You may have felt safe in recent months, but what you do not know is how many times Christian has protected your life without your knowledge. I cannot offer invincibility with a guard, Silver. I can only offer the best protection available."

"Logan *can* protect me, Novis. He's capable and trustworthy, someone who's come to my aid more than once."

Novis lightly touched the scar on his cheek shaped like a backward L. I could see why Adam thought of him as an exemplary Creator. He had a way of explaining things that made it difficult to prove him wrong, but our conversations were filled with patience on his part.

"Silver, you need to trust me on this. It's only for *two* days. Surely life with Justus can't be that painful?" His eyes went dramatically wide before he rolled them and I laughed.

"I guess not. I'll have Logan stay over if that gives you peace of mind."

"Actually, no. I'm requesting that he go with Christian as backup."

"Wait, hold—"

"Listen for a moment," he said, raising his hand. "Only a small circle of individuals are involved, and Logan is one of them. Leo is now affiliated with HALO, and they're working on an important case for the Mageri. He's highly respected among his kind and I don't wish to put him in a position that could jeopardize his standing. This is not official Chitah business, so it is customary for me to seek permission from the eldest in the family. I'm working very hard to bridge the gap between our people and mend those gates."

"Fences. Mending fences."

Novis laughed loudly, but it was short-lived. "I love idioms, but I can never get them right. Silver, it's a two-day excursion, and you should know that I empathize with your situation. It's not easy, and only children should be told what to do. But in all fairness, you *are* a child in our world. I promised that I would not be a restrictive employer, provided you had a guard to allow you such freedoms. I don't see a need to quarrel when our burgers are cooling."

"You do realize that Christian and Logan hate each other."

Novis raised a shoulder, indicating there was nothing he could do about that. "Leo is talking to him about it tonight."

"At the Red Door, where everyone can hear?" I asked in shock. *Royally stupid idea.*

"No, that's a ruse. They'll have drinks and then talk later in private. Stay home. Watch the snow. Read a book," he suggested.

Outside, the snow glimmered like billions of crushed diamonds blanketing the city. It didn't seem possible so early in the season, but I wondered if a large congregation of Breed and their energy influenced the weather. What impact did we have on the world without even knowing it? Answers I'd never have, but suddenly the world blossomed into an ocean of possibilities.

When I looked back at Novis, a distant expression filled his eyes as he gazed at the street. In the blink of an eye, the moment was gone and he pulled the red straw from his tall glass and sucked the chocolate from the other end.

"Adam won't visit us," I said, leaning back in my seat.

He pushed the shake away and wiped his mouth. "Adam isn't the same man. Events like that change us, and he hasn't been responsive to my suggestions."

"What suggestions? That he attend a party and put on a happy face with all his scars?"

Novis twisted his mouth. "Perhaps I am not as empathetic to such things, as I have been witness to a lifetime of suffering. The strong endure. I chose Adam as my progeny because of his bravery and resilience. He was willing to give up his life for honor, but now he cannot live his life with imperfections."

"He's *hurt,* Novis. Not just from being rejected by that tramp you kept in your house, but…" I shook my head.

I almost went blind, so I knew how Adam must have felt facing a future with a visible affliction. A Mage isn't born, but made of the strongest men. This is how our kind survived through the years—the best of the best. He would not just be treated differently, but his gifts would be rejected. I could see Novis's side of things because Adam had always been a warrior. But now he sat in the corner of the ring, feeling defeated by life and pummeled by Karma. Sometimes the worst beatings we endure are never the physical kind.

Novis pinched his bottom lip between his fingers.

"His talent as a Healer is no longer secret," Novis said. "There have been one or two who have offered to employ him, and I will not lie, it's out of pity. Despite the reasoning behind it, Adam should snatch up this opportunity to prove himself, but he's refused. It's an honor to be so young and selected for private services. I wanted his gift to remain a secret, fearing it would endanger him. But I'm recognizing that it could keep him safe. Adam resists. He locks himself away or spends hours running."

"Yeah, he always liked to run."

"At some point, a man must learn that running will get him nowhere. I will give him time, but I have no words of comfort and cannot coddle my progeny. He must stand on his own feet and find his way in this world, or else I have failed as a Creator."

A clamorous sound of metal pots rang out from the kitchen and Novis leaned to the side, keeping a close eye on the cook. The expression on his face reminded me of how ancient he really was.

"I'll keep you informed when Christian returns; we'll have a meeting and discuss whatever he uncovers."

"Has he left yet?" I peered out the window at the dark shadows between the buildings. The cold air from the frosty windowpane made me shiver.

"No. He'll leave tomorrow morning. Is there anything you think would be valuable to ask Grady?"

I looked at him appreciatively. Novis respected me, and that meant something. "Ask him if he loved my mother, and if he did, why he put her through that. I want to know what he got out of ruining her life."

Why didn't he take a woman *willing* to be inseminated? Plenty of women would have loved to have children, and some might have loved the idea that immortals existed. My mom lived with him for months, so why didn't he immediately take her to the lab? Why did he make her cross an ocean just to have her impregnated?

"You heard her, Christian." Novis's blue eyes were fixated on something behind me and I turned around.

A tall figure in a long black trench coat swirled out the door into the snowy night.

CHAPTER 2

"It's late for a checkup," Justus said to the Relic. His large hand ran across his clean-shaven head. Around the house, he normally wore cotton shirts. But tonight, Justus wore a blue dress shirt tucked into a pair of dark slacks.

Page lifted a scolding eyebrow in response to his tone, placing a slide beneath a small microscope that she carried in her oversized bag. She turned the focus knob and leaned in for a closer look. "Relic hours are unpredictable, Mr. De Gradi," she replied in a soft voice. "It's the only time I could squeeze you in."

Page La Croix had worked as my Relic after saving my life from a Chitah bite, and it wouldn't be accurate to call her a doctor since a Relic did more than mend the physical body. Ancient knowledge lived in a Relic's DNA, passed down through the generations of each family. They didn't have a prolonged life and were as mortal as any human.

I'd hung around immortal men long enough to know that some were abrasive and often objectified women. Page once confided how challenging her job had been in the beginning. Many either refused her services or belittled her. Relics worked hard to instill a trusting relationship with their clients that would last for the rest of their lives, but being bullied was not part of the job. Her partner had ended up with the difficult ones, but over time, she'd learned to stand up for herself. "*It's unfortunate, but if I'm soft and allow them to walk all over me, they will,*" she once told me. "*If they don't respect me, then I can't effectively treat or counsel them. Most Relic women have toughened up over time because of this.*"

She ran her hand through her choppy brown hair and moved the slide.

"Well, any ghoulies in there?" I asked.

"Still looks clean, Silver. I want to continue our checkups. Your situation was unique—not just surviving three Chitah canines in your neck, but the consumption of so much Vampire blood. Not to mention the healing light you borrowed from a Mage. A weird combination of factors was at play. I need to study and learn from it. I've never heard of anyone's eyes turning Vampire the way yours did, even for a brief period. It shouldn't have happened."

"Maybe no one ever had a cup of Christian."

Justus groaned from his corner of the dining room. It wasn't a room illuminated with electricity, but there were plenty of bright candles on the table to provide Page with all the light she needed. I could tell he was displeased with my comment; the visual of me necking with his former guard had probably scarred him for life.

Page sat back in her chair and pinched the inside corners of her eyes. It looked like she was running on coffee and a few hours' sleep.

"I'm going to take a sample to the lab."

"No," Justus cut in. He dragged a chair from beneath the table and sat across from her. "I forbid it. Review what you need to, but none of it leaves the premises."

"How do you justify that? We could learn a lot from her blood. She may have some unique properties."

"And what exactly is that going to do for *you*?" He let the words roll off his tongue slowly, like an accusation.

Her brown eyes met with his. "Not a man of science, are you, Mr. De Gradi?" She shook her head and dismissed his attitude, as if she'd encountered it a million times. "If you think I'm seeking out a Nobel, you can wipe that idea out of your head. Relics understand Breed genetics, but not *everything*. Humans have a better grasp on their own species than we do of ours. There is so much magic within us—so much *possibility*. Something remarkable transpired with Silver."

Page's eyes lit up; she was passionate about her profession and you could see it whenever she spoke. "We know that Breeds go extinct, but every so often, there's a genetic leap, and a new Breed is born. It happens. You know it, and I know it. Sometimes it peters out and nothing comes of them if they can't reproduce or pass on their abilities, but sometimes it sticks. We've never actually *seen* the birth of a new species from inception; they've just appeared over the years without knowledge of their origin. Wouldn't that be the most spectacular thing to witness?"

"It would, except Silver is a Mage," Justus countered.

Her eyes fell away and she rubbed them again. It was going on two in the morning and I didn't need a clock to tell me that.

"I guess it's up to my Ghuardian what I do with my own blood," I replied with annoyance, directing a frosty glare his way.

Justus shook his head, conceding defeat. "Take what you need, but only this once. Show it to no one else. You'll dispose of her blood once you have personally examined it under the proper equipment. If you are not skilled in that sort of research, then—"

"Don't doubt my skills."

Color bled into his neck and he laced his fingers together, resting them in front of his face.

She swiveled in her seat and touched my arm. "That's all I need tonight, Silver. Call me if you experience unusual symptoms or if something doesn't seem normal. No matter how small, I'm here for you. You're as healthy as a horse as far as I'm concerned, so I don't see a need to make these visits weekly anymore."

Those visits were on Justus's orders.

I couldn't help but notice the furrowed brow that appeared on his face when she made her announcement. Justus placed his large hands flat on the table and pushed himself up as if he might make an announcement of some kind. Instead, he turned around and went out the main door.

"Page, do you mind if I ask you something? Our books don't teach me half of what I discover through personal interaction."

"Books will only teach you so much," she agreed.

"Did you go to a special school for Relics?"

She smiled a little. "I went to Harvard. It's important to acquire a modern education, but school had to take a back seat and I dropped out. It would have been a waste of my life to spend it in school when I could be more useful among the Breed with my inherited knowledge. My life isn't as long as yours." She blew a strand of hair away from her face.

"You don't have kids?"

Her lips thinned. "No, and all Relics are expected to continue the lineage of knowledge."

"That's a lot of pressure."

She shrugged and twirled a pen on the table. "All Breeds who procreate have the same instinct of preservation. Relics are very ancient and because of our average lifespan, the importance of children is always stressed."

"Can Relics only have children with other Relics?"

"Well… we can't have children with *humans*. Relics may be mortal, but we have that spark of Breed magic—for lack of a better word—in our DNA. No Breed can procreate with a human. Nature seems to make small exceptions within the Breed, however. So I've heard, but it's very rare. It's preferred that we stick to our own kind in order to retain that magic and knowledge."

"It's been done?" I asked.

She tilted her head side to side. "Those who have made that choice are turned away among their own kind, and they are considered traitors."

"How are you a traitor? You're living a decent life, having children…"

"The magic cancels out when two opposite Breeds come together. We can only pass on our knowledge to *Relic* children. Full-blooded Relics. It's the only way to preserve our heritage and each family specializes in different things. If I had a child with a Shifter, the child would be neither Relic nor Shifter. In any case, it's rare. Our genetics don't mix easily and a pregnancy is unlikely."

"Those children won't inherit a drop of knowledge?"

She smiled. "That's the interesting part. It's muddied down, but they would acquire a little. They'd still be human, though, and no one wants their child to be rejected among their own kind. Not to mention a Shifter would outlive their child. We haven't done enough studies because interbreeding just doesn't occur very often."

The door swung open and Justus appeared with snow caked

on his boots and a dust of white powder on his broad shoulders. "Learner, set up the guest room. The Relic will be staying with us tonight."

Page's eyebrows nearly shot to the roof. "Pardon me?"

Ignoring her complaint, he ran his hand over his head, now wet from melted snow. Some of it dripped on the floor with a loud smack as Justus cranked on his internal thermostat. "The road is impassable and we have a foot of snow on the ground from the drifts. The sleet is coming in," he said in a baritone voice.

"Then I better get moving," she insisted, zipping up her medical bag. "I have an important client I'm scheduled to see in an hour. I swear, this is the craziest weather I've ever seen."

Justus laced his fingers around the handle of her bag and hauled it off the table. For a moment, I thought he was going to help her obligingly to her car, until he headed toward the bathroom. Guest rooms were upstairs, and if you took the secret lift in the bathroom to the lower level, you'd only find a few rooms, including a study with a foldout bed.

She bolted from the table and followed behind him—her arms swinging along with her hips.

"Wait a minute. Wait just a minute. Give me my bag; I'm not staying here. I have appointments that—"

"Can wait," he insisted.

I heard the bickering all the way to the bathroom and then it quieted. *What a turn of events*, I thought.

Once Page resolved to the fact that she wasn't leaving the house, I talked with her briefly and showed her how the elevator lift operated. She had work to do, so I headed back upstairs. I found Justus in the kitchen drinking a tall glass of water with a wedge of lemon.

"Did Novis talk to you?"

"Yes," he replied, taking a short sip of his water. "I've raised the security level and the monitors in the living room will remain on at all times."

Max strutted in and circled around his ankles with a meow. Justus set down his glass and stared at my panther boy, who started licking his wet boots.

"Ghuardian, I'd like to go outside before the snow melts."

He chuckled and rubbed his hands up and down his face. "Let me guess, you want to play in the snow?"

I scrunched my mouth. "I grew up in hell and we rarely saw winter."

"Tell you what—I'll escort you outside once it dies down."

"Gracias," I said, bowing to him.

Maybe this kind of thing got old for those who grew up in it, but I wanted to enjoy the thrill of throwing a few snowballs at his head.

I made my way downstairs and offered Page a set of silk pajamas. They were a make-up gift from Sunny after the embarrassing lingerie she bought for my birthday, which I returned. It was Sunny's way of giving me the middle finger because they were purple with giant orchids. We had an extra toothbrush and razor lying around, which I set aside for Page. She was upset that Justus wouldn't allow her to try to make it out of there in that beat-up Toyota of hers.

I grabbed an extra pillow from the closet, a soft green throw, and a pair of blue slippers. Justus ambled down the hall on his way to bed.

I peered in the guest room. "Page, I got you…"

Page was fast asleep. We hadn't turned down the bed yet, and it looked like as soon as she sat down and curled up, exhaustion consumed her. I draped the throw across her legs, setting the pillow on the floor in case she woke up with a stiff neck.

Justus loomed in the doorway.

"She's asleep," I whispered. "Let's go to bed."

The next morning, the house felt uncomfortably warm. Justus usually kept the thermostat at level Siberia, so I wasn't about to complain. The electric bill was doubtfully his motive because as a Thermal, he had the ability to regulate his body temperature. He never took my complaints seriously, only telling me about when *he* was a child, he once slept outside without any shoes during a blizzard.

Sweet cocoa warmed my tongue, but what a shame there were

no marshmallows left. Justus strode into the kitchen, sweating like a bull in his black workout pants and tank top. His chest and shoulders were ruddy, a telltale sign he'd been working out harder than usual.

"Who won? You or the punching bag?" I warmed my fingers around the cup, my mood ring tapping on the edge.

He lifted a tall bottle of water from inside the fridge, gulping down several swallows between pants.

"You should take a day off from that, you know."

"Just because you've been slacking in your training doesn't give me permission. I'm disciplined, Silver. You should try it."

I nearly spilled my drink when Page appeared in the doorway. I wasn't used to someone else being in the house besides Justus.

"I'd love an explanation of how I ended up in the bedroom at the end of the hall." She brushed a swath of messy hair away from her face.

My eyes landed on Justus, who was avoiding eye contact. There were two bedrooms on that floor, and she sure didn't sleep in *my* room last night.

Justus wiped the sweat from his brow with his forearm and crossed one foot over the other as he leaned against the counter. "Are you hungry? We should eat," he asked and declared, all at once.

I blew on the froth of my cocoa and slurped down another delicious sip.

"No," she said, massaging her wrist. "I'll pick up a bite at McDonald's on the way home."

We followed her into the living room and I plopped down on the long sofa, covering up with a red blanket. Max's tail stuck out from beneath one of the leather chairs, sweeping left and right.

"You're not going anywhere," Justus informed her. "The snow tapered off last night, but the roads are treacherous." He pointed at the monitors. "They rarely send the city trucks this far out to clear them."

"Look, I really appreciate your hospitality and putting me up for the night, but snow is snow. Frozen flakes of water are not going to keep me from getting back to my job."

Justus laughed boldly and chugged a mouthful of water. "You're mortal. If that *object* you call a car slides off the road, you could freeze to death."

"Not if *you* carry her, Ghuardian. She won't have to worry about freezing."

I gave a wide, toothy grin and immediately felt like running when he cut me a glare so sharp that it could have split atoms. He was used to the banter, but I crossed the line when I did it in front of company. Maybe the jaw-clenching tipped me off.

I leapt up and Max flew out from beneath the chair and skidded between Justus's legs. I snorted, watching Justus lift his knee and turn to watch him go.

"Ghuardian, I'm going to get dressed and head outside."

I dashed to my room—as much as one can dash going down secret lifts—and bundled up in a pair of jeans, a heavy white sweater, and knee-high black boots. Not the kind made for snow, but for coolness. When Justus had stockpiled my wardrobe, practical items for winter weren't considered. I lacked a decent pair of waterproof gloves and thermal *anything*. I grabbed my coat and tucked a black knit hat over my head.

When I made it back upstairs, Justus was stretched out on the sofa, already showered and watching the monitors on the wall. I glared at his snow boots, nylon pants, and thin shirt with long sleeves and a hood.

"Is that going to be warm enough for you?"

He cocked his head at my inane question. Justus the Thermal could go outside naked and enjoy a lovely glass of frozen margarita while sitting on a glacier.

Page came up from behind and looped her long white scarf around her neck. "I'll go with you, Silver. I want to see what all the fuss is about."

Justus lowered the security to allow us out of the house; stealth meant no one in and no one out. Once we got topside to his oversized garage that housed only a few cars, the door lifted and I ran into the snow. It crunched beneath my feet and I wasn't thinking about lifting my knees, so I tumbled facedown. Even with a face full of snow, I could barely contain my laughter.

"Holy shit, Page. Where's your car?" I yelled out, looking at a giant snowball.

"I guess that mound over there." She hiked through the snow in her flat sneakers and knocked off a chunk from the hood. It was buried in snowdrift. "Hey, can someone get me a broom or something?"

I heard the insistent crunching of heavy boots trudging through snow as Justus plowed his way to her side.

"Hey, Justus!" I yelled. "Why don't you just lay down on the car? That should—"

A snowball hit me in the face. Beneath his stoic expression was a hint of a smile. I wasn't supposed to address him by his given name while under his Ghuardianship, so that was my warning.

"Oh, it's *on*," I declared.

I retaliated with a few snowballs and he ducked, but the last one clipped the back of his head and Page let out a high-pitched, melodic laugh. When Justus turned his head, all I saw were teeth. The man was actually *smiling*—with his teeth! It wasn't the fake smirk or the wide grin he gave the women at the bar. I hated to dwell on such a thing, but Justus concealed his emotions and I rarely got a glimpse of the real guy beneath all the layers of Armani and cologne. He looked five years younger.

Justus began breaking up the snow and clearing it off the roof of her car. Page used her bare hands to clean the windshield, and snow covered her arms. Mine were already red and swollen from the biting air, so I cupped them together and warmed my fingers with a heated breath. The snow wasn't as deep in the woods, and branches hung low with the heavy weight of winter.

I scooped up a handful and tasted it.

"Avoid the yellow snow," Justus said without a hint of humor in his voice, which made it funnier.

I lost my balance and fell backward. As miserably cold as I was lying in a pit of snow, I took a moment to admire the silent clouds drifting overhead. My life had turned so serious that I needed to cut loose and laugh.

"Ghuardian," I panted, blowing out a white, frosty breath as I approached the car. "Do you want me to start digging out the driveway?"

I glanced at a yellow triangle hanging on the back windshield that read: *Genius on Board.*

Page had a sense of humor. Especially given that most geniuses wouldn't be caught dead driving that beat-up car.

He lifted his blue eyes toward the winding path. "No, allow me to take care of that. We should move inside and change into dry clothes. I'll work on the path later." Justus lifted his face to the sky, squinting at the billowy clouds. "I think we'll be okay," he murmured to himself, as if he could read something in the sky. Sometimes I got a glimpse of the man who had lived many lives, in different eras. How surreal to think of all the changes in history that Justus had witnessed in his lifetime.

Once inside, we stomped around in the outside hall to knock off the snow from our shoes so we wouldn't track it into the house. I collapsed in the entrance hallway, lying on my back.

"I'm exhausted." I unzipped my ruined boots. "Sorry to report that these are going into the trash."

"Here, let me help you." Page crouched beside my feet and gripped the heel, giving it a tug. I slipped out of my coat and shivered.

"Page, look at your hands," I said, noticing how swollen and red they were.

"It's fine."

Justus closed the door and towered over her. "Let me see your hands."

When she didn't obey, he crouched down and clasped his strong hands around hers.

A moment passed and her doe eyes lifted to his. "Is that heat coming from *you*? Silver made a few remarks, but I've never actually met a Thermal. That's really an amazing gift."

Justus wasn't very good at containing an emotion called pride. It showed in the subtle way that he straightened his back and his eyes glittered.

She pulled away. "It stings… maybe too much heat."

At the break in contact, Justus stood up, grabbed the pile of wet clothes, and left the room.

"You have free rein over my closet, Page. I'll throw your clothes in the dryer, but we're pretty close to the same size if you want to borrow mine."

She tugged at my other boot and I peeled off my socks. "You're very kind, Silver. Don't ever lose that quality with age. Even some of the Learners that I meet have an air of superiority about them, as if they are the *chosen ones*." She unlaced her shoes and threw her wet socks beside mine.

"Probably because they *were* chosen." Her eyes latched on to mine in surprise. "My Creator made me against my will. I choose my life now, but I wasn't a *chosen one*." I emphasized my words by using my fingers to make quotation marks in the air. "That's why I'm like one of those wild stallions—always running off and kicking my heels. At least, that's what Justus tells me. This is my life now, but you have to admit we have some pretty ridiculous rules."

"And Justus took you in? It just seems so…"

"Unlike him? I know. I thought he was a prick when I met him too."

She smothered a laugh and pulled off her scarf.

"He's an honorable man who wants to do the right thing," I said. "You get used to his personality after a while and eventually learn to love the grumpiness that is Justus."

Page stood up, pulling off her coat. "If you say so. I'm going to switch out of these jeans before they adhere to my legs."

"Do you ever go out?" I asked out of curiosity. "For fun."

"Umm, on occasion. Why?"

"Just wondering if you'd like to do a girls' night out with me and Sunny. I'd love to have some of those again. Being surrounded by all this testosterone just isn't good chicken soup for the soul."

Page pressed her lips together and gave a short smile. For a bookworm who wore reading glasses and avoided makeup, Page shined in her own lovely way. Her light brown hair had an edgy cut that tapered off around her neck and a long swoop of bangs parted on the side. It was a practical haircut for a woman who didn't like fussing over her appearance. Page had feminine features with delicate hands, and an elfin smile that reminded me of Finn.

"I might enjoy that, Silver. Sounds like fun."

CHAPTER 3

I
T WAS REFRESHING TO HAVE another woman around the house. Besides Sunny, I didn't really talk to many women as most of them latched on to my Ghuardian like Velcro.

Page spent the morning having consultations with her clients. Justus set up the webcam in the study so she could have virtual meetings. He disappeared for hours in a private room to work, and there must have been progress since he came out at one point with victory splashed on his face.

By afternoon, I'd heated up some soup and delivered Page her third cup of coffee. Once in a while, I passed by the room and saw her nose in a book. For reading, she wore a fashionable pair of black-framed, rectangular glasses. Strange to think I'd never have to worry about failing vision, suspicious moles, or the million other things average people dealt with over the course of their lives.

I lazily collapsed on the sofa, watching the snow on surveillance before flipping it to the aquarium screensaver. Large monitors covered the wall on the left, and while each ran independently, they could also produce a single image. When I realized that we could watch movies on them, I had paid a visit to the store and grabbed a bunch of random titles. Watching period pieces with Justus was painful because he'd always remark, "*That's not how it really was.*" He hated modern comedies and tolerated some of the action films. But I caught him standing in a quiet corner by the hall whenever I put on *Sense and Sensibility*, *Braveheart*, or something with amazing cinematography.

Justus shoveled snow for hours before coming back inside. He showered and changed into a cotton shirt with skintight long sleeves that hugged his muscular build. Not his usual color either, but white as snow. His beige trousers were a little loose but showed off his athletic legs.

His arms looked like they wanted to rip free from the confines of the cotton that was stretched to the max. Justus settled his weight against his right shoulder and leaned on the doorframe, staring at our faux fireplace.

"What's wrong, Ghuardian?"

"Why do you continue running coffee down to the Relic? You should feed our guest."

"She said she was too busy and didn't want me to go through the trouble. I guess she's not much of a cook and mostly grabs takeout or fast food; maybe a homemade meal isn't what Page is craving."

Justus turned on his heel and walked out of the room. I followed close behind as we went into the kitchen. Justus stood before the open fridge, staring at a bag of potatoes, deli meat, and a dozen soda cans.

I'd learned to whip up a few basic meals, but we often lacked the necessary ingredients. I wasn't a patient person in the kitchen, but I did make a good enchilada that Justus enjoyed. Logan made cooking seem effortless and often fixed me a meal when we were together. I loved the way he always needed to reach for something in the very place I was standing. He'd ease up behind me and kiss my neck as he pulled a spatula from a drawer.

Needless to say, I blocked the utensil drawer on a regular basis whenever he was over.

"I'll make omelets or something," I volunteered, pulling his arm so I could grab the eggs.

Justus bullied me toward the door. "Tell her to wrap up the work she's been doing and get off my computer. Bring her upstairs," he said gruffly.

I shrugged and went to the secret lift in the bathroom shower that lowered into the training room downstairs. Page scribbled in a small notebook, sitting behind the grandiose desk in the study. Justus had recovered a few things from the old house that weren't damaged by the intruders, one of which hung on the wall behind her. A sword.

"Do you normally work this much?"

She scrunched her hair but didn't look up. "It's my life."

"It's almost dark outside."

Page set her glasses on the desk, pinching the bridge of her nose. "I didn't realize it was so late already; without windows or clocks down here I lose track of time."

"Yeah, it's like a casino around here." I chuckled and leaned against the doorframe. "A Mage doesn't need a clock," I reminded her. "I'd love windows, but Justus has a point. He works for HALO and has good reason for the elaborate security."

I scooted up a chair and we chatted for a while. Page revealed that as an only child, her parents had placed an immense amount of pressure on her to have children. Relics had children because of genetic obligation and not for the sole reason of loving a child. Her parents had died many years ago, and the inheritance had allowed her to attend medical school for a short time. The cost became overwhelming and she'd eventually dropped out. I admired the dedication she had to her profession and her perseverance through everything. Page didn't elaborate on the details of her job because it would break the confidentiality of her clients.

It took a little convincing, but she came upstairs and as soon as we stepped into the hall, a strong odor made me wrinkle my nose.

"Oh shit," I muttered, running toward the dining room. It smelled like a fire had broken out.

My jaw hit the floor.

Food filled the table on the china plates we rarely used. Burnt toast, steamed vegetables, wine, and a large bowl of what looked like rice, but I wasn't sure.

Justus appeared in the doorway with a plate of chicken slathered in barbecue sauce.

"Leftovers?" I asked, taking a chair.

The plate tapped against the table as he set it down. Justus uncorked a bottle of red wine and filled the crystal glasses. I was astounded when the realization hit me. "You cooked this yourself?"

"Looks good," Page complimented, standing by the table.

Boy, she had *no* idea what a rarity this was. In the past year I had lived with Justus, he never once cooked a meal that wasn't reheated leftovers or cold cuts. This was like Halley's Comet, or spotting an unconscious leprechaun at the end of a rainbow with a pot of gold.

Page put her knee on the chair and leaned over the table, snatching a piece of toast and scraping off the black crumbs. She had a wildish look to her without her glasses on, almost like how I imagined a pixie's face might look. She had the impish grin and wide eyes, all she lacked was a set of fluttery wings and fairy dust.

"I usually just eat in the car when I'm between appointments," she said, almost talking to herself. After filling her plate, she read the label on the expensive bottle of wine and glared at Justus. "Aren't you going to sit down?"

He cleared his throat and shifted his weight on his right leg.

No. He wasn't.

Not until she did.

I watched with avid curiosity; Page was the only other woman I'd ever met who was not susceptible to a Charmer. Our gifts had limitations, and a rare few possessed something that negated our energy.

Justus was a sexual lawnmower who ate up the attention of every woman within proximity. What do you expect a man who's treated as a plaything to become? None of them cared what came out of his mouth, and because of that, he'd developed poor social skills with the opposite sex.

Page irritated him. Even more interesting was that he irritated her. His frustration with her comments, opinions, and actions was written all over his face. She didn't listen to him, or maybe "obey" was the operative word.

Justus looked like an ancient oak tree as he stood behind his chair with his arms crossed, waiting for Page to seat herself.

He wasn't being chivalrous or a hospitable host. He *liked* her.

Page gave in and slid onto her chair, sitting on one leg.

"What in the name of HALO is this?" I scooped a spoonful of a thick mash onto my plate and it made an audible smack.

"Rice," he said proudly, taking his seat at the head of the table.

"It looks like grits. What did you do to it? Or should I say, not do to it?"

"Those instructions are not accurate," he argued, flipping his napkin open. "Someone should speak to the company that fabricates them."

His cheeks flamed and he rubbed his jaw to conceal his blush, so I put a sock in it. Justus made the effort and that's all that mattered.

The tall candles flickered in the dining room, illuminating the painting on the wall behind him. Despite his inadequate cooking skills, Page went for seconds. Justus had thrown a frozen chicken into the oven, and I'd never tasted anything chewier in my life.

He was a man who enjoyed eating meat with his hands, but when I glanced over, I saw they were clean. Justus held the silverware like he intended to murder something, and a few jerky arm movements sent half his chicken onto the floor. He picked it up, dropped it on his plate, and looked at it contemplatively.

To my relief, he didn't continue eating it. Instead, he set down his utensils and leaned back as he often did when he couldn't eat another bite. The chair creaked in the quiet room.

"I never have time to cook," Page remarked, killing the silence. "I'm always too busy to figure out how to boil an egg. What I really need to do is to marry a chef." She arched a brow. "Especially if they can prepare a good steak or sushi."

"You and me both," I said, trying a sip of overpriced wine. "I'm lucky. The man I'm seeing enjoys cooking for me. Maybe it's customary with his kind, but I'm not complaining."

"I'm jealous." She buttered the crunchy toast and took a bite, spraying crumbs all over her plate. "Does he have any single brothers?"

Max slinked around my leg and I gave him a good scratch on the head. The lift in the bathroom scared him, so he mostly hung out upstairs. He'd officially claimed one of the chairs in the living room, which became the "hair chair." Justus balked about the litter, meowing, and even the revelation that cats shed whiskers.

Didn't matter. I caught him a time or two cozied up with Max.

"Do you not have a man to take care of you?" Justus asked.

Oh yeah, he was trying to figure out her *situation*. I smiled at my plate and listened astutely.

"You can't depend on anyone to take care of you, Mr. De Gradi. I take care of myself."

Justus replied in a baritone voice. "You don't take adequate care of yourself, so it would appear that you need someone to do it for you."

When she narrowed her eyes, her lashes looked like a Venus flytrap closing. "*You* don't need to take care of yourself because your light does that for you. The rest of us mortals have to make do with what we have. What use would I be sleeping away the morning when I could be providing invaluable services to the Breed? A person only requires a certain number of hours of sleep per night. I eat enough to keep me going, and avoid overindulging in the necessities."

"You spent all day in that room avoiding the necessities," he said smoothly. Justus placed his forearms on the table. "Consider this a vacation and set aside your duties."

"If I did that then—"

The alarms suddenly blared and Justus arrowed to his feet. Page looked at me wide-eyed as he hurriedly got up and moved into the hidden control room. I found him leaning over a monitor with a vertical line creasing his brow.

"What is it?"

"Maybe a deer," he said with uncertainty.

"Who the hell is *that?*"

In the upper left-hand corner of the monitor, a man was hiking up our driveway through the snow. A hood obscured his face so neither of us could identify him.

"That looks like Slater," Page said. "What's he doing here?"

By the time I turned around, Page had left the room.

"Who is Slater, and how does he know where I live?" Justus demanded. Arms folded. Looking pissed.

"Slater is my partner." She slipped into her coat. "He's a Relic and because we divide our cases and rotate shifts, we have to share information on our whereabouts. I called him this morning to let him know I'd return tomorrow, but *nooo*, he just wouldn't listen." She rambled on, almost to herself. "He can be such an asshole sometimes." The extreme manner in which she yanked her shoelaces told me she didn't care for him much.

A hard look rolled across his face. "He has no business on my property."

I grabbed a pair of Justus's oversized boots and clopped alongside Page as we went up to the garage. It required walking down a dark hallway and taking a short elevator ride. I tucked my hands beneath my arms as the garage door lifted.

Justus had cleared a path so that it was passable, but he hadn't made it all the way to the main turnoff. The man was a machine.

Slater kicked up snow as he approached the driveway. Fairly tall, sunglasses, and a short, scruffy beard. The closer he got, the more I noticed his smug look. His messy hair was an indistinct color of faded brown, and the stinging wind had reddened his cheeks as if he'd been slapped. Slater looked like one of those guys going on an expedition to the Arctic Circle. He squeezed his gloved hands and it made a gritty sound.

Justus stopped short and held out his arm, forcing us to stand behind him.

"Page, my car's up the road. Get your bag and we'll go," Slater said, blowing out a thick plume of frosty breath.

"I told you everything was under control," she said loudly. *Defiantly.*

Slater shook his head and took a few steps before Justus did the same, the snow crunching beneath his boots.

"You're trespassing, Relic. I want you off my property."

Slater sized up Justus top to bottom. Without looking away, he shouted, "Do what I say, Page. Go get your bag and we're leaving."

"I don't think you heard me," Justus growled.

"I heard you, Mage, but I don't give a fuck who you are. Got it? This is Relic business and I'll take it from here. We have clients waiting and work to be done, and thanks to you, we're days behind."

Page walked around Justus and hugged her arms. "Slater, I can't leave my car here. I've been able to keep up with most of my appointments through conference calls. I'll be heading home tomorrow."

"Are we gonna fucking do this here?"

"You don't own me." She emphasized every word. "Don't you dare just show up out of the blue and start ordering me around."

Page walked closer to make her words private, but we heard everything. I glanced down and saw the snow melting around my Ghuardian's boots.

"Are you seriously telling me, Page, that you want to be trapped in the middle of absofuckingnowhere? You should *appreciate* that I came all this way for you." Slater sighed with resolve. "Leave your bag here; I'll pick it up later."

Slater grabbed her elbow and she snapped it out of his grasp.

What happened next was too fast to track. In the blink of an eye, Justus knocked Slater to the ground, pinning him with his forearm.

"Do that again and I'll cut off your hand and mount it on my wall," Justus said in a placid voice.

"Let him up, Mr. De Gradi. He's right; I need to catch up with my appointments before we fall behind and upset our clients."

Justus twisted his neck around, creating lines in the back where the skin folded and stretched.

Page shivered. "I've got obligations. I'll pick up my car and bag tomorrow. Please, just get off him."

"Kind of a bite in the ass having a woman order you around, isn't it, Mage?" Slater provoked.

Justus pressed Slater's neck hard enough to make him gasp before rising to his feet. Little did Slater know that in that very spot, Justus had cut a man's throat.

Page left with Slater, and I got the impression that her clients were the least of her problems. She was in an abusive relationship with her partner, even if it was just verbal or manipulative.

Justus spent an hour sitting at the dining table, staring at the half-eaten food before he finally retired downstairs.

Hours later, I passed him in the training room, pounding the sin out of a punching bag.

CHAPTER 4

TALL MEN LOVE TINY CARS. Levi was no exception. It's one of those great mysteries in life, like where your missing sock went and why men in uniforms are always so damn sexy.

Girls' night out had been derailed. Novis called and requested a group meeting at the Red Door; Christian had returned with news. It was our favorite club and they'd recently added on a dance room. Novis made arrangements that would allow Knox entry, given the owner had thrown him out the last time for starting a fight. We all met up at Logan's condo to share rides, and Justus headed out separately in his Aston Martin.

Levi grinned from the driver's seat of his little red car as I stood on the curb. Novis claimed the front and I peered into the back where Logan and Christian sat beside each other. I was two seconds from taking the bus when Logan tugged me onto his lap. Novis had to pull his seat all the way up to the front to accommodate for Logan's long legs. Meanwhile, Christian looked like a panini sandwich with Levi's seat shoved all the way back.

This kind of outing required club gear—tall boots, a bomber jacket, and a sassy black skirt that fell just above my knees. Levi blasted the heater so high I unzipped my coat, leaned against Logan, and scooted down on his lap.

Big mistake.

Logan never wore aftershave, and yet he always smelled amazing. I drew in a deep breath and suddenly his mouth nipped and sucked on my earlobe. Despite Muse thumping on the speakers, the loud conversation about a badass movie that Levi had watched with Finn, and the sound of Christian's noisy candy wrapper twisting between his fingers, I could hear Logan purring.

Not only that, I could *feel* it against my back.

The car made quick turns that had me sliding all over his lap. At one point, his right hand settled on my upper thigh and each hard stop caused his index finger to press between my legs. Accidentally, I'm sure.

My heart pounded eagerly and heat flushed over my body. His mouth moved around my ear until he found the soft spot on my neck that weakened me. I arched my back and he grew uncomfortably hard beneath me. Logan scented my arousal and his entire body responded.

Levi flashed an irritated look over his shoulder. He had Logan's blond hair, except darker and very short. Sometimes Levi reminded me of a cop.

"Put a cap on that, Lo; you're burning my nose."

Logan lifted his left hand and gave Levi the finger.

The car pulled into the parking lot and when we got out and headed toward the club, Christian distanced himself from me.

Logan wrapped his arm around my back and lifted me onto the curb without breaking his stride. Moments like that made my heart flutter.

We walked past the line of humans hoping in vain to get inside. They didn't have a clue it was a Breed-only bar.

Novis led the way and the crowd parted. His status as a Councilman was clearly known among all—either that or he was a regular who liked to get his boogie on.

Levi suddenly halted and spun on his heel, causing me to crash into him. He gripped my shoulders and stared at Logan. "Fuck, my ex is here."

"Why is that a problem?" Logan asked quizzically.

"Because dollars to donuts he's going to confront me and start some shit in here." Levi's expression tightened. "I'll be…" He glanced around. "Shit, I'll just be somewhere. I'll come hang when he's gone."

"Wait," I said, gripping his brown jacket. "Which one is he? I want to see the idiot who let go of a good thing."

He leaned in and kissed my cheek, glaring up at Logan. "If this jackass doesn't mate with you, I will," he said with a wink.

I laughed softly and watched him disappear into the crowd.

We passed several Shifters, Vampires, and other Breeds who looked at our motley crew with skeptical eyes. Maybe the intimate way that Logan held me close offended them. I didn't care.

The new dance room was dim and attractive with dark walls and ample seating around the floor. Novis folded his jacket over the back of a chair across from Sunny, who was preoccupied making out with Knox at the round table.

I cleared my throat and dropped my purse on the table. Knox glanced up, wearing a proud grin and half of Sunny's lipstick. A few empty beer bottles were in front of him while Sunny worked on a bottle of orange soda.

"How's it hanging?" Knox greeted the men.

Typical Knox.

They exchanged a few words and I settled in the chair beside Sunny while Logan called over a waitress and ordered a round.

"When did you get here?" I yelled over the music.

She leaned in close and I could smell her new perfume. Logan preferred my natural smell, so I rarely wore any. "We got here over an hour ago. What took you so long?"

"Don't ask. Where's Page?"

Her strawberry-colored lips curved up into a *wicked* smile.

"What did you do?" I leaned in with a punishing stare.

"Nothing," she said in an innocent voice riddled with guilt. "That's a woman who needs to cut loose once in a while."

"Why am I having flashbacks of my twenty-third birthday?"

Sunny guffawed and everyone looked at her. "Girl talk," she said, shooing them with a flick of her wrist.

I scooted closer. "I still have to see her professionally, so I hope that you've been nice to her."

She snorted and plucked a cherry from a small dish, rolling it around on her tongue. "Jack Daniels was *real* nice to Dr. Page."

I sighed as she turned around and planted a kiss on Knox, his fingers threading through her wavy blond hair. When they finished, he had the cherry between his teeth.

Logan abruptly got up and stalked to a nearby table. He lifted a short glass from a woman's hand and dumped it on the floor. My mouth hung open at his impulsive behavior. After whispering something in her ear, he returned to his chair. The blonde stood up, angrily brushed the ends of her black dress, and slapped the man in the face.

"What was that about?" I asked, tugging on the sleeve of his shirt.

Logan angrily drank a swig of beer and put his arm over the back of my chair. "*That* was a Sensor. He swirled his finger in her drink and spiked it."

"How do you know?"

"I see it all the time," he said, scanning the crowd. "People shouldn't use their abilities to take advantage of others."

"How very noble of you, Mr. Cross." Not being sarcastic either, but I didn't have to explain myself because he could scent that kind of thing.

A sexy song rolled through the club and Logan slid his eyes over to mine. A little tension built up before Christian moved in and took a seat.

Novis suddenly announced, "Justus is here."

"*Feck me*," Christian exclaimed in his Irish lilt, twisting around in his chair.

Justus walked through the door and heads turned. What I immediately noticed was the bow tie. Not the large goofy-looking ones I'd seen on weathermen, but *vintage*. Only Justus could work a bow tie and make it the sexiest fashion statement imaginable.

Christian snorted. "I haven't seen him wear that tie in a hundred years or so. He thought he was the cat's meow when he went prowling about town in that thing. Jaysus, that dolt really kept it all these years."

"So what if he wants to look good?" I said in his defense.

"He only wears that when he means business. Down to business," Christian said, twirling his finger at me in a small circle. "*Lady* business."

"I get it."

Everyone rose from the table except for Sunny and Knox. As I moved around my chair, a woman on the dance floor snagged my attention. Her arms waved in the air and the lights switched to azure blue. She was captivating, dancing with a man who moved like a lion closing in for the kill.

"Oh. My. God." I spoke to Sunny but never took my eyes off the dancing woman. "What have you done to Page?"

Novis turned a curious eye and watched her sway to the music. He concealed a grin and said, "Gentlemen and lady, shall we? I'd like to have my dinner in private quarters. There's too much noise and smoke for me to enjoy a good meal."

The walls in our private room were impenetrable, blocking out all the noise in the club. Almost all Breed clubs had private rooms that were soundproof from a Vampire's ears. Christian tested it before we went in. It wasn't uncommon to use the rooms for a private party or a meal, so few people gave a second thought when someone made a reservation. Asymmetrical chairs the color of the Atlantic Ocean curved around like a horseshoe. Trays of hors d'oeuvres covered the black table sitting low to the ground. If not for the sconces illuminating the black walls, the room would have been depressingly dark.

We chose to sit at a round wooden table with leather-seated barstools. There weren't enough stools for Christian to join us, so he paced about the room and gave us a rundown of his trip. Sunny and Knox remained outside as they were not part of these private matters.

"So that's all Grady told you?" I sighed with disappointment.

Christian peeled off his leather gloves and stuffed them in his coat pockets before plopping down in a blue chair in the seating area. He had used his Vampire charm to extract information from the man who had taken my mother, years ago, to the fertility lab where I was made.

"Not quite." Christian ruffled his disheveled brown hair. His smile looked more like an invisible hook was tugging at the corner of his mouth. He still hadn't grown fond of shaving and always sported a scruff that wanted to be a beard when it grew up. "Your

Grady knew nothing of the experiments initially. He really did like your mum."

Novis sipped on a cup of coffee while Logan pulled his loose hair away from his shoulders and tied it with a band. Logan had gone as protection but wasn't privy to the interrogation that Christian held with Grady.

Christian went on. "The poor bastard had no clue his woman would be the first offered up in the experiments until they baited him. They promised the child would be his."

"His? A Mage can't have children, can they?" I looked at Novis and he shook his head with absolute certainty.

"They *told* him otherwise, and his curiosity and need to procreate got the better of him." He shrugged indifferently. "I suppose dear ol' mum was in for a shock."

"So he met my mom and it was love at first sight?"

Christian scratched his short beard and threw his feet on the coffee table with a thud, his dirty black shoes disgustingly close to a cheese tray. "I think he's been tampered. Em... scrubbed. Something's missing I couldn't get from him. I suppose it may have to do with how they met; perhaps it was arranged or he was given a list of women to find and they erased those memories. Maybe he kept your mom in hiding before he gave her up. He liked her, but he obviously didn't love her. Grady was your spark daddy," Christian said with a dark chuckle. "When you were conceived, it was known from the start you would be female. Grady said it had something to do with how they created the embryo—Breed magic and all that shite. That was to his disappointment, and he washed his hands of it."

"Because I was a girl?" I dropped my eyes to the table. "So I have an actual father, but..."

"Not quite, lass. You're not paying attention. Grady put his light in you, but he wasn't positive if he was your sperm da. You have mixed DNA. Hell, Silver, you're a fecking cocktail." He snorted and swayed his feet left and right on the table.

"Can we not laugh at my genetic flaws and my father disowning me because I'm a girl?"

It shouldn't have mattered, but it did.

"You're not a flaw," Novis assured me. "Grady provided us the location of one of their labs. They kept in contact with him over the years because of his involvement. That's why we suspect his mind has been tampered with and selectively erased. Perhaps they thought that Abigail, your mother, would one day try to contact him. They wanted to find you, study you. You were their first patient."

"Where's the lab?" I tapped my boot on the rung of the chair.

"Simon is there as we speak," Novis said, gliding his finger along his bottom lip. "He's doing what he does best. We might find out who's coming and going from that location."

Justus always had an opinion and his silence bothered me. I nudged him with my shoulder. "What's up?"

He lifted his cobalt eyes to Novis and pushed his unopened beer to the center of the table. "She has a father... who is a Mage?"

Their eyes met and shared an enigmatic moment.

The light from a Mage was as unique as a fingerprint, and even if that's the only thing I acquired from Grady, part of him lived within me and that's what they saw.

One thing that didn't escape my attention throughout our conversation was that across the table, Logan's face was painted with disappointment. I knew he wanted confirmation that I had Chitah blood in me. This would validate his claim as kindred spirit and more importantly, he could officially claim me in front of his elders. Chitah laws only granted us partial rights because I was a Mage, therefore we would never be protected by their laws since they did not legally recognize the pairing.

"Logan?"

He startled me when he abruptly stood up and pressed his fingertips against the wooden surface.

"Your Mage father is despicable," he said with restrained anger, his lips peeled back. "Only a worthless male abandons his young. Among Chitahs, it is the greatest privilege to have a female child. They are the givers of life and unite the family; it is an *honor* to bring a female child into the world." He struck his chest with a closed fist.

Logan's words weighted down the conversation.

Justus placed his hand across my back with a light pat before easing out of his chair. Either he was being supportive, or he actually approved of Logan coming to my defense.

An unexpected emotion surfaced—guilt. I'd never be able to mother his children if he stayed with me. In the end, he would want a family, and that was something I couldn't give him. Nothing held more importance among his kind. I touched my brow and turned my head away.

Logan inhaled a slow breath, reading all the emotions in the room. Immediately, he strode around the table and leaned in close, brushing my hair away from my ear. "I meant what I said, Little Raven. I would have you no other way," he whispered.

After the meeting, we rejoined Sunny and Knox in the dance room. Levi sat to the left of them, scarfing down a messy chilidog with cheese fries.

"Love these," he said with a mouthful of food. "You guys want me to order a round?"

My stomach turned at the quantity of chili sliding off the dog as he shoved it into his mouth.

"I'll pass," I said, taking the chair next to his. Novis sat beside Sunny, across the table from me, folding his arms. I couldn't help but notice a melancholy expression on his face.

Knox abruptly stood up and lifted Sunny's hand, pulling her out of her seat. They made their way to the dance floor, exchanging flirtatious looks.

"Now this I have to see," I said, pivoting around in my chair. Simon would just have to get the recap of the night that the Red Door came down because Knox was breakdancing. I was sorry he was missing this.

Knox slipped his strong arm around Sunny's lower waist and stood still while she danced around him.

Typical.

"Did your ex leave?" Logan asked his brother.

I turned around and reached for Sunny's bottle of soda to keep an eye on it.

Levi wiped his mouth with the back of his hand and licked his thumb. "Doubtful, but he never had all the right moves anyhow, so I won't have to worry about him showing up back here," he said with a private snort.

"Who broke it off?" I tried to be sensitive, as I didn't know how serious they were.

He took another wide bite of his chilidog and scrunched his nose. "I can't deal with Shifters who are wolves. They're too damn territorial. Maybe I need to find me a cat, or a bear." Levi wiped his hands on the napkin and smiled. "Dollars to donuts if I had me a bear, then I'd at least get the perk of a winter vacation while he's hibernating."

We laughed and clinked our glasses together.

"Excuse me," a man said behind my left shoulder. "Would you care to dance?"

Wow. Awkward with Logan right beside me. "Um, no thanks," I declined, glancing up at him.

But he wasn't looking at me.

"Hell yeah," Levi nearly shouted, shoving his plate forward and standing up.

I turned my blushing cheeks to Logan. "Well, that was embarrassing. I guess I don't have the touch anymore."

He lifted my chin with the crook of his finger. "You shouldn't rely on others to validate your worth as a woman. If it makes you feel any better, three males tried to approach you."

"Tried?"

His lips eased into a grin as he stroked my bottom lip with his thumb. "I stared them down and they changed their minds. You are a desirable female, but I'll be damned if I'm going to watch any man grind with you on that floor."

I lightly bit his finger and smiled. "Next time, *let them* ask me. A woman likes to feel a little fuss over her once in a while. I'm not interested in dancing with anyone tonight."

His brow arched. "Is that so, Little Raven?"

CHAPTER 5

J ACK DANIELS MAY HAVE BEEN *a strong drink, but it only took one shot of Green Dragon for Page La Croix to loosen up.* She rarely got out, so it felt great to let go of her inhibitions and dance. No stress, no work, no obligations. Just music.

Few people really considered the life of a Relic, knowing that their purpose was only one of servitude. Yet the knowledge that thrived within her made it difficult to walk away from a life that she was born to live.

Page should have never let Sunny talk her into the second shot. Being new to the club, Sunny had no clue just how legendary Green Dragon was.

Slater had tried to call her five times, so she turned off her phone. He had always been a control freak, scheduling appointments *for* her and deciding how to divvy up their clientele. It was as if she had no mind of her own around him. Page knew some Relics had it worse, so she was apprehensive about requesting a new partner.

The music vibrated through her body like a massage, and it didn't matter that she was dancing with a complete stranger. In fact, that made it better. He didn't know anything about her problems, and he didn't care. He also had a phenomenal smile—although she was too busy having an out-of-body experience to dwell on it.

"I'm a Shifter," he said against her ear. "You?"

"Relic," she said proudly, throwing her hands in the air and turning around.

Her black snow boots with thick tread on the bottom were great for winter, but not for dancing. Her feet were beginning to hurt.

Snow boots or not, Page was having a blast. Except the man behind her enjoyed his position a little too much; she should have known better than to turn her back on a Shifter, and based on his reaction, he was probably a wolf. It was an open invitation to his kind, and his arm hooked around her waist.

The crowd ahead of them began to part as someone made their way through. Flashes of colored lights sprayed across a sea of moving bodies until the only thing in her line of vision was that cantankerous Mage.

De Gradi.

That man rubbed her the wrong way with his arrogance and aristocratic lifestyle. Most of the older ones were like that, Remi being an exception—to a degree. He's the one who asked a favor of her to treat Silver after the Chitah attack. Remi was a Gemini and because of his dangerous nature, he was forced to close off his emotions, but in no way did he have a superiority complex.

Unlike De Gradi, who charged at her like a bull. Or maybe it seemed that way because she was drunker than a skunk.

"Is everything all right?" he asked in a controlled voice, threatening the man behind her with his stare.

Her eyes hooded and she smiled. "Peachy." The Shifter's hand tightened around her waist and Justus engaged in a staring match with him.

"Is Silver here yet?" Page wondered aloud.

"We have a table. Come with me," he said, offering his arm.

But Page wasn't ready to sit down. How often did she get to go out on the town *and* wind up dancing with a handsome man? Almost never.

"Let me finish out the song."

She shuddered when the man blew against her neck and tugged her short hair. If it's one thing she didn't like, it was a man getting overly familiar with her.

"Dance is over," she announced over her shoulder. "It was lovely."

"Not done," he said, still moving.

Justus caught the man's wrist and twisted his arm away from her. "You're done."

Page outstretched her arms. "No violence," she slurred. "I can smell the testosterone brewing, gentlemen."

A couple of hiccups made her pause, but the sickly feeling subsided and she turned around to face her dance partner. He had a golden tan and midnight eyes, and was watching her in a ravenous manner that made her uncomfortable. Most Shifters sought out their own kind, but they were notoriously territorial when it came to another man encroaching on their prize, regardless of what Breed she was.

Time for a new tactic. "I'd love for you to meet my two kids," she blurted out.

His eyes widened.

Page smirked. "They're five and two. They'd just adore you."

The Shifter took a few steps back and shook his head, walking away. Page knew how to get rid of persistent men through logic, not so much experience. Most Shifters didn't like women who had borne another man's child. They wanted to claim and conquer their women without any male competition. Children meant there was a father in the picture they wouldn't be able to get rid of.

Her feet were hot and she wiggled her toes and frowned. Page turned back around and saw a wide-eyed Justus staring down at her. Wide, *beautiful* eyes. They glimmered in contrast with his shaven, lightly stubbled head and hard features. His gaze was like finding a blue diamond in a war zone.

"I don't have kids, so don't look so appalled," she grumbled, waving a hand. Then she blew through her lips making a sound similar to a horse, followed by a snort and chuckle. What a joke. If he *only* knew.

"I think you should sit down, Page. You're... inebriated."

Page laughed so hard she bent over, clutching her side. A woman accidentally bumped into her and almost knocked her down before Justus caught Page by the arm.

"I'm having fun," she argued, standing up straight. "I'm also tired of men thinking they can boss me around, so you can clip that tone with me right now. If you want me to sit down, then you'll have to dance with me until I get tired enough to feel like sitting," she said in a soft and playful voice. "Otherwise, take a walk, Mr. De Gradi. I'm busy having fun. Nothing here to see. Move along."

A beautiful blonde in a slinky green dress floated between them to talk to Justus, so Page closed her eyes and began to dance. Slow movements this time, going with the groove of a popular song. Small strands of hair stuck to her face from the heat, and her red button-up blouse had come down three buttons so that she could cool off.

It felt strangely hotter, and the heat melted against her in a way that relaxed every muscle in her body—like being in a sauna. Page opened her eyes and gasped.

Justus was dancing with her.

Bow tie and all, that man could move his body in such a divine way that the gods would have watched in awe. Masculine, but not showy like the other men with all the bumping and grinding. He swayed with such a hypnotic and subtle rhythm that she couldn't look away.

Page touched the lapels of his suit jacket, peeling them back until it fell to the floor. His arm slid around her lower back and he reeled her hips in until their bodies were close but not touching. As sexual as his moves were, he kept a small buffer of air between them.

Air she was certain was charged with energy.

They moved in rhythm. She'd never felt this in tune—this in sync—with someone else. To the point where she wasn't sure who was leading whom. By the slow rock of his hips, Justus defined himself as a man of experience.

Of course he was. With his fat pockets, expensive clothes, angled jaw, and a confident attitude that many women would have fallen in bed with. He smelled better than any man she'd met, wearing expensive cologne imported by Adonis himself.

Here she was, drunk and ogling Mr. De Gradi, her *client*. Page reluctantly pushed him away.

Justus remained motionless, staring at her in such a way that made her touch the back of her sweaty neck with embarrassment. Then he did something unexpected. He lifted his left hand for her to take it. Confused, Page lifted her right hand, and he slowly closed his fingers.

"Now what?" she said with a short laugh. His right hand came around to her upper back, leaving a distance between them of several inches.

In the middle of a modern club, where couples were rubbing against one another like dogs in heat, Mr. De Gradi began to waltz.

Page clumsily followed his moves as he stepped forward, to the side, and back. She had never waltzed before but had seen it on television. Maybe it was the Green Dragon, or the magnetic look in his eyes, but Page danced and laughed, forgetting everything and completely letting go.

Until the heavy tread of her snow boot squashed on his shoe and she stumbled, almost falling on her back. But he caught her, and they stopped dancing.

Justus bent forward, lifted her off the ground, and threw her over his shoulder. She stared at the floor where he left his jacket behind.

"Let me down!" she yelled, slapping his back.

And without hesitation, he did. Justus set her down and she slid against his chest. The smell of his dark and wonderful cologne ended up all over her.

"I'm not a concubine," she huffed, straightening out her blouse. "Handle me that way again, Mr. De Gradi, and I'm afraid I'll have to deny you any further services."

His brows quirked and she noticed the crooked bow tie coming undone. "My apologies if I've offended you," he said. "Join us and I'll order you a meal."

"I can afford to pay for my own dinner, and aside from that, I don't think I could eat anything after all those drinks."

His lips pressed into a thin line and Page walked around the flustered Mage who held the attention of every woman in that club.

I stayed at the Red Door for hours and had the privilege of watching Levi doing a few illegal dance moves, trying to bait Logan onto the floor. Logan had no interest in that style of dance, but I teased him endlessly to give it a whirl. Page stayed long enough to call a cab and unfortunately, girls' night out was cut short because her happy hour had begun hours before mine. According to Levi, there had been drama on the dance floor. I missed out because Sunny and I were visiting the ladies' room. Levi didn't elaborate; it just became a private joke between him and Knox.

Page's phone kept ringing and she finally answered, yelling at someone on the other end as she left the club.

Sunny and Knox shared a slow dance in a dark corner, and Novis watched them for a while before heading out. Since Novis had left his car at Logan's, Levi drove him home and I shared a passionate kiss with Logan as we said our goodbyes near the front door.

I talked with Sunny and Knox for an hour, sending Adam a few text messages. He kept in touch with me a little more and wanted to know how things were going, even if he didn't feel ready to hang out with us. I was just glad we were getting on better terms again.

Eventually, the party wound down just after one in the morning. On the drive home, Justus shifted gears and made a right turn where he should have made a left.

The trucks had shoveled and sanded the streets until they had become a slushy mess. It was sad to see how ugly it became, all for the sake of us being able to drive to the grocery store. Snowmen of varying sizes and degrees of menace guarded the park. The kids had run amok, building forts and waging war against the snow people, leaving behind evidence of their battle.

The car slowed in front of a red brick building.

"Where are we?" I squeezed my bare fingers.

Justus threw the car in park and shut off the engine. I opened my door and stepped into a pile of dirty sludge that clung to my boot. When I tried to stomp it away, I slipped and landed hard on my rear end. Without a word, Justus gripped my arm and helped me to my feet. I wiped the street off my skirt while he walked up to the door and pressed a button. That's when I noticed a black bag in his hand.

"La Croix. Who is this?" a voice said through the speaker.

"Justus De Gradi."

She waited a few beats before answering. "It's late for visitors."

"Then we'll wait." He scraped his shoes on the stoop.

I glared at Justus. "She could have been sleeping, you know. It's moon o'clock."

The door buzzed and I followed Justus up a set of stairs to the second level. I didn't ask how he knew where she lived because Justus worked for HALO; he probably had the latitude and longitude for Santa Claus. The halls were frigid, and nothing about the building was upscale. The polished floors looked like something you'd see in a gymnasium, and the walls were scuffed and in need of a fresh coat of paint. Was this how a Relic lived? He stopped at one of the doors and rapped his knuckles on the wood.

A dark brown eye peered through the crack. "What are you doing here? I'm working," she said in a shaky voice.

"I wanted to be sure you arrived home safely, given your condition."

"I'm fine."

Justus had his hands clasped behind his back, still holding the bag. "If you're available tomorrow, I can bring you your car. You should be home so I can hand you the keys."

"Thanks, Mr. De Gradi. That's very considerate."

"I brought your bag. If you have appointments, then you'll need it."

"You didn't have to go out of your way. You two shouldn't be driving around the city in this weather."

Justus brushed his left hand across the coat sleeve on his right arm. "It was on the way home. No trouble."

"Oh," she said softly, staring at her bag. "Here, I'll take that."

The door creaked as she bent over and reached for the bag. When Page straightened up, Justus made an unexpected move that caused her to jerk back. He reached out and ran his hand through her hair, brushing it away from her face.

Revealing a fresh bruise on her eye.

She stepped back when Justus leaned on the door and forced it open. It looked like fireflies were dancing in the irises of his blue eyes. Page flinched when he reached out to touch her face and Justus stiffened.

"How did you get that bruise?" he asked in a voice that made me shudder.

"I slipped in the snow?" Sarcasm dripped from her voice. We

were all adults and it wasn't a mystery that someone had hit her.

Justus yanked off his coat and tossed it on the floor, revealing his dress shirt, sans tie. "Learner, bring me a bag of ice and a clean towel," he said, rolling up his sleeves.

I walked into the kitchen by the front door and reached into the freezer, cracking open an ice tray. I lifted a thin dishrag from a drawer and ran it under cold water, squeezing it out before wrapping up a few cubes of ice.

I found Page in a small chair in the hall with Justus kneeling before her. When I handed him the ice, he carefully adjusted the cubes and pressed it to her cheek.

"It's complicated," she explained. "I'm not the kind of person who allows a thing like this to happen."

"Neither am I," Justus agreed.

"Is Slater your boyfriend?" I asked. "He doesn't seem like your type."

"He thinks he is. When my parents died, he took over making decisions for me. I let him at first because I was in shock from their death, and he handled the funeral arrangements and finances. I was young, and he was a family friend. Slater has wanted to make babies with me for eons." Her eyes rolled a little and she shook her head. "My family has a lot of knowledge on rare Breeds and he thinks I'm an agreeable match with his genes. It's all very scientific."

Justus lowered his eyes. "Why did he strike you?"

"Spending the night at your house really provoked him like I've never seen before. It started an argument that's been going on for years. I didn't tell him where I went tonight, but he heard the club music on the phone. He's afraid I'll find someone else so he tries to keep a tight leash on my whereabouts." She ran her long fingers through the ends of her honey-brown hair and averted her eyes. "I got out of the cab and he was waiting for me. I said some things I probably shouldn't have because of the alcohol and he lost control."

Justus's arm dropped like a guillotine, slamming the ice on the armrest as he rose to his feet. "I'll pay him a visit."

"Oh, *no, no, no,*" she said, rising to her feet. "He's never done anything like this before, so there's no need to start World War III all on account of a bruise. He's not stepping foot inside my house again. I may have to work with him, but that's as close as he'll get to me. I'm not the kind of woman who lets something like this go. Hit me once and I will *never…*"

Tears glistened in her eyes and she turned her head away. Page had that familiar look of embarrassment, like she should have seen it coming and it was her fault for allowing it to happen. "Please don't do anything; it'll only make it worse. It's not going to happen again."

"You're right about that, Page." Justus allowed her to take the ice from his hand. "This *won't* happen again."

"Thanks for bringing my equipment, Mr. De Gradi. I'm sorry I can't offer you anything to drink, but to tell you the truth—I'm beat." A short laugh popped out and then she sighed heavily.

"Ghuardian, we've imposed here long enough. I think we all need some sleep."

Sometimes you didn't want all the drama, all the fuss, and Page had a lot to think about. I doubted she wanted to be chastised for not wanting Justus to rectify the situation with more violence. As chivalrous as it was, it could potentially make things worse for her.

"Page, I'm sorry about tonight," I said. "I thought it would be fun for us to hang out."

She smiled. "I really had a good time, Silver. Maybe next time we can just catch a movie."

"Sounds good." I looked at Justus, but like a bag of concrete, he didn't budge.

"Please," she coaxed. "I'm grateful that you thought to stop by and see how I was doing." Her fingers grazed his arm for just a moment. "Let me get your coat."

The air warmed ten degrees.

CHAPTER 6

"TAREK CHALLENGED FOR THE POSITION of Lord of his Pride... and won."

"He *what?*" I gasped in a broken voice. My heart raced within my chest as I looked at Logan beside me on the sofa in his condo.

I had assumed that when Logan met with his older brother, Leo, they were discussing the trip with Christian. That was partly true, but there were also major political shifts occurring within the Chitah territories.

I once raised suspicion that Tarek might have killed his older brother in order to secure his claim for the position of Lord. He was in a top-ranked family among his Pride, and only the eldest brother retained the right to challenge for the position of Lord. In Logan's family, Leo would be the one entitled to that privilege, should he ever choose to accept.

A Lord has authority over all his Pride. However, the Overlord rules all Chitahs. The frightening part was how close Tarek was to that rank, and his greed and treachery made his current position even more dangerous. Tarek's younger brothers had privately disowned him after he raped his kindred spirit, but now they were forced to heed his call.

"How can he be a leader after what he did to me?"

Logan shook his head angrily and the black rims around his amber eyes intensified. "You're not a Chitah, so nothing he does to you matters in their eyes. Female or not, we cannot impose punishment on other Breeds. Crimes like these fall through the cracks because leaders don't want to instigate war between one another. With Tarek in a position of authority, there's nothing we can do. He'll be in power for fifty years. Until the next open challenge, the only ones who have a right to challenge for his position are his brothers."

"Fifty years," I breathed. "What about your Pride? Did anyone challenge your Lord?"

Logan explained that each Pride alternates years so a complete shift in leadership wouldn't occur all at once.

"I'm not sure if Leo will go for it. We have a fair leader, although his views are old-fashioned. He's respected."

"Tarek can't come after you, can he? Now that he's in power?"

"He only has power over his own Pride. We're divided by territories, and he has no dominion over mine."

"Maybe his people will stage a coup," I said hopefully.

Logan slid his hand around the back of my neck and lightly ran his fingers against my sensitive skin. The oversized window in his living room loomed behind the sofa, offering little privacy from a curious eye.

"I wish there was more progress with Nero," Logan murmured. "It burns me to know he walks this earth."

I touched his wrist. "Justus said there are dozens of Neros out there, and eventually all of them will be caught." I paused for a few beats. "Eventually. We had a long talk about it and I see his point. I can't live my life for revenge, or else I'm not living at all. Someday..."

"Yes, someday. He's hurt you once, and I don't like that he's still free to do it again." Logan squeezed my leg. We couldn't accuse Tarek of associating with Nero to help bring him down because slander was punishable if not proven.

"How's Finn getting along with Lucian?" I noticed a small wooden carving of a cheetah on the table that I'd never seen before. "It's so quiet around here; I wish he lived closer so I could see him more often."

The Cross brothers had been rotating Finn between homes so they could each bond with him *and* his animal. Shifters and Chitahs—while similar in nature—faced different challenges. Chitah siblings often live within the same house or building when there is a sister to protect. Finn was a wolf, and it suited him to live in a pack environment. He had never received formal education, so

Lucian, being the brains in the family, tutored him.

"Little Wolf is doing well. He's got it in his head he wants to be a lawyer," Logan said with an unwavering smile.

"He does?" I asked, poking my head up. "Seriously?"

Logan nodded. "I wouldn't put it past him. He has drive that most men only dream of, and after what he's been through, he wants to protect those who the laws have not. The Breed can always use good lawyers."

"Ugh... Breed law. I should invite him over to take away all those bigass books that Justus keeps on his shelf. Our history is biased, making other Breeds look bad. Makes me wonder what you guys have on *your* shelves; no wonder all these rivalries exist."

Logan laughed and nudged his fingers against my rib. "I think we should encourage him, don't you?"

"Now that you mention it, we have to make sure our child gets nothing but the best in this world." I sniffed out a laugh.

The motion was so fast I could only gasp; Logan pulled me onto his lap and locked his luminous eyes on mine. A look of possession crashed through him.

"What's this about?" I saw the serious look on his face and dropped my humorous tone.

"Hearing you say the words *our child.*"

I swallowed.

Hard.

"Logan, I can't give you one of those."

"I didn't ask."

"Do you want them?" It was a stupid question because I knew he did. His former mate had been pregnant with Tarek's child and Logan was willing to raise it as his own. But maybe I wanted to hear it from his lips.

His eyes slanted away. "Having young would bring me satisfaction."

"I don't think you should waste your time chasing me when I can't give you what you want."

Several small kisses tenderly touched my lips, awakening the butterflies. "You're my lemon cake," he whispered across my mouth.

"Children would only be a scoop of ice cream on the side, but I don't require any. You're more than enough. You'll always be everything that I want."

I leaned back a little. "Then why the enthusiasm?"

He traced his finger across the small ridge on my upper lip. "Hearing your admission to sharing something with me in life, whether we can have it or not, *that* is what stirs the male within me."

I closed my mouth around his finger and gave it a little suck. He pulled it out quick. Awareness flared in his eyes, along with restraint. "I'm going to court you the right way, Silver. I've gone about it all wrong."

Remembering the intimate moment I'd shared with Logan sure didn't feel wrong, but it had weighed heavily on his conscience. He felt that he wasn't honoring the Chitah ways of courtship. I hadn't accepted his claim because that was as good as marriage. We had so many strikes against us—being mortal enemies, for one. Still, I craved him whenever I shut my eyes at night and thought of his body tangled with mine.

"Don't you want me?"

Logan's chest vibrated like a bomb about to go off. His lips fell across my collarbone and savored me like melting chocolate under the summer sun. I weakened at the feel of his soft mouth consuming the taste of my body. His kiss was insistent and rapturous.

"More than you know, Little Raven."

He lifted his warm golden eyes. I traced the outline of his strong cheekbones and curled my fingers around his ponytail. Logan nuzzled his smooth jaw against my cheek while caressing the side of my neck with his hand. It felt wonderful to be so close to him.

"How long do you think you can hold out?" I tugged roughly on his hair, pulling his chin up so I could run my tongue over his Adam's apple.

Logan's body responded whenever I took control—something a Chitah male was not used to, but it drove him wild. I slid to the floor between his legs and his entranced eyes dragged down to my mouth. With a swipe of my tongue, I wet my lips and continued running my hands up his thighs until my fingers curled around his shirt, slowly rolling the ends away from his stomach. Every move I made was dramatically slow, and I never looked away from the raw power pulsing in his eyes. It became foreplay, where the longer I held his gaze, the more aroused he became.

My lips kissed the soft patch of skin just below his navel and I smelled his skin and tasted his energy. Logan's breathing grew heavy and his hand trembled when it touched my shoulder.

"Silver, stop."

His words were caged.

I popped the button free on his black cargo pants and slowly pulled the zipper down. He grew thick beneath the fabric and I stroked him while trailing my kisses around his abs.

Logan gripped my hair and pulled me away. "I can't control myself if you keep doing that." His canines slid out and a primal gaze painted his face.

My tongue circled around the firm muscles on his stomach and he let out a ravenous moan.

My argument would not be in words, but actions.

I pulled the band down on his boxer briefs, revealing my first glimpse of him. Logan was beautiful, and my admiration stirred something prideful on his face. Some of his hair had pulled free from the ponytail, sliding in front of his eyes in thick strands.

I wrapped my fingers around his shaft. Every touch, every breath, every shift of my body against his would elicit a wild reaction in him. I looked up beneath my brows and we locked eyes.

Never stare at a man that way and not expect to feel swallowed up by his power.

Logan battled against his animal with every ounce of energy, gripping my hair to pull my head back. His breath was heavy, as if he'd run a mile. "I don't know what will happen. I've never done this."

And he hadn't.

"Let me do this for you," I whispered. "Technically it doesn't break your rules; it's not sex by your standard definition."

Before he could argue, I wet my lips and his eyes followed the movement of my tongue. Most female Chitahs weren't into this type of bedroom play for reasons I just didn't understand.

A unique spotted pattern, the color of honey and sand, rippled across his stomach and arms—something that occurred when a Chitah's emotions were heightened.

My eyes focused on his deadly fangs and we were both thinking the same thing.

"I trust you, Logan. I know you won't hurt me. Let go and give yourself to me."

I wrapped my mouth around the head of his shaft and Logan's switch immediately flipped. The bright golden-amber color in his eyes was swallowed up by obsidian black. I'd never felt more powerful than having someone as deadly as Logan look at me with dark, sexual eyes—completely in my thrall.

The wild Logan that ran on instinct watched me and the air between us charged. I took him deeper, gripping him at the base while he loosened his hold and stroked his fingers possessively through my hair.

I quickened my motions, taking time to outline every ridge and line with my tongue. Logan's fangs had slid all the way out and his entire body tensed. I felt his heart pounding when I stretched my arm out and placed my hand on his chest. The look of arousal on his face as I pleasured him was more exciting than I had imagined.

And yeah, I had imagined it.

Logan didn't throw his head back or close his eyes. He watched so intensely that I got aroused. His nose twitched and he took in a deep breath.

Now Logan knew that I wanted him too.

Suddenly, his phone rang. It was Leo's ringtone and his eyes flickered between black and gold. I released my grip and ran my hands all around his stomach, pulling down his shirt with a frustrated groan.

"Answer your phone," I said with a chuckle, tucking him back inside his briefs. "It might be important." If Leo was calling, it probably was.

Logan lifted his hips and reached in his back pocket. He turned the phone off, grabbed hold of my arms, and pulled me onto his lap.

I wasn't sure if it was a relief or a curse that I was wearing jeans instead of a skirt as I straddled him. I waited for his words—ones that always melted me. Logan admired me with his hands, and the simple stroke of his thumb over my eyebrow felt more intimate than any other place he could have touched me. The way the backs of his fingers caressed my cheeks, how he outlined my mouth with his thumb, and then Logan softly kissed the scar on my neck. A deep and wonderful sound hummed in his chest.

He slapped my hip playfully. "I think you've broken enough rules for the evening. Come on, my female. It's too late for you to be out and I want you safe at home."

"Mmm, I like it when you call me that."

Logan tensed and the rims of his eyes expanded. "Female… or *my* female?"

"Sorry, Logan. I know how important your customs are and I'm not trying to imply—"

His lips mashed against mine in a molten kiss and before he could slide his tongue in, he pulled back. "Imply all you want, my female."

"Walk me to my car, Mr. Cross," I said with a smile in my words.

Logan buckled me up in the cheap little car that Justus had recently purchased for me. And truly, it was cheap. I had refused to let him waste his money on something extravagant. Having Christian as my guard allowed me to zip around town and run errands—provided I kept Justus updated with my whereabouts. I still had to ask permission to use the car. I could never win with that man.

I hated to leave Logan in his condition, but better to leave before he scented my guilt. He wanted to do the honorable thing and court me properly, and I always seemed to be leading him down the path of temptation, like some kind of Pied Piper of Sex.

I dialed Page and waited for her answer.

"Hi, Silver. Are you in need of my services? Is everything okay?"

I laughed. "Yeah, just fine. Actually, I called to see how *you* were doing." I cleared my throat. "I'm sorry we barged in like that; I didn't know Justus was planning on stopping by."

"Don't be sorry. Look, I'm glad you called. I'm coming over in the morning to pick up my car, so let Mr. De Gradi know I'll be there no later than nine."

The back tires lost traction when the car turned a corner.

"Hello?"

"Sorry, Page. I'm listening. Are you sure that you don't want us to come get you? It's no trouble."

I heard her clicking her tongue as if she were thinking. "I'd prefer a cab."

"Why? That's just a waste of money."

"The wet spots on the road will freeze tonight and I'd rather you not risk your safety. I've had to deal with more accidents in the past day with clients. Not all Breeds heal as quickly. Shifters can only do it when they change into their animal, and a Shifter doesn't go through the change until they're an adult, so I get a lot of kids."

"I guess you have been busy. Are you doing okay otherwise?"

I slowed at the intersection but my car continued sliding. I tapped the brake and turned into the skid, causing the car to straighten and grind to a halt. The tires spun in place, kicking up bits of ice in the back. "Shit."

She sighed. "It's—it's fine. Nothing I can't handle, and I think I have an important decision to make. Hello? Is something wrong?"

"Sorry for cutting you off but I need go." Luckily, everyone in the city had the good sense to stay home so no one was around to hit me.

"Do you think your Ghuardian has jumpers? Hopefully my car battery hasn't died from frostbite," she said with a laugh.

"That man *is* a jumper."

The tires were spinning in place, so I threw the car into neutral and unbuckled my seatbelt. "We'll see you tomorrow, Page. Have a good one."

"Take care."

I shoved the phone in my purse and popped the door open, looking around. "*Dammit*," I muttered. It might have been helpful if Justus had shown me how to maneuver a car on ice.

Then again, I drove a tin can with no traction.

The stinging wind bit my cheeks when I got out and decided to push the car. I'd seen it done in the movies; how hard could it be?

Car in neutral: check.

My door made an awful complaint when it closed and I walked like a penguin to the rear. Maybe if I rocked the car a few times and then threw it in reverse, it would make a difference.

I bumped my rear end against the trunk repeatedly until the car began rocking back and forth. This method seemed like a good idea since I didn't think I could push the car with the shoes I had on. I felt like an ass, but since there was no one to bear witness, I had no qualms with embracing my assness.

My foot slipped and I hit the ice on my right shoulder. Without warning, the car began sliding backward.

I screamed, scrambling to get away from the tires.

Suddenly, a metal croak sounded. Christian stood at my feet, holding up the end of the car as if he were fluffing a blanket out for a picnic.

"Car trouble?"

After a few attempts, I managed to stand on my feet and wipe the sludge away from my face as he dropped the car. My jeans were wet, but I couldn't do anything about that.

"Thanks, Christian. I thought I was about to get squashed like a bug."

"Now where*ever* did you learn that technique? I don't seem to remember them teaching that in defensive driving."

"I got that from the offensive driving class," I said, wiping my nose.

He stood very still in his long black trench coat, the edges flapping in the wind like a moth's wings. The winter ensemble was for appearances since cold weather had no effect on a Vampire. His black liquid eyes settled on me, and a crooked smile animated his unshaven face. Christian loved his scruff, letting his whiskers spread down his neck like a man who just didn't care.

"Let's grab a bite," he offered.

"I need to get this car out of the—"

Christian whirled around and pushed the car like it were a

matchbox until it settled by the curb. He reached inside, pulled out my purse, and locked it up.

"I'll not take no for an answer, lass, so don't sit here and rabbit on. I can hear your stomach growling from blocks away. There's Italian just up the road. It's a beautiful night for a stroll, is it not?" he declared in a serious voice, spinning around with his arms outstretched.

It was out of character for him to be considerate. I hurled a sludgeball at his shoes and matched his pace.

"Always got to have the last word," he accused.

"I didn't say anything," I pointed out. "I've only got five bucks on me, so I hope this is a cheap place."

"Jaysus wept. Doesn't Justus give you a fatter allowance than that?"

"I don't see you much these days." I tucked my hands into my coat pockets and blew out a frosty breath.

His shoes crunched on the ice with every step and he kept his chin tucked in. "I can't stay shacked up in your underground bunker; it goes against my principles."

"It was just a bed and a warm place, Christian."

"It was a sweet gesture, to be sure, but I'm of little use if I'm not performing my duties to the fullest."

"Yadda yadda," I muttered.

"Your fella was a real joy to travel with. I thought *you* were a barrel of monkeys, but that one is the whole fecking zoo."

"We're here," I said, glancing up at the neon light.

The Italian restaurant advertised they were family owned, and the moment we stepped inside, the spices made me salivate. My shoes squeaked on the linoleum floor and Christian gave me a dirty look.

A short man with a black mustache greeted us and I leaned forward to give him my order when Christian suddenly spoke up. "She'll be having the spaghetti combo."

"Do you have a few extra garlic cloves?" I asked. The cashier appeared confused and I slapped Christian on the back. "They're for my friend."

Dinner arrived quickly at our small table in the back. Christian set the warm breadsticks in the center and watched me stuff hot noodles into my mouth.

"I want to hear more about your trip," I said, licking the pasta sauce from my fork. "You didn't find out anything else?"

He scratched his jaw and looked out the window. "Just what you already know."

"You're not keeping anything from me, are you?"

Christian watched me closely and his voice softened. "You don't have any desire to meet your da? He's an interesting character."

"Do you know how hard it was growing up without a father? Wasn't he even curious about what I looked like? Now after everything I've found out, the only thing I feel is contempt. Regardless of whether Grady donated his sperm or his light, he's *not* my father." I sipped my lemon water through a white straw and pushed an ice cube around.

"After getting a look at Grady, the mystery of your ginger hair is not yet solved, lass."

He was baiting me. When I was human, I had red hair. It didn't come from my mother or her side of the family. Upon my creation as a Mage, my DNA shifted and I permanently acquired many physical traits of Samil, my Creator.

Christian laced his fingers and watched my reaction intently.

"I'm not that girl anymore, in case you haven't noticed," I said, flipping a strand of my black hair. "That's in the past."

"It was more fetching when it was long," he muttered, sitting back.

"Logan likes it short."

"Maybe he doesn't want the competition; looks like Goldilocks is giving you a run for your money with his tresses."

I took another bite of pasta. "Why don't you order some food? You need to cram something into that big mouth of yours."

Christian pulled a noodle from my plate and let it dangle from his mouth. "Ever seen *Lady and the Tramp*?"

"Well, if I'm the lady in this scenario, then I guess that makes you the tramp."

I flipped the end of his noodle and it stuck to his face. A man at a nearby table lifted his head from a small book when he heard me laughing. Sometimes Christian needed to lighten up a little.

"You are a venomous child," he said, dropping the noodle onto the table. "Now I know where you get that temper of yours from."

I slammed my fork down. "Why are you baiting me on this? The only thing I want to know about Grady is his involvement, but anything personal I just don't want to hear. *Why* do you continue to bring him up?"

Christian lowered his brows and they almost smothered his eyes. His open collar exposed his smooth and delicious neck. I remembered the intimacy of the blood sharing and felt myself flush as I looked away.

"Perhaps I think you're being spiteful to a man without giving him a chance."

"You're my guard, not my therapist."

He stood up and tossed a wad of money on the table, along with my car keys.

"I've taken out five juicers this week who tried to come after you. One of them planned to sell you on the black market for two hundred grand. Drive home safely."

CHAPTER 7

THE FOLLOWING DAY, JUSTUS KEPT close watch of the security systems.

I thought about the way he acted around Page and wondered how serious he could be about a woman who wanted nothing to do with him. Justus liked to be in control and required a compliant woman. It's why we butted heads so often, and those were the moments that he liked me the least. Page didn't succumb to his gifts as a Charmer, and the peculiar thing was—he hadn't even noticed.

Of that, I was certain.

Just after eight in the morning, a sensor alarm went off at the main entrance of our property. The cab driver dropped Page off and she hiked through the snow up the private road. I watched on the monitor as Justus broke into a full run until he came within her sight. Then he slowed to a casual stroll.

Yeah, the man was smooth.

I went into the kitchen and made a pot of coffee.

The first thing I heard when the door opened was a dramatic sneeze.

"Page?"

She stood in the hallway, sapped out. Her bright red nose looked sore, and her brown eyes were sunken in and bloodshot. Especially the bruised one.

"You look awful."

Justus glared at me and I shrugged.

"It's just a cold," she muttered in a stuffy voice.

Something I'd never have to experience again, thank God. I watched as she removed her coat in slow motion. Justus shook it out and hung it up neatly on a hook he'd installed that morning.

"Does coffee sound good? I've got some cocoa if you'd rather have that."

"Coffee sounds fine," she said in a monotone voice. "It hit me in the middle of the night and I didn't get much sleep. I decided to… to…" She sneezed again and wiped her nose. "To pick up my car before it got worse."

Justus stood helpless in the hall, a man who didn't have a single cough drop in the house. A man who hadn't had a cold in more than five centuries. "Learner, check if we have any soup."

Luckily, that was one thing we *did* have. I put a pot of chicken noodle on the stove and brought her a cup of hot chocolate instead of the coffee. Page's brown hair was unkempt and stuck up on one side. My guess would be that she crawled out of bed, got dressed, and came straight over.

"Here, try this. I put tiny marshmallows in it. Does your throat hurt?"

She held the brown mug and leaned against the wall in the dining room. "I just feel achy and tired. Once I'm back in my own bed, I'll feel better."

"The soup will take a few minutes to heat up," I said. "Have a seat."

All men have an unspoken rule: never sit at the head of the table that isn't yours. Page had apparently never heard of this rule or didn't care. She relaxed in Justus's chair at the far end of the room in front of the painting, and I sat to her right. Not my usual spot, but it wasn't a usual morning.

Justus spoke in his lusciously masculine voice. That's the only way to describe it, because he was being uncharacteristically soft. I had learned not to complain about pain around him because he never offered sympathy unless he was the cause of my injuries. Even then, our training sessions had progressed enough that there was no need to borrow light from him when I could tap into the sun or just heal naturally.

"What can we get that will ease your discomfort?" he asked.

"Morphine." She laughed and rubbed her face in her hands.

"You know, that cab driver took the long way so he could get more money out of me," she said as if talking to herself. "Nothing, Mr. De Gradi. Unless you have some aspirin—my head is killing me."

No, we didn't have any pharmaceuticals in the house. A Mage suffered the occasional bout of stomach upset, but otherwise, medicine had no place in our lives.

"A cool cloth?" he suggested.

"Perfecto," Page mumbled.

"That's a yes, Ghuardian."

He left the room and quickly returned with a neatly folded towel. She placed it across her forehead and blew out a breath while Justus lit a few candles. The buzzer went off, so I hurried to the kitchen and brought her back a bowl of soup.

Page had no more than five small sips before she pushed the bowl away. "I better go," she announced, standing up on shaky legs. "Thanks for babysitting the car even though it needs a wash."

My confused eyes flicked over to Justus and I touched her flushed cheeks. "She's burning up." No wonder Page was talking incoherently.

Justus reached for the keys and she clutched them tightly.

"No, I want to go home. *My* home."

She suddenly gripped my shoulders and her brown eyes went wide. "I'm going to be sick."

The keys hit the floor with a jingle.

I rushed her to the bathroom where she flew in front of the toilet and retched. I closed the door and suddenly had a vivid image of what Christian must have gone through that night he sat with me for eight hours, watching me puke.

No wonder he despised me so.

"Here," I said, wiping her chin with the rag. "I think you've got the flu. I had it once when I was a kid and it knocked me out for several days. You shouldn't be driving on ice when you can barely walk."

"I'm not staying out here, Silver. I want to go home. You know what it's like when you just want to be sick in your own bed."

"Then I'll drive you, okay? I can take a cab back home; no big deal."

"Thanks," she whispered before the rest of the soup came up.

I vowed to never eat chicken noodle again.

"Page is a little better." I spoke quietly into the receiver, telling Logan about the turn of events. "She came down with the flu and I was about to take her home when Justus put up an argument about how I'd end up in a ditch."

Logan chuckled on the other end. "He has a point."

"He insisted on driving her, something I have no doubt he'll regret. Page is lying in the backseat of her car with a garbage can. I think Simon is going to pick him up and bring him back home. He didn't say."

"Simon won't be coming," Logan said.

"Why's that?" I paced across the living room and landed in the swivel chair.

"He's watching the lab, remember?"

"Oh yeah, the stakeout." I wondered how incognito a man in a leather collar with a tongue piercing could be. He tamed it once in a while with some sharp clothes of a European fashion, but Simon loved his bad-boy look.

"Do you need me to stay with you? I'm on my way."

"No, Logan. Stay where you are. I like being alone sometimes. It's nice and quiet around here. Except for Max."

"How's he doing in the new home?"

Chitahs didn't typically own pets, but Logan had bonded with him. Sometimes Max would leap onto his shoulders, which I never saw him do with anyone, and rub his face against Logan's cheek. I loved seeing that because Max was a piece of my past—the only piece I had left. Logan bringing him back into my life was the most thoughtful gift anyone had given to me.

I curled up and played with a loose thread on the pillow. "I think he missed his mommy. What are your plans tonight?"

"I'm meeting with Leo. If you need anything, you have my number."

"Will do, honey."

He growled approvingly and we hung up.

Not more than a minute later, I received a text from my employer.

> Novis: Meet me at the diner at three. Burgers and fries are on me.

Novis possessed a unique sense of humor few could appreciate; rhyming had become his signature style in a text message.

It's a good thing we weren't meeting at twelve, or elves might be on the menu.

CHAPTER 8

J USTUS GLANCED AT THE RELIC in the rearview mirror. After ten minutes of groaning, she buried her face in the crook of her arm and fell asleep.

The heater in her car barely functioned and she'd left her coat at the house. Justus focused on his core light and released a comfortable degree of warmth within the vehicle, but it didn't ease her tremors.

In his time, colds were often deadly. What once wiped out villages now kept mortals at home with a bottle of medicine and tissues. That offered him little comfort. Page was mortal and required proper care, but he didn't trust human hospitals.

Once he shut the engine off, Justus got out and stepped in a pile of muddy sludge. The city had done an inadequate job at clearing off the roads, and he kicked around a few heavy drifts of snow beside the car.

He hooked his hands beneath her arms and pulled her out of the backseat. The frigid wind blew around soft tendrils of her hair, so he adjusted his core temperature and held her close.

Justus used her keys to get inside the building. He hadn't paid attention to her living conditions on his last visit. The apartment had a simplistic feel with a quaint sense of style—a quality he admired. Bookshelves lined a wall from floor to ceiling. Page didn't have all the little trinkets and flowers most women collected. Her decorations were books, papers, pens, and small bundles of colored yarn. They were the types of books that Simon liked to read. Science books. Justus had a small library, but his pleasure derived from the classics.

The bedroom connected to the living room and he stared at a plain white bedspread covering a twin bed.

Up close, there were delicate freckles on the bridge of her

nose that he hadn't noticed before. Finding himself unnecessarily distracted by her heart-shaped face, he placed the Relic on the small bed and wondered how she shared the space with a man, due to its meek size.

The Relic tucked her knees against her chest and Justus glared at the bathroom door connected to the bedroom. He rummaged through the cabinets, pulling out soaps, towels, and toilet paper until he found medicine. It promised to eliminate all her symptoms, so he set the bottle on the wooden nightstand and closed the heavy draper. He had no clue how to care for an ill person. Even in his human life, it had never been a responsibility put upon him. Women took care of the infirm, and doctors were summoned for those with money. Justus came from a poor family, and his own mother had succumbed to a feverish illness at twenty-seven.

He slowly peeled away her wet socks and noticed her chalky-white feet. The boots she'd worn the other night at the club were tucked in the corner of the room, and Justus grew angry with himself for having made her walk to the car. He should have carried her.

His fingers curled warmly around her ankles and Page suddenly flew up with lightning speed, clutching her stomach. Justus stepped back, afraid he'd crossed a line of professionalism with the Relic like the incident at the club. When he saw her face sour, he grabbed a small waste can from the bathroom. She bent over, and without a word, vomited into it. While it should have disgusted him, he rubbed his hand across her back soothingly.

Strands of hair clung to her sweaty face, covering the ruddy mark around her eye that made him want to put Slater into the ground.

"I'm sorry," she said weakly.

"You're ill, not sorry. Will you permit me to help you, Page? Look at these bottles and tell me which one will heal you."

She tapped her finger on a milky, green liquid and Justus filled the small plastic cap.

Why were her living conditions inadequate and small? Relics had an advantage over many Breeds in that they could earn a respectable living through the wealth of their clients, acquiring a substantial income. Sensors were traders, and Shifters often ran their own companies, although they felt inherited land outweighed monetary gain. But Relics, they possessed knowledge that was sought after. When the parents died, the money exchanged hands to the next in line. Why did Page live in a one-bedroom apartment that could barely accommodate his car?

He had HALO business to attend to, but those plans dissipated the second Page stripped out of her pants. She was oblivious that anyone else was in the room, eyes closed as she kicked off her jeans.

Her state of mind bothered him. Women in this condition were vulnerable and anyone could enter the house. It happened all the time, and human television used it as nighttime entertainment. What honor would he have in leaving her alone? It plagued his conscience, even though she was only a Relic.

Justus rubbed his smooth jaw and returned to her side, helping her out of her shirt. She might have thought him a lech, but Justus had seen more women naked than he could count, so it hardly mattered.

Hardly.

He changed the wastebasket and placed it beside the bed. Then he stood by a small table with his arms folded, deciding what to do.

That morning he had dressed himself in a cream-colored shirt with a wide opening in the front and drawstrings. Women liked this look on him and thought it was romantic, so he'd chosen carefully when assembling his wardrobe. Now such trivialities hardly mattered.

In the corner, a brown sitting chair looked like a favorite spot with a book on the armrest and a knitted blanket folded over the back. Justus could have taken a seat, but his feet became cement blocks.

He thought about leaving. He thought about how frail humans were. He thought about the dagger strapped to his lower leg. He thought about Slater.

"Wow," I remarked, staring at my phone.

"What is it?" Novis asked, dipping a chicken strip into his milkshake.

I wrinkled my nose. "Now that's just plain disgusting."

"You mixed and mingled."

"Yes, but there are rules."

His smile thinned out. "Yes... rules. I thought you didn't care for rules?"

"Don't blame me if you get sick." I set my phone on the table beside the glass ketchup bottle. "Justus sent me a message. He said Page took a turn for the worse and he's going to stay for a while. I hope it's not serious." I looked up at Novis. "We think she might have the flu."

Novis nodded, "Centuries ago, we didn't have medical care for such simple things. People died. Infants and strong warriors were given no preferential treatment by death. Of course, living conditions were unfavorable then. If the Relic grows too ill, she should call her partner."

"Why don't they work alone?"

"Relics are paired up early on, and for most of them, it's a lifelong relationship. They share information and serve as each other's backup. There are no Breed hospitals, so Relics are the equivalent of private doctors. They retain clients throughout their lives. Most partners marry and their children take over caring for their immortal clients. It's preferred; we like to keep our secrets within the family." He pushed a crumb around on his plate. "The word *immortal* is thrown around when it simply means we have an extended lifespan. Nothing is forever. Except atoms."

"I met her partner. He socked her in the eye."

Novis looked up and his brows slanted. "I wouldn't let Remi know about that. A Gemini closes off his emotions for a reason, and if they're as good of friends as you say they are, he might do something regretful."

"Never mind," I said. "Let's not get sidetracked. Am I here for an assignment or are you just craving my cheery companionship?"

It was between lunch and dinner, and a young mom a few tables away tried to calm her screaming baby with a stuffed lion that squeaked.

"Only three people work in the lab," he began. "They rotate schedules like clockwork. Simon's been concealing his light after sensing two of them to be one of us; we're not sure what the third could be."

I glanced around. "Is it okay to discuss this in public?"

He quirked a smile and pinched his lip before responding. "I'm well-guarded for such conversations."

"Maybe your guards are lying in a ditch."

His smile stretched and he looked down at the table, shaking his head. Novis tugged at some of his dark hair that he kept spiked in every direction. "Never worry about such things in my company, young Learner. You must take my word when I tell you that we have the utmost privacy."

Hmm. Novis was full of secrets. "Do you know the names of the scientists?"

"No. Their cars were unmarked and Simon couldn't follow them without raising suspicion. He's tracing the plates, but it's doubtful they're complete imbeciles. We're not able to obtain a warrant without motive. Our laws are not like the human world, as you know. The Mageri will not serve warrants without a testimony and documentation. We cannot arrest until there is sufficient evidence to convict. Once a name is ruined, it's hard to recover one's good-standing. For immortals that has always been imperative due to our social circle being much smaller and our lives being much longer."

"Do you think that's the only lab there is?"

He broke a chicken strip in half and looked at it closely before popping it into his mouth. "Can't be sure." Novis licked his finger and wiped his hands on a paper napkin.

"This doesn't seem like groundbreaking news to call me here."

"We want a peek in the lab."

"Simon's a good peeker," I said with a smile. "I bet he can pick the locks."

"We can't risk tripping any alarms they may have. It must be unlocked from the inside."

"And how do you propose to do that?"

He nudged his head sideways and gave me a look, prompting me to think about it.

"Oh… you think I could move the locks inside? I'm not sure; it's not something I've had much practice doing." It wasn't so much the metal that I could move, but I had the ability to manipulate residual energy left from a Mage who had recently touched the object. "I've never tried moving something from the other side of a door—I don't know if it will work."

"Think… or know? Why don't you go home and practice? You'd be surprised what you can do when you put your mind to it. It's time you learn to focus that talent you have and put it to good use. No one can train you on your telekinesis; you must learn how to develop it on your own."

"What if they catch us?"

"Simon knows their routine. You'll have four hours to conduct a search and get out. I'd prefer if you finished up quickly so that no residual energy is left behind. If the third man is a Sensor, he'll be able to pick up any emotions left behind. Be sure to keep that in check—no fights, and don't touch the equipment. I doubt the third man is a Chitah based on the descriptions, so we won't have to worry about anyone tracking your scent. Keep it clean, in and out. If you can't find anything useful in an hour, then leave."

I smeared my fry across the plate, picking up pepper flakes. "I'll give it a try, but that whole hour could be wasted with me trying to get the lock open. I might trip the alarm."

"The most self-damaging words in the English language are: try, might, and if. These are words of uncertainty. Will you fail? That is possible. But continue doubting your abilities and you'll never succeed."

"How do you know they don't have security cameras?"

"Simon checked it out."

"Micro cams?"

"Like I said, he checked it out. So did Logan."

"Seems Logan has been up to a lot of things without telling me."

His pale blue eyes brightened. "Likewise, I'm sure."

Novis had a point, except Logan didn't work for him and I did. Then again, Logan was a good negotiator and might have received payment for his services.

"Have you warmed up to your name, Silver?"

I shrugged indifferently.

"It took time to get used to mine," he admitted. "A name is only something you're called, it's not who you are. Many of us retain our human names, such as Justus and Simon. If Justus had been renamed Peter, would it change the man he is?" Novis tapped his long finger on his plate. "I think I'm going to pick a new location next time. Do you like Chinese cuisine?"

CHAPTER 9

MY WINTER WONDERLAND WAS TURNING into a slushy nightmare. The novelty of fresh powder was replaced by the reality of wet pants, dirty shoes, frozen cheeks, and slipping and falling on my ass. Novis left the diner with his driver and I trudged out to my car, thinking about putting a blanket and a few survival items in the trunk, just in case. Which struck me as funny, being an immortal.

I texted Justus that I was on my way home and offered some tips on how to starve a fever and all that. The last thing that poor woman needed was a man shoveling a steak down her throat.

A cold blast of air snuck up from behind and caused me to shiver as I approached the car door. The key wouldn't go in the lock at first, so I jiggled it. That's when I heard footsteps approaching from behind. *Crunch. Crunch. Crunch.*

"I'm not hungry, Christian."

"Well, I'm famished. I could really use a… *bite.*"

My heart didn't just skip a beat; it froze and forgot how to work again. My blood pressure plummeted and I nearly fainted. The gravelly voice, the way his words cut like razors at the end of each sentence, and the deep intake of breath were the distinctive sounds of a person that I knew all too well.

Tarek had just walked back into my life.

My eyes skipped around the empty lot, searching for Christian. He said he'd only intervene if there were an imminent threat. Tarek had plunged three venomous fangs into my neck not long ago, almost ending my life.

That felt pretty imminent.

"Tarek." I greeted him, turning on my heel. The snow flattened beneath my boots and I tucked my arms around my body protectively.

A tan coat with a fur collar replaced the sinister look of the black wardrobe he'd once sported. I suppose that his new position entitled him to finer threads. He still had the short black Mohawk, except now more hair grew from the sides of his head as if he might be growing it all out. Most Chitahs had light features, but Tarek's hair was dark, and it made his golden eyes ominous. His brows furrowed and his lip curled. "Out for a *bite*, little Mage?"

The joke was getting old.

He laughed and I charged up my light, knowing I'd never outrun a Chitah.

"What do you want?"

He widened his stance. "Now *that's* a question I'm hearing more and more these days," he said, dusting off his jacket with his leather gloves. I couldn't help but notice his tall, *heavy* boots.

"Sorry, sweetie, but I learn from my mistakes." Tarek tapped his heel on the ground. "These boots are specially lined, so I don't think you'll be having any luck if you intend on cutting my heel again."

He lifted a silver case from his pocket and pulled the lid back, putting a hand-rolled cigarette in his mouth before snapping the case shut. With an etched lighter, he lit the end and watched me with steady eyes as the paper crackled. After a consuming drag, Tarek tucked the lighter in his pocket and chuckled privately. Smoking didn't seem like a smart habit for a Chitah who relied on sense of smell.

I once asked Logan why he chewed on mint. He explained that he'd discovered that mint cleanses the palate and sharpens the emotional flavors on his tongue.

A white cloud of smoke hovered between us.

I cursed myself for looking away, unable to hold his menacing gaze. It made me feel inferior and Chitahs fed off those emotions. "I have no business with you, Tarek. What's done is done between us. Nero is wasting his time if he's still looking for me."

Tarek sucked in another drag and the end of the cigarette pulsed orange. With a flick of his wrist, he dropped it in the dirty snow and aggressively stomped on it until the poor little thing was squashed from existence.

"Maybe my business with you doesn't involve Nero. I'm sure you've heard the splendid news about my promotion." He pinched his gloves over his tongue, picking off a stray tobacco leaf as he raked me over with his eyes. "A man in my position can have whatever he wants."

"You can't have everything."

"Can't I?" He cornered me between my car and a brick wall outside the diner and I looked around the dark parking lot. He brushed a wave of hair away from my face with a sweep of his hand. "What does Cross see in you?" he asked himself. "Why would he lie for you?"

My heart raced as he drew uncomfortably closer.

"Leave us alone, Tarek. If you don't have business with Nero, then you don't have business with us."

A smile parted his lips. "Your distaste for me is a turn-on, you know that?"

"I don't know why you have the audacity to despise Logan so much. Just because your kindred spirit didn't choose *you?*" *I was really stirring the pot now.* "He loved her, and you should be ashamed of your crime. Katrina's death almost ruined him, but he's managed to move on, despite what you did to her. Logan didn't steal her from you, Tarek. You threw her away."

Faster than a heartbeat, his hand clamped around my throat. My chin rose, feeling the hard push of his fingers against my jawbone. He slowly relaxed his grip and smoothed his gloved hand down my neck. I grabbed his wrist and threw a burst of energy into him.

Tarek grimaced and then shook his head as if I'd only slapped him. I didn't put half as much energy in him as I normally would have because I didn't know the repercussions of attacking a Lord.

"When Cross knows what it is to lose, I'll sleep at night—however that loss comes. Your Vampire friend is distracted at the moment and can't hear our conversation, so this is just between me, you, and the fucking wall." His finger pressed against each object he pointed out. "I will cut out your heart and everyone you love. You will see their deaths before you see your own."

I couldn't seem to draw in enough air. "What do you want?"

His lips hooked into a grin. "You." Tarek brushed his hand across my cheek and pinched my chin. "You can either choose to watch your entire life ripped apart or you can choose me."

"If I say no?"

"I'll start with gutting that cat of yours and spilling his insides on your doorstep. Oh yes, I know you have a mangy pet because I can smell it on you," he said with a wrinkled nose. "Then I'll hunt down the Cross brothers and kill each one of them, starting with the youngest. Logan will witness their deaths before it's his turn. It'll be slow, painful, and you'll watch every horrifying second of it. But he won't be allowed to take his last breath until you take yours; I wouldn't want him to miss that for the world."

A frosty breeze tangled a few strands of my hair and I felt more frozen than a glacier.

"Choose me and your friends will be safe. I won't touch a single hair on their heads. That means you'll be mine. No one will have any right to challenge me if you *choose* me."

"Logan will challenge you, Tarek. He's already claimed me as his kindred. That means—"

"Nothing. There *is* no kindred outside of our kind. He lies to you, and you're a fool to believe him. If you accept my claim, no male can legally challenge me because of my title. I'll be sure the mating ceremony is quick, as I wouldn't want to have to kill your boyfriend if he tries to attack me. Our mating won't be legal in many ways, but I'm a Lord, and I've got a few ideas on that obstacle."

"Wait a minute… stop." I held my hand up defensively. "You want me to be your wife? And if I don't, you'll… Why are you *doing* this?" Tears welled in my eyes.

"Because I can?" He shrugged and a tiny snowflake landed on top of his head. "Cross is my sworn enemy and that *means* something. I will not relent until I taste my revenge. Tell no one of this or I will remove your choice. I will take that away from you and *all* will die. I am Lord of my Pride, Mage. Consider that. I can make it happen with a snap of my fingers and you won't be able to bargain your way out. I have far too much protection and you have no evidence. Tell one living soul and I'll spend the rest of my life making sure that everyone you love is put into the ground, either by my hand or that of my men. And I'll find out; I have eyes and ears everywhere."

My head swam. Tarek would hold to his word. If just one life were lost because of me, the blood would be on my hands.

He scraped his boot along the concrete, rubbing a hand over his mouth. "My terms are conditional; you can never tell Logan the truth. He must believe that he's not worthy enough, that he didn't meet your standards as a suitable mate. If I suspect for one minute that you've told him about this—and I will scent it on him—then I'll follow through with the original plan. You will cradle his neck as he takes his last breath, and he will know that the blood of his brothers is on your hands. They'll all die, Mage. Everyone you love. No mercy."

I hadn't even noticed that my right hand was raised, as if I might revoke his threat with five splayed fingers. He held my wrist, lowered my arm, and leaned in so close that his sour breath touched my cheek.

"Tell Cross you're attracted to something that he doesn't have: power and position. I'll be generous and give you time to think about your answer. The next time we meet, be ready to give it, or I'll make it for you. Choose to be my mate. I have other conditions that you will follow through with—no exceptions. Or we'll start with your human friend, Sunny."

Then, just as suddenly as he appeared, Tarek stalked off.

He saw me as nothing more than a means to an end, a trophy of his battle with Logan. Even if I broke it off with Logan, Tarek would fulfill his promise.

Now that he was protected by guards and in a position of influence and authority, Tarek had absolute power.

<hr/>

The gritty sound of heavy footsteps running in my direction came up from behind. A shadow of a man, his coat flared in the wind against the white contrast of snow. *Damn, I had to get it together.*

"Hey, Christian. My car wouldn't start, so I'm just giving it a minute."

He quirked his brow and glanced at my locked door. "Another Vampire gave me chase. You all right?"

"I'm fine. It's just this stupid car. I should have listened to Justus and got the BMW," I said in a flustered voice. "What Vampire?"

"He attacked me without provocation. We're not typically aggressive to one another, but he continued shoving me down the street and attracting too much fecking attention. I couldn't risk a human pulling out a camera and recording what I would have liked to do to that fanghole," he said with disgust laced on his tongue.

"Maybe you should have put the garlic in your pockets the other night," I said, walking to the car.

Christian spun me around and laid his right hand across my clavicle. His black eyes scoped the parking lot. "What happened just now?"

"Nothing happened. Now quit feeling me up."

He released his grip and I slid my key into the lock. This time, it went in without complaint.

Christian leaned over my back and spoke in a low voice beside my ear. "Your heart is racing a mile a minute. A little car trouble wouldn't cause that kind of reaction. There are tiny beads of sweat on your brow that you probably aren't even aware of; your hand is trembling, and if I tasted your blood," he said, holding my wrist to his mouth and smelling of my skin, "I would know just how afraid you are."

I snapped my wrist out of his grip. "Don't threaten to bite me, Christian. That would not end well."

Before I could slam the door, he caught the frame. He looked at me long and hard. Studied me the way you might look at the inner workings of a watch. When I turned the engine over, it hopped to life without a stutter.

CHAPTER 10

P AGE LAZILY OPENED HER EYES, warmly wrapped up in her grandmother's blue afghan. The last thing she recalled clearly? Trudging through the snow outside Silver's house and then vomiting in the bathroom. That must have been when her fever spiked.

She remembered getting up several times that night and chills racked her body relentlessly. Her muscles still ached. Relics were at a disadvantage because they were one of the few Breeds susceptible to human disease.

At least the worst of it was over. She wanted to kick herself for venturing out at the onset of symptoms.

Page glanced over her right shoulder and gasped at a man looming next to her bed. It took a second to realize she knew him.

Justus stood with one hand tucked in his pocket and the other in the fold of his armpit. His body swayed slightly, but his eyes remained closed.

Dear God, the man was asleep.

Dawn peered through an opening in the drapes, dividing the room with a ray of hazy light. Her window faced east, so that meant from the time she went to Silver's house, twenty-four hours had passed.

"Mr. De Gradi," she whispered.

Page slowly sat up and peeled the blanket away. Startled by the sight of her bra and panties, she yanked the blanket up to her chin. Gradually, her memory returned.

Oh no, she thought. *Did I really strip in front of him?* Page could have died from embarrassment. Building a respectful relationship with clientele was critical, and she had essentially given him a peep show.

"De Gradi," she said firmly, pushing the flat of her hand against his stomach.

In a swift movement barely visible, his hand flew out and snapped around her wrist. Fear slapped her in the face and she gasped.

After three hard blinks, he immediately released his grip and took a step back.

"No need to be frightened," he said, rubbing his weary eyes. "You were ill. What can I get for you?"

She wrapped the cover around her exposed back and said, "I need some privacy." Justus lowered his eyes and turned away.

With the blanket wrapped tightly around her, Page hopped off the bed in a hurry, not thinking that her legs might be weak. She wobbled unsteadily and when Justus caught her, she wriggled out of his grasp.

"I'll leave you," he said, turning away and closing the door behind him.

Her reflection in the oval mirror above the bathroom sink startled her. What a sight. Mangled hair, pale skin, the bruise on her eye was starting to turn *green*, and her eyes were sunken in from exhaustion. Not the look of a woman of twenty-six. Other women her age looked vibrant and young, while Page's lifestyle of stress had taken its toll. She dressed conservatively so the immortals wouldn't see her as such a child.

The fever must have caused her skin to become sensitive, so she passed on the shower and slipped into a blue robe. No point in running a comb through her hair since he had already seen Page looking her worst, but she did brush her teeth.

Page had been told a number of times that if she ditched the reading glasses for contacts and put on something sexy, she'd have no problems getting a man. She had once dated a guy named Gaston who told her the smart look was hot—until a girl with double D's walked into his life.

School had always been a critical step in her career path until the day she discovered she was infertile. That changed everything and Page dropped out of school to work fulltime. That knowledge fueled her desire to become the best at her job; if she couldn't pass on her genes, then she would serve her Breed *well* before her genetic line ended. As she had no siblings, the La Croix family knowledge would die with her.

When Slater found out her secret, he insisted that she undergo fertility treatments and try to conceive with him. Slater wasn't attracted to her, and yet he expected her to carry his child? Combining their genetic knowledge to produce brilliant offspring became his obsession.

That was enough to make her nauseous all over again.

Page opened the bathroom door and noticed the sheets had been changed and the bed turned down. She tightened the belt around her knee-length cotton robe and crossed the living room.

"What are you doing here?" she asked, entering the kitchen.

"You need to eat," he ordered, standing by the stove. No, he *demanded*.

"There's no need for you to stay here, Mr. De Gradi. I had no intention of putting you out." She took a seat in the nearest chair and stared at the linoleum floor. "I can take care of myself; I've been doing it for years."

"If you took proper care of yourself, you would not be sick." He twisted around and gave her a scolding appraisal. She hated that look on men. It was the primitive "me man, you woman" sentiment and implied that women were just no good on their own.

"I do fine."

He turned around and said quietly, "You could do better, Page." She glanced at his long-sleeved shirt with the V-neck opening in the front. The casual style reminded her of Robin Hood or something.

"Why do you address me by my first name when I never gave you permission to do so?"

It was inappropriate for a client to address a Relic informally unless told otherwise. Some just called her Relic, which was acceptable.

"Would you prefer that I call you Mademoiselle La Croix?"

Her breath caught.

His pronunciation of her French name, along with the appropriate title, was *perfect*. So much so that it straightened her spine like an arrow.

"Are you of French origin?"

He turned away and scraped the skillet with a spatula. Page stood up and noticed he was victimizing the hell out of a couple of eggs that never did any wrong to him.

"Here, let me do that," she said with a smile.

He shifted his body between her and the pan.

"You're murdering the eggs." She looked up at him and realized this was one battle she wasn't going to win.

The tips of the hairs on his head captured the light and were dark blond. Thanks to spending all night at her house, he'd also gone without a shave and the stubble on his face was the same color.

"Then tell me how you prefer them. Tell me what to do and I'll prepare them the way you like," he offered.

The open part of his shirt around his collarbone caught her attention. It seemed like no matter what time of day or night, Justus De Gradi was always at his best. Fresh shave, sharp clothes, expensive watch, and designer shoes. Something about this look on him was rustic and simple.

"No," she said, reconsidering. "What you have is fine."

This Mage had been more than generous in not only driving her car home, but also taking care of her while she was sick. Page wasn't about to put him down for making her a meal.

He stalked over to the trash can and dumped the eggs inside. "No, it's *not* fine. Tell me how you like your eggs."

"You just wasted them! I would have eaten your eggs."

"Tell me how you want them cooked. But first, I want you to sit in that chair."

While his words were curt and demanding, he made no move to force her. He wasn't trying to boss her around in the wrong kind of way; Page was on her feet when she should have been lying down. She often used that tone with her more stubborn clients. Doctors always make the worst patients.

Too tired to argue, Page gave in and eased into the chair. While scraping her fingers through her tangled hair, she gave the Mage instructions on how to cook eggs and he followed them to a T. Right down to the correct amount of butter, milk, and pepper.

The real question became a matter of whether or not she could stomach this splendid meal. It would be a shame for him to have gone through all that trouble only for her to hurl it back up.

How delicious it looked! One taste was all it took and the engine started up in her worn-out body, craving nutrition and rest.

"Make yourself something to eat, Mr. De Gradi. Anything in the kitchen is yours for the taking."

"Not before you," he said, stealing the chair on her right.

When her fork scraped up her third bite, Page felt self-conscious. "Could you stop watching me chew? It's impolite."

His eyes flicked away and rested on a ballpoint pen sitting in the center of the table. "Are you missing work?"

She considered that. For the first time, in fact. "I am, but my partner will fill in for me. We're busy right now, but it's not as bad as we anticipated."

"Do you enjoy your line of work?" he asked conversationally.

It seemed cozy having a personal chat with Justus in her small kitchen, away from his extravagant home and without her work hat on. "I do. What I enjoy the most are the pregnancies with Shifters and bringing those sweet little babies into the world. And then cases like Silver's come along every so often that really have me earning my keep. They challenge my intellect." She took another bite of food. "These eggs turned out really good."

"Your partner is Slater?"

"Yes, the jughead who showed up at your place." She chewed slowly and pushed the eggs around with her fork. "Relics partner for life—it's not something we switch around on a whim. We build a trusting relationship with clients that could be broken if the partnership is severed. They're suddenly put in an unfair position where they're forced to choose between us, and I hate doing that… but I'm going to put in a request for a new partner. I can't work with Slater anymore."

Justus nodded and clasped his hands together on the table. She noticed how strong they were, how masculine. My God, he could crush tennis balls with those things.

He stretched and stood up, setting his chair beside hers and taking a seat again. Page shrank a little when he leaned in close.

"May I assess your injury?"

"I've already examined it. Nothing's broken; it just looks ugly."

He reached up and cradled her head in his left hand, gently touching her face with his right. When she winced, he leaned forward. Close enough that she wondered if her breath was bad and quickly shut her mouth. For a moment, tiny sparks glimmered deep in the irises of his eyes—a common trait for an older Mage.

He released a heavy breath and sat back. "It will heal."

With a history in medicine, this came as no surprise, but it soothed him to be able to conclude she wouldn't perish from a bruise. Page smiled appreciatively.

"I think I better lie back down," she said, rising from the table.

Justus followed behind her as she made her way into the living room and curled up in her favorite spot on the sofa. Page hated dark rooms and always made it a point to have the curtains open in the daytime, even on cloudy days.

"Will you open those for me?" she asked, pointing at the window on her left. "I enjoy the light."

Justus silently crossed in front of her and pulled the curtains open. Tiny snowflakes the size of peas sifted through the air like powdered sugar.

"Did you turn up my heater? It's warmer in here than usual; maybe I'm still feverish."

His face turned scarlet and he quickly left the room. It seemed like the moment he walked out, the air chilled ten degrees and Page shivered. When Justus returned, he walked over and draped her blue afghan across her legs. *Who was this guy?*

"I know I've already imposed my brashness on you, but do you mind if I call you Justus, or would you prefer Mr. De—"

"Justus," he said, sliding his hands in his pockets.

"Really, Justus, you don't have to hang around here and fuss over me. The medicine you gave me really helped." Page surged forward and sneezed in her hand three times. "Sorry," she grumbled, hating the sound of her weak voice.

"Do you need more medicine?" He sat on the edge of a leather chair that wasn't one of her favorites, but most of her clients felt comfortable sitting there when they visited her home on rare occasions.

What she really needed was to blow her nose, but no way was she going to do that in front of him.

"No man looks after you?"

The steady sound of a clock ticking in the kitchen ate up the silence.

"Um ," She cleared her throat a few times and sniffed. "I don't need a man to take care of me; I'm not an invalid."

"So you keep pointing out. I didn't ask if you needed one, I asked if you *had* one."

Page shivered and pulled the blanket over her shoulders. A sudden blast of heat touched her face and settled into the blanket.

"Are *you* doing that?" The sensation felt similar to heat wafting out of an open oven.

He nodded.

"Handy little gift you got there." Page didn't have many Mage clients, and their gifts never ceased to amaze her.

A pounding at the front door crushed the silence.

Justus stood up and looked like the Rock of Gibraltar. "Are you expecting anyone?"

"No, but if it's not my landlord then it's probably Slater. He's the only one with a key to get in the building. I might as well get this over with, so go ahead and let him inside. Please keep it civil; I'm not feeling well enough to break up a fight."

"On my word." Justus crossed the room and reached for the latch on the front door.

"What the fuck are *you* doing here? Page!" Slater shouldered by Justus and cut through the living room to stand on the other side of the coffee table. "Well isn't this just cozy," he said, shredding her apart with his hostile eyes.

Page recoiled and sat up straight. "Slater, did you pick up my appointments?"

"You bet the hell I did. Why didn't you call? Oh wait, I see… you've been *busy*." He emphasized every syllable of the last word with sexual innuendo.

"Slater, I'm going to put in a request for a new partner. You've grown too volatile and frankly, just a little too possessive. We can talk out the details on the phone later tonight, after I've had some rest and a shower. Let's not have this discussion in front of company."

"Is that what you're calling it these days? *Company?*" Slater laughed and rubbed the palm of his hand over the scruffy beard on his chin. "I've pursued you for eight years, and you fuck the first guy who comes along."

Justus stepped forward until he was nose to nose with Slater. He moved so deliberately and slowly it made her nervous.

"You got a problem, Mage? You should be careful not to put your dick in other people's business."

Justus curled his hands into solid fists but kept them at his side. She cleared her throat to remind him of his promise.

"Slater, I don't want any trouble. Just leave the key on the table as you go. This has been years in the making, but no one will ever lay a hand on me twice. We're going to have to split our clientele, so I'll contact them to put in their formal request with our Council. Call me later and when we're done hashing out the details, I want a clean break. That means you don't contact me anymore. We're done."

"Over one fight," he said smoothly.

Page lost it and her voice cracked as she screamed at him. "You hit me! Do you think I want to take a chance of you doing that again—or worse? I can't even believe you would stand there like it means nothing."

Justus positioned himself between her and Slater, who rocked on his heels as if he might make a sudden move. She almost wanted him to because she was within arm's reach of a very heavy candy dish that she'd never liked anyway.

"You heard the lady, get out," Justus said in an authoritative voice. "*Now.* Drop the key and leave the premises. I'm an official member of HALO, and I'll report any trouble. There's not going to be any trouble though, is there?"

Slater wasn't winning this battle, so he slapped the key down on the table in a pissed-off fashion and stalked toward the door. "It's not over, Page. We're not finished with this by a mile."

CHAPTER 11

I COULDN'T PROCESS EVERYTHING TAREK HAD thrown at me, and as a result, I broke a date with Logan with some lame excuse that I wanted to study.

Saturday rolled around uneventfully, and I hopped into the passenger seat of Simon's Maserati.

As the interior light went out, I caught a glimpse of Simon and opened my door back up. He sighed dramatically and dared me with his eyes to say something. I wasn't quite sure exactly *how* to broach the topic.

"Simon, you have a penis on your head."

I stared in astonishment at a tattoo that ran straight up his forehead to his hairline. Realistic and impressive, albeit not that endowed.

"I lost a bet."

I shut the door and smiled. "I don't know—that looks like a win to me."

He scraped his hair over his eyes. "I knew I should have worn the bloody hat."

"It's not permanent, is it?"

He snorted. "My body will absorb it within a week."

"That's what she said?"

Simon's contagious hyena laugh filled the car and he cranked on his stereo. "Perhaps the ladies will see that I actually think with the right head."

When he grinned, I poked my finger in his dimple and he tried to bite it.

"You're going to get yourself in trouble with that dimple someday, Simon."

His car growled like an angry dog, and he shot me a wink. "I'm counting on it."

It took us two hours to drive to the lab and we arrived thirty minutes before the last person closed up for the night. Simon wanted to make sure they had left the facility and kept to their routine. The windowless building had two concrete steps that led to the main door. We parked the car across the street to wait it out. I debated for a long time whether or not to tell Simon about my situation, but I'd catch shadows moving around outside and get second thoughts. I was certain Tarek had put a man on me—and probably the Vampire that tangled with Christian. If so, nothing I'd tell him would be private as Vampires have a keen sense of hearing.

Simon texted a few messages to Knox and cracked up laughing. Meanwhile, I looked through his glove compartment and found useful items like a dagger, adult magazine, leather conditioner, cotton balls, Sensor lollipops, and a map of the Grand Canyon.

Simon was so random.

"You know, that's a really annoying habit you have," I said to Simon as he popped his jaw. "One of these days it might come unhinged."

"Only if you start wearing latex. Don't believe all those wives' tales. I can also tell you that you will not go blind from repeated—"

"Look, they're leaving," I interrupted, turning the radio down. "Are you sure the third guy isn't a Vampire?"

"If he is, then he's a ninny for not confronting me on more than one occasion when I've been on my stakeout." Simon snorted. "Now I think I know where that term derived from."

A man in an oversized coat turned away from the door and walked to his car. He was a shadow moving through the darkness, face obscured and of average height. Moments later—after a sputter of smoke coughed out of his exhaust pipe—he drove away.

"Like clockwork," Simon sang, hopping out of the car. He skidded on his left foot and made a quick recovery.

"Don't you have snow boots?" I asked, looking down at his tattered brown shoes straight out of Oliver Twist."

"Love, unless he's climbing Mt. Everest, a grown man wearing snow boots should be shot on sight."

At least my cute tan boots were water resistant and had good tread. Simon's shoes were comfortable for flashing, but I didn't think he'd get far on ice. His brown hair was tousled and gelled, like he'd been standing in the rain and just ran his fingers through it.

"Are you sure we weren't followed?"

"Only by your fangtastic sweetheart sitting on his three-speed up the road," he said, jerking his thumb back at Christian's motorcycle. I snorted because it sounded like he said *sweethot*. Simon didn't trust Vampires, evident by the aviators perched on the bridge of his nose.

"Are those necessary?" I said, glaring up at him. "You look ridiculous; he's not coming in, so you can take those off."

Simon reluctantly tucked them inside the pocket of his leather jacket. "Have you been practicing?" he asked as we approached the door.

"Yeah, but…" I gave him a worried look and brushed my hair away from my face. "I'm not skilled."

"Need I remind you of the sword?"

"Lifting that out of Justus was sheer luck. I have more control over objects I can see—this is different."

"No time, love. We need to hurry before the energy on the door evaporates. Give it a go."

I removed my gloves and dropped to my knees, trying to avoid looking up at Simon because I knew he wanted to make a joke. The flat of my hands touched the door, and almost immediately, the tips of my fingers tickled as the energy from two places on the other side of the door crackled. I'd never done anything as intricate as manipulating energy to move in specific directions. While I'd practiced at home, the locks weren't the same.

I focused my energy and rotated my wrist clockwise before realizing that I was thinking backward, so I turned it the other way.

A metal click caused Simon to stir.

"Bravo!" he whispered excitedly. "Is that it?"

"No, there's one more. This one's… different. I can't tell what kind of lock it is, so I'm not sure how to focus." I glanced over my shoulder. "Simon, what if I can't do it? Novis is expecting me to complete this task."

"Then we have four hours to kill. Got any ideas?" He rested his hands on my shoulders and sensually massaged them.

"Get your hands off me, Simon. It's distracting."

"Now you know why the ladies go for the Hunt."

I turned my eyes on him like a shark. "Your energy leaking all over me isn't exactly helping."

He stepped back and after several long seconds, there were a few more clicks and a slide. My shoulders sagged as that level of concentration was the equivalent of lifting a boulder.

"Okay, try it," I said, out of breath.

I stood anxiously as Simon opened the door. "Atta girl!" he praised me with a hug. We stepped inside and closed the door behind us.

"Smells like my sock drawer," Simon muttered in disgust.

It looked like a doctor's office with maroon chairs along the left wall and front desk. Below our feet, a green carpet full of stains carried a heavy aroma of mildew.

We hurried through a second door and my mouth hung agape at what I saw. The spacious room had been gutted of its interior walls. Three metal tables with straps hanging from the sides filled one side of the room. White curtains divided the room into sections—the kind that slide along the tracks like you see at hospitals. Someone put a lot of money into this place based on the computers, microscopes, and lab equipment on the left.

Simon began with the file drawer. Since my job was to get us in, I stayed out of the way and looked over the setup. The tables had restraints and I wondered if the inseminations still went on and if so, how voluntary they were.

At the end of the hour, Simon had begun taking photographs. A white refrigerator with biohazard stickers on it snagged my attention, only the contents were not edible unless you were a Vampire. Vials of blood filled the shelves along with unidentifiable liquids. A sports fan had placed a basketball decal on the fridge door.

"I wonder what all this is used for," I said, staring at a cabinet filled with tiny bottles—the kind that doctors used to extract medicine for their injections. I opened the fridge and peered in again. The vials were numbered, but not all of them.

"Simon, you should take a few pictures inside here."

He nudged me out of the way and finished up the job.

Simon talked a mile a minute when we got home. He and Justus went into the study for a satellite conference with Novis to schedule a private meeting. Simon believed that computer connections could be compromised, so he didn't want to take any chances discussing their findings over the Internet.

I wandered into the control room hidden in our hallway and watched the monitors. Not a shadow stirred in the misty, dense woods. I jumped when a man with a long black coat suddenly stepped into the frame. Christian stood very still, watching the camera. It was eerie, as if he were looking right at me, so I leaned in closer.

"What the hell are you doing, Christian?" I whispered.

A smile relaxed his face and he lifted his hand and curled his finger in a *come here* movement. I stepped back, terrified to say the least.

Throwing on my coat, I marched down the hall and headed up the elevator that led into Justus's oversized garage. He had a couple of nice toys, but nothing that paralleled his previously destroyed collection. I had plans to rectify that. The garage door opened and revealed Christian's black shoes, long legs, coat, short beard, and finally his smug expression.

"Exactly how did you do that?"

"Concentration," he replied mystically.

Sometimes I wondered if the blood sharing we'd done had any lingering effects. He never mentioned it, but Simon said that Vampires were secretive about such things.

"Well, don't do it again. It's creepy."

He shrugged and dropped his hands in his coat pockets. "Do

you want to talk about what happened?"

It wasn't the lab he wanted to know about, but Tarek. I didn't answer.

"Is that how it's going to be?" he said, narrowing his black eyes at me. "Your business may not be my affair, but it is very much my business to know if you're in danger."

Christian tilted his head and focused on my chest. I mentally commanded my heart to slow down as I took a shallow breath and sighed.

"Don't bother," he said. "If you can't trust me, then I hope there's someone you *can* trust enough to tell. Whatever it is, you shouldn't keep it to yourself."

If Tarek had a Vampire following me, then talking to Christian would be all the permission needed to spill blood in my name.

I wanted to confide in someone more than *anything*, but fear kept me quiet.

CHAPTER 12

I N A QUAINT LITTLE SHOP on the corner of Mockingbird Street, I discovered a world of gourmet cocoa flavors I never knew existed. It felt warmer that morning and frozen puddles of water glistened beneath the sunshine. But the chill still clung to the air as a reminder that winter hadn't sunk its teeth in just yet.

I ambled down the sidewalk with my sack of goodies, thinking about how proud Justus had looked when I told him how I'd used my gift to open the locks. It was a tremendous feeling to know that my gift was more than just a novelty.

A dark, sleek car with tinted windows pulled up on my left. The rear window lowered and Tarek stuck his head out, curling his finger for me to get in with him.

Without a word, I complied.

We sat in absolute silence for ten minutes. While uncertain of what had happened to Christian, I knew if Tarek wanted him dead, it would have already happened. The car veered off the road close to the river and the driver stepped out and took a short walk.

A black fedora sat on Tarek's head, covering up the hideous haircut. It appeared that a wardrobe consultant had forced him to ditch the biker look and put him in a charcoal-colored suit, tailored to fit his formidable physique.

"Your time is up. I want an answer."

I had thought about it.

A lot.

It was *all* I'd been able to think about. I'd eat my meal and go to my room, worrying myself into a stomachache about what the right thing to do was. Each decision came with risk and consequence. If we tried to expose Tarek without evidence, it would compromise the safety of Logan's family and everyone I knew. I couldn't live with myself if he hurt someone close to me. Not one life would be worth my freedom.

I knew it.

Tarek knew it.

I exhaled and wrung my hands together angrily. "What are your conditions?"

He relaxed against the door and spread out his legs, giving him an air of authority he didn't deserve. He'd grown a tuft of hair on his chin, something his fingers pinched at during our conversation. "First, you will sever your trust with Logan." His eyes rested on mine. "Cheat on him."

My head involuntarily shook.

"Are you backing out of our agreement?"

A fleck of tobacco on the floorboard caught my attention, distracting me from reality.

"This isn't a negotiation, Mage. You will bed another male, and it must be someone Cross knows—not a stranger." Tarek rubbed his finger across his chin, his grin widening. "Tell him he doesn't satisfy you. Tell him he's not worthy. If I can't have my revenge in blood, I will ruin his heart."

Tears stung my eyes as he continued.

"I'm hosting a social gathering and you'll attend as my date. Our courtship will be brief, but believable. After you accept my claim in public, we'll make it official. Those are my conditions and you'll not deviate from them by a hair." He leaned forward and hardened his eyes. "Don't think for a second I won't find out if you've broken our agreement and told someone about this. Do exactly as I say or blood will rain down upon you."

I wiped the back of my hand across my sweaty brow as the true terror of what was unfolding became vividly clear. "They won't accept a union between us; I'm not a Chitah."

Tarek chuckled. "You let me worry about that."

My hands were fully charged and had I touched him, I could have easily knocked him out. But I didn't have the stomach to remove his head—one of the few ways to kill an immortal. The driver would be a witness, and I would be executed.

"This begins immediately, Mage." Tarek abruptly leaned so close that I looked away from his rabid eyes. A satisfied growl fluttered in his throat at my submissive reaction. "You have three nights to drop your panties and tell Cross all about it. If you fail, I will not award you another day. I think I've made my intentions clear. How you want to play this out is your choice," he said, pointing his finger. "Now get the fuck out of my car. You can foot it from here."

Tarek left me on the side of a rural road twenty minutes from home, holding a bag of peppermint cocoa. The wind snagged my hair and flung it about carelessly. Each step was a reminder of the uncertain path that lay ahead. I was finally gaining the respect of my Ghuardian. Logan was teaching me to trust again through his patience. A position with Novis provided me with opportunities I'd never dreamed possible.

Ruined. All of it.

Once home, I tossed the plastic bag haphazardly on the floor and went quietly to my room. The house still smelled like morning coffee and I found Max downstairs for a change, sitting in the hallway.

"Silver!" Justus barked from his study. "Your guard just called and said you disappeared."

"I felt like walking," I mumbled against my pillow.

He came into the bedroom and stood in the doorway. "Why would you walk home in this cold?"

"I can't freeze to death, so what does it matter? I'm not feeling well, Ghuardian. Something I ate."

Three days, only three.

Three days until I ruined my life, betrayed a noble man, and became someone that I wouldn't recognize in the mirror. A choice lay before me and I immediately ruled out Logan's brothers. It would have destroyed him.

Justus was out, and also Finn—they were family to me. We didn't have many mutual friends, so this narrowed down my choices. Remi remained a possibility, but he was Justus's friend. Plus, he intimidated me. I lingered on Adam's name for a while, and that would hurt

Logan because Adam once carried a torch for me. The only problem was I didn't have the stomach to use Adam so heartlessly—not after all he'd been through.

It boiled down to two names: Simon and Christian. The problem with Simon wasn't getting him in bed, but his strategist brain figuring out that something wasn't right. Plus, the only way to pull that off would be to get him rip-roaring drunk, and even then, the idea of ruining our friendship made me sick.

Then again, once I married Tarek, I had no doubt that my relationships would be severed.

I stuffed the pillow over my head and cried the kind of tears that are shed when you're mourning a profound loss.

The next evening, Justus busied himself installing new security locks on Page's doors and windows. I didn't really get what all that was about; he said they were just basic reinforcements that would prevent intruders from strong-arming their way in.

Page called and asked if I could talk him out of it, but once Justus got something in his head, there was no stopping him. He told her to accept it as an alternative payment for her services; this way, he would know that his money was being spent wisely.

Naturally, this rubbed Page the wrong way.

After he left, I watched the surveillance monitors in the control room. A shadow emerged from the trees and stood in the clearing by the motion-sensitive light, staring up at the camera. It was as if Christian could see through those electric wires, but I knew that wasn't the case. I ran my finger over the keyboard and punched in the code to disable the entrance alarm. Within a minute or two, the front door opened, and I reactivated the alarms.

"You want a drink?" I asked, filling my glass with vodka.

"I don't drink on the job," he replied. "Dulls the senses."

Yeah, dull away, I thought, downing my glass and pouring a second. Christian shook off his coat, hung it on the hook, and followed me into the living room, pausing at the entrance.

We'd chatted on a few occasions like this because I hated the idea of him standing out in the cold all night. It gave me a guilt complex. Despite his brassy personality, Christian was conversational and someone I enjoyed listening to when he wasn't needling me.

I sat on the white flokati rug spread before the sofa. The only source of light emanated from the faux fireplace.

"Take a load off. This place is locked up tight."

Christian accepted the invitation and sat on the floor with his arms over his bent knees.

"Want to tell me what's going on with you?" he asked.

"Just having second thoughts about getting permanent with Logan, that's all." The vodka was already racing through me.

"Is that so?"

I rinsed my throat with another long sip and he took the drink from my hand. "You don't need to get plastered to talk to me; I'll listen to whatever you want to say." Christian set the glass down on the far table and shifted to face me. "What vexes you, girl? Am I to worry about your safety, because I'd like to know why I'm being shadowed by a Vampire? Each time he's done with me, I find you in such peculiar conditions."

It was a now or never moment. There wasn't enough alcohol in the house to dull the ache in my heart.

"Did you ever think about being with another Breed, Christian? I never imagined it would be so hard."

"Well, now, I'm no Dear Abby, but I think I can tell you with absolute certainty that I'm not the person you should be asking for relationship advice." He snorted, leaning against the sofa and straightening his legs.

I risked a glance in his eyes. "So I'm not comparable to Vampire women? You once said that I wasn't classy or sexy."

"I was being cruel, Silver. Don't dwell on stupid things I've said, please God."

"The truth is cruel. I'm definitely none of those."

"Cheer up, lass, you're not so bad." He dropped a friendly arm around my shoulder.

"Christian?"

"Yep."

"When you were in my bed that night, was it just the blood, or was it me that turned you on?"

Something dark played on his features; a memory of the night when he shared his blood so that I might live. What transpired in that exchange remained a mystery to me, but not to Christian. I'd tasted his emotions toward the end and he thirsted for more than blood.

I seized the moment and sat up, throwing my leg over his lap to straddle him. My lips mashed against his throat and he shuddered as I scraped my teeth gently against his skin.

"Because I think about it, Christian. I think about tasting you again."

I ran my tongue along his neck, feeling the rise in his pulse where my fingers rested on his vein.

"Stop what you're doing," he breathed. "*Stop this.*" His hands clasped around my hips; he could toss me off at a moment's notice.

But he didn't.

My tongue glided over his neck once more before I slowly dragged my mouth across his bristly jaw until our lips joined. Our breaths met and he closed his bottomless eyes, allowing my tongue to run over the edge of his teeth. Christian's fangs punched out and pierced my tongue.

This was how you seduced a Vampire. I was learning that men had erogenous zones specific to their Breed.

I melted a kiss against his mouth, arousing him with blood. By the firm way his fingers pressed into my hips, I knew that he was urgent to take it but resisted—throwing his head back.

Perfect.

I lightly bit his neck, tasting his salty skin. A moan vibrated against my lips as a battle raged between reason and instinct. Beneath my short skirt I wore no panties; not my usual attire, but Christian hadn't known me long enough to have figured that out.

My mouth sucked on the soft skin of his throat just above the vein, feeling every muscle in his body tense and move all at once.

"Ever had a Mage?" I whispered, wrapping my fingers around his wrists and placing his hands on my chest. He dropped them to my hips again, as if unwilling to participate. Christian became a combustible package of dynamite that I was desperately trying to blow up.

Deepening the kiss, I tore open my shirt and the buttons tumbled down his chest and rolled across the floor. I hissed, not expecting how painful his grip would be.

Christian quickly let go. Breathing heavy. Glossy, black eyes hooded. His mouth parted and fangs extended.

I wanted to get it over with, and fast. I unzipped his trousers and wrapped my hand tightly around him.

"Ah, Christ," he groaned. Christian bucked beneath me. Our energy had no effect on Vampires, but then again, there was no sexual energy rushing through my body. I wasn't as aroused as he was, and because of that, I wasn't sure if I could take him. He didn't smell like Logan or touch me in the same reverent way. Christian also didn't have that faint trace of mint on his tongue.

It was all wrong.

"Slow down," he said. "Slow…"

I closed my eyes, trying to forget who I was with, stroking him against me. Nothing worked and my frustration rose. I finally gave up and lifted my hips.

"Wait, Silver, you aren't ready." Christian began pushing me away.

"I'm *so* ready." I said, kissing his jaw.

"Stop this. *Stop!*" His loud voice shook with frustration and anger. In a swift motion, he tossed me onto the white carpet like a heap of dirty laundry.

And that's exactly what I felt like.

"This isn't what you want. I can sense it in your touch, I can hear it in your heartbeat, I can see it in your capillaries, and I can taste it in your blood. What is this all about? Don't use me for your games," he said, straightening himself up. "Do you think I would take a woman who doesn't even want me? I'm not desperate. Or are you so insecure that this is a feeble attempt to convince yourself that you could have any man, and you aren't as undesirable as I once suggested?" Christian rose to his feet and zipped up his pants. "I have little patience for a woman's whims of insanity."

"Just go," I croaked.

He stood over me and his face soured. "I wasn't thinking with the right head when we got this started up. Had I been, I would have remembered that I don't find you attractive in that particular way. Not to say that men won't take a shine to you, but…"

Christian cut himself off and his black eyes glimmered.

"Something else is behind this," he said decidedly. "Does this have to do with Tarek?"

I shook my head. "Leave."

CHAPTER 13

A S PLANNED, LOGAN ARRIVED AT the house shortly
thereafter. I lowered the security to allow him entrance and
changed into a new shirt, not even bothering to put on a
pair of panties. I may not have had sex with Christian, but Logan
would be able to smell the sexual intent all over me. It wouldn't
matter if I had consummated the act or not.

In my mind, I had cheated with Christian. Tarek would never be
able to scent the lie because it was something I wholeheartedly believed.

I wanted to scream.

I wanted to throw up.

I wanted to kill Tarek.

When the front door swung open, Logan's nostrils flared and his
face became placid. Before I could close the door on him—having
had second thoughts—he caught my arm and pulled me into the hall.

His pupils were engorged, fluctuating between black and gold.
Logan bent forward and ran his nose along my hair, down my neck,
and drew in a deep breath. A frightening sound rumbled from
within his chest, the kind of sound a man might hear just moments
before death. Logan had developed his skills over the years—able to
pick up layers of emotions the average Chitah could not.

"Why is the smell of sex and guilt all over you?" His monotone
voice gave me a fright.

I jerked my arm away. "Let go of me."

A door crashed open from down the hall and Christian
stalked forward.

"I command you to step back. As her guard, I will only give one
warning." His eyes flicked between us, and I knew if it were anyone
else, Christian would have already thrown him to the ground.

Logan turned away from me when something else caught his attention, and that was *my* smell all over Christian.

He cocked his head to the side, stepping forward once.

Twice.

And then a third step. When Logan turned to look at me over his shoulder, his eyes were blazing with rage and betrayal.

In one second, every beautiful moment between us crumbled at my feet. The way he would stroke my cheek as I told a story, his boisterous laugh, the way he watched me with such adoration whenever I entered a room. Every memory we had together that laid out a path of the unknown—a future I'd been afraid of—was blackened. In that instant, any choice I ever had with Logan was removed. Any resolution I had hoped to find in my heart was destroyed.

"Logan, it's my life and you can't control what I want. You're only courting me, but I'm a woman of free will and this isn't working between us. I don't want a man who takes his time because deep down, he's not serious. You can't satisfy me the way a woman needs to be satisfied." I looked at Christian and thought of him so that lies didn't bleed into my scent.

Logan winced, and my anger at Tarek fueled the fire on my tongue.

"This isn't right," I said, waving a finger between the two of us. "It was just an infatuation, but it's stagnant and going nowhere. I need more in my life than what you can offer. I've made my decision, and I reject you, Logan Cross. I want you to leave before we say things we'll regret."

An observant Chitah could sense a lie, but not amid so many complex layers of strong emotions, including his own.

He didn't lunge after Christian as I had expected. Logan Cross turned his back and made a memorable walk down the long hall until he vanished from my life.

The person Tarek really murdered was me, because I had to hurt someone I cared deeply about. Logan would one day recover from this and move on. I never would.

I closed the door, turned the security back on, and went into my room. I slept beneath the covers for two hours before Justus stormed down the hall.

"Silver! Explain why my retinal scanner is destroyed," he shouted from outside my door. A scanner that Christian had damaged when he broke down the door.

A low volume of murmurs in the hall caused me to roll over. "Move out of the way, Christian. Then allow me to see for myself. Is she in there?"

I listened to the tumble of voices outside the door, rising and falling in volume

"...happened to the doors?" *That was Justus talking.*

"...discuss this in the morning... getting upset so you need to fecking go to... and let her..."

"Then leave the house and stand guard. The security alarms will..."

"...staying right here all night," I heard Christian reply firmly. But the words drifted in and had little meaning.

"The hell you are."

Christian raised his voice so that every syllable was felt more than heard. "I am *not* moving from this door. If we have to fight, then let's be done with it. I have known you too many years to swing against you, but so help me, I will. You're not taking one step past this door without going through me, and that is on *my* order as her guard."

After that night, Christian no longer hid in the shadows and guarded from afar.

Logan didn't call, but Levi did. The emotions were still raw, so I quickly hung up without explanation. Logan's brothers were probably patting him on the back and telling him he did the right thing. It would have never worked out between a Chitah and a Mage.

Let them hate me. Let them despise me for what I did. But let them live.

Regardless of how Christian might have felt about me after what

I did, he performed his duty to the fullest. Using him was horrible, but it didn't cause any irreparable damage, not the way it might have with someone I loved. I think he was mortified he was so caught up in it that he forgot his place as my guard.

I had to give Justus the impression that I'd been seeing someone new, so each night I dressed up and went out. He questioned me relentlessly until I admitted I broke it off with Logan. He didn't seem surprised as he'd warned me long ago it wouldn't work out between us.

Tarek's invitation arrived on a heavy card with fancy lettering, announcing the new Lord of the Youngblood Pride. It came with a long box and when I untied the ribbon and lifted the lid, I stared at a wine-colored dress lying on soft tissue paper. A small note indicated the hour he would arrive to pick me up.

The night of the party, I slipped into the expensive gown. It was a flattering fit, but for this occasion, I felt like a whore. Burgundy fabric draped past my knees and a long slit ran up the side. The neckline plunged past my breasts, fastened by a silver chain that wrapped around my neck. A chain that I discovered rather quickly was infused with magic to suppress my powers.

Justus knew I had a black-tie event to go to, but he got nothing else out of me. Now that I worked for Novis, he couldn't be demanding with his questions since some of my secrets could be work-related.

With my hands tucked in the pockets of my long coat, I walked down the driveway at sunset with Christian three paces behind me. While I didn't ask him to dress up, he wore black slacks and polished shoes beneath his trench coat. At the end of the road, Tarek's black car slowed to a stop.

I opened the back door, relieved to find he wasn't inside. Christian left the bike behind and joined me in the backseat. I watched a beautiful sunset with streaks of orange-sherbet and raspberry clouds melting into the darkness.

Tarek's mansion required me to turn my head left and right in order to see the whole thing. Each Lord in his Pride had acquired the same house and property during his term. I counted three floors with windows that were trimmed in tiny gold lights. Inside, guests were laughing and holding wine glasses, savoring a celebratory moment as leadership changed hands for the first time in fifty years.

Tarek waited out front, wearing a black suit and a cocksure grin. Christian wedged between us and the Chitah laughed heartily.

"Vampire, move out of the way. Silver is my *date*." He punctuated *date* with his canines. I took his outstretched hand with as much grace and dignity as I could salvage. Christian's expression told the story—he never saw it coming.

"Remove the jacket; it's not doing a thing for you," Tarek complained, unlatching the buttons on my coat and yanking it to the ground. He belted out a dark laugh as I stood in the cold wearing his dress.

"Silver, what you are doing?" Christian asked in disbelief.

"She's attending a party. Vampire, I'm not sure that you're on the invitation," Tarek said, clucking his tongue.

Christian's body language showed his intent was to step forward, but he merely leaned. "Where she goes, I go. By order of the Mageri, I am assigned to protect her life, and there is *no* exception. You know as well as I do the law entitles me entry."

"Very well. Shall we?" Tarek slipped his arm around my back. "Sweetie, you're shaking," he said with a smirk.

Christian's hand slapped around Tarek's wrist so fast I would have sworn he crunched every bone in it. Tarek yanked his arm free and scowled as four Chitahs surrounded us with lightning speed.

Guards.

"Do that again, Vampire," Tarek dared. "Lay your hand on a Lord and see what happens."

Christian's expression hardened and he reluctantly backed down.

Within the lavish home, a spectacular chandelier illuminated the center of the main room. Cream walls made the oil paintings pop, and adorning every available table was a stunning arrangement of fresh orchids. Guests nibbled on desserts and sipped wine that was placed in specific areas, if not brought directly to them by a servant.

Tarek babbled in my ear about how most of the men present were high-ranking officials, and that they'd never permit all Lords in one building at the same time due to the security threat. If there were a Mage in the room, they wouldn't have sensed me as the chain around my neck smothered my light. Not everyone was a Chitah, so I guessed Tarek was keeping his enemies closer.

"Tarek! My good man." One of them greeted him, clapping his hand on Tarek's back. "We're delighted by the change in power. It will be a good thing," he said with a toothy smile. Not everyone at the function seemed to like Tarek, but they all respected the position of his family enough to know it wasn't in their best interest to make an enemy of a Lord. "And who is this young specimen?"

"This is my female," Tarek said, tightening his grip around my waist. "A Mage. Lovely, is she not?"

"Ah," he said with a twist of his mouth. "But you cannot bear young with a Mage. How will you continue your family line?" They spoke as if I weren't even there.

"There *are* old laws that will entitle me to more than one mate, Niles." Tarek winked. "I think it's time we fully embrace our heritage and restore some of our old customs. Out with the new and in with the old."

The man with the fat belly and beady eyes patted Tarek's shoulder. "Good man. I quite agree. It's always nice to have… *tokens*." He winked back at Tarek and raised his arm to grab the attention of a man across the room. This Chitah was tall, lean, and much older than the rest.

"Peter, come say hello." Niles beckoned the man over and he strode up with his arms hanging stiff at his sides, flicking his light brown eyes between all of us without a hint of expression.

"Tarek, you haven't met Peter. He's Lord of the Inman Pride. Peter, this is Tarek Thorn, our newest addition." An elegant smile spread across his face as he watched the two men bow to each other.

Peter straightened his back. "We look forward to a long partnership with you, Tarek. It's good to see a shift in power. Introductions?" His eyes dragged all the way down to my red shoes. He might have only slept with his own Breed, but he was a man, and he liked what he saw.

"This is Silver, my female."

When he said it the second time, I heard the creak of Christian's shoe taking a single step forward. Tarek's eyes narrowed at him.

Niles eyed me and rubbed the side of his pug nose. "I can't help but think she looks familiar, Tarek. Where did you find her?"

Tarek beamed and puffed out his thick chest, dressed in a tailored black suit and tie. He had been waiting for this moment. "She was once claimed by Logan Cross."

Niles laughed, slapping his hand on his knee. "Of course, the Mage at the Gathering! I congratulate you," he nearly growled. "What an excellent choice she has made—the obvious one." His eyes lingered on the open part of my neckline. "For her to deny a male who staked such a public claim on her? Poor bastard. You are a worthy male indeed, Mr. Thorn."

Tarek's hand owned my hip. Why did this have to be such a production? Why not just send an announcement that we were getting hitched? Oh God, I felt nauseous just thinking about it.

Hushed murmurs surfaced through the crowd and Peter cleared his throat. "The Overlord," he whispered. "What a *rarity*."

A statuesque man with citrine-yellow eyes and coal-black hair glided in our direction. He wore a long, dark trench coat and carried a walking stick. Not that he needed it, but he did appear more seasoned than most of the men in the room. If I had to guess, he was close to a thousand years old and looked to be in his late fifties. He had peppered hair mixed in with the black, but just on the sides. Logan said that aging five years every one hundred was not an absolute; there was no exact science behind it and it varied from family to family.

My knees trembled as he crossed the room. You could feel the power emanating from him like an aura.

Each male he passed bowed submissively while the women lowered their heads.

"Sire, it is an honor to be in your presence," Tarek said in a voice thick with admiration.

The Overlord placed his hand on Tarek's shoulder and the room fell to a hush. "With power comes great responsibility, young Lord. Use it wisely, and be good to your people." His citrine eyes burned like fire as he looked upon me and then Tarek. "One day, your reign of power will end. Leave a legacy that your family will be honored by, one that will flourish within your Pride and bring unity. Good evening."

And just like that, the Overlord and his entourage left the building.

Tarek still held his breath as he whisked me into another room. "Someday, that will be my title," he murmured to himself.

If it weren't for the tight grip he had around my waist, I would have bolted out of the house and across the thousands of acres of property. A tall man with reddish-blond hair and no suit jacket politely tipped his head at a woman as he leaned against the fireplace mantel. He held a regal disposition that few Chitahs did, despite his rugged appearance. A short beard accented his wide jaw and strong features. He turned and his face lit with a smile, but when his golden eyes spotted me from across the room, the champagne glass nearly slipped from his hand.

I froze.

"Leo Cross!" Tarek shouted. "It's good to see you found time away from your new job to come out this evening."

I stared at the shoes of Logan's eldest brother because I couldn't bring myself to look him in the eye. Tarek ushered me across the room in his direction.

"I believe you already know Silver. Shame how things worked out between her and Logan; it must be an embarrassment for you," Tarek said in a mocking whisper. "She's a splendid female and I see why he gave chase. The circumstances in how we met were unfortunate, but we've put all that behind us. I'm sure Logan knows a little bit about that feeling, especially given how they met. Silver is a forgiving female."

I was stunned. Nero once hired Logan to kidnap me, but I wasn't aware it was information that Tarek could have known about.

"Tarek, may I offer you my congratulations," Leo said with zero enthusiasm.

While I admired the gold band on his right hand that symbolized he worked for HALO, I felt Leo watching me as he made the remark.

"You should challenge for Lordship, Leo Cross. Your time is coming soon and this will be your chance to move into a seat of power. There are many perks that go along with the position," Tarek said, tracing his finger along the curve of my shoulder. "It seems that power and money are very attractive qualities to a female." When he pinched the back of my arm, I looked up and smiled cordially.

"Good to see you, Leo," I said, testing my voice.

"Silver," he replied softly, almost questioningly. "You are well?"

I shrugged. "I didn't want it to end the way it did, but we move on."

After a few brief words, Tarek escorted me into an empty room. As the door closed, he grabbed me by the throat and backed me against the wall. Christian remained outside the door—forbidden entry.

"I can smell your fear and I know how nervous you get at these social functions, sweetie." He narrowed his eyes when he said the word fear, meaning that doubt was leaking from my pores and making his fantasy less believable. "It's just a formality, so play along." His finger touched the scars on my neck and trailed down my open neckline. "You look good enough to eat in this dress."

To add insult to injury, he threw his scent on me. For the last hour of the party, I had to endure the secretive stares as I paraded through the house that would soon be my new home.

CHAPTER 14

"Have you at least tried sitting down and talking to Silver?"

Page peppered her baked potato and poked it with her fork. It had taken three full days to get over the flu, and Justus had dropped in a few times in the days since. First, it was to fix the broken dryer, then it was changing out her loose doorknobs, and the next thing she knew, he wanted to upgrade her security system. She'd insisted on paying for the cost because she was left with no choice as he had already purchased it.

A waitress hurried by and the smell of fresh steak trailed behind her. Page hadn't had a meal like this in ages and she wanted to show her appreciation to Justus. It was the least she could do for someone who'd watched her stomach turn inside out.

Justus appeared to be a closed-off man with no desire to know her on a personal level. She had to twist his arm to get him to agree to go to dinner. When she decided on the chicken salad, Justus ordered her a steak and announced he would be collecting the bill.

That infuriated Page, but she decided it wasn't worth arguing over.

"Silver has no desire to speak to me," he said. "She sulks."

"Women do that." Page smiled. "It's called the feminine mystique. You'd be surprised how quickly we open up when someone lends an ear without saying a word. Maybe she thinks you're going to criticize her."

"I don't criticize."

Page laughed, tugging at her earlobe. "No, you don't. Not even when you chewed out the alarm guy for not setting it up correctly."

Justus tapped his palm on the bottom of the steak sauce bottle until a few dollops of thick sauce covered his steak. "He was an amateur."

"Was that a criticism?" Page smirked, taking a bite of her potato. Panic set in when the potato burned like fire on her tongue. She fumbled for the glass of ice water and took several long gulps.

Justus froze mid cut; arms held up to the side like two massive weapons as his eyes widened at her.

"Hot," she replied, feeling the sting on her tongue. "I better stick with the salad until it cools. So, Justus De Gradi, tell me about yourself."

He coughed and looked ready to choke. "I have been a Mage since—"

"No, no, Justus. Tell me about *you*." She looked up at his baffled gaze. "You know… *you*? What's your favorite kind of music? What are your hobbies and what's your favorite dessert? The things that make you tick; this isn't an interview about your Mage career, it's just a little small talk to pass the time." She pushed a tomato wedge to the side. Page enjoyed light conversation; it put her clients at ease.

The waitress hurried by and abruptly slammed on the brakes mid-step. Her head slowly turned and she devoured Justus with her hazel eyes, lids sparkling with purple shadow. She leaned over his side of the table and softened her voice. "Could I refill your wine? You know, one steak isn't going to hold a man your size over," she said, tracing her finger around the waistline of her skirt. "You look like the kind of guy with a voracious appetite."

Page lowered her eyes to her plate. Technically, this wasn't a date, so she didn't meddle. Crunching on a red pepper, she wondered why a restaurant salad always tasted better than the ones she made at home. No wonder she ate out all the time.

"What if I brought you another juicy steak?" The waitress whispered the last part, because clearly doing him a culinary favor would earn her the right to mount him.

Page wanted to laugh but kept an indifferent expression.

A piece of lettuce flipped off her fork and stuck to her bottom lip. She glanced up and jumped with fright. Justus sat with his fingers laced together and his chin resting on his knuckles—watching her as if the waitress didn't exist. Page quickly wiped her mouth with a napkin.

The waitress was a persistent little tart with her noxious perfume and heavy eye shadow. She leaned over so far he could have sampled her wares with his mouth.

"No, thank you." He dismissed her, retaining eye contact with Page. His eyes were hypnotic up close, and she could see why all the women were at the mercy of his gaze. "Would you enjoy some dessert, Page? I can arrange for them to prepare whatever you want."

"Um, no I'm not in the mood for anything sweet. I haven't even started my meal."

"Well, if you need anything, I'll be back to check on you," the waitress said. She was young, curvy in all the right places, and clinging to Justus as if he were a lifeboat on the *Titanic*. When he didn't respond, she clicked her heels on the wooden floor and made a memorable exit.

He leaned back and the chair creaked. Since the restaurant wasn't fine dining, there was no need for formal attire. Page wore her favorite jeans with a black V-neck sweater. After he'd seen her at her worst, she made an effort to style her razor-cut hair and wear her favorite perfume. Nothing fancy, just a bottle she'd picked up for ten dollars at the grocery store, but it smelled fresh and clean. Page had sprung the invitation on him and since he was at her house, Justus had to go with the clothes on his back. So he sat across from her in black jeans and a white undershirt with a dark blue button-up over it. He'd undone most of the buttons, and she preferred that look to the expensive duds he normally wore. If he had hair, she would have mussed it up.

Justus was clearly a man who liked to be admired. Who could blame him? If he spent that much effort toning up, then he deserved the admiration that fell on him from women.

Page had no time to indulge in the whimsical fantasies of a single woman. Some days she was lucky if she even ran a comb through her hair, which was why she kept a short, choppy style.

"So, tell me something about yourself," she pressed.

"Why do you want to know about me, Page?"

Her toes curled at the buttery texture of his voice.

"Why are you evading my questions? I didn't realize getting to know the real Justus was top-secret information," she said with a lift in her voice. "This isn't a date; you can relax. I like to get to know my patients. Well, you're not a patient, but you're her… family. Sort of. I just wanted to pay you back for taking care of me and you won't even let me do that much."

"You seem to be concerned with making sure you're even with people."

"I don't like being in anyone's debt. I'm sure you understand the dangers of that," she pointed out.

"Are you going to eat your dinner or just poke at it?"

"Don't take up the fatherly role with me, Mr. De Gradi. I'll eat it when I get hungry. I didn't want this." Page pushed the plate of uneaten steak forward an inch.

"You don't eat enough."

"What was it you were saying earlier? Oh yes, you don't criticize." Page lifted her fork and stuffed a cherry tomato into her mouth.

Justus pinched the bridge of his nose and a vertical line appeared on his brow. The tomato wasn't nearly as bitter as her tone, and her face soured. Page's no-nonsense attitude worked with clients, but it didn't carry over well in social situations. She couldn't even have dinner with a man without starting an argument. Or maybe it was something more, because she didn't seem to lose her cool with anyone else in private conversation. She felt a blush rising on her skin.

Justus suddenly dropped a hard fist onto the table and she jumped in her seat. When she looked up, he was laughing.

Laughing! He threw back his head and a few people turned to look.

"What's so funny?"

He lifted his silverware and shook his head. "Nothing," he said, sawing into his steak. He had a wide smile, appreciating something mighty secretive. "Just something I hadn't noticed before. Something I should have." He chuckled and shook his head again. He possessed a bold laugh: deep, warm, and full of life.

"Good to see you smile for a change," she said observantly. It relaxed her to see him more human.

"Why isn't a woman of your merit bonded... ah..." He cleared his throat. "I apologize, that's a Mage term. What I meant is *married*."

Page was suddenly famished. Hell, she felt like stuffing her face until she went into a food coma.

"Work doesn't allow me much time for socializing. And, well, I'm just busy most of the time."

"You were going to say something else?" he pressed.

"No, I'm workaholic." Page looked up. "That's all there is to that story."

Justus set his fork down and leaned in. He gave her the look all men have when they know someone is wasting their time with skirting around the truth. His gold ring tapped impatiently against the table.

"I'm not the cat's meow, Justus. Among Relics, I have certain... deficiencies. Anyhow, I *choose* to be single. I like my life." She crunched on a cucumber.

"You," he snapped, pointing his finger at her, "are anything *but* deficient."

Page held her breath. He caught the attention of two women at a table to her right and one of them interrupted the conversation.

"Would you mind? I never can get these to open." She handed Justus her steak sauce bottle and smiled flirtatiously.

Without removing his eyes from Page, he twisted the cap off and handed it back to the woman.

"I should have known," she muttered. It was so obvious and yet she had completely overlooked it. He wasn't just about confidence and money, Justus was a womanizer.

"Known what?"

She pinched a small cucumber from the salad and nibbled on the end. "Never mind."

"I refuse to finish this meal until you tell me what you were thinking."

She took a bite of steak and then another. "You're one of *those* guys—those Don Juans who play women like a fiddle," she said, waving her fork at the women in the room for emphasis. "Don't bother with the compliments, Justus. I'm not here for your amusement."

When he rose from his seat, Page knew the evening had finally come to an end. She tossed her napkin on the table and the next thing she knew, Justus had wedged himself into the booth right beside her, forcing her to scoot to the left. He lifted her plate and glass and set them both in front of her, moving his own dinnerware in front of him.

"What are you doing?" she said gruffly.

"Joining you for dinner. I prefer to sit at a woman's side rather than across the table. Too many objects to throw. I will not sit there while you decide that my interest lies in your body when that is not the case."

That was possibly the least romantic thing a man had ever said to her.

Ever.

Justus saw nothing attractive about her, and to prove it, he chose to sit beside her. Or maybe she'd bruised his ego and he was trying to win her affection so he wouldn't feel so inadequate.

She pushed at his shoulder with her own. "Dinner is over, Mr. De Gradi. Let me out."

"A good meal should not be wasted." He looked at her over his shoulder and sharpened his gaze. Justus looked like he could have been a marine, although he smelled more like a walking *GQ* ad.

She scraped her short nails on her jeans, trying to remain calm. This was her client's Ghuardian, after all. "Do you think sitting within close proximity will make me behave like one of those women who keep sexing you up with their eyes? How long are you going to keep me penned in here?"

"Until you finish your dinner," he said, breaking apart his roll and stuffing it into his mouth. "I'd like to try out the conversation thing. I'm not sure that you—"

His words suddenly cut off.

She crammed the baked potato in her mouth, sawed the steak to pieces, and then chewed it fast and hard. If this was the only way to end this humiliation, then so be it. Page almost choked until she washed it down with a glass of water. She managed to break a record by finishing her meal in less than a minute. Steak sauce smeared her lip and chives were sprinkled all over her lap.

While something out of the norm could always be expected at a Breed restaurant, a few people from surrounding tables turned in their chairs and gave her a disgusted look.

"What are you doing?" he growled in a quiet voice.

She gave him a frosty glare. "*Move.* I'm done."

Justus stood up and dropped a fat lump of cash on the table, no doubt to avoid the embarrassment of waiting for the check.

Once they were outside, she wrapped her wool coat around her tightly and hurried up the road toward the train station. The cold air burned her ears and she sniffed as her nose started to run. It usually did when the temperature dropped like that.

She had no intention of sitting inside his expensive car for an awkward drive home. Tonight reminded Page of why she never dated. Relics looked for a good match of genetic knowledge, and didn't dwell on things like appearances or money. And yet here she was, a wealth of knowledge and could offer none of it to a future husband. Even a Mage saw her as inferior, but for reasons other than her inability to have children.

Women's lib hadn't quite made it to most of the races. Having to sit through dinner and converse with a man who admitted that he didn't find her attractive became more than she could stomach.

"Page," he called out from behind. "The car is not this way."

"I can see myself home." Her ankle boots punished the sidewalk with an angry stride. They passed a bakery as the inside lights shut off.

"Allow me to escort you. The streets are dangerous at this hour and it's not safe for you to be alone."

She turned her attention to the curb just ahead. As they crossed the street, she asked, "What are you trying to prove with me? I have too much going on in my life as it is. Do you know what a big deal it is to have to explain why I can no longer work with my life partner? They don't just pick anyone to pair you up with; it's a tedious process to match the right people based on their skill set and it's usually decided by the time we're in our teens. Now I have to start over and I'll probably have no luck in finding a good match. I don't want you messing with my head just because I'm some kind of a conquest for your ego."

"Page, stop. Right now."

He stepped in her line of vision, and the two of them were facing off in the middle of a side street. Justus wasn't even wearing a coat and the wind blew his button-up back, exposing a thin undershirt. A chill hung in the air and his breath came out heavy and thick like white smoke.

"What?" She lifted her hands in the air. "*What?*"

Justus was so smooth in how he went about it that it took her a second to realize that she was being kissed.

He captured her lower waist and pulled her against him. His body was warm and so was his mouth against hers. Page forgot to breathe and merely hung in his grasp as his lips softened against her own.

Justus De Gradi was a phenomenal kisser.

There was no tongue action because he wasn't getting that serious with her. It was old-fashioned and romantic, the way every woman dreams of being kissed. Just not in the middle of a busy street with snowflakes falling on their noses. Her fingers curled around the opening of his outer shirt as if he might flee at any moment.

Page let him caress her mouth with his soft lips. Justus delivered a fervent kiss wrapped in tenderness, as if a firestorm raged beneath his calm. She shivered when his warm hand curved around the slope of her neck, and she rose on her tiptoes to get closer to him.

The planet silenced around them. Nothing existed except the hiss of his rough hand rubbing against her skin, the sound of her heart pounding against her chest, the crunch of ice beneath his boot, and the release of air from his nose. He let go of her waist and cupped her cheek with the palm of his hand. Page melted like frosting on a warm cake, forgetting everything else. His touch was a flame against the frosty chill of the night.

Just as his lips were.

"Get a room!" a cab driver shouted from his open window.

Abruptly, their kiss ended and a car whizzed around them.

Out of breath, she held his gaze for only a moment. It was the most romantic moment of her life and part of her doubted that it was genuine. "I guess that makes us even for dinner," she murmured.

Page brushed by him and after just a few paces, he shouted, "Am I *that* undesirable as a man?"

For a microsecond, her heart stopped.

Justus walked away and she knew that his question wasn't directed toward her. It wasn't ego she heard in his voice, but rejection. None of it made sense.

"No, you're *perfect*. That's the problem. I'm the one who doesn't meet the gold standard." Page turned and continued walking, mumbling to herself. "I've never been good enough."

Tears stung her eyes and suddenly strong arms folded around her from behind. Justus radiated heat against her back and she forgot that snowflakes were falling. His grip wasn't threatening but reverent.

And then his deep voice melted against her ear in raspy words. "Why would you say something to belittle your worth? You have it all wrong. You're intelligent, strong-willed, sure of yourself, *beautiful...*"

"I almost believed you, Justus, but you blew it with the last bit." She wiggled to get free, but he only allowed her to spin around and face him. "I'm decent-looking, but beautiful is not an adjective that accurately describes me. Why are you saying all this? I don't understand what your interest is."

"I *want* you to look at me the way you do now: mad as hell."

Was he serious? She looked into his distant eyes, and they weren't entirely on her, but skated off to the right.

"Women don't see me, they're *affected* by me. You cannot comprehend the torment of having to go through life knowing that the only reason women show affection is because it cannot be helped."

"You aren't making any sense."

A car horn blared and she jumped, heart beating wildly as he escorted her to the sidewalk.

"I'm a Charmer, Page. Do you know what that is?"

"I've heard of it, uh... you can make women like you."

"No. I have no choice in the matter. They *all* like me."

"And that's a problem because why?"

His brows pressed down and hardened his stare.

Page had two Mage clients and saw them infrequently, and only for consultations. She didn't understand Mage issues because it was never her area of expertise.

"I don't want them to like me. I want to be able to walk into a room and have a woman throw a glass of wine in my face, or roll her eyes at me, or tell me that my clothes are all wrong and I should do more pull-ups because I'm not strong enough. Because *that* would be real."

"What does this have to do with anything?"

He slipped his warm hands behind her neck and she softened her gaze. "Because aside from Silver, you are the only woman I have ever met who has not been affected by my gift. It is a simple joy to hear you criticize me and to know when you smile or say something kind, it's because you mean it. I don't understand why you throw away my compliments as if you are undeserving. You are nobility and grace. In another time, another life that I have lived in, a woman like you would have been coveted by kings. I am only sorry—" He cut himself off and his lips tightened. "I have not set a good example of how a gentleman should live." Justus stepped back and tucked his chin against his chest.

The wind gathered up a few scraps of paper and scattered them about. They stood quietly, facing each other. Page struggled to absorb the gravity of the moment.

She hadn't considered how lonely life could be if the opposite sex only wanted you because of an imbalance of energy. At least, that's how her scientific mind thought of it. There must be chemistry in Mage energy, which would explain the variety of abilities among them.

"Apologies. I have offended you," he said.

Page brushed away a brown tangle of hair that caught in her eyelashes. "No, you just…" She sighed, not believing the admission she was about to lay on him. Maybe then he'd realize that he was wasting his efforts. "Everything you just said about me—that was really beautiful. But I'm nothing to be coveted. The truth is, Justus…" She lowered her head and turned to the right, facing the street. "I've never been with a man."

The silence was so deafening that every snowflake hitting the cement sounded like a grenade exploding.

"I'm an outcast among Relics because I can't have children. I'm not the sort of girl that other Breed men go for because my job is demanding. I'm a dedicated worker who doesn't have time for socializing or even cooking. My shoes aren't designer heels—they're a pair of scuffed-up boots and dress shoes. I read. I knit. My favorite kind of music isn't the popular stuff on the radio—it's Etta James and Billie Holiday. Most nights I get home so late that I fall asleep on the couch almost as soon as I walk in the house. I haven't exactly had anyone knocking at my door."

The admission hung in the frosty air like linen frozen on a line. Page had always been forthright with her thoughts and opinions, but now she felt exposed. It was a real moment—one where she didn't think about the right or wrong thing to say. It was putting herself out there, right on the edge of the cliff. The wind stung against her lips and she stared at the empty sidewalk before her. The moon peered from above as a dark cloud passed over it, and it was bright and watchful.

A loud rapping sound startled her and she clutched her chest, spinning around as her boots scraped against the concrete.

Justus stood with his arm outstretched to the glass window of a candle shop. His closed fist rapped on the glass twice more.

"*I'm* knocking, Page. Let me in."

CHAPTER 15

I SPENT HOURS AT SIMON'S APARTMENT to see how much progress he had made in reviewing some of the photographs. His place wasn't huge, but he had a spectacular view from the fifteenth floor of his high-rise apartment building. Casual was an understatement when it came to his taste in décor. A chocolate-brown couch ran along the wall, and the shag carpet covering most of the living room floor looked like an original out of 1970. He only owned one television set. If you sat on the couch, you faced the front door with the kitchen area to the far left and the hall and a computer station to the immediate right.

Simon was in the middle of cataloguing the photographs of the lab. Word searches didn't help with images, so I typed information for each picture on a spreadsheet for quick reference and filed accordingly.

Most of the photographed files contained medical jargon I didn't understand—patient this, hemoglobin that. Not all the shots had come out clear, and I thought to myself that Adam would have been perfect for the job.

"This is going to take forever," I groaned.

"I enhanced the images to remove shadows and blurry spots."

After clicking through a few images, I leaned back and glared at him. "What kind of editing software are you using? You put a happy face on this picture. That's not very professional."

He snorted. "I was protecting her dignity."

Among the documented images, Simon had taken a few shots of an adult magazine. "Unless they're brewing porn stars in that lab, I fail to see the connection."

His office chair squeaked as he leaned back and stuck out his pierced tongue.

I was beginning to think that Simon just had a bad case of OCD, ADD, and PMS. With a little BS and OMG mixed in.

"Simon, whatever happened to game night?" I rubbed my weary face with my hands.

"This is why real life is a drag. Anytime you feel like getting owned in Battleship, just give me a ring."

"I think you should get some kind of audio translator that puts all your words down on the computer."

"Do you really think a bleeding scrap of digital bits could understand my accent?"

"When you have it? No. But then again, you swear so much you're liable to muddy up the files anyhow."

"Bugger off," he grumbled in a weary voice. "Doesn't seem to bother the ladies none. In fact, most like it when I constantly talk in their ear while I'm changing their oil."

I slapped the tattoo on his forehead and stood up. "You can be such a dickhead sometimes."

Simon leaned his head back and soaked me in with his caramel eyes. "You're so mature. I had a woman tongue my forehead in a way that I'd never quite experienced. So laugh it up, Chuckles."

I snorted at the mental image of Simon walking into a bar with that embarrassing tattoo and what his pickup line would be.

"What's your Mage gift, Simon?"

He pinched his fingers together and moved them across his lips, zipping them closed. Didn't hurt to try, and I sometimes asked in moments when I'd catch him off guard. It's possible he hadn't discovered them yet, as Justus told me some realize them right away, while others it takes years before their ability develops.

"Justus still training you?" he asked.

I nodded. "I'm learning to use my energy a little bit more. See?" I held my hand up and rubbed my fingers together, creating a trace of blue light between them that was an energy spark. I had acquired the knack of summoning my light at will, learning to harness it properly, and leveling down as needed. Justus had also taught me how to extract healing energy from sunlight, although he advised against crutching on energy to heal. I still had a long road ahead to get anywhere near on the same level as these guys, but patience is a virtue, and I was not without virtues.

"Excellent progress," he said in an impressed voice. Simon shifted around in his chair. "Where is Justus?"

"He sent a text that he was with Page, installing alarms or something."

"Justus likes her, you know."

"Who, Page? I don't see it."

He snorted. "Some men say it with roses and candy. Justus says it with Tasers and deadbolts. I don't hear much of Logan these days. Sorry bastard not wooing you hard enough?"

With a heavy sigh, I slipped into my leather coat and pulled up the zipper. "Don't ask me another question about it, but we broke it off and I'm kind of seeing someone else. Look, Simon, I'm whipped. I can give you a hand tomorrow, but my eyes are starting to cross. Don't work too hard," I said, messing up his hair as he flipped his laptop shut.

Simon had a hunch something dramatic had happened. He was the one who'd done the system check on the new retinal scanner while Justus spoke privately with him in the outer hallway. He rarely pried in personal matters, something I simply attributed to him being male.

I glanced at a shot glass on the desk. "You know, you don't exactly have top security in this apartment. You should think about that while you're up here putting sensitive data on that laptop of yours."

Simon was challenged by my accusation. "Throwing down the gauntlet, is that how it is?"

"I'm not attacking your ability as a strategist; I'm merely pointing out that a flea could break in here. Maybe you should store this at our house. And don't look at me like that."

His tattered red shirt with ripped sleeves said "Undercover Lover," which was more than what he had been wearing when he answered the door. He'd made some croquettes on his brand-new countertop and we'd nibbled on them while looking over the evidence. But I could only stare at a computer for so long.

"I'm going to head out, so call me when you want me to come over and give you a hand. I do miss our game nights," I said softly, leaning over to kiss the top of his head.

Simon arched his brows so that his forehead wrinkled and I scraped his hair in front of his face to cover up his hideous tattoo. Without warning, he clasped my fingers and scrutinized me with serious eyes. A muscle in my face involuntarily twitched and I jerked my hand away.

"See ya later, Simon."

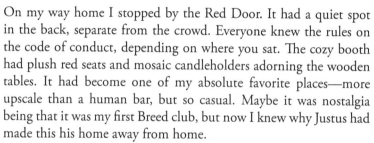

On my way home I stopped by the Red Door. It had a quiet spot in the back, separate from the crowd. Everyone knew the rules on the code of conduct, depending on where you sat. The cozy booth had plush red seats and mosaic candleholders adorning the wooden tables. It had become one of my absolute favorite places—more upscale than a human bar, but so casual. Maybe it was nostalgia being that it was my first Breed club, but now I knew why Justus had made this his home away from home.

I ordered a Green Dragon that was always too strong for me to handle; a green concoction that looked like liquid kryptonite. Sickly sweet and one small shot glass was all a person really needed. I hated the stuff, and it hit the spot. Christian slid onto a stool at the bar several feet away, peering at me over his shoulder while the bartender wiped down the surface with a white towel.

Tarek's threat loomed over me like an ominous cloud. My second glass arrived on the table and I grimaced as it sailed down my throat.

"I thought you didn't care for the specialty drinks."

My eyes lifted to a man with color-shifting eyes, now resting on hazel. His ultra-soft brown hair polished his shoulders, and the menacing dragon tattoo that stretched around his neck punched out like a waking nightmare.

"Remi, I didn't expect to see you here. Is Justus with you?"

I only saw Remi on the rare occasion. He was a Gemini—a Breed with a detached personality, and good reason for it. Maybe that's why Justus wanted me to keep my distance from him. They had a switch not unlike a Chitah, except instead of running on animal instinct, something dark and dangerous took over. The only way a Gemini could return from that state was to spill blood. I'd never seen it, nor did I care to.

"Justus has been busy." He bowed, keeping his eyes on me. "May I sit?" He removed his long jacket and folded it across his arm. Remi was dressed like everyone else in the city—warm. His long-sleeve cotton shirt fit his body well—a charcoal shade with a wide collar revealing the tattoo he wasn't afraid to show off.

"Sure. It's a free country."

He quietly slid across from me and laced his fingers together. "Sometimes it is, and sometimes not so much."

"I'll drink to that," I said, raising my empty glass. I felt a peculiar, almost dreamlike effect that promised me hours of sleep.

"I've mentioned to you the importance of retaining your humanity, Silver. More than once, if I recall."

I lifted a brow, sensing the direction of conversation. "Yeah, I remember."

"In your presence, I feel the need to mourn. It's an intuition, one that often comes with loss. Whatever pain you're enduring, don't shut yourself out. When you close off your emotions, you become like—"

"You?"

I blanched when the words escaped and I shut my eyes in disgust. Remi had selflessly helped us on more than one occasion and I'd just insulted him.

"I'm sorry," I said in a low voice.

"No need to apologize, Silver. I'm not offended by the truth. It is the way of Geminis to shut out our emotions, our... humanity. We are not able to control them as easily and as a result, there are consequences. But you have a choice. I miss the charm you once possessed in your humor, and there was a light in your eyes that is much dimmer now." Remi lowered his gaze thoughtfully and wrapped his fingers around a glass he had brought to the table, taking a small sip. "I would very much like to quietly sit here with you and share a drink."

Which he did.

Remi offered a mental hug even though I barely knew him. Sharing silence with someone is underrated. Sometimes words are not enough, or they're not the right ones.

Geminis were one of the most feared races among us. I found nothing threatening about him except the level of control he possessed. It was almost robotic, and even his compassion felt devoid of emotion.

My eyes closed and a sea of voices pulled me into a relaxed state of mind. When I opened them, Remi was gone.

"Stop it," I complained, leaning against my car and turning my back on Christian.

He wasn't tolerating my defiance. Christian slapped his hand around my wrist and took the car keys, walking me to the passenger side and shoving me in.

"What's the big deal?" I yelled out. "I'm immortal."

"Aye, you're immortal. But you're also langered. A woman and child crossing your path wouldn't be so lucky."

When he cranked the engine, it didn't start. After a few seconds, I opened my eyes and saw he had popped the hood open. I had my doubts that Vampires were very handy with a dead battery, so I pushed open my door and got out.

"Where's your bike?"

His hands were spread across the engine and he glanced up. "Think I'm letting you hang on to me in your condition? Liable to fall off the back and end up as roadkill."

"Come on, Sister Christian. Let's take a walk and we'll catch the soul train and walk the rest of the way home. Don't be such a big baby."

I shuffled down the road like a drunk zombie, my eyes closing like hammers striking a nail—forcefully and without hesitation.

"I'll have Simon take a look at it tomorrow," he said, coming up from behind. "Why don't you get Justus to buy you the newer model?"

If my eyes hadn't been glued to my lids, I would have rolled them.

I stumbled on the curb and fell to my knees. "Ah, shit. That was almost a faceplant."

Christian had finally had enough of the public intoxication sideshow act and picked me up.

Every muscle relaxed into a pool of bliss. My plan when I got home was to sleep on my red chaise, just for old-times sake.

Ten minutes into the walk, Christian abruptly stopped. I had tucked my face in the crook of his warm neck and could feel his pulse thumping faster against my cheek. I opened my eyes and noticed tiny specks of snowflakes glistened like diamonds against my clothes.

"Stay back," he said in a low, almost dreamlike voice. "I know you've been following her. Keep your distance."

I grew alarmed when I heard a distant growl that sounded like a Chitah.

"We could stay like this all night or you could let us pass," Christian said in a thick voice. "If you have a problem, then it's with me, and we can settle this whenever you like. Just say the word. But I will not stand here a minute longer, enduring your tantrum. Move away."

When the voices grew louder, my eyes snapped open. I was pretty damn sure that dreams didn't vibrate your skull with profanities.

Christian held me with only one arm. In the other hand, he palmed a knife. I twisted my neck around to see what the situation was.

The situation was Logan.

He held an aggressive posture with his arms heavy at his sides and head tilted down. Blond hair hung freely over his shoulders, tempted by the touch of the wind as it spun in its play.

"Put me down, Christian." His arm relaxed and my feet hit the concrete.

I had to play my emotions carefully. Logan could jeopardize this if he questioned the truth out of me, or worse, continued to pursue me. He needed to let go, because holding on to me would only bring death.

"It's over between us, Logan. I want you to stop following me."

He tilted his head to the side and locked his savage eyes on mine. It was the same riveting gaze as when he'd appeared at my doorstep one rainy night to capture me for a price. His shoulders were broad and his stance was confrontational. His cheekbones cut into his profile, giving him an animalistic expression.

"I'm sorry it had to come to this, Logan. I really am. But your claim on me is bullshit and you know it. I don't know why you fabricated such an incredible story just to win me over."

"I spoke to Leo."

Of course he did. I'm sure Leo couldn't wait to tell him about Tarek. In many ways, I was doing Logan a favor. Now he could be with his own kind and have a chance at a normal life with a family. But what rubbed the salt deep in his wound was that I chose the man who had not only tried to end my life, but had also raped Logan's former mate.

"Then you know, and there's nothing for us to discuss."

"How *could* you!" he roared.

"Because of free will. You said from the beginning that I've always had the choice. And I chose Tarek." Logan continually lifted his nose, drawing in scent, and I knew I had to be careful about not lying. "Tarek has power, Logan."

"But he *bit* you."

"And you *kidnapped* me. Your point?"

He lowered his head, his gaze, and his volume. "Am I that expendable? Tell me why I wasn't enough."

"Stop following me. Stop thinking about me, and just let me go. I'll *never* choose you." My words were nothing short of gunfire erupting over the surface of his heart. "I'm not the person you think I am, Logan. You promised that if I chose another that you'd accept it and not seek revenge."

Words he'd spoken the night we'd laid in my bed when he tenderly kissed the rib my ex once broke with his fist. Before I lost it, I let rage consume me to extinguish the pain. "You *promised* me that. And yet here you are, lurking in the shadows like the ghost of relationships past."

My eyes swallowed every visual inch of him. Lips I would never taste again, the feel of his face as it nuzzled against my neck, and the tiny laugh lines carved in his cheeks that I could only see when curled up against him.

And that hair—that beautiful, long hair that had become a symbol of hope for winning my love.

"Come on," Christian said. "Let's get your drunken arse home."

Logan's hands trembled, but he kept his animal in check as we moved around him and I walked regretfully out of his life.

CHAPTER 16

"WHERE ARE YOU TAKING ME?"

I wiped my sweaty palms against my jeans, glaring at the large ring on Tarek's hand that the passing streetlights illuminated. It was the next day, and he had picked me up in a short limo without giving me any information on our destination. Christian tailed behind on his motorbike. I'd confirmed with Tarek that I'd kept my end of the bargain.

Tarek pushed his hips forward in the seat across from me and smiled a wolfish grin. His finger tapped against the window. "Soundproof, you know."

I looked around, noticing the peculiar lining on the doors and seats. Of course it was soundproof. He had access to all the amenities a Lord was offered.

The car rolled down a busy street where people scattered, clutching their scarves and kicking up dirty flecks of snow as they hurried through the darkness to get to their destinations.

"I'm very impressed with your follow-through, Mage. Although in retrospect, I might have suggested you bed Leo." Tarek rubbed his Mohawk and cursed. "Damn, why didn't I think of that before," he breathed.

I shuddered.

"But, the Vampire was an interesting choice. It's a slap in the face to choose a male who is not even a Chitah, so that went over well, I'm sure," he said with a malicious grin. "I think you should speak to your employer about getting a new guard. It's a conflict of interest to be sleeping with a man you employ."

"Christian was assigned to me by the Mageri, not Novis. Are you going to tell me where we're going?"

"Our first date, of course. Informal, as promised. We need to be visible, and I have the perfect location picked out."

When the car rolled in front of a building with bold red letters on the window, I slid down in my seat. It was a Chinese hole-in-the-wall restaurant near Logan's apartment. He visited that place all the time with his brothers—the same restaurant that he'd ordered takeout when he held me captive in the cave.

"Your friend comes here a lot. Every Thursday night around..." He looked at his watch and grinned. "Right about now."

"I'm not hungry," I protested with a whimper.

He snatched my wrist. "You're fucking starving. *My terms, my* conditions. Refuse and I'll call it off. No second chances. Don't forget who you're dealing with, you little battery charger. I'm a Chitah, and I think we both know what I'm capable of," he said, pushing a meaty finger against the scars on my neck.

"Why the parade? If we're going to marry, let's just do it and get it over with. You've had your revenge."

He slid his hands down the lapel of his jacket. "What would be the fun in that? I want you to make it believable, so wipe that fucking sad face out of my sight. Make it smell real, because if you don't pull this off, then I won't hold to my end of the agreement. There are droves of women who would kill to be in your position, and soon enough, there will be."

I reached for the handle and Tarek leaned forward and pinned me against the seat. His scent was thick and filled the car as he rubbed up against me. "This will mask any emotion you leak," he said decidedly.

It was a quaint restaurant with square wooden tables and booths lined up along the outer edge. Various images of dragons and women holding fans decorated the walls, but nothing helped the tacky green carpet underfoot. That aside, the food was excellent as far as buffet goes, and they would prepare anything fresh on order.

Tarek led me to a table dead center in the room. I hung my purse over the back of the chair and when I lifted my eyes, I saw Logan sitting in a booth with Finn. He was wearing one of my favorite outfits on him. It was a light brown knit sweater with a loose turtleneck collar—one that was sentimental because he dressed me in it on the night we met.

His plate was half-eaten, but his eyes were full as they took in the spectacle of our entrance. Finn turned his head to look and his eyes widened.

That's when my heart fluttered. Finn's animal was still volatile, and so help me if Tarek so much as laid a pinky on him, I would lose all control.

Four of Tarek's bodyguards positioned themselves near the doorways, and Christian stole a booth on my left.

Tarek made three trips to fill our plates and seated himself on my right.

"Eat," he said as he shoveled a forkful of fried rice into his mouth. "Not bad for a dump. But then, we Lords can't eat caviar every night, now can we? Smile, Silver. It relaxes the face." He thinned out his eyes with a cruel expression and I tried to relax and twirl a few noodles, imagining myself strangling him with them.

"Next time, I'll take you to one of my favorite places," he said. "It's one of the most extravagant Breed restaurants in the city, and I can always get a table at short notice. How's your Ghuardian these days?" I watched his jaw work like an iron machine. "Does he know I'm taking out his Learner?" Tarek laughed and licked his finger. "I'll have a man-to-man talk with him."

"He knows about us, Tarek."

"Good, good," he said agreeably. "As it should be. We make an acceptable match, even with your shortcomings."

The candlelight melted across our table like a pool of fire. I sipped my water and concentrated on my plate, studying each pea as I removed it from the rice.

"Some of the formalities of my position can be dull. Meetings, making connections... it all gets to be a little excessive," he said, feigning small talk. "I like getting out and having a meal with my female." His voice rose, wanting me to respond. I took an unnoticeably deep breath and smiled at him.

"When do I get to meet your brothers?" I asked hopefully. Maybe Tarek was corrupt, but from what I'd heard, his brothers had disowned him. I held on to the hope that his family might look after me.

A muscle in his cheek twitched.

"If we're taking this to the next level, then I'd love to meet my new brothers. I've heard so much about them, they sound like—"

His fist dropped on the table, not so loud that it would catch anyone's attention, but enough that I could tell I'd hit a nerve. The vein in his forehead bulged and his lips thinned. I was walking a thin line, but considering the history with his brothers, there was a remote chance they might offer me protection.

Christian leaned forward to get a better visual.

Tarek placed his hand over mine and stroked it softly. "Of course you can meet my brothers, I'm honored that you want to meet my family so soon. It lets me know you're as serious about us as I had hoped."

His fingers pinched a small piece of beef from my plate and he held it in front of my mouth. "Have a bite."

"No thanks."

That was an intimate gesture for a Chitah that you only shared with someone you trusted. Letting him feed me was as good as having sex on that table.

He dropped the beef and looked over our plates, holding his hand like a claw in one of those quarter machines kids play that gives false promises of winning a purple elephant or yellow teddy bear. My heart thumped.

"Cross, what a surprise to see you here," Tarek said, twisting around in his chair. "Who is your friend? You must join us. I *insist*."

This is not happening, I thought.

At the request of a Lord, Logan rose from his table with his plate and glass and sat in the chair across from me.

"My friend is a Shifter. He prefers to eat alone," Logan said.

When his eyes fell on mine, they rolled completely black and popped gold again. He picked up Tarek's scent all over me, judging by the flare of his nostrils.

"You should talk Leo into challenging for the position when it comes up in your Pride. Imagine, if he became Lord, we would almost be family! Hope you aren't harboring any resentment, Cross. I decided to let things go between us. Fuck, man, you can't go around in life holding a torch for someone. Katrina wasn't the only one for me," he said, squeezing my hand. "Funny how things work out, isn't it? Shame what happened with that Vampire," he said, leaning toward Logan and lowering his voice to a whisper. "Silver told me all about it. If I were you, I would have gotten rid of that problem a long time ago. You catch what I'm saying?"

My insides felt like a monster-truck rally, due to my fear that Tarek could push Logan over the edge. We spend our lives standing on the precipice, one foot on the ground and the other hovering over the unknown. All it takes is the gravity of a moment to change the course of our future—to either pull us to safe ground or cast us into a perilous fall.

"How did it start between you two?" Logan asked with a curiously neutral expression.

Tarek chuckled and bit into an egg roll. "We agreed to meet and bury the hatchet about what happened. After all, it was only business. Damn shame that didn't work out in your favor. Sweetie, why don't you tell him the rest?"

His hand squeezed mine ever so slightly.

"Well, we just started talking. Tarek is a convincing and persistent man."

Tarek knew I couldn't lie with Logan, so he quickly took over the conversation. "She has a strong will—I like a little fight in my women," he nearly growled. Logan stiffened in his seat. "Obviously a man in my position has a lot to offer. It's taken a serious turn, and I believe we've reached a mutual agreement."

Logan slowly lifted his chin and a steady, cool voice moved past his lips. "Does he treat you well?"

Before I could conjure up an answer, Tarek interjected. "I treat her like the Lady of a Lord she will soon become."

With that one admission, Logan knew exactly how far Tarek intended to go with me.

All the way.

Ignoring Tarek, Logan repeated his question in slow, private words. "Does he treat you well? If I am to accept that you have chosen another, then I must know that he will properly care for you."

Logan's nostrils flared as he sought a reason to challenge Tarek.

"He treats me as I deserve to be treated. Tarek has money and he can financially care for me better than you."

Tarek straightened up in his chair and stretched his arms over the back of it.

"Are you looking to win back my female, Cross? It sounds as if she's made her choice, so don't get any plans to bed her before I do. Oh, don't worry," he said with a laugh. "I'm a perfect gentleman with this one, unlike you. Perhaps your endowments fell short, or maybe you just couldn't offer her the comfort that only money can bring. I plan to select just the right moment for our consummation."

Tarek winked, and it suddenly dawned on me with absolute clarity that sleeping with him would be part of the deal. A permanent part.

"And how do you plan to mate with a Mage, Tarek?" Logan provoked. "For one, it's not legal. And as a Lord, you are required to provide offspring, which you don't have."

I glanced at Logan, who looked noble and stunning. He no longer wore his hair tied back. It was as wild as the look in his eyes.

"There has never been an official mating with another Breed that has been acknowledged by law," he continued. "It would bring embarrassment to your Pride."

Tarek ran his hand over his Mohawk. "Things I have already considered. There are older laws, ones you may have forgotten that will allow me more than one mate. As Lord, I have full authority to revive these laws. They will bear sons for me, but every man likes to cozy up to something warm at night. I don't plan on doing that with a female carrying my young; a pregnant woman does nothing for me."

"It won't be *legal*," Logan said, lips curling angrily.

Tarek snorted softly. "That certainly didn't seem to stop you. As I said before, I've considered these things. Come here, sweetie," he barked at me, patting his leg. I rose from my chair and Tarek pulled me onto his lap. His arm snaked around my waist and a possessive growl rose from his throat as his fingers stroked my belly. I almost shuddered.

Almost. Tarek was testing my willingness, perhaps hoping I would ruin the charade so he could spill blood.

"Normally I don't like sloppy seconds," Tarek purred, running his finger along my cheek. "But this one is something special. I'm guessing you know that already. Can't say I'm sorry for how things turned out."

His scent pushed out again and he nuzzled his face against my neck. I turned so that my hair spilled across my face and hid that I was scrunching my nose. It looked like a private moment between lovers when I was simply playing out the destruction of Logan's love for me to the bitter end.

I slipped my arms around Tarek and nuzzled against his sweaty neck.

"I'm done eating; let's go," I whispered. Something stirred in him and he squeezed my thigh. Tarek smelled victory.

"I'll be sure to send you the invitation, Cross. Take care."

When I lifted my head, I heard the bell on the front entrance jingle.

Logan and Finn were gone.

CHAPTER 17

"THAT WAS QUITE A SHOW you put on, Mage. Quite a show!"

Tarek belted out a laugh while rolling up the divider between his driver and us. He shuffled out of his suit jacket and took down a few buttons of his white shirt. We sat facing each other and I folded my arms.

"I'm beginning to have more fun with this than I had imagined. I have a gift for you," he said, handing me a thin, flat box.

I lifted the lid and pulled at the white tissue paper. At least it wasn't a dress box. "What is it?" I asked in an unpleasant voice, staring at a delicate chain.

"Custom made," he said casually. "Here, let me put it on."

Tarek plucked the chain from the box. It reminded me of the mesh that knights might have worn as armor, only it had a feminine quality. The small chain slipped around my neck and had several thin rows of silver in the front. Not like something I'd wear to Club Hell, but classy.

He fastened the jewelry with an audible click. Tarek leaned back, holding a tiny key between his fingers.

That's when I felt it. Like turning down the volume at a rock concert. I'd worn something like this once before.

"Where did you get this?" I said in a breath.

"Nero has a distributor that negotiates only with him. This is a rare piece. You should feel special."

"Why the hell would he sell you jewelry to give to the one person he's been hunting for himself?"

Tarek chuckled darkly. "It's all about building alliances, and at the moment, my title places me in a position to provide Nero with information that is of greater value than a scrawny Mage such as yourself. He may want you, or want to kill you, but he's not a stupid man. Nero sees opportunity, and part of that comes with respecting my wishes if he wants me to cooperate."

"You can't make me wear this," I raged. "I need my energy to protect myself!"

"You don't need protection, sweetie. You've got me and I'm all the protection you need."

"I'll pick the lock," I said, tugging at it.

"Afraid not. You won't be able to get that thing off with the Jaws of Life. You know, I'm beginning to reconsider my plan to mount you. After tonight, I think you deserve a reward."

"I'm never going to sleep with you, Tarek."

He laughed boisterously and clucked his tongue. "Who said anything about sleep?" His finger slid over a button and the divider lowered. "Driver, pull over and give us privacy."

The car turned off the road and the driver stepped out, leaving us alone in his soundproof, tinted-windowed, bulletproof vehicle. I tried the door handle but it didn't open. He captured my wrist in his hand and brought it to his nose, taking in my scent.

"You are ridiculous," I said, snatching it away. "I'm doing this because I have no alternative—none that a human being with a conscience would choose. But mark my words when I tell you that I will make your life a living hell."

"And for each hell you bring, I will take a life."

"That was *not* part of the deal; you can't keep holding them over me for the rest of my life!"

"Can't I? That is one thing I did not give my word on. This isn't a movie where someone will save you, Mage. Every decision you make affects a life and you have to ask yourself how much you're willing to sacrifice for them." His fingers slipped into the hem of my jeans.

"If you harm a single hair on anyone's head that I love, then you'll pay for it. I don't care if you *are* a Lord."

His eyes vanished to slivers and his grip tightened. "Hence the collar," he ground out. "Don't you ever threaten me again, Mage. I don't like the way your mind works, and I don't plan to take any chances with my life. *Never* trust a Mage."

Just then, a tapping on the glass snagged our attention.

He flipped the switch and rolled down the window. Christian's face peered through the opening.

"It's time for Silver to go." His voice was cool, like a peppermint, and sent a chill down my spine. His black eyes flicked to mine briefly, scanning the situation.

Tarek ignored him and lit up a cigarette. "I want you to talk to your employer and request a new guard."

"I'm going to quit my job," I stated. Something I'd been mulling over, but I could never serve Novis while mated to Tarek.

Tarek rolled the window back up and leaned in close. "Absolutely not. All that important knowledge you would be forced to give up? No, I'm afraid that's one of the perks." He blew a plume of smoke in my face and touched a round button on the armrest. Seconds later, the driver eased into the front seat and started up the car.

"If Novis doesn't assign me a new guard, then you'll just have to live with Christian."

Any trace of humor he held on his face was completely erased by a penetrating stare that bored into me like hell itself.

"I don't have to live with anyone. Accidents happen. It would be a shame."

Tarek left me at the main turnoff to my house. I was all but stomping the ice and gravel to China. Halfway up the driveway, Christian yanked my arm and pulled me into the dark woods before we reached the motion detectors. I stumbled behind him as he walked me to his motorcycle and threw his leg over the seat.

"Get on."

Christian knew how to handle a bike. It moved effortlessly in his control, gliding around corners and picking up terrifying speeds as his head periodically searched behind us. The streets had been mostly cleared, but a few icy patches remained, which he somehow avoided. At one point, I was certain we were going at speeds over a hundred miles per hour.

The bike veered off the road, taking us on a bumpy ride up a dirt path that cut straight through the woods. I shut my eyes—terrified—because Christian kept the headlamp off. Only a sliver of a moon lit the sky, not enough to light our way through the darkness. The Vampire could see everything, but I couldn't. Christian skidded to a stop and I leapt off as he walked the bike behind a set of bushes. From there, he took my hand and led me to a cement building with no windows.

Christian locked the door while I paced to the center of a pitch-black room. The sound of matches rattled on my right and then there was the rough scratch of a wooden stick sliding along gritty sandpaper. With a hiss, light burst into the room from a tiny flame, and Christian lit a few red candles and set them on the floor. Shadows danced on the ceiling and walls as if they were extensions of the physical world leading separate lives. My breath fogged before my face and I cupped my elbows.

"Is this where you live? It looks like a prison," I said.

A mattress covered the floor in the far left corner, and to the right a small table and chair completed his furnishings.

Christian's black coat dropped on the floor and I studied his attire. He had once dressed in showy leathers and full Vampire gear to rile me up, but the real Christian didn't give a shit. The sweater had a torn collar as if he'd taken a pair of scissors and made the hole wider to show off his strong shoulders. He reached out and ran his fingers over my necklace.

"Turn around," he ordered.

I complied, and the chain tugged against my neck. Christian's arms shook as he attempted to break it, and the silver bit against my skin. I coughed and he released his grip, turning me around with his hands on my shoulders.

"This structure is soundproof, and never you mind how. No Vampire could hear us if they dared to follow, and I'm certain the one who has trailed me on two occasions did not follow us, because he's a dolt and drives an SUV. We're alone." The lilt of his Irish tone fell flat. "I'm your guard. This means keeping your confidence. We're not leaving this room until you tell me everything. Logan may be daft to what's going on, but I'm not."

"I'm going to ask for another guard. Novis will agree when he found out what we did."

Christian shook me so abruptly that my mouth hung open. "You do *not* have to act with me. Novis isn't going to take me down from my post on your request. It won't be the first time he's heard about diddling with a guard."

"Tarek will kill you."

"I've seen a great many things in my day, and blackmail is not a new concept. Neither is my life being in mortal danger." He scratched his beard slowly, the other hand cupping his elbow. "I thought about what happened, and it was the only conclusion I could draw from you throwing yourself at me. Drunk or not, I know you're not the sort of girl who would drop her knickers if it meant risking her relationship. It wasn't regret I saw in your eyes that night, it was defeat." Christian walked me to the chair and folded his arms. "Sit down. What you tell me will never leave this room if it means putting your life in danger."

"My life is not in danger."

He gently pushed my shoulders until I was sitting in the chair. Christian knelt down and sat on one leg, speaking in his usual dark voice. "Then whose? Logan's?"

"Everyone," I whispered. "I have to do exactly as he says. All of this is an elaborate play to get back at Logan. Years ago, Tarek had a kindred spirit that he was ashamed of—one that he never claimed in front of his elders. She fell for Logan and they mated, and Tarek never raised a challenge because she wasn't good enough for his family. He raped her, she got pregnant, and through another set of circumstances, she was murdered. In Tarek's mind, he thinks Logan stole her away… even though he's the one who let her go."

"And the threat?"

I released a heavy sigh and looked at his dark lashes. "I had to betray Logan. But that wasn't enough because now he keeps taking it further. Now he plans to mate me, and that's as good as marriage. Yeah, a Mage," I said, nodding as the stoic expression on his face slid away.

"Why haven't you told Simon? He's a strategist and this is his area of expertise."

"He'll tell Justus. Tarek laid down a threat that if anyone finds out, or if he even suspects that anyone knows, he'll carry out the murders. You know as well as I do that a Chitah is good on their word. I can't take that chance. *I don't know what to do,*" I said in a defeated voice. "I can't have even one person die because I made the wrong decision." Tears welled in my eyes and I angrily wiped them away. "He's Lord of his Pride, and you know by law I can't accuse him of anything without evidence. All that I have is my word, and that isn't enough because he hasn't committed murder. He hasn't committed anything, just made threats. I don't even think the elders of his race would care if he did kill me because I'm a Mage and beneath them."

"So disappear."

I shook my head with a ghostly expression. "He'll do it to spite me. He'll always have this ace up his sleeve. Anytime he wants me to do something, all he has to do is pull it out." I slammed my fist on the table. "And now he's got me wearing this damn slave collar! I can't even fight him."

Christian lowered his eyes. "So that explains it," he whispered.

I pushed my face into my hands. "I'm so sorry. There was no one else I could choose and I feel so embarrassed for what I did." My face flushed when Christian's hand touched my knee.

"It's already done and forgotten. It's more shameful to know you were forced upon me and I went along with it." A muffled crack came from the floor and I glanced down at a fissure in the concrete where Christian's fingers were splayed.

"He's already won. Even if I were to kill myself, he's won."

"Don't talk like that, lass, or I'll kill you myself."

That roused a smile on my face. "Can you wipe his memory of me, or—"

Christian shook his head and his voice fell to a lower octave. "He's too protected now. Without knowing the specific moments to erase, it would be too dangerous. Tarek or someone else will notice he's been scrubbed and all hell will rain down on you, or perhaps the Mageri. Attack a Lord and not even the Mageri could protect you. It might instigate war."

I rubbed my cold nose and looked at a broken cobweb in the corner. "Why do you have a bed? I thought Vampires didn't need to sleep?"

His eyes skated away.

"Oh."

"Vampires can be particular about our privacy."

"So you bring the luscious ladies to a dirty mattress on the floor?"

He shrugged and I changed the subject. "What if you ask Novis to leave your post? He can't force you to stay."

"Fecking *not*. Now start from the beginning—I want every detail."

CHAPTER 18

"HE DOESN'T CARE THAT I'M spending the night with you?" I asked.

"You know Justus," Christian assured me. "Always full of questions. But he trusts me when it comes to my job. It's not to say he didn't give me a thick ear."

The chair wobbled as I rubbed my lower back and stretched. "How long are we staying here?"

"Until we work out a solution. If you think I intend to watch this go down, then you're a piss-poor judge of character."

"Maybe we should bring Simon in after all."

"No, you were right to not tell anyone. We can't risk it. Tarek's a cunning bastard, and if you have a Vampire on your tail, it won't be hard to track Simon's leathery arse and pull the truth from him."

"The Vamp could get that information from you. A stake might change your mind."

"I rather enjoy steak, now that you mention it. But my secrets are not easily given up, and I've already knocked him around once or twice—enough to know that he couldn't pull a tooth out of a six-year-old's mouth."

"Hardy har har."

"So nice to see your nasty temper again. I missed it," he said, taking a seat on the edge of the mattress.

"Do you know anything about Chitah laws or history?"

"I'm afraid I would be of little help there." His knuckles rubbed the soft hair on his chin. "Why *not* have Logan challenge him?"

"Hell no! I don't want anyone hurt, especially him."

Christian snorted. "It's a bit late for that."

I turned my head away, rubbing my drowsy eyes. Candlelight

had a soothing effect—maybe that's why Justus clung to that lifestyle. "The only way Tarek might drop the façade is if Logan chose another woman. He thinks Logan was lying to me about being a kindred spirit, and it was nothing more than an infatuation."

"Do you believe it?"

I picked at a splinter poking up from the table. "I don't know what to believe anymore. Maybe he's got his wires crossed. If I no longer matter to Logan, then Tarek loses."

"Do you think Logan would take another female?"

Christian flopped onto his back with his arms folded behind his head, blinking at the ceiling with scheming eyes. "Think about it very carefully, Silver. Do you think there is any small part of Logan that wants to be with another woman?"

"I don't know. It might be appealing for him to date a Chitah. Less drama, no stress, it would make his family happy. What's your point?"

"Consider it. If Logan fell in love with another woman, then Tarek would be defeated. Why would Tarek continue ripping your life apart if none of it mattered to the one man he wants to destroy? You're merely the hammer he's holding to beat down the nail. If Logan has any doubts about your relationship, if you think there's any small hope that he would take another woman, then I can plant the idea in his mind and erase our conversation."

"You mean—"

"Charm him. If it doesn't work, then nothing's lost. It means you won't get him back, Silver. But at this point in the game, I don't think he'll pursue you much longer. You belong to Tarek now. You've refused him, and a man's pride cannot be mended."

Charming was how a Vampire could weasel into your subconscious. "What are my choices?"

"Stay with Tarek and live in fear and keep those around you alive. Or give Logan a woman and gain your freedom. Either way, you'll lose Logan, but perhaps it might be a bittersweet parting; you'll be free and he'll be happy." Christian put his hands over his face, elbows in the air. "You don't have to decide now. *Jaysus*. What a load to put on someone." His voice fell to a soft murmur. "I should be hunting men like him. I always thought about that line of work."

I got up from my chair and sat at the foot of the mattress with my back against the wall and my knees bent. "Can you clean his memory of me?"

"No, I don't recommend it. Long-term memory removal renders one insane. To remove so many moments that are weaved in your life and embedded in specific places in time leaves gaping holes like Swiss cheese in your head. If I'm part of a particular event in their memory, that is preferable. It's clean, like an eraser on a chalkboard. Intense memory cleaning is like using whiteout in a thick book, you're going to miss spots and they're going to notice several pages are missing unless you clean them all. Your mother took some time, but I left the romance with Grady intact and only removed that last bit at the end."

"The last bit being my conception," I grumbled.

I reached behind my shoulder and picked at a chip in the wall. My decision would sever any hope that Logan would wait for me, as he once promised he would. I had a rebellious streak in me that was difficult to overlook, and he would endure criticism from his own kind. In time, Logan would eventually want children. The closer I came to a decision, the more I knew.

I'd wasted every precious moment of opportunity. Logan came into my life as a man who couldn't be trusted, and ironically, he was the man who taught me to trust again. And yet I was the one who wasn't worthy of him.

"Will he love her?" I whispered.

"If he chooses. I can only plant the suggestion, but if any part of him is willing, then it's out of my hands. Do you think he is hurt enough to take another?"

"No. There's something I have to do to finalize it."

"Don't fret over it, lass. Hearts are made of glass, and once broken—no one can reassemble it for you. They can cut themselves trying, but it's better if you just sweep up the pieces. Nothing good ever lasts for long."

Maybe Christian was right, but now that things were set in motion, there was one last thing I had to take care of. "Do you know how I can get some liquid fire?"

It displeased Justus when I quit our early morning training sessions. He kept my body conditioned through workouts and taught me maneuvers through our sparring. Sometimes they were simple moves to escape an attacker, other times he focused on teaching me how to control my energy. With the chain locked around my neck, I wouldn't be able to flash or heal, and he would know something was up. I kept it tucked beneath my shirt since it wasn't a heavy piece of jewelry.

He wanted to groom me into a warrior, but refrained from showing me complex maneuvers I'd seen him perform. It was just enough to fight off juicers—rogues living outside Breed law who were energy addicts, stealing light from young Learners. I'd had several encounters with juicers, although Justus had always stepped in to protect me.

"What is this supposed to mean?" Justus shouted from my doorway.

An invitation had arrived in the mail, announcing my acceptance of Tarek's claim.

Our engagement party.

Tarek had invited everyone close to me, moving his chess pieces strategically around the board in case I decided to back out. I had argued with Justus for an hour before he stalked off, and now I was facing the cooled off version.

"You can read, can't you?"

His face was uncharacteristically red and blotchy. "If you think I will agree to this then—"

"We went over this, Ghuardian. It's not your choice who I marry," I replied calmly, brushing my hair in front of my bedroom mirror. He stood behind me with an angry vein protruding from his forehead.

"I am your Ghuardian, and that means I have control over your welfare while you are in my custody. I have say in the matter."

"Once we mate, I'm no longer in your custody. You have limited control over my care, but you can't control who I'm going to marry.

I won't have independence until you officially release me, but you know as well as I do that if I marry, then that law is overruled. Your job will be done." If a stone could be sliced with a sword, I knew what it would look like. Justus lowered his head. "Ghuardian, we all move on eventually. Now you'll have your life back. Don't worry about me." I turned to face him. "I want this more than you know. So much has changed in the past few weeks, and I need you to trust that I'm making the right decision. People aren't always who they seem to be; you above anyone should know that. I'm not asking that you like it—I only want you to accept it."

Confusion streaked across his face like lightning and I smiled. "Never underestimate the decision of a woman," I told him. "Sometimes we do the most surprising things. You have to let me make my own decisions when it comes to matters of the heart; love is unpredictable and makes you do things you never imagined."

I had to put him at ease and somehow, my words and reassuring tone did.

He folded his arms and leaned against the door. "If this is your decision, then what more can I do to stop it? I've known you long enough, Learner, to have figured that much out. But know this: if Tarek Thorn or any man ever lays a hand on you, then I will rip a hole in his universe."

"How's everything with Page?"

Justus spun around, and I could have sworn I saw that man blush. "She's... ah..."

"Yeah, yeah, I know. All that and a bag of chips."

Justus tilted his head over his shoulder and threw me a smile. The man had charm. Blue eyes that could give the sky a run for its money, chiseled jaw, shaved head, masculine cologne, expensive clothes, and a flashy smile. He never needed the gift he was given as a Mage—the one he considered a curse. Justus was a natural-born charmer, whether he knew it or not.

I had caught him surfing websites for flowers, so I had a feeling that while he admitted nothing, Justus was considering a little wooing of his own. I felt wistful that I would miss out on so many things. Then again, Justus would probably back out or drag it on for years.

This part of my life was ending, and I would miss the banter I shared with Justus. He was a Mage who upheld the laws, and I was an obstinate young Learner who broke them. Still, he was confident that he would one day shape me into someone he could be proud of. It would take time to squeeze out the impulsive nature that was so ripe within me.

Justus despised Tarek to the marrow. My Ghuardian had witnessed an attempt on my life by this man. I'd come close to dying in his arms, and that kind of thing haunts a man. How I met Logan was no secret, and Justus had eventually accepted our relationship, as I'd pointed out to him in our previous argument. Immortals differ from humans in that we are more likely to accept the improbable and more willing to believe that a person can change.

When Justus left the room, my heart thundered in my chest. HALO, the organization that Justus worked for, brought down men like Tarek. But they had no power to protect lives—it's not what they did. If the Mageri found out about this and sufficient evidence was provided, it could instigate war.

The scar on my neck burned and I covered it with my hand. The door suddenly swung open and Christian came in and leaned against the wall.

"It's done," he said in a quiet voice.

My heart sank.

Logan had plenty of beautiful women from his past to choose from, and Christian had given them all a little Vampire hypnosis to win him over again. It took very little convincing because Logan was a prince among his kind—his family was coveted by Chitah women.

No one ever thinks the last time they're with someone intimately could be the *very* last time. I thought a lot about our time together at his condo that night and regretted that I wasn't more attentive. Why hadn't I just thrown caution to the wind and shared a night of passion with him? I would have let him remove my clothes and see all of me, because my modesty was one thing he tried to protect. I would have spoken sweet words to him and not held back on my feelings because of fear. I would have made love to him in front of that open window for all the world to see, because now I'd never have that chance again. I would have savored our time together and run my finger across the tiny laugh lines on his face as he held me close while we pillow-talked.

I would have loved him.

I would have told him.

"There's just one problem," Christian said, scratching his jaw and widening his stance.

I raised a brow.

Christian walked toward me with a pensive gaze. "He's got the idea that there might be a chance between you two. After everything, he's clinging to a hope that's preventing my magic from taking hold. He told me he'd wait for you, and I wasn't sure what he was rambling on about."

"Then maybe I need to sever what he's holding on to."

Christian tilted his head.

"I know what to do to make this final between us. I can't have him holding out for me. It wouldn't be fair for him to waste his life pining over someone who isn't worth it. I refuse to see him live his life feeling defeated by Tarek. Maybe this won't affect him the way I think it will, but he deserves better than that. I need privacy to do this, so I want you to be a shadow and out of sight. No matter what happens, Christian, stay out of it."

My tone was serious, and he nodded in response.

"Before I go through with it, there's something else I want you to help me with. You might know a little bit about this kind of thing, but I want to do it tonight. I'll handle Logan tomorrow since we have two more nights until the party."

"Just say the word and I'll make it so."

CHAPTER 19

"**I**S IT GOING TO HURT?**"**

Paul gave a thin-lipped grin and winked, flashing his silver tooth. "It only hurts the first time, but I think you've heard *that* before," he said with a smoker's chuckle.

"Ha. Funny." I glanced around at the art on the wall while Paul got ready to ink me. I'd never gotten a tattoo before, not that it was a big deal for a Mage since our body would gradually absorb the ink because of our healing abilities.

"Why don't you get *this*?" Christian said, sitting on top of a cabinet, holding up a thick book.

"Because *that* is a penis."

"Isn't that what all you ladies want?"

Paul snorted. "I had a guy come in recently who got one of those put on his head. I don't know what the hell the story was with that, but it was the funniest shit I've ever been a part of." He rolled up his chair. "Kept calling me a wanker or some shit, so I made his dick crooked."

I glanced up nervously at him.

"Don't worry, I take my job seriously. His will go away, but yours won't. You sure about this?"

He had already drawn the outline—no sense in turning back now. Finn sat on the other side of me, holding my right hand. When I had told him I was getting a tattoo, I made him swear up and down not to tell a soul, especially Logan. Christian was going to alter his memory of what I got tatted on me anyhow. I needed someone with me besides Christian, someone who wouldn't ruin the experience with jokes.

Justus wouldn't understand. Adam was out for personal reasons, and Sunny once told me that she'd disown me if I ever got myself marked up like some biker chick.

All my resources were tapped, except Finn. He was curious to see how the whole process worked. I thumbed through the designs while Finn stood in front of the television watching rap videos for twenty minutes.

According to Paul, Breed tattoo parlors operated a little differently. I had to sign a consent form promising not to sue, maim, or kill him since I was paying extra for liquid fire. Paul instructed me to remove my pants, and that didn't fly well with Finn. Once he calmed down, Paul covered up the important parts with a towel. He claimed he was the kind of artist who didn't like stuff in the way.

Personally, I think Paul was just a big ol' perv. He looked intimidated by Finn—a curious reaction because Paul was also a Shifter, although he didn't reveal to us what his animal was. Finn wasn't an intimidating kid.

Kid. I kept calling him kid because something about him exuded innocence. He once guessed his age to be in his lower twenties, but something else to consider was that Shifters aged slowly.

Finn stood an inch taller than me, had beautiful hazel eyes, unruly hair the color of cinnamon, and an elfin smile that made him seem as if he'd sprung out of a fantasy book.

He squeezed my hand.

"I'm okay, Finn. You look more nervous than I do." I bit my lower lip.

I didn't consider that this might have been upsetting for him, but a couple of times, he touched his arm where the brand was.

"Is it that important?" he asked in a low voice.

I replied in a soft breath. "Yeah."

The crinkle of a wrapper sounded from across the room and I lifted my head. Christian tossed a yellow piece of plastic into the wastebasket and popped a butterscotch into his mouth. "I'd never be caught dead with a tattoo."

"People get inked for all kinds of reasons," Paul piped in as he switched on the needle and began. I grimaced. "Some like to decorate their body like a work of art, others want to remember a moment in their life. And for some, it's private. It's like wearing a visible scar that marks their heart. Sometimes the stories are good, and sometimes they're shitty. And sometimes they don't tell me a damn thing." His eyes fixated on the moving needle. "Then there's love."

"Feck love," Christian spat. "Love fades and then you're stuck with a rabbit or someone's name on your arse."

Paul shut off his pen and burned Christian with a hot gaze. "Unlike a human, you can't have a tattoo removed when liquid fire is applied. If you haven't met a woman worth marking your body for in her honor, then you know diddly shit about love." He lifted the sleeve of his shirt and displayed a beautiful tattoo of a flower with a name on it. "You haven't lived until you've met that woman who will spark your fire and turn your entire world upside down. The one who makes you reconcile with your past and become a better man. If love fades, it was never meant to be. When it sticks to you like gum on your shoe, then that's lasting love. It's the one you weren't expecting, the one you can't scrape off no matter how hard you try. It will either destroy you or fulfill you, but it *will* change you. You think when I ink a name on someone's skin that it means nothing? That the person wouldn't bleed and die for that name? You haven't *lived* unless you've loved."

Christian rolled his eyes and crunched on his candy.

"Can we get this over with?" I asked. "He's just trying to provoke you so I'll end up with a blob."

Finn stroked my hair to the side.

"How do you like Lucian?" I asked him once Paul resumed his artwork.

Finn shrugged with an uncertain expression. "He's different."

"How so?"

"He's book smart but he's kind of an a-hole. I mean, he says whatever without thinking because in his mind he's always right."

"Ah, one of those. Doesn't have a filter; reminds me of Simon."

"No," Finn corrected. "Simon's funny. Lucian is… I don't know how to describe him. He's kind of my height, so he doesn't look like the others. And his hair is blacker than yours."

My brows arched. "Really?"

No wonder his older brothers were so protective of him. Lucian would have been singled out for sure. Not just because of his hair, but also his height.

Finn rubbed his nose against his shoulder. "Uh huh. He's just scary smart. Like a mad scientist or something."

"That's dramatic," Christian mumbled.

"Let's see you live with him," Finn snapped back. "He's got insomnia, so he paces at night and my animal can't get out," he said, flicking his eyes at Paul. Finn didn't reveal to just anyone what his animal was, but I had a feeling Paul knew. It explained his strangely submissive behavior when Finn spoke or looked at him.

"That's not a bad thing, is it? I never got the impression from Logan that Lucian was a bad seed."

"Naw," Finn said, relaxing in his chair. "Lucian's just different, that's all. He's strict with the tutoring and always thinks he's right, even when he's wrong."

"That sounds familiar," Christian blurted out. I gave him a frosty stare and he lifted his eyes to the ceiling, studying the cracks.

"I like him," Finn continued. "But his insomnia is starting to make me nervous. I need to get out, if you know what I mean."

His wolf needed to get out. A Shifter wasn't supposed to cage their animal when it wanted to play or else it would try to take over and not allow them to change back. A streak of rebellion, if you will. So there had to be harmony between man and animal since they shared the same spirit. I could already sense that Finn was restless from not having shifted—he was more temperamental than usual.

A slow rap song came on and Paul's needle hit a sensitive spot. I sucked in a sharp breath and actually wanted to smile. It was empowering to mark my body with something that would last forever. A feeling I hadn't known since Tarek walked into my life. I reflected on the permanence of some things, and the impermanence of others. It gave me hope that maybe a few hundred years from now, I'd be at a different place in my life.

"Does it hurt?" Finn asked, the needle buzzing in the background. I sensed hostility in his tone. When his eyes flicked over to Paul again, I squeezed his hand.

"Hardly. You should see what Justus does with me in the training room," I said with a snort.

"You ain't seen nuthin' yet, honey." Paul looked up and grinned.

Tattoos covered him from neck to wrists. Everything from one of those justice scales to a bleeding heart. But there weren't any animals on him, such as dragons or snakes.

"This is the easy part," he said. "The liquid fire is going to burn like a sonofabitch."

"Will you *shut up*?" Finn growled.

Paul lowered his head and continued with his artistry.

"How come you don't put the liquid fire on the needle?" I asked. "Seems like you could kill two birds with one stone."

Paul laughed. "Doesn't work, honey. Liquid fire won't hold to metal for long; it's funny that way. Otherwise, we'd all be walking around with daggers coated in that shit. Life just can't be that fucking easy. Plus, I want to make sure you're happy with the final product before we seal it."

"So put it in the ink," I suggested.

He swung his eyes up to mine. "You'd be screaming, and we'd have one hell of a mess tatted all over you."

I sighed and looked over at Finn in his dark blue sweatshirt. "Logan says you're into law."

He gave me an impish grin and his eyes sparkled. "Yeah. I kind of like reading about the different Breed laws. Some of them don't even know that they contradict one another."

"You going to pursue that? You should. I think you've got a lot of potential in you, kid. I'd be proud to see you—ah!" I hissed between my teeth as the needle hit a sore spot.

Faster than I could track, Finn shifted into his wolf.

"Jaysus wept!" Christian shouted, standing on the counter. "Get your fecking puppy under control, Silver."

"Shut up!" I yelled back.

Finn's red wolf snarled as he stalked around the table and sat beside Paul.

I'd never seen a man sweat so much. He carefully wiped his brow and lifted his eyes to mine. Finn growled, and Paul immediately lowered his gaze.

"Do me a favor, Mage. Try not to make a peep and upset your friend. I'm just a guy trying to earn a living, not get himself torn up by an alpha."

Justus tightened a loose pipe beneath Page's sink, listening to the sound of her fingernail clicking against the kitchen table.

"It doesn't matter what you want anymore, Justus. You can't take over the steering wheel when someone else is driving without causing a wreck. Silver has to make her own choices and her own mistakes. I have to agree that it doesn't make sense, but I've seen people make poor choices before, so she wouldn't be the first. Maybe he *has* changed; I know how some of you immortals turn a new leaf. Do you think her feelings for him are genuine?"

"No," Justus bit out angrily from the floor. He peered down the length of his body and noticed her bare feet. She had on a pair of grey sweatpants and a loose shirt; Justus was dumbfounded by how attractive she looked in something so casual.

"What did your friend Simon make of it?"

"He's stealth at the moment, working on another project. I haven't spoken with him about this, and not sure I want to."

Page sighed—the breathy kind that had no answers. She mystified him, and his chest tightened whenever she looked at him with those chocolate eyes.

Women had always been nothing more than piranhas, nipping at him everywhere he went. Page didn't nip. She listened. She responded. She occasionally disagreed, and he could barely comprehend how much that actually appealed to him.

"There's nothing to decide, Justus. You *must* go to the party. If you don't, your relationship with her could be damaged. Maybe she won't be in your custody, but as her Ghuardian, she'll always have a connection to you. Don't sever that. Men come and go. She may need you someday, and you should be there for her. If Silver means anything to you, then accept her decision even if you don't agree with it. I lost a friend that way once. She got involved with some loser and I kept going on and on about how she needed to break it off with him. It was back in school and the sort of thing friends argue about—except she suddenly stopped talking to me. They broke up a few months later, but she never let go of the judgment I held. That's when I learned that I can't be a stoplight in someone's life; I need to be a welcome sign."

The phone rang and she reached around.

"Hello?" She waited a few seconds. "Hello?" Page pressed her lips tightly together and slammed the phone in the cradle. "Want something to drink?"

The abrupt change in topic signaled something was wrong and Justus slid out from beneath the sink. Page pulled open the fridge door and analyzed the contents while pursing her lips.

"Who was that?"

"No one important," she said, grabbing a small can of grapefruit juice. "All I've got is juice or coffee, unless you don't mind a glass of water?"

"Number one: You need to keep this place stocked with food and drinks. You don't—"

"Yeah, yeah, I know. Take care of myself." She laughed softly and sat at the table.

"Number two: How often are you getting those hang-up calls?" He placed his strong forearms on the table and leaned forward.

She peeled the top off the can and flicked it in the trash. "Every night, but it's nothing to worry about. I know who it is."

If Page hadn't been in the room, his fist would have slammed against her flimsy table. Instead, he sat down and smoothed out the edges in his voice. "Is it Slater?"

"He'll stop when I change my number, but right now he's having issues letting go."

"Has he come by?"

"No, he couldn't get in if he had a bulldozer," she said with a chuckle. "Not with the deadbolts you installed on my door."

Page was too relaxed about the situation. Justus had lived a long life, long enough to know that men who displayed this type of obsessive behavior were unpredictable and unwilling to give up what they coveted.

"Let it go, Justus. Some people just take longer to get the point." Page sipped her drink and grimaced. "Yuck. They say this stuff is supposed to help you lose weight, but I don't see that happening with my fast-food runs. I might as well go back to soda and live a happier life."

All Justus saw was a slim figure with lovely breasts.

He arched a brow. "You don't need to lose weight. I would prefer it if you—"

"Wait a second," she said, throwing up her hand. "If you tell me that you would prefer me packing on a few pounds, then we're ending this little chitchat."

"In my time, a full-figured woman was revered."

"Let me know when they invent a time machine, because I'll be sure to reserve a seat on that ride." She wobbled the can between her fingers on the table. "I'm not really obsessed with it either way."

Justus wanted to argue, but a small barrette clipped in her hair distracted him. Page had a lovely curve to her neck where it met her shoulder, and she had a habit of resting her fingers on that spot and lightly stroking it during casual conversations. Instead of glossy tresses, Page kept her hair short and practical. Her attire at work was professional—nothing like the revealing outfits that many women wore. It reminded him of a time when it was scandalous for a woman to show her ankle, and clothing left a lot to the male imagination.

"The orchids were gorgeous." A smile tugged at her lips, but she shyly studied the juice can. "Truth be told, no one's even given me a rose. Getting just one would have been romantic—not those bouquets with all that tacky baby's breath. It's a shame such a lovely phrase was wasted on garnish that looks like a wild weed. Baby's breath—isn't that a nice thing to call a flower?"

"It was nothing," he said dismissively, but his chest tightened.

"Nothing? I bet they cost you a fortune," she said, rising from her chair. It was the same tone Silver liked to use—the one that implied he was materialistic.

Certainly the flowers were expensive, but he was not about to waste his efforts on something cheap. A thoughtless gift is a display of indifference.

By the restless way she fumbled with her shirt, Justus anticipated that he was about to get the boot. Since the night he kissed her, the energy between them had changed. He sometimes caught her looking at him, only to quickly look away. But she made no attempt to rekindle that fire. She wasn't a Mage, but Justus was attuned to the spike in energy whenever they shared a quiet moment.

"It's getting late, Justus. I have appointments in the morning and I don't want to keep you, I'm glad that you stopped by to confide in me about Silver."

"Will you accompany me to the party?"

"Um... maybe," she said, ruffling up her hair. "I'm sorry I can't give you a definite answer, but my schedule can be so unpredictable. Don't think twice about asking someone else. I'm busy playing a little catch-up. Plus, I have to get things in order with my separation from... um..." She touched her cheek, as if she'd said something wrong.

Page had a duality to her that he enjoyed. Edgy and strong willed, yet at the same time she could be blushing and thoughtful.

"I'm on call twenty-four hours a day; this is my life."

Justus approached her and she backed up. Maybe he *was* assertive, but that's what a few centuries will do to a man.

Page stood with her back against the wall and when her lips parted, he heard her draw in a deep breath. In the quiet kitchen, he listened to the sound of her feet nervously shifting on the sticky tile floor. Justus did something he'd been thinking about ever since he noticed that barrette in her hair.

He took it out.

After slipping it into his pocket, he ran his fingers through her short hair in an upward motion, exposing her unblemished neck. It ruffled a scent in the air—a subtle sweet flavor on her skin. Was it her natural smell, or a cream? Maybe it was her shampoo.

He wanted to know.

"What are you doing?"

He liked the sound of her breathy voice, and a pale rose tinted the apple of her cheeks.

Justus placed his heavy palms on the wall behind her, leaned in close, and froze. An intense scarlet spread rapidly across her collarbone and neck.

When Page blushed, she blushed *all over.*

Her arms hung lax at her sides and Justus moved a little closer, finding her presence to be extremely engaging. He tilted his head and placed a delicate kiss against her soft neck.

One. Small. Gentle. Kiss.

The heat from her blush warmed his lips. That's when his heart unexpectedly fired off in his chest, and he was so certain she could hear it that he released a slow sigh to calm himself. Page shuddered.

With expert hands, he placed the crook of his finger below her chin and moved her head to the right, exposing the left side of her neck. Justus brushed his knuckles very tenderly across her jaw and neck, listening to the soft hiss of their skin coming in contact. Page's nervousness showed in her quickened breaths. He watched every minute reaction, from the flutter of her long eyelashes to her dilated pupils. The telltale sign of arousal was never more evident than when she slowly blinked and then finally closed her eyes.

Justus planted a lingering kiss against her slender neck. Never had such a simple act felt so intimate. He tasted her with his tongue and his heated breath bounced back against his face. The quietness of the room stilled him, and everything about her filled his senses. The round shape of her breasts showing off two hard tips that pressed against the fabric of her cotton shirt. How silky her hair felt when it brushed against his cheek. The sweet smell of her skin filled his nose like a bouquet. She was like nectar, and he couldn't pull away.

Page was an orchid standing before him, full of grace.

Fragile.

Mortal.

His strong hand leisurely traced down her neck, the curve of her shoulders, and then fell to his side.

A pulse in her gaze caught his attention—one of inexperience. "Page, tell me you have at least been kissed."

"Um, *yes,* I've been kissed. Just not quite like that," she said, a secretive smile curving up one side of her mouth. "Not so… gently like that."

Justus knew that he wanted to please this woman in every way. Every. Conceivable. Way.

He cupped the sides of her neck and took a step forward, resting his cheek against hers. "Will you let me kiss you on the mouth?" he whispered against her ear.

His thumb traced along her jaw, feeling the motion of her head as she nodded. Had he sensed one flicker of reluctance, he would have backed away.

Page watched his mouth instead of his eyes and it didn't look like she had taken a breath. Her eyes were so rich and dark that they ensnared him, drawing him into their mysterious depths. He noticed a tiny mark near the corner of her eye, and her upper lip had a pronounced Cupid's bow.

She trembled against him.

"Cold?" he asked, immediately adjusting his body temperature to warm her.

Justus didn't like to be touched. He tolerated sexual advances, but affectionate gestures were out. Page kept her hands to herself, and something about that bothered him… because he *wanted* her to touch him.

The moment their lips joined, a surge of power rushed through so many nerve endings that he stiffened. So much softer than he remembered and Justus broke contact, afraid that his power wasn't quite in check.

Page began to babble nervously. "Oh, I forgot to mention that the blood that I—"

Justus cut her off with a passion-filled kiss. Wet. Soft. Tender.

He placed the flat of his hands against the wall, stroking his tongue against hers—coaxing her to do the same. And she did. Desire ached at the base of his spine when the kiss deepened.

The entire kitchen could have been set on fire from the heat licking off him, but Page didn't back away as many women did at the sudden increase in his body temperature. In fact, she leaned in closer. His energy was under control, but his hands never floated south. Page was a woman of virtue, and only the scum of the earth would wipe his hands on her like a dirty dishrag.

"Justus, wait. *Stop.*"

He stumbled back and tipped over a chair. Panic seared him like a third-degree burn; he should have never pushed her. "Apologies. I should leave."

"No, wait. It's not you. I'm just not used to feeling so…"

Adored?

"I don't know how to act with you, Justus. I can't figure out why you keep coming around, *especially* after seeing me so sick. I'm not…" She struggled with a thought before shaking her head. "I'm a Relic. You're a Mage."

He stepped forward until they were inches apart. "I'm a man. You're a woman."

"But I'm not like *those* women," she said, pointing to the side as if one might appear in the room. "This is me; this is all that I am."

Justus wasn't about to have this woman spend another second thinking that she was anything less than the luster of a diamond.

"You have a brilliant light that is unparalleled by any Mage. You *shine*. If men have not treated you well, it's because they were blind. You are… radiant," he said in a voice that fell to a breath. Justus dipped his head low so that he spoke against her temple. "We're different, but we're not so different. I feel a connection with you, Page. One I've never felt with a woman before. You intrigue me, and it has nothing to do with the immunity you possess. I had a dream you were standing on the edge of the earth, and I have this feeling even now that you might step off and I'll lose you. If a kiss is all I'm allowed, then it is all that I deserve. Oh, *mon ange*," he whispered in a rough voice. "I want to show you how beautiful you are."

She looked up at him contemplatively.

Had he really just spoken to her like some kind of poetic fool?

"I need time to think about it."

He bowed his head respectfully. "As you wish."

CHAPTER 20

THE HORN ON THE L train blared in the distance. Darkness filled every crevice of the street corner, from the cracks in the sidewalks to the sides of the buildings where trash piled up. There was a bakery a few beats up the street, but I needed privacy and chose to meet Logan in front of the old apartments on Thirteenth that caught fire several years back. They never sold the property, nor had they demolished it. The windows were boarded up and the fire escape had been dismantled to deter the squatters.

Despite the chill, my hands were toasty warm inside my coat pockets.

Footsteps behind me crunched on freshly fallen snow—only enough to sheet the sidewalks, but the wind blew it around like dandelions caught in the summer breeze. By the long stride, I knew it was Logan.

"I'm glad you came," I said, keeping my back to him.

"Do you want to tell me why I'm here?"

I didn't have to look to know Logan was mad, and it oozed off his words like venom.

"To talk it over privately. We haven't officially ended this; we keep racing to our corners, waiting for the bell. But I don't want to swing anymore, Logan. I want you to know that I've chosen Tarek and I'm not going to change my mind."

"*How* do you know that?" he interrupted. Even a few feet apart, I could feel the raw emotion as he towered over me. "People change. I've changed."

"Maybe I should have accepted you the way you were. I want you to know that you deserve to find someone who can give you all the things you need; I'm just not that person."

"Clearly," he said in a cutting voice. "Turn around and face me."

I kept a cool head, but I'd also strategically chosen the side of the street where the wind would be in my favor. When I turned around, I stared into a hunter's eyes. Logan wore a stylish black jacket, unzipped, with a dark green T-shirt. A leather belt caught my eye because of the silver buckle that looked like a paw, but then I realized it was a common style with men and was supposed to be brass knuckles. He looked so handsome that I wanted to run into his arms one last time.

He lowered his head, his arms hanging at his sides. "I've taken another female."

"Does this mean you'll leave me alone?"

He bit his lower lip.

My hands made tight fists in my pockets. "Say what you need to say; this is your chance."

Logan stepped forward with the power and confidence that he always exuded. He sucked in a deep breath that sounded like a hiss. "I don't think I will ever understand why you chose him. I have turned my life around to be a better man—a *worthy* man—and while I could forgive you for Christian…" He lowered his head and shook it adamantly. "I cannot forgive you for Tarek."

His eyes were those of a prosecuting attorney and I was the defendant.

"Tarek knows what's important to me, and he's promised me things. As a Lord's mate, I'll have everything I could possibly want. Tarek can offer me absolute protection, and I wouldn't have to constantly be on the run or hiding from Nero."

Which was true. Tarek might not have any feelings for me, but he was possessive enough that he wouldn't let another man have me.

"So then it's money? I would have never thought you for a gold digger. You wouldn't even let me buy you an expensive dinner!"

That burned.

"Buying me an expensive dinner was nothing but an attempt to impress me with money, so don't be a hypocrite. You know that wealth and power mean something to an immortal, and Tarek has more than you do."

Logan stepped close enough that I got nervous he might pick up my scent, but the wind blew from behind him. I feared that I would somehow be transparent and he'd see through all this and take me into his arms, swearing to protect me. Deep down, a part of me wanted that and was saddened it would never be.

Logan brooded. "If I had power, would that be enough for you to choose me? If I challenged to be Lord—"

"Where is that even coming from? You can't be Lord; you aren't the eldest."

"There are other ways if the eldest refuses to challenge."

"Don't start this, Logan, because you'll end up being a lonely Lord. I will never choose you and I'm so fucking exhausted from having this argument." I stepped forward until we were in arms reach. "Never. *Ever.*"

Logan reached out and lightly touched my shoulder. Faster than a heartbeat, my hand unsheathed a dagger from inside my jacket. I gripped his long hair and held the sharp blade to his throat, just below his right ear. Logan might have been taller, but I had the upper hand.

He tilted his neck and offered himself, eyes glittering with ferocity, but still gold.

I angled the dagger and swiped my arm in a quick motion. Logan jumped back in shock, eyes wide as I stood with my blade in one hand.

In the other was the long length of his blond ponytail, sliced from his head.

With that one action, I cut his chances with me. He reached around, stroking his fingers through the ends of his short hair. I couldn't read his expression, and I didn't want to. This was the only way to extinguish the torch he carried for me—the only way to keep him from harm.

His beautiful blond bundle of hair fell to the wet cement. A symbol of his love placed at my feet to tread on.

I didn't think that a word could possibly move past my lips that wouldn't be followed by tears.

The length of my walk up the street never felt so arduous. I glanced once over my shoulder and in the distance, Logan stood with his back to me, staring down at a pile of hair that rested at his feet like a forgotten dream. A quiet snow began to fall within my soul as I watched him motionless on the corner of Thirteenth Street.

The man who had once wrapped his generous arms around me and called me his Little Raven would finally close his heart to me.

Now and forever.

The following day, a package arrived from Tarek filled with the contents of what I would be wearing to my engagement party that evening. As my neck was already adorned with a silver necklace, he sent no jewelry. This chain would likely be hooked around my neck for the rest of my life. I lifted the champagne-colored gown from the box and tiny sparkles caught the light. Unlike the harlot dress, this strapless gown would fall to my ankles and float with elegance. A smaller black box sat inside the larger one, and when I opened it up, I lifted a golden hairclip and turned it between my fingers. Shaped like a flower, tiny diamonds were meticulously placed within each petal.

After applying my lipstick, a panic attack took over and I raced into my bedroom and slammed the door. I'd never hyperventilated before—there wasn't enough air and my hands were shaking. Justus had left thirty minutes prior upon my request because Tarek would be sending a car to pick me up. He was still upset with me, so it would have made the wait unbearable. I held a convincing argument, but I could tell Justus was embarrassed by my decision and no longer respected me the way he once had.

I'd had little sleep the night before. I tossed and turned in the bed as my mind raced and continually replayed the devastating scene of slicing Logan's hair. When I finally fell asleep, I dreamed about it. I saw images of myself falling into an abyss until I landed in a pile of blond hair. Sorrow consumed me, and anger. A figure emerged from the darkness and I looked up, expecting to see Tarek. But instead, it was Nero. He merely watched, shaking his head as the soft hair below my feet transformed into baby's breath. Something happened after that, but I couldn't remember it. I woke up from the dream feeling strangely calm and safe, and I was able to sleep for a few hours after that.

"Silver, open the door," Christian said impatiently.

I staggered, dizzy as the room began to spin. The dress itched and the necklace felt like it was strangling me. The pounding on the door grew louder.

Right before he kicked it in.

Christian walked in like a breeze, gripped my shoulders firmly, and swallowed me up with his serious black eyes. I was distracted by the fact he was wearing a formfitting black suit, skinny tie, and had neatly combed his dark hair. Now he just looked like a Vampire going to a ball.

"You can't afford to panic yourself. Tarek will scent your emotions," he warned in a steady, calm voice. "Shut 'em off for the night, you hear? Let's play this game out. Once he sees that Logan has settled on another woman, he'll reconsider spending the rest of his days with a Mage whom he reaps no personal gain from."

"This necklace," I said, tugging at it. "It makes me feel mortal. I don't like not feeling my gifts, Christian. I'm too vulnerable this way. Something could happen."

"Calm yourself, lass. You forget that I can keep a paper doll safe in a raging inferno," he promised with a crooked smile.

"I'll hold you to that."

We had arrived at Tarek's home for the party. It was atrociously large, filled with expensive paintings, furniture, and décor. Everything about it reeked of the braggart who stood at my side, clasping my arm in his. Most of the women present were Chitahs, and every single one of them speared me with her gaze as I took the place where a female Chitah should be.

The men were skeptical of the pairing until Tarek assured them that he would be taking at least one female Chitah to mate with and bear his young.

"It was such an unfortunate accident with your eldest, Torin, but some things happen for a reason. It is a great honor to see you as the Lord of our Pride," a man said, bowing meekly. Tarek ate up the groveling, although he tried to look bored by it as he floated his attention elsewhere.

A beautiful woman in a long black gown approached. She wore no perfume, but her skin shimmered with some kind of fairy dusting. As she walked by the men, their noses lifted in the air, as if a heavenly scent trailed behind her. She had glossy hair that was almost white, and her attention was all over Tarek.

"Good evening, Sire," she purred. "It's been a long time. I see you've been doing well?"

"Not as well as you, Jasmine. You look good enough to eat," he growled. After a moment of familiar silence between them, he absently jerked me to his side. "This is Silver; she is to be my mate."

Jasmine barely flicked an eye at me as she ran her long red nail across Tarek's hand. Female Chitahs always had their eye on the prize.

"So nice to see you again, Tarek. Do call." I felt a tremor go through him as she turned away, and his greedy eyes watched as her hand stroked down her shapely hip.

"That's the kind of female you should be," Tarek mumbled.

"Desperate?"

An hour into the party, a few business associates pulled Tarek away. I dragged Christian into an empty hallway by his tie. "Where the hell is Justus?" I said through clenched teeth.

"Something came up. He won't be making it. Nor Simon."

Disappointment flared. Sunny couldn't attend because they had taken a short trip out of town for the night to close out some storage space Knox was renting. "So that's how it is?"

"It's an emergency; that's all I know."

"What happened?" I glanced over my shoulder to confirm we had privacy. "Please tell me no one is hurt or in trouble."

"Remember what I said about bottling up those emotions, lass? I don't know a fecking thing. I only got the text."

"Why don't you get your lucky charms and see if you can find out what happened?"

"You know, the Irish jokes are getting a wee bit old," he grumbled. "That mouth of yours will get you into more trouble than you know."

I folded my arms. "I have a black belt in sarcasm, Christian. Deal."

Not a moment too soon, Tarek briskly walked up on us. His Mohawk had been trimmed shorter and the buzz on both sides of his head looked like his hair was finally meeting up at the same length. He tightened his fingers around my upper arm and pulled me down the hall.

"We have an important guest, so try not to wander off."

I nearly tumbled over my stupid heels as he hurried me into the next room.

Tarek's arm slid down my back like cream, but that's not what made me shake. Across the room, my eyes fell upon a tall man with a penetrating gaze. His short blond hair had been shaped into a choppy cut, but it was still longish on top. Logan looked devastatingly handsome. The short hair brought out the strength of character in his face; the hard, cut jaw; and the deep-set eyes that absorbed the light and glimmered. He usually kept his face shaved, but stubble had grown in. He had managed to steal Tarek's thunder by drawing the attention of every woman in the room.

Logan's presence radiated power.

Without the distraction of his long hair, his shoulders were remarkably broad and assertive. Logan didn't go all out with his attire but dressed in a casual white button-up and grey slacks. I glanced down and noticed his trademark black sneakers. A hint of anger sparked on Tarek's face when he caught sight of him. Maybe he was trying to process the new hairstyle and meaning behind it, but he most certainly did not appreciate that Logan Cross was the center of attention at Tarek's own engagement party.

"Cross," Tarek bellowed. "I see you made it, and not a moment too soon. The little woman was getting tired so I had to give her a little waking up, if you know what I mean." He winked and kissed my shoulder.

Logan stared at him, a man bored by childish attempts to instigate a reaction. When his voice melted out, it was so sincere that my chest burned. "Congratulations to the both of you."

I looked up at Tarek, whose eyes were fixated on the woman clutching Logan's arm. I tried not to look at her, but I *knew* who she was.

Red Dress.

When I had gone to the Gathering where Chitahs went in search of their kindred spirit, I'd found Logan encircled by a group of women. Red Dress was the blonde in the red gown who had decided Logan was hers.

Now he was.

She delivered the most satisfactory smile when she recognized me standing beside Tarek. I imagined a glint of light sparkling off her tooth to the sound of a bell.

"Sire, I would like you to meet Eva."

Eva lowered her head respectfully at Tarek. "It's such an honor to meet you," she spoke softly. "This is an exquisite home; you are a man of great taste."

Tarek would have enjoyed the compliment had he not been so perplexed with what exactly was going on.

Logan's hand cupped just below her ribs and he leaned into her in a familiar way. "Eva and I have known each other for many years and she has accepted my offer to be her mate, bypassing the traditional courtship."

Tarek froze, and his hand squeezed my waist painfully, but I was numb.

"Mate, you say? But how can that be when Silver here is your *kindred spirit?*"

Eva laughed with closed lips. "Surely you're kidding? Didn't *you* claim her at the Gathering?"

"I did," Tarek boasted, pulling me against him, a trace of his scent leaking onto me. "Silver is my mate, and I had every right to claim her. Not before Logan tried, but he was not man enough for her. Silver made the wiser choice, as I'm *sure* you would have."

Tarek's words softened and I realized his backup plan was to woo

Logan's woman. If I had to share a house with Eva as Tarek's mate...

Logan shook his head lightly. "Silver could never be my kindred spirit—this I know now. She's not a Chitah, and I can't be sure what influence her Mage energy had on me. Eva embodies a selfless quality that I admire, and any man would be lucky to have a woman who is so attentive to a male's needs."

I couldn't help it, but I involuntarily snapped my gaze at Christian standing at the far end of the room. His shoulders lifted in a guilty shrug until he saw how pissed off I was. Then I got his nasty glare. Surely Logan didn't come to his own conclusion that Eva was perfect in every way. Christian had only planted the idea for him to find a mate—at least, that's what he *told* me. If Logan could fall this quickly for another, then I had doubts that his feelings for me ran as deep as he once proclaimed.

Tarek scratched his chin and studied Logan in a serious manner. He looked up because he didn't match Logan in height. He was huskier in size and exuded strength in other ways.

"A fine woman Eva appears to be, but I'm surprised, Cross. Silver has only recently broken it off with you. Mated?" Tarek snorted. "Surely not."

"You're not mistaken," Logan replied, eyes piercing Tarek like arrows. "I'm pleased to see Silver has found someone who fulfills her needs as I have. What's between you and I will never be right, but my interest in pursuing the Mage is over. You have my best wishes for a successful mating. If you don't mind, I promised to show Eva around."

Logan bowed his head and stepped back, disappearing into the thick crowd with his new woman. Before losing sight of them, I saw Logan lean in and nuzzle against her neck. I hadn't been as prepared for that moment as I thought.

Tarek looked like he had a timer in his eyes, seconds from detonation.

He yanked me into a private room and as he slammed the door, I released a sorrowful breath, devastated by Logan's resolve. Weak in the knees, I sat in a plush chair and stared at my shaking hands.

"What is this game he plays?" Tarek ground through his teeth.

"Why is he not strung out on you?"

"I don't know," I whispered, looking at my hands, turning them to fists.

"Don't you?" he roared.

"No, I don't! Do you think I want to see him standing in the arms of some tramp? You think it's so easy for me to sit here and accept everything I've had to give up because of you? It doesn't look like it went your way, and now you've ruined my life and made an ass out of yourself," I shouted. "His feelings for her are not a lie; I could see it on his face and I'm certain you could scent it."

Tarek held on to the fireplace mantel as if he wanted to pry it from the wall.

"Maybe he's the biggest liar of us all. I thought he would have loved me more," I whispered. "I honestly believed that he was willing to wait for me."

"I apologize for the intrusion, Your Lordship. The guests are asking for you," a man interrupted from the door.

"Stall them," Tarek replied, and the door closed. "What kind of worthless woman are you that a Chitah who *claimed* you would not fight for you? Do you know the resolve of a Chitah for a claimed female, even if she is not his soul mate? We do not back down that easily."

"I'm not a Chitah."

Despite the women who must have offered themselves to Tarek over the years since Katrina's death, he had never mated. The instinct among males was strong to have a family. Yet here he was, settling for a Mage in a plot gone awry.

I cupped my arms tightly. "I can't give Logan children or satisfy him the way he deserves. It would have never worked out. I guess you were right all along—I was just a curiosity."

"Fuck."

"What's the matter, honey? Cold feet?" I began laughing maniacally. "Your friends may shake your hand for toting me around like a prize, but they laugh behind your back. You're making yourself out to be a joke. No dignified Chitah would settle for a Mage. Let's get back to the party. I'm beginning to like the idea of having caviar and champagne all the time." I walked past him.

He snatched my arm bruisingly and flung me across the room. I stumbled, catching myself on a marble table.

"Careful, Mage. *Nero* is also in the house. I'm sure he'd love nothing better than to juice you up. I'm possessive over what's mine, but I might be willing to make an exception if I'm pushed far enough."

CHAPTER 21

"Ladies and gentlemen," Tarek announced from the main room. "I want to express my deepest gratitude in having you here this evening to recognize my chosen mate. However, it is with regret…"

I pressed my ear against the door, anticipating words that I'd waited so long to hear—words that would release me.

"I must tell you that the celebration will have to be cut short." A few groans sounded amid the crowd. "Please, yes, I know. There will be more elaborate celebration at a later date. Silver is not feeling well, and I must tend to my female. I'm sure you can understand my concern. Our valet attendants have your cars ready. Please take a complimentary bottle of champagne as you leave, and thank you for coming."

The murmurs grew louder—talking… moving… leaving. When I attempted to leave the room, Tarek pushed his way in.

"Where's Christian?" I asked.

"Taking a walk," he answered. "My Vampire employee cuffed him with that wonderful metal that hangs from your neck so he won't be a nuisance to us. A Vampire's cockiness makes them so easy to bait. He didn't know the cuffs were… special."

"Why didn't you tell everyone that the engagement was off?"

"Because, Mage, I'm not a pussy. We're going *all* the way." He reached out and brushed his knuckles down my chest. I hopped back a step and his eyes widened.

"Logan won," I said.

"Sorry, sweetie, you're talking in a language I don't speak." The doors opened and two of his men stood at his side. "Take her upstairs," he ordered. They gripped my elbows and Tarek announced, "You'll be spending the remainder of your engagement in my home. It's time that we took things to the next level. I'll have your Ghuardian properly notified and one of my men will pick up your things."

"Why are you doing this?" I shouted, struggling against the guards hauling me away.

"Because I can. Because I *will*."

"Let me go! Walk away with some dignity!"

His fingers snapped and the men stopped. Tarek walked up and narrowed his hateful bright eyes on me. "Dignity is exactly why we're going to follow this to the end."

"I'm still in my Ghuardian's care and you can't take me without my consent. Without *his* consent!" I said, still struggling.

"Of course I can," he replied indifferently. "You are to be my mate and that makes us practically married. Husband trumps Mage daddy."

"Please, Tarek, just let it go. Let *me* go," I begged.

His face filled with understanding. "I'm a man of my word, unlike Cross, who so readily dropped you like a soiled handkerchief. I've already seen to your accommodations. Take her away," he ordered the guards.

The men shoved me into a room upstairs and locked the door.

Tarek was not only going to keep me, but he was going to try to win Logan's woman. I fell against the door and slid to my knees, staring at a windowless room with pumpkin walls. A large canopy bed made of wood sat against the wall with oval mirrors on either side.

The necklace not only blocked my Mage abilities, it also prevented me from visiting the Grey Veil—the in-between realm where I could speak with Justus. Then again, what could I tell him that wouldn't land me in hot water with Tarek?

My fingers clawed at the silver chain and I cursed. Tarek should have conceded defeat, or at least realized that his efforts with me weren't worth the trouble. I had gone over this a million times with Christian, and this outcome had not been expected.

If only I could speak with Simon.

The door swung open without warning and I backed into the

corner of the room. Tarek turned the lock and threw his black jacket over a beige chair.

"What do you think of your boyfriend now?" he seethed, coming at me like a hurricane out of control.

My heart leapt when Tarek threw me onto the bed. He snatched the end of my long dress and ripped it all the way up to my waist. Hearing the fabric tear brought back a memory I had long tried to bury, one that made my mouth dry and caused me to fight harder. One that had never played out in its entirety, but still gave me nightmares.

I kicked out my legs and Tarek descended over me, slapping my face until I was temporarily stunned. I punched my fist and clocked him good in the eye and then got him again in the jaw before he nearly knocked me out.

The moment I felt a tug at my panties, he froze.

"What the f—"

Dizzy and nauseous, I ignored the sting on my cheek and realized what he was looking at.

"Do you like it?" I smiled and laughed silently.

Tarek rose from the bed, immovable for what seemed like an eternity.

His eyes locked on to a tattoo of two cheetah paws that were inked just beneath my panty line. Being that I mostly wore boy shorts, that would be a little higher than most women's panty lines. An indelible mark that not only staked my claim on Logan, but served as a reminder to Tarek that I would never be his.

Paul was one of the best tattoo artists in the city, and instead of a solid black design, it was detailed with dark edges. Inside the left paw was the letter L, and inside the other was a C, but not inked. The shading was carefully done around it so the letters stood out as my skin tone.

The more Logan Cross slipped through my fingers, the more I wanted to hold on to him. Through all my indecisiveness, it wasn't until I had lost him that I knew without a doubt that I loved him.

The liquid fire had burned like hell and Christian had been forced to hold Finn back from attacking Paul. In the end, the pain of the tattoo hadn't hurt near as bad as the pain in my heart.

I shut my eyes, waiting for the next moment to come. One that would either seal my fate or dismiss it. As it turned out, it was dismissed.

Tarek pivoted around and stalked out of the room.

"Check the surveillance footage," Justus ordered. "There are four cameras set up and I want everything analyzed." He slid the lock shut on Page's front door. He'd already gone through the apartment four times from top to bottom, but came up with nothing to explain her disappearance.

Abduction was more like it. Justus had arrived, dressed in his finest suit, hoping she would be available to escort to the party. Instead, he found her front door ajar, the kitchen chair turned over, shards of glass all over the floor, and everything inside him shifted to something dark.

One of his HALO brothers was a Sensor and stopped by as a favor to confirm that from the residual emotions, there was a confrontation, but not as much fear as he would have expected. She must have opened the door to him as the alarm had been disabled. Leo didn't recognize the scent and said the trail cut off at Twenty-Second Street and Marsh.

Simon dropped a large bag on the table. "It'll take a minute to load and transfer the data over. How far back you want to go? Twenty-four hours?"

"Minimum," Justus said. "Dust the doors and everything in the kitchen."

Simon didn't just have the equipment to dust for fingerprints—he had the technology to compare the prints in any human or Breed database.

"Who do you think did it?" Simon asked. "What kind of manky bastard would mess around with a Relic? They're healers, for Christ's sake."

"I want to know everything about Slater, starting with where he lives."

Justus hadn't stopped pacing since he arrived over an hour ago. They searched the building and reviewed the messages on her answering machine. Simon thumbed through her appointment book and suggested a client could be the culprit.

"Sit down, mate. You're going to end up touching everything in this whole bleeding house and make my job a nightmare." The long chain on Simon's black jeans clinked from his seated position on the floor in front of the television.

Justus went into the kitchen and sat down, scrubbing his hands across his bristly scalp. He stared at a broken cup on the floor and then glanced up at the mistletoe hanging above her doorway. When his phone vibrated, he quickly yanked it out of his pocket. Christian had left him a text message.

Had he been a worthy Ghuardian, he would have gone to the event to celebrate the new life of his Learner. Silver would soon be leaving his care, and Justus hadn't sat down to decide how he felt about it. Taking her under his wing in the beginning was one of moral responsibility, but over the course of the past year, he had grown fond of things he hadn't expected. Not just her progression in training, but listening to her slide down the hallway in her socks, the sound of her laugh erupting during a movie, and even the blow-dryer late at night when he was trying to sleep. It was having another life in his home—one to care for, one to guard, and one to mentor. Now he would be alone again.

Justus could not overlook that Tarek had attempted to end her life. He'd almost watched her die in his arms. Their world was different from the human one, and with their extended lifetimes, men changed. Even Logan had earned himself the right to be trusted, all things considered.

No matter how much Silver tried smoothing it over, Justus still wanted to wrap his large hands around Tarek's neck and squeeze until there was no more breath.

He sent Christian a vague message of an emergency that would prevent him from attending.

"Justus! Take a look at this," Simon shouted.

He shot out of his chair and walked in front of the TV where Simon sat, watching the images play out like a silent movie.

A figure in a dark jacket spoke with a woman outside the building. He helped with her paper bag and slipped through the main door. The next shot was in the elevator. The hood on his jacket obscured his face. The next angle was in the hallway, and he slowly walked down the hall until he reached Page's apartment.

Simon fast-forwarded through a thirty-minute time lapse as the man stood by the door and occasionally paced around. He was holding his phone and sending messages, and sometimes he'd place his ear against her door.

"Who is he calling?" Justus wondered aloud.

Simon put it on pause. "Two calls to the Relic's house phone match up, but I haven't tapped into her cell phone. The number on caller ID was blocked." Simon resumed the video and Justus nervously folded his arms.

Page opened her front door and the man pushed himself in.

"Hit pause!" Justus roared. It was that split second moment when he wanted to stop it from happening—as if he could stall a moment in time with a press of a button.

Simon warily looked over his shoulder as Justus blew out a controlled breath. He didn't know if he was ready to see what was about to unfold on the video.

"Play it," he said in a caged voice.

Page walked backward in the kitchen, defensively holding out her right hand. There was arguing and then… he pulled a gun on her.

When the man glanced into the living room, Justus immediately recognized the attacker.

"It's good we got this on video, Justus. Evidence," Simon pointed out.

Justus was too transfixed on the screen to hear a word he had said. Slater's arm stretched all the way out, leaving a foot of air between the gun and her chest. A few moments passed of swaying as the two spoke calmly. Page was trying to defuse the situation. He could see it in her relaxed face and casual body language. Smart woman.

Until she panicked. In a split second, Page dodged his aim and ran toward the door. Slater came up from behind and threw her to the ground, pressing the barrel of the gun against her back. A chair tipped over along with a glass that sat precariously at the edge of the table. The last thirteen seconds of footage showed him dragging her to the door, forcing her onto her feet, and them leaving the building side by side.

There was nothing voluntary about it, because he aimed the gun at her from beneath his coat.

"Slater's address. *Now*."

"She won't be there, Justus. He wouldn't be that stupid."

Justus rose from his seat and tightened the ropes of muscle in his arms. "Find out every doorstep where he's ever wiped his feet. I want to know where he sleeps, who his clients are, where he has a drink, and anyone he associates with."

"Did you call Silver?" Simon unhooked the cables from the television to his laptop.

"I have no time to attend an engagement party," he replied.

Simon slid his laptop onto his legs and leaned against the leather chair. "Just as well, the sodding *bastard*. If you want to know where I put my invitation, it's floating in the toilet. Tarek? Of all the manky bastards," Simon muttered in a low breath. "Women change their minds more than their knickers. She must be on the rebound and he must be one hell of a sweet talker. Did Logan sleep around? Maybe she's doing it to piss him off, because that would do it. I don't know why you won't talk about it."

"Wrap it up, Simon. I'm heading out to Slater's house and I want you to back me up. Collect what you can and move to the next step. I'm paying you for your services—"

"If you ask me for a personal favor, then I'll do it. Cause that's what friends do, right? I don't need a fucking penny in my pocket to prove my loyalty."

Simon stood up and cracked his neck, tossing a pillow angrily to the sofa and mumbling to himself.

Justus still paid him.

Twenty minutes later, Justus arrived at Slater's house on the east side of town. It was a small piece-of-shit house with a door that he could easily kick in.

And did.

After tearing apart the living room, he moved to the bedroom and emptied every drawer without a clue of what he would find. Frustration sliced into him like the edge of an axe—a tension that abated when Simon arrived. By then, Justus had lost track of his suit jacket and tie, and the top buttons on his shirt were missing.

Simon meticulously analyzed everything on Slater's computer while Justus went through his mail and personal journals. Nothing yielded any clues.

"I've seen all I need to see," Simon finally declared. "We've been running around for the past three hours and I need to go over some of this data before we lose time. Let me review the footage and look for a match on the fingerprints. I'll put the word out to a few people I know. You should go home and get some shut-eye."

"Not good enough!" Justus threw his energy into the television, causing an explosion. Out of breath, he stared at the broken pieces, realizing that his actions were a clear admission of his feelings for the Relic.

"I'm doing the best I can, but if you want to spend the night redecorating in here, then by all means, have a go," Simon said, waving his arm. "I'll check if there are any street cams that might have caught something, but on this side of town, I seriously doubt it. For pity's sake, go home and sleep. You'll have a better head in the morning. And do me a favor—call Silver."

"What for?" Justus said in a raspy voice.

"Something isn't sitting well with me and I can't put my finger on it. As much as I'd like to yell her bleeding ear off, it's none of my business who she wants to shag. She's young and makes mistakes, but I don't see her shacking up with the man who tried to kill her, even if he was working for Nero. Maybe she's trying to get close to him to get to Nero, and if so, I don't like that she isn't including us in her plans. I've taught her so well in chess that I'm no longer able to predict her moves. If you don't say something to her, I will," he said, shaking his head and pacing in circles. "Just call her."

CHAPTER 22

I POUNDED ON THE BEDROOM DOOR for what seemed like an hour. Tarek never came but my purse and a bag full of clothes did, minus my phone. Not *my* clothes, as they were a little bit big for my narrow frame. After putting my hair in a ponytail, I slipped out of that ridiculous gown and put on jeans and a sweatshirt.

Suddenly the door clicked open.

Christian eased in with his back to me as he kept his gaze on the guard outside the door who looked entranced. Silver cuffs were locked on his wrists with infused metal that blocked his Vampire abilities. Or at least some of them.

"Christian, are you okay? What are you doing here?" I whispered.

His fangs descended, startling me a moment as he stalked forward and gripped my shoulders.

"Is this all he did?" he asked, holding my chin and staring at my bloody lip.

"I don't think he liked the tats."

"Damn right he didn't." Christian bit into his wrist and offered me his blood. "The metal binds only some of my gifts, but not the power in my blood. Drink so your face will heal."

It was awkward to be standing in the middle of a room, sucking on someone's wrist, but that's exactly what I did. I couldn't help but notice the possessive look in his eyes as I ingested his blood.

"I can't hear a damn thing and my strength is gone."

"Were you charming the guard?"

"I got a free pass to visit. Tarek seems to like your position as an apprentice. I don't know what inside information he could possibly want, but if Nero's involved, then Tarek's pockets are getting fat. I filled your fiancé's head with happy thoughts that Novis would cut you from his employment if he found out you broke Mage tradition."

"What tradition?"

"Moving in together before the bonding ceremony. Now he's scrambling with what to do."

I glared as I continued suckling from his wrist. One thing I knew was Mage law, and that wasn't in any of the books I'd read.

Christian shrugged. "So I fibbed a little. I told him I wanted to see that you were unharmed." He brushed a loose strand that had fallen from my ponytail. "You can stop now; it's healed."

I Ic ran his rough, wet tongue across the bite where my blood mingled with his. When he pursed his lips, his tongue rolled around in his mouth and his expression changed. It was a private look, as if he tasted something familiar, because I knew he was getting nothing from me otherwise. He lifted his black eyes to mine and I blinked. I didn't like a Vampire watching me, nor did I care for the look of ownership on his face that he couldn't conceal.

"I really thought this would work," I said in a defeated voice. The room grew eerily quiet as a memory from the party came back. "What happened with Justus? You didn't tell me what the emergency was."

He clasped his hands in front of him and lowered his chin. "Page has been kidnapped and they think it was her partner."

I stood up and paced. "I feel so useless here."

It was then I realized I'd no longer be involved in Justus's life the way I had been before. I was taken out of the game and forced to sit on the sidelines in both personal matters and investigative ones.

"They went to Slater's house and turned up nothing."

"Slater?" I touched my lip absently in thought. Christian remained quiet, watching me cross the room as I leaned against the far wall with my eyes on the floor.

"What are you thinking?"

"Page told me Slater only wants to make intelligent babies with her," I said, rolling my eyes. "But she revealed that she was infertile. Not only that, but Slater knew it. I got the vibe he didn't really like her otherwise, so I don't see this as some possessive male thing. Why would he kidnap a woman he doesn't even like, who can't give him the one thing he wants?"

"You don't think it was him?"

I shook my head. "I don't know, I'm just thinking out loud. How much longer are you allowed to stay?"

"Five minutes." There was a stretch of silence before he spoke again. "But you're coming with me."

My heart knotted in my throat. "What?"

"To be sure." Christian smiled, and something slipped out between his lips. "I'm pretty handy with pocket picking. When I first came to America, it was a way of life and put bread on the table. You had to be able to do it so effortlessly that it wouldn't break their stride. I've got magic fingers."

He slid the key in the lock and his cuffs fell on the bed.

"I can't."

"You're refusing to be free?"

"I can't, Christian. If I leave, he might…"

His Irish accent became so thick I could barely understand him. "He might anyway, ever thought of that? Tarek is stewing over what happened, and with Logan's fecking paws on your panty line, he's going to take it out on you. It's time to come clean, lass. Your friends should be made aware of the danger they're in. Silence is power, Silver. Don't give him your silence."

"We'll never get out. He's got Chitahs for guards!"

"Who will not lay a hand on you, and on that you have my word."

Inching toward him I whispered, "They're fast, and I can't outrun them with this necklace on. I can't fight."

"Which is why you'll do exactly as I say," he replied in a stern voice.

Christian shook out of his trench coat and removed his jacket and tie.

"I want you to shadow behind me and keep your emotions covered up. There are two guards between the front door and us. Once we take out the dolt standing in the hall, that'll leave us with Curly."

"Curly?"

A crooked smile graced his expression beneath the scruffy dark beard. "Never watched the Stooges?"

"What about the Vampire who's been tracking you?"

In a grandiose gesture, Christian swished his coat around my shoulders. I slid my arms through the long sleeves while he rolled up the cuffs. "Tarek sent him out since he thinks I'm contained. No matter what happens, I want you to trust me."

His fingers worked the buttons through the holes and he stopped on the last one. "That won't do," he muttered, staring at my bare feet. "Got a pair of sneakers in the bag?"

I shook my head.

Christian double-layered my feet with socks. "Ready yourself, girl. I'm going to let him in. Stand behind the door so he doesn't see you."

I took a deep breath, preparing for a fight without any of my abilities of flashing or regenerative healing. I glanced at Christian, who had rolled up his sleeves like a guy who was ready to kick some ass in a street fight. And with his strength, he could.

"Wait," I stalled, grabbing his arm as he motioned to knock on the door. Christian gave me a rather charming sideways smile as he shooed me with his hands. His knuckles lightly rapped against the wood twice.

I sucked in a calming breath of air. We didn't need the Chitah picking up a scent of fear and adrenaline. I casually picked at my thumbnail as the key slid into the lock and metal clicked. It was like a scene out of a horror movie as the doorknob slowly turned. Christian's hand hovered over the handle, and his black eyes shrank to slivers as he yanked it back.

The door obstructed my view, and I heard a gasp and a hard fist pounding against someone's face. Christian turned around and dragged the unconscious man to the bed where he cuffed him. The left side of the Chitah's face was sunken in from crushed bones. Chitahs heal slowly, but it was a gruesome display of a Vampire's power.

"Come on," he said.

I followed behind Christian as we moved into the hall. I bumped into him a few times, but I kept quiet as a mouse in my socks. It seemed too easy as we looked down the staircase. Christian cocked his head, listening with his keen Vampire ears.

Knowing I was in a house full of Chitahs, I pressed my face against his back and thought of all my preferred flavors of gum. Grape was tasty, but the flavor never seemed to last. Anything strawberry or raspberry was always a good pick, although once I had tried a foreign brand I bought in an Asian store and while I couldn't pinpoint the flavor, it was the most delicious gum I'd ever tasted.

I used these thoughts to distract me from putting out any strong emotional scents that would be noticed. Christian was undetectable to them, but he never looked stressed.

We went down the stairs, one careful step at a time. He'd pause and listen on every third step. Once my foot touched the bottom, I looked at the home stretch. Three steps and we'd be out the front door.

Christian positioned me against his hip so that I was between him and the wall. I reached for the door handle and he caught my wrist, holding it like an iron lock. But he wasn't looking at the door or me. His neck snapped toward the hallway on our left.

From the shadows, someone moved so fast that they were on us in seconds. Christian backed me up against the wall and shielded me with his body. The guard lunged with his teeth bared. Christian swung out his arm, but missed. The Chitah stopped moving long enough for me to see the shine on his bald head.

"Christian, we have to get out of here," I hissed.

If the Chitah called out to the other guards or Tarek, the game would be over. Christian was an immovable force to be reckoned with.

The Chitah charged twice and made the mistake of reaching out to grab me. Christian caught him by the neck and an audible snap later, the man fell to the floor.

"Will he die?" I whispered.

"He'll wake up with one hell of a headache. Come on," he said, rushing me outside.

Christian had the ability to shadow walk in dark places, but the moon was out, and I wouldn't be able to keep up with him with the chain around my neck. I ran so hard that the frosty air burned my lungs. We crossed the main stretch of property and I grabbed at his white shirt to slow him down.

"Wait, I can't run like this." I bent over and coughed, struggling to catch my breath. "Are you sure those were the only guards?" My feet ached from having tromped over acorns and twigs.

"Would you like me to set up a tea party out here so we can talk about it? Let's not dwell on the details. Run your arse off!"

I balled up my hands and sprinted like an Olympic champion. At first, it was easy with the cold air adding a little zing in my step. But eventually, I got a stitch in my side and slowed down. A blast of wind came up from behind and I shivered, but the wind didn't make me tremble. I turned around, heart racing.

"What's wrong?"

I stared into the blackness behind us, in the direction of the house. "Do you hear anything? It feels like we're being watched."

Christian's silhouette was barely visible and he clamped his hand across my mouth to silence my breathing.

"Run!" He shoved me forward and I stumbled in confusion. "As hard as you can, *run!*"

Panic moved through me like a riptide and I hauled ass, leaving Christian behind. I reached a slope and climbed to the top, looking both ways as I stepped onto the asphalt. On the left, a VW sputtered in my direction, looking like nothing short of the cavalry.

I waved my arms. None of Tarek's men would be caught dead in a Beetle, so I frantically ran down the road, hoping they didn't run me over.

"You need a lift?" a young guy asked. He poked his head out of the window and I walked around quickly to his door. He looked like a college kid with brown hair combed down over his forehead and a university T-shirt.

"My car broke down," I panted, smiling as much as I could. "It's freezing out here and I need a ride."

He glanced at my socks so I had to think quickly. "I didn't think the car would conk out on me. I had a craving for nachos and couldn't find my shoes. That's what I get." I laughed, trying to make it sound like something we've all done once or twice late at night.

"Hop in," he said, rolling up his window.

Jesus. He bought it.

I ran around the car and sank into the bucket seat, staring at his large, round wheel. "Wow, I didn't think these things ran anymore." I tried to swallow but my throat was sticky and dry.

"Were you running?"

"Yeah. I didn't want to get stuck out here alone, so I just started running. Gump style, ya know?"

He laughed and I relaxed a little, wanting to scream at him to hit the gas. Muscles jumped in my legs and I slid down the seat as he cranked the heater up and started to drive.

"Thanks for stopping. Three other cars tried to run me over," I lied.

"No biggie," he replied. "I'm Nate."

I almost said my name, but caught myself. "Ember."

"Cool name," he said, shifting gears.

Nate was probably out on a beer run or something. I kept swallowing and breathing through my nose. My mouth was so dry that I couldn't summon a drop of spit if I tried. He reached around back and handed me a bottle of cold water. I cracked it open, taking welcoming sips of the nearly frozen water he must have kept in his car for emergencies.

"I'm not sure where you're going, but I've only got a few dollars in the tank."

"I won't put you out," I promised. "Just drop me off wherever you want once we get into town and I'll be fine. I spent all my money on snacks, so I can't give you anything for gas unless your toy car runs on Oreos."

He howled with laughter and did one of those long "ahhhs" at the end, which made me smile. "No, but I do."

I looked over my shoulder at the dark road behind us and saw nothing but pavement rolling away. My heart sank as I thought about what might have happened to Christian.

CHAPTER 23

Nate dropped me off in front of an all-night market. I strolled inside and sat down at the blood-pressure machine, wondering if it would explode if I slid my arm in the cuff. Christian didn't give me a plan if we were separated. The store felt safe because if trackers found me, they might not cause a scene in a human establishment with security cameras.

"Can I help you find something?" a man in his forties inquired with a polite smile, adjusting the rim of his glasses.

"No, I'm just waiting for someone. My car broke down and it's freezing out there, so I'm just going to wait inside if that's okay."

"Perfectly fine, ma'am. Have a good evening," he said robotically, heading down the diaper aisle.

I stared at the screen filled with information on systolic and diastolic pressure. An old slow rock song played on the intercom and I sighed, uncertain of what to do next.

"Excuse me, sir. Can I use your phone?"

A clerk with acne walked by, reached behind the customer-service desk, and placed a phone within reach. I nodded with a courteous smile as he disappeared.

If I had money, I'd have gone to a hotel. Instead, I dialed Christian and it went to voicemail.

"Hey, it's me. Where the hell are you? I'm at that corner market by Sully's Books and I don't know where to go. I'm on a store phone and I'll be here for another twenty minutes. If you're not here by then, I'm leaving. It's almost morning and I feel like I'm on a merry-go-round," I said, talking to myself. "Twenty minutes and I'm outta here, Christian. Stay safe."

I walked the aisles like a zombie, trying to stay awake, anticipating that Tarek's trackers could burst in at any moment.

My socks were caked in wet mud from running through a soppy field. It was then that an idea came to me—a place that I would be safe that would give me time to think.

Jail.

I casually strolled over to the perfume aisle and shoved a bottle in my pocket, but got annoyed when I saw the expensive ones were locked up. When the clerk came into view, I stuffed a few tubes of lipstick in my coat pocket. The only problem was that these items would only get me a slap on the wrist. So I hit the meat department and tucked a steak down the front of my pants.

The DVD aisle was next and I stuffed a couple Eddie Murphy and Mel Gibson movies in the back of my jeans, lifting up my entire coat to do it. If I was going down as the stupidest shoplifter in history, my legacy would be that I had great taste in movies.

"Ma'am, you're going to have to come with me."

"Why?" I yelled in a belligerent tone.

"I've got you on camera shoplifting; the cops are on their way."

"Don't you have anything better to do than accuse people of a crime they didn't commit?"

When I moved toward the door, he grabbed my arm. Maybe they wouldn't arrest someone for shoplifting, but they certainly would for assault.

I pushed him and he stumbled backward. I didn't want to hit the poor guy. Ernest—according to his nametag—looked like he'd just experienced his first fight. Now was not the time for the sympathy card to slide onto the table. I narrowed my eyes at him but Ernest got spooked, went to the main door, and locked it.

Good man.

"Hey, what do you think you're doing? You can't lock me in here like some kind of an animal!"

I almost wanted to laugh when *Lethal Weapon* popped out of the ass of my jeans and slapped onto the floor.

Blue lights flashed from the parking lot and I silently rejoiced.

Ernest gave a victorious smile, and I thought about what a great story he was going to have for his wife and friends. I'm sure by then he'll have embellished on the details.

A large man wearing a puffy coat with a police badge stitched on the arm peered in the window at Ernest and then at me. I tucked my coat tightly together and with perfect timing, Eddie Murphy fell from between my legs and landed at my feet. The cop pointed at the lock and Ernest opened the door.

"I'm Officer Stone. We got a call for a shoplifter."

"Uh, yes sir. She also shoved me. That's assault, isn't it?"

"Hmph," the cop murmured, giving him a judgmental look. Officer Stone was a thick man, maybe an inch taller than my five-foot-nine stature. He had a classic buzz cut that I could see from the sides of his brimmed hat. When he approached, one hand covered his gun.

I stepped back and tightened my coat.

"Is what he says true?"

"It sure is!" Ernest answered, puffing out his chest.

It deflated the minute Officer Stone snapped his fingers. "Shut up, Ernest. I'm talking to the suspect; let me do my job. Unless you think you have it under control?"

Ernest quieted.

"Kind of late to be out—what have you got in that coat?" His grey eyes scanned my body and stared at the movie that I kicked behind me. I could hear it swishing across the floor down the aisle.

"I bet you'd like to know," I replied.

A grin quirked on his face just beneath his mustache.

"Make this easy on everyone. You and I both know that you're not going anywhere because Ernest over there has locked the door. Isn't that right, Ernie?"

The store manager locked the door again and watched with wide eyes.

"Now, this doesn't have to be hard." Stone's eyes flicked down to my muddy socks and his brows pushed together for a fraction of a second. "Let's start with your pockets."

Officer Stone relaxed his posture and leaned against a register as if we were engaged in a friendly conversation. But I wasn't about to make this easy for the copper, as Simon called them.

I pivoted around and ran full throttle across the store. His shoes hammered against the floor as he chased close behind. I tried to turn the corner, but my socks lost traction. I grabbed a rack of animal crackers and hit the ground, smacking my forehead as the boxes toppled over.

Not a moment later, Stone was cuffing my hands behind my back.

"Lipstick, perfume, more lipstick…" He listed off every stolen item from my pockets. Then he patted me down beneath the coat. "DVD, steak… Hey, this was a good movie. I'm going to roll you over."

Stone had a perplexed look on his face. "How the hell did you get a steak in your pants?"

I just blinked at him.

"I didn't take you for a T-bone girl myself." He squatted a moment and looked me over. "I need to search your jean pockets. Do you have anything in there I should know about? Needles, knives, razors?"

Razors?

I shook my head and he slipped his fingers into my pockets. "Where's your ID?"

My head was pounding and I grimaced.

Officer Stone peered in my eyes. "You don't look like the druggie type."

"I was going to sell a few chick flicks on the black market to support my habit, but they were all sold out of Meg Ryan."

He had a friendly laugh and when he sighed, I broke his train of thought. "We just going to lie here all night, or are you taking me to jail?"

"If I didn't know better, I'd think you were *trying* to get yourself arrested." He lifted his thumb and forefinger to his mouth, rubbing at the corners. "Someone after you?"

"No."

He didn't look convinced. "Your socks look pretty tore up, and that might lead me to think that you were homeless, looking for a fresh cot and a meal. But this is a mighty fine coat and I can still smell the damn detergent on your clothes. Boyfriend trouble?" He touched the sleeve. "A man's coat doesn't fit you."

"Look, I know my rights. I don't have to tell you shit."

He reached in the collar of my shirt and tugged at my necklace. "You steal this too?"

"If you can take it off, I'll buy you a beer."

Stone pulled back my eyelids and gave me a hard look. "Come on then." He lifted me up by my armpits and hooked his arm around mine. "Let's go for a ride. Ernest, open the door," he yelled out.

"I want to file charges for assault."

Officer Stone stepped up close and Ernest blinked nervously. "You look all right."

"She *pushed* me."

"Sleep on it and then decide if you want to lock up a young woman for battery. Feel free to bring your surveillance footage to the station, because I'm sure the boys would love to have a look," he said with a stout chuckle.

Ernest chose to retain his dignity.

As we crossed the parking lot, Stone tapped his hand on my cheek. "That's a nasty bump you got. Don't fall asleep; you might have a concussion."

I also hadn't slept in twenty-four hours. A jail cell with a nice cot sounded great, until I started thinking about cavity searches and public showers.

"What's your real name?"

I answered him with silence.

"So that's how it is," he muttered.

"Pretty much," I replied.

"If you want to post bail, I'd suggest you start remembering."

"Hey!" Christian shouted as he crossed the parking lot. "What's going on here?"

"Sir, you need to step back," Stone demanded of the man walking around in the freezing cold with nothing but a white dress shirt and slacks.

Christian switched his accent to the local one. "She looks like a real tough one, officer. Didn't mean to interrupt the wheels of justice turning."

"Mind telling me where your coat is?" Stone asked, as his fingers tugged at my sleeve.

"Ask your wife."

Which might have insulted the cop had he been wearing a wedding ring. I rolled my eyes at Christian and gave him a severe look that told him to *shut up*.

"Is that blood on your shirt?" Stone questioned.

Christian grinned politely as he looked down and flicked his finger at it. "Ketchup."

Stone looked at me and lowered his voice. "Do you know him?" He didn't care about my answer because he was watching my eye movements and facial expression.

I pulled my elbow a little closer to my body. "If I do, does that mean I can go?"

"No, but it might mean that he'll take a trip with us."

"I don't know him."

"Why did I think you would say that?"

Christian's strict features made me wince as he rolled down his sleeves. He was *pissed*.

"If you two don't know each other, then you need to get your ass moving," Stone said.

We were standing too far apart for Christian to entrance the cop, and it was against the law to kill a human—especially law enforcement.

My guard paced off with a menacing stride as the cop helped me into the back of his cruiser. I whispered under my breath so only he could hear. "Trust me, Christian. I'm safer this way. I need time to think it through."

He raked his hands through his hair from back to front, a peculiar gesture I'd seen him do before. Then again, everything about Christian was peculiar.

———◆———

CHAPTER 24

"ADAM!"

From across the bar, Adam watched Sunny illuminate the room with her radiant smile. She had her blond hair pinned up in a messy knot, and Knox was by her side—as he always was. It could be thirty below zero and that man would be wearing a formfitting shirt that barely had a thread count.

Adam had claimed a table in the far corner of the human bar.

Novis disapproved of socializing with mortals. While he had opened his door to Sunny and Knox because of their friendship to Adam, Novis was indifferent to humans. He'd told Adam on a number of occasions that he shouldn't get too attached to someone who will die; that it wasn't good for the soul. The only things worth holding on to were things that you could count on to last: laws, Breed, wisdom, and possessions.

After the bombing, Adam had been left with his own conclusion about what immortality meant. He watched opportunities wither away. A Mage is chosen—selected by their Creators for their admirable traits and strengths. Therefore, not many of them came with the kind of imperfections that Adam toted around on his face, arms, and chest. The judgment he had endured was brutal. The most painful part about it was losing Cheri—one he had grown to love and trust and who betrayed him. Adam loved too easily, and it would be for the best if he didn't give away his heart so foolishly.

Two days after the bombing, Novis expected him to make a public appearance as if nothing had happened. Adam had just recovered from the excruciating ordeal of his scars healing up. He needed time to deal, especially when the guards gave him the cold stares and most definitely when the offers for a Healer were withdrawn.

Adam felt at ease in the human bars. They stared but eventually got over it. They also didn't walk right up to you and address it like a Vampire would, or another Mage. He could have a drink in peace and feel like a regular guy just hanging out. Adam wasn't the only one who'd walked away that night with injuries; he'd heard rumors that at least six of the survivors had committed suicide rather than living life scarred or disabled. That didn't paint a rosy picture.

He took a hard sip of his beer as Knox and Sunny approached. Her painted smile told the story. Women had an admirable way of holding a torch in the darkness.

"Hey, brother." Knox greeted him. "How's it hangin'?" He spun the chair around and sat with his arms over the back. "Ready for me to blow your mind?"

Adam politely stood up until Sunny settled in her chair. She was busy unwrapping herself from a white scarf that was knitted for a giant. Once the hat and matching gloves were neatly folded on the table, she claimed the chair on his right.

"Hi, Adam. How are you?"

"Not bad. Is he treating you right?"

Her shimmery lips smiled wide and she leaned over and kissed Knox on the cheek. "He treats me like gold."

Knox's eyes went half-mast and the tips of his ears turned scarlet. He pulled the ends of his knit hat down, covering them up before swiping Adam's beer and taking a drink.

"Adam, how have you been, really?" Sunny pressed. "We haven't heard from you and Silver's been wondering when you're going to come out with us." She briefly spun around to look at a man singing on stage who was getting a lot of catcalls from the women.

Knox didn't look like he wanted to tread on this topic and waved at the waitress to bring him what Adam was having.

Adam leaned back and rubbed his short, patchy beard. "I'm here. I don't know what I can tell you."

An uncomfortable silence hung between them and quickly ended when the waitress clicked a few bottles on the table and left her card. Her name was Mimi and she couldn't take her eyes off Knox. That never used to happen, because Knox was a hard-looking man, all rough around the edges. Maybe it was the fact that he smiled a lot more now with Sunny at his side.

"So what's up?" Adam asked, tipping his bottle of beer and taking a sip.

Knox cleared his throat and leaned forward on his elbows. "I got offered a position with HALO." He watched Adam's expression and gave him a toothy grin. "No shit. I got contacts all over the place—we both do. In fact, if you'd show interest, they'd snatch you up because your name was mentioned more than once. Remember the dealer we talked about in our old group who's selling that fucked up magic metal shit on the black market?"

"Yeah. You find out anything?"

"I'm on it, and getting close. HALO knows they may never confiscate what's already out there, but maybe they can stop production."

"You accepting the job?"

"Of *course* he is," Sunny answered for him, but in a tone that told Adam they'd argued about it.

Knox gave her a reassuring look and said, "They don't have any human representation. I can shed light about what we did in the Special Forces and help them out with some of their investigations whenever they hit a wall because it's on human turf. I'm telling you," he marveled, leaning back, "this shit just gets weirder and weirder. Who would have thought a year ago I'd be sitting on the side of the people we were taking out."

Sunny cleared her throat and got up. "Ladies' room," she announced, and swung her angry hips away.

"Problems?" Adam smirked.

Knox chuckled. "Nothing that can't be taken care of later on tonight when I put my mouth on her."

"You don't deserve a woman like that," Adam said in a humored voice.

"You speak truth, brother," Knox agreed. "I'll never understand why that woman puts up with my shit, but the God's honest truth is that I love her more because she does. She still tosses my smokes in the toilet; we can't seem to come to an agreement about a man enjoying a cigarette after sex."

"Or steak. Or a car drive. I'm surprised you hung on for all those months smoking menthols." Adam snorted and polished off his beer.

"I'm down to a pack a week," Knox said proudly, muscles flexing in his dark green T-shirt. "Women don't want to kiss a smoker; I get it."

"So you're taking the job?"

Knox picked at the edge of his tight hat. Some called it a beanie, but whatever it was, Knox never left home without it. "Can't deny the pay is outstanding. It'll be more behind-the-scenes shit so my woman won't have to worry about me getting up in the middle of the night, strapping on guns, and going on a raid. This is right up my alley."

Then the weird silence loomed again.

Knox cleared his throat and leaned in privately. "Is it something you'd want to do? Hell, I'd love having you in. It would be like old times."

Adam shook his head. He had something else on his mind and didn't need the distraction of playing cloak and dagger.

Knox rubbed his jaw and released a disappointed sigh through his nose.

"When did this all happen?" Adam turned around at a few shouts coming from some obnoxious pool players. The singer had left the stage and the jukebox played at a tolerable level.

"They gave me a practice run to test out my skills. My first job was—get this—Marco Fucking De Gradi. Justus doesn't want to deal with him. I think after taking out Merc, he's afraid he'll do the same to his own Creator."

Adam cursed. "There're laws against killing your Creator."

"Exactly," Knox said. The chair creaked and he curled his hands into fists, deep in thought. "I'm glad I gave that bastard what he had coming. You don't mess around with my girl and walk away."

Knox had put the man's lights out in a short-lived bar brawl not too long ago. One that gained him a little respect with some of the immortals because Marco was a Mage and Knox was just a human.

"Why did he come back?"

"Guilt. I went down to Texas and questioned him—told him who I was affiliated with and he wasn't on board at first because I didn't have one of those rings they wear. But you know I'm a convincing man," Knox said with a wry smirk. "He said finding Silver was a fluke; her energy as a human was way off. That's why he kept asking Sunny about Zoë's father, because there were always rumors floating around about crossbreeding and he wondered if there was something to it. Samil had given him a list of names to locate, but it was time-consuming."

More claps sounded at the bar and the both of them looked up with alert eyes. Some habits are hard to break.

Knox continued. "Anyhow, he thought Silver would be like a bonus or some shit, but it backfired on his ass. He knew Samil was working for Nero and tried to go directly to the man to resolve some shit they had between them, but Nero didn't want to deal with him."

Adam ran his finger along the scar on his jaw. "Why did he show up in Cognito?"

"To strike a deal with Justus."

Adam didn't like the sound of that. "What kind of deal?"

Knox lowered his voice. "He doesn't want the Council or anyone else involved because he's barely able to fly under the radar anymore with some of the shit surfacing. Marco knows how to get in touch with Nero when he needs to, and he wants some woman back. He found out how valuable Silver is to Nero and wanted to do a little swap. He thought the whole situation with Justus taking in a Learner—a *female* Learner—made as much sense as a screen door on a submarine."

Adam folded his arms and leaned back in his chair. A woman with a good heart deserved better than the way the men in her life had treated her. Abused. Abandoned. And now he discovered someone wanted to trade her off. No wonder she didn't trust men.

"Marco came up to bribe Justus."

"With what?" Adam sniffed and shook his head.

Knox took another swig of beer and grimaced. "Everything. He was going to give Justus his entire fortune. Justus is a materialistic guy—look at all that shit he has. Cars, homes, all those suits and watches. Christ! If he has that much money, you can only imagine what his Creator has. Marco wanted to pay Justus for Silver."

Adam's jaw muscle flexed. Anger bubbled in that nasty way that made a man do stupid things, so he rubbed his face and looked over his shoulder at the pool players.

"Why did he tell you all this?"

Knox's gravelly voice lowered. "So I'd relay it to Justus. He wanted to put the idea in his head and see if he took the bait."

"He better... fucking... *not*," Adam growled, watching Sunny pick up a menu at the bar.

"No, he's not on board," Knox confirmed. "I had a private talk with him and he's a man shamed. I don't blame him, because I get that your Creators are like fathers or some shit. That's a heavy load to lay on a man, and after he finished tearing up my office, he wrote me a check for the damages and told me to keep it between us. But I'm telling you because we're tight like that, and I trust you. He appreciated my tactics at getting what he needed, and we started talking more seriously about my future interests."

Adam tipped his beer. "Well done." The sentiment lacked enthusiasm, but Knox deserved a pat on the back. He was motivated, intelligent, and always wanted to do something for a greater cause.

"You know why we did all those hits?" Knox said discreetly. "To test out their weapons. Not all of them worked—you remember that as well as I do. My ex-partner dug up some seriously disturbing shit in those Trinity files. Most of the metals have a shelf life and weaken over time, but they're not telling that to the people they're selling it to."

"Damn," Adam breathed. It made him want to get involved again to get some revenge against the men who had used them like guinea pigs. They both shared a disgusted look, knowing that was a part of their past they'd never be able to erase.

"You need to snap out of it," Knox blurted out.

Adam's eyes flicked up and caught Knox staring at the scar on his temple that ran straight down to his jaw. It was the most prominent one that couldn't be covered with facial hair. "Don't worry about me." Adam brushed him off.

"Quit doing that," he grumbled. "If these pricks won't hire you, I fucking will. What did you plan on doing before you found out you were a Healer? Think on that shit. You got a long time to work it out, but you got way too many talents to ignore."

"Well," Sunny chimed in, strolling up to the table. "As much as I've complained, I will finally admit that Breed bars have better food. This place is a dive and they don't even have nachos on the menu. Is this where you hang out, Adam?"

Adam shrugged. He came on a few occasions, but he preferred a bar a few blocks up the street called Northern Lights. Local musicians were allowed on stage after nine. He loved watching these humans get up and belt out their soul, only to go back to their regular job at the bank. Otherwise, his routine hadn't changed much. Two hours each morning, he went on a hard run. After that, Novis usually had an agenda. Sometimes they practiced with weaponry, but without a job or purpose, Adam had become listless. It made him want to pick up photography again, but he'd lost the passion.

Sunny covered her stomach with her hand and blushed. Knox looked like a fishhook had grabbed the corner of his mouth and pulled it up. He winked at Sunny and whispered something softly in her ear.

"Extra-large," she said privately to him.

"With cherries, baby girl," he promised, kissing her nose.

"Watch my purse." She got up and headed toward the bathroom.

Adam rested his chin in the palm of his hand. Sunny's stares made him uncomfortable because her eyes were filled with pity. That's not the way a man wants to be looked at by any woman.

"I'm going to marry her," Knox said quietly.

"Yeah, so you keep saying."

Knox fished in his pocket and slid a tiny black box across the wooden table.

Speechless, Adam lifted the lid and admired a modest heart-shaped diamond ring with a platinum band and two pale amethyst stones on either side, sparkling beneath the cheap lighting.

"You dirty dog," he said with a wide grin.

Knox pulled the ends of his hat down, brown eyes staring at the box. "You think she'll like it? It's not one of the big ones."

"You're serious?" Adam was still in shock and trying to process it. Knox had sworn he'd *never* marry a woman, but that was before Sunny. "She's going to fall over for this."

Knox blew out a relieved breath and closed the box, slipping it back into his pocket.

"What are you waiting for?"

"Shit, I don't know. I don't want to blow it and I'm not good at planning all that romantic stuff. I'm just waiting for the right time. Women have all those fantasies about vineyards, carriages, roses, and violins."

Adam leaned in tightly. "She's not going to say no. You could propose to her sitting on top of a tobacco truck, swearing your way straight into hell, and that woman would say yes."

Knox laughed and rapped his knuckles on the table. "Where are you staying these days, brother? Novis says you don't come home some nights."

"Here. There." Adam swished the liquid in his bottle and watched a woman leaning over the pool table, taking a corner-pocket shot. She had more curves than the ball she was aiming for.

"People are wondering what you're up to is all I'm saying," Knox said in slow, pronounced words. "I know that shit you carry around, and you got that look in your eye. Talk it out with me here or later, but don't do something stupid that's going to make you one of my cases."

"I thought you were a man who believed in justice."

Sunny appeared from the bathroom door and headed toward the bar. Knox kept a close eye on her at all times and when she slid onto the stool, he turned his attention back to Adam. "Someday, Razor…"

"Adam," he corrected.

"Don't be funny with me, brother. You'll always be Adam Razor in my head. The guy that took a knife in the gut for me. The guy who told me to quit fucking around and find a good woman. The guy who told me that someday he was going to have some property and watch his kids play on a tire swing. The guy with a conscience. I'm not seeing that conscience in your eyes these days." Knox waved a heavy finger at Adam's face and scraped his lip with his teeth. "I don't want to see you do something stupid for revenge."

"My sister's killer is out there; I have a right to find him."

"You think that's going to make your problems go away?" Knox asked.

Someone cranked a rock song on the jukebox and they both leaned in closer to hear each other. Knox had no right to judge him because he'd never lost anyone that mattered—let alone a twin.

Knox sighed heavily. "Is that what you've been doing at night? You think you're just going to find him wandering around on the street outside human bars in a city where the crime didn't even happen?" he asked incredulously.

Adam narrowed his eyes and shoved the bottles to the side. "Samil was his maker, and I got a good feeling that he'll come back home eventually. I've got his face burned in my memory and I've lived here long enough to know our kind eventually comes home. It's where most of Samil's progeny is, and if that sonofabitch is out there, then I'm going to find him. I'd sure as hell know his mark if he's changed his appearance."

Knox's large arms rested on the table and his face softened to one of resolve. "I get it. Just promise me something," he said in a low voice.

"Yeah?"

Knox lowered his dark eyes to the table and nodded to himself as he came to some kind of conclusion. "When you do find him, do the right thing. *Whatever* that might be, brother. I'll always have your back."

CHAPTER 25

"How long will you keep me locked up?" I asked Officer Stone from the back seat of his squad car. "It's not a hotel, you know."

The hell it wasn't. Although the idea of a strip search as part of the check-in process was losing its appeal. The police radio squawked and the car made a wide right turn.

"Remembered your name yet?"

"Jane Doe."

"Well, Jane, why don't you tell me why you were stealing a bunch of worthless shit at an ungodly hour?"

I avoided looking at his piercing eyes in the rearview mirror and winced as I stupidly rested my forehead against the glass. The monstrous bump began to throb all over again.

"Doesn't this have trouble written all over it," he mumbled as the car slowed down.

I leaned over and looked through the front windshield. A black car was parked ahead of us with a man signaling for the cop to pull over. He wore a long tan coat with black gloves and a fedora, one that covered his Mohawk.

Tarek grinned when he spied me in the back and I slid down in my seat.

"Sit tight," Stone said.

"Take me to the station first. You're not supposed to make stops, are you?"

"Do you know them?" he asked without turning around.

I didn't answer. Stone got out of the vehicle and slammed the door. He was a fearless man, always in control of the situation. He approached Tarek with his hand covering the gun at his hip and I could hear the conversation through the glass.

"What's the trouble?" Stone demanded more than asked, stopping at a safe distance.

"No trouble. I just happened to be out driving and noticed you had my fiancée in the back seat of your police car. I'd like to take her home. What has she done?"

"You mind stepping away from the car and removing your hand from your pocket?"

Tarek lifted his hands as if under arrest. I peered through the small space between the headrest and the seat. A protective panel divided the car, and claustrophobia was rearing its ugly head.

"How much is her bail? I can pay it here and save everyone the trouble. My wallet is in my pocket," Tarek said, reaching around his waist. Stone tightened his grip on his gun when Tarek slowly opened his wallet and removed several bills. "For your... trouble."

Stone flashed his light on the money and then back in Tarek's car. "If you know this woman, then what's her name?"

Tarek narrowed his eyes. We all had fake identities we used in the human world so our real names wouldn't be documented. Tarek didn't have a clue what mine was.

"I assure you she is my fiancée. I can bring you witnesses if needed, although I think Ben Franklin is witness enough, don't you?" He reached in his wallet, tugging at it several times until he rolled up a wad and held it out toward Stone.

The cop backed up. "If you know that woman, then you can swing by the station in the morning. I'm going to ask you to get in your vehicle, or I'll arrest you for bribing an officer."

Stone hadn't a clue he was up against a Chitah Lord, but he was a man undeterred. That might have provoked Tarek, but he seemed to play by the rules when it came to human law enforcement. Taking Stone out in the middle of the street wouldn't bode well if there were a witness or a street camera.

Tarek straightened his back and drew in a deep breath through his nose. His golden eyes gleamed in the headlamps and white plumes came out each time he spoke. "Very well, we'll follow you."

"You do that and I got a cot with your name on it. Fond of

cavity searches? Because there's a guy at the station who is, and he'll *love* you. Get back in your car. Now."

Tarek flashed teeth for a second, but to my surprise, he did just as the officer requested.

Officer Stone returned and sat in the front seat, turning around to look me over. "You sure have a lot of boyfriends who don't know your name." His coat made a rustling sound as he buckled up. "You stole that shit on purpose, didn't you?"

"How long will I stay in jail for?"

Stone forced out a tight breath. "I don't really like locking people up for stealing worthless crap. Do you want me to call the women's shelter?"

"No. How long?"

"Would getting locked up make you feel safer, is that what it is?" His eyes read me like a book. "Why don't you tell me who these men are? You're wearing Bachelor Number One's coat, but I suspect he's not your main problem. Dickhead Number Two just tried to pay me off. He's lucky I didn't shove him in the trunk, because if I'd had another cruiser with me, he'd be under arrest."

"Look, my head really hurts, so if you don't mind, I'm going to stop talking now."

"Where do you live?" he asked.

I shook my head and he grew increasingly impatient.

"Tell me where you live and I'll take you home. I haven't called this in or filled out the paperwork yet. I got more hardcore criminals out at this hour to worry about. No harm done, outside of offending me with your poor taste in movies."

"I don't have a home," I lied.

He removed his hat and tossed it in the seat beside him. His buzz cut had a flat top. Stone's brows slanted, giving him an apologetic expression. "You sprang forth this very night? Hallelujah, it's a fucking miracle!"

"I could spit in your face and call you a pig if that'll make our trip shorter."

He carved me up with his eyes. "Fair enough," he replied, turning around in his seat as the car sped down the road.

"This isn't the way to the station," I said as I watched the buildings become more unfamiliar and thin out.

"I'm taking you to a shelter; that boyfriend of yours will be coming to the station, and I don't think you want to see him, do you?" His eyes darted to mine in the mirror.

"Just take me to jail. I don't want to go to a shelter."

"And why not?"

"Because he'll *find* it—now take me to the fucking station!" I yelled, kicking the doors.

"Cut that out and settle down! You'll be safe there."

"I don't have time to argue, just take me to the station. You don't know that man; he can find a speck of lint in the Sahara Desert. He'll be at that shelter within ten minutes of my arrival."

"Fair enough."

I slid across the seat as the car made a sudden U-turn in the middle of the street.

When we arrived at the station, Stone hauled me in and sat me down on a bench, uncuffed. A few minutes later he reappeared and took me by the arm, dragging me back outside.

"Where are we going?" I looked around and noticed dawn was on the horizon as the colors began to change. I shivered as Stone pushed me into the passenger seat of a blue sedan.

Did this qualify as abduction? Somehow, I didn't think it was part of the booking process.

"You're coming with me," he said matter-of-factly, starting up the engine.

"Um, look… I don't know what you're up to, but you can't—"

He reached over and grabbed my hand before I could open the door. His face was just a mere inch from mine and I leaned back to create space.

"Let me help you for one night so I can sleep knowing I didn't send you to an early grave. If you want to come to the station later, I'll drive you myself and make up charges. I've been around the block and then some; I know that look and maybe I got a soft spot for helping out a woman in trouble. Maybe if someone had done it for my mother, she wouldn't be sitting in a mental institution. So come get a good morning's sleep, and maybe by then you'll remember your name and where you need to go. Deal?"

"It's not safe. I can't go to your house."

"I'm a cop who's pissed off a whole lot of people. I keep my house locked up tighter than a prison." Something softened in his expression. "I see those marks on your neck," he said, motioning toward the Chitah scars. "That's a world I know a little about, one I'm ass-deep in on a daily basis. Boyfriend Number Two was a tall sonofabitch with a unique eye color, wouldn't you say? And your Vampire friend is a real jackass."

Before I could formulate a smart comeback, Stone turned the wheel and backed out the car. He knew about Breed. He knew I was in trouble. And for Good Samaritan reasons I'd never understand, he wanted to help.

I used to doubt the existence of angels, not realizing they were men and women walking among us.

Stone lived in a modest house with tall iron gates along the sidewalk. A small key unlocked the gate that secured his front porch. He had all but built a cement wall around his property. Once inside, he flipped on the lights.

My eyes widened at the guns all over the room.

"These are my babies," he said unapologetically. Stone went into the kitchen and put on a pot of coffee. "Take a load off on the sofa if you want to sleep. My room is off-limits, and if you want to use the bathroom, hold the toilet handle down."

"I think I'm past sleep at this point. I'll take the coffee."

"Fair enough, have a seat. Let's start with your name."

Ah, to tell or not to tell: that was the question. My false name would come up in one of the Mage databases if he reported it.

"Let's not."

"You got any family?"

I shrugged.

"Is there *anyone* who can help you out? You might start by telling me what you are. I'm trusted among Breed and I could get you the right kind of help. I don't know why you're mixed up with a Chitah, but that's the wrong kind to tangle with."

I sat on his musty plaid sofa from the 1970s and dropped my feet on the coffee table. Dirty feet with holes snagged in the socks. Embarrassed at my lack of manners, I crossed my legs, peeled off the wet socks, and stuffed them inside Christian's coat pockets. I couldn't help but imagine what delightful things he'd have to say when he discovered them. It was getting warm, so I unfastened the coat and slipped out of it.

"Put your feet up. I don't care," he said from the connecting kitchen on my right. He tossed a frozen bag of tater tots at me. "Sorry, I'm all out of peas."

I stared at the bag and my stomach growled.

"For your head," he said, tapping his skull.

"Thanks."

I pressed the frozen bag to my aching head. Stone returned with two white mugs, setting mine on the end table to the right and switching on the lamp. It was the most hideous thing I'd ever seen—celery green with a hula girl on it.

Stone was a weathered man with silver hairs sprouting through the dark color of his youth. He appeared to be in his late forties, and time was not on his side. His features were strong, but his face looked like a man who'd seen too much and a boy who had once had an acne problem. His nose had been broken a few times and his lips were nonexistent. Yet there was something pleasant about him, and it had to do with integrity.

I took a sip but wasn't in the mood for coffee. *Especially not his.* I pulled one of my dirty socks from the coat pocket and tossed it at him.

"Thought you could use a coffee filter," I joked, picking the granules from my tongue. "I could be some lunatic, you know. Cut you up in your sleep and ship you to Taiwan."

His lip twitched and he raised his cup. "My sister was strangled with an extension cord by her boyfriend. Let's just say I didn't cuddle up to the idea of sending you home with Dickhead."

His mother *and* sister were victims of abuse?

"Some people would have taken his money." I wondered what made him stand apart from those kind of men. "He would have offered more too. He probably would have given you his damn car."

"Maybe I should have held out," Stone said with a chuckle. "Does he own a Mercedes? Always pictured myself in one of those. Someday... when I retire." Stone had a three-second daydream as he sipped his coffee.

"Why don't I call him and find out," I grumbled.

He leaned forward in his chair and moved the bag on my head. "You need to keep the tots on this end and hold it firm."

"Is this going to be breakfast?"

"Are you hungry? I got sausages, ham, bacon, and leftover pizza."

"Sounds like a heart attack. No thanks."

"When's the last time you ate?"

"Probably around the last time I slept. I'm way past that now. I just need to sit for a while. My head hurts too much."

Suddenly, the lights shut off, submersing us in total darkness. I dropped the bag on the couch and strained to hear anything out of the ordinary.

"Stay put," he ordered in an authoritative voice.

A flashlight flipped on and shone in my eyes, forcing me to throw up my hand.

"You stay here while I check it out," he said. "Don't move."

My eyes followed the bright stream of light as he reached up and pulled a large gun off the wall. Stone walked out the door, and the waiting game began.

CHAPTER 26

T HE MOST FRIGHTENING SOUND YOU can hear in the dark is silence.

I felt my way around in the tight space, using my memory to lead me to the door. This was a process I was familiar with, having been temporarily blinded not too long ago. Officer Stone had gone outside, and I admired how brave cops were to run into the face of danger while the rest of us cowered. It had nothing to do with a uniform or a gun—the badge of character was one they wore beneath their skin.

I pressed my ear against the door.

Another minute passed, then another. My heart steadily thumped against my chest like a basketball being dribbled on a court.

All of a sudden, the power switched back on and I gasped, turning in a circle to look behind me. Stone must have reset the breakers, something I knew a lot about from an old apartment I once lived in.

I opened the front door and peered through the locked iron door on the porch, my breath floating into the predawn light that was subdued by a heavy fog. There was a slight breeze as wisps of my black hair floated about, and I wedged my face through the bars, squinting at the movement ahead.

With haunting clarity, I saw Tarek standing behind the gate that circled the yard. He was distanced from the house, but the unblinking gaze made it feel as if he were standing right in front of me. My heart sped up and a terrible feeling of dread washed over me in waves.

"Open up," he called out.

"Where's Stone?"

"The human?" He chuckled. "He's having a chat with me. Why don't you join us? Open up."

"I don't know how. You didn't hurt him, did you?"

"Of course not, sweetie. Not yet, anyway."

Tarek removed his gloves and tucked them in his pockets before folding his coat and dropping it at his feet. He slowly unbuttoned his shirt and stood as a mass of muscle like I'd never seen. Tarek was more than a man or a Chitah—he was an abominable demon unleashed on the earth. His pecs flexed as one of his men brought Stone into view.

"Don't hurt him!" I screamed out.

Tarek faced the human and in a calm voice said, "Open the gate and I'll let you live."

"Fuck you," Stone spat, his face bloody and bruised. Tarek's guards held him tight.

God... No, no, no.

"Officer, please open the door and let me out!"

Tarek lowered his eyes to Stone and ordered the guards to release him. His men stepped out of sight and Stone wobbled unsteadily. Then a calm fell over him and he stood up, looking Tarek straight in the eye.

"Last chance, Mage," Tarek warned. "Let me in and save his life."

"I can't!" I yelled from the porch, my fingers wrapped around the bars. "They lock from both sides. Officer Stone, do what he asks and give him the key. He won't hurt me and you don't need to be involved in this." My heart raced as I watched Tarek's fists relax. "Tarek, *please* don't hurt him. He doesn't know who you are."

My voice croaked and I trembled, watching how calm Tarek was standing in the freezing cold, wearing only a pair of slacks. If only I could use my gifts, I'd be able to slide the lock open.

"Last chance, human," Tarek said, shoving Stone toward the gate.

Stone lifted his eyes to mine and delivered a glance I knew well. Defiance.

"Stone, *no!*"

With a smooth turn, Stone faced Tarek and mumbled something I couldn't hear. Tarek's canines punched out and his switch flipped.

A unique pattern rippled across his skin as rage consumed him. The colors were intense, dark spots that covered his torso and shoulders.

Before I could scream, Tarek tore out his throat.

My fingers squeezed the metal bars and I soaked in the pain of a good man who died for nothing.

Blood sprayed over Tarek's chest and Stone's limp body twitched as Tarek sliced him up with his fangs. I had seen enough.

I stumbled back inside and locked the door behind me. I'd never felt such a coldness stir within me, such a feeling of dread that settled on my skin like a sheet of frost.

Stone lived in a desolate area of town where most of the houses were condemned and abandoned. Tarek's roar over a fresh kill was chilling, and my hands trembled as I fumbled through drawers in search of a cell phone. I laughed when I glanced up and saw he had a regular phone on the wall with the curly cord.

Who was I going to call that could possibly stand up to a Chitah? I tried Christian, and on the third ring, I heard a click.

"Silver, what's wrong?"

"How did you know?"

"I can hear your fecking heartbeat through the phone. Where the hell are you?"

"He took me to his house. He was going to... oh God." My voice trembled. "Tarek is here. He killed the cop outside and now I'm trapped in the house."

"Your location!" he demanded. "Christ, I can *hear* him."

I held the receiver away to listen. Tarek roared and it sounded primal—like a caged animal, thirsty for a kill. With the taste of blood buzzing in his head, I knew that nothing would stop him from getting inside.

"He's flipped, Christian. He's... I'm going to die. I can't get this necklace off!" I said in a shrill voice, pulling at it until I grimaced in pain.

"Silver, *calm* yourself down." Christian's voice was rich and dark, scaring me to silence. "Tell me where you are."

I gave him the directions, but I had no idea where he was and knew he didn't have a car. No one could reach me in time.

I dropped the phone when the locks on the door clicked. The brass knob slowly turned and Tarek appeared in the open doorway.

Which meant he had found the keys on Stone.

Blood that once filled Stone's body with life was now splattered on Tarek's bare chest like a shirt. His eyes were soulless and black.

I wasn't sure if his instinct was to kill me, tear me apart, or drag me to an altar, but none of those options sounded agreeable.

He blew out a steady breath and a ring of gold appeared around the black orbs, framed by heavy brows. But all my eyes could see were his fangs, and the scars on my neck burned like phantom pains.

"What a convenient setup the human has; the gates are impenetrable. At least without this," he said, holding up a small bloody key. "Did you know he actually swallowed it?"

A blanket of chills swept over me and I shuddered, blocking away the images that flooded my mind. While I looked at him—at least as much as I could with his intense gaze—my peripheral vision was working overtime to assess where the weapons were in proximity to my position in the room.

Tarek reached for the phone on the floor without breaking eye contact, pulling the cord until the receiver was in his hand.

"To whom am I speaking?"

I heard a garble of obscenities through the line.

"Likewise, Vampire. Let me give you a piece of advice: stay away. I'd like some private time with my fiancée. If I hear so much as one sound, I promise you on my word as a Chitah I will tear her apart."

He placed the phone back in the cradle and pulled a cell phone from his back pocket, pressing a number and holding it to his ear. We stood only five feet apart. I couldn't outrun him, and I was locked inside with weapons that probably wouldn't kill him.

"Good morning, Cross."

I gasped, and Tarek grinned.

"Is that any way to greet an old friend? Shame. How are things working out with you and the little miss? I just wanted to express my congratulations that you have found a replacement."

Tarek stalked forward and corralled me in the corner of the living room. My eyes scanned the weapons hanging on the wall, weapons I had no clue how to use.

"If you mean to kill me then just do it. Quit playing these games," I hissed under my breath.

"Would you like to talk to Silver? She's right here. Say hello, sweetie."

I pinched my brows together when he held the phone to my ear, wondering what his intentions were. "Logan, whatever he says, *don't* listen to him."

Tarek smiled and pulled the phone back. "Yes, don't listen to me. I know you have plenty of things to be doing. Laundry, picking up groceries for the new lady love—all that relationship bullshit. You have my condolences."

I blanched, wondering if Tarek meant to kill Logan's intended mate. "Tarek, don't," I said, adamantly shaking my head.

He smeared his hand down his bloody chest and brushed a finger across my cheek. I jerked away from his ruthless hands. He smelled like bitter sweat, earth, and something metallic.

"For? Your loss, of course. I know it doesn't mean much now, but you carried a torch for Silver once, even if she isn't your kindred spirit. In lieu of flowers, you can give me your girlfriend, if you like. But... Hold on. No need to yell," he said in an amused tone. Tarek patted his Mohawk and left a streak of blood across his scalp.

I was close to hyperventilating.

Tarek nodded at me as a man who had just won. When I reached for the phone, he backhanded me, and I yelled as the crack of his knuckles hit my cheek.

"Ah, you know how it is. She's not really my type; I guess I don't do sloppy seconds after all. Not to mention, she's a lying whore who would bed a man beneath my nose. But I guess you know all about that, don't you? That's what I get for choosing a Mage, such an unworthy mate compared to a Chitah. What honor could I have in walking away? None. That's what. A sinner deserves to be punished, don't you agree?"

If Logan had any residual feelings for me, Tarek was baiting him.

"Logan, don't listen to him!" I screamed, but he shoved me to the ground.

"What?" Tarek plugged his finger in his other ear theatrically. "Sorry, I wasn't able to make out what you said. I was preoccupied with beating my woman. Have you ever hit Silver? Feeling her skin break beneath my fist feels spectacular. I can give her a smack on your behalf—just say the word. Maybe I should cut out her tongue," he said wonderingly as he watched me on the floor.

"Tarek, stop," I whispered. "I'll do whatever you want, just don't bring Logan into this."

He smiled lazily before all expression melted away. "Godspeed, Cross. We've had a lot of bad blood between us over the years and I wanted to mend the rift by giving you a chance to say your last goodbye. Although in time, she would have sabotaged your new relationship. You know how a Mage mind works—they have no respect for what's honorable and good. Here she is."

Tarek tossed the phone at me and I hung up, throwing it across the room.

With Chitah speed, Tarek retrieved it before I could move an inch.

He pinned me down and held me to the floor by my hair while he dialed Logan.

"Do that again, bitch, and I promise Cross will die. He might have been able to pretend the rest of his life away with another female, but let's see if he can deny his love for you under the blade of a knife. Talk to him, or I promise you he will die. A broken heart is better than one that is cut out. You decide."

I held the phone to my ear. "Logan, I'm so sorry," I whispered.

"Where are you?" Quiet rage filled the dark corners of his voice.

"Don't cling to honor over something that was never meant to be. Don't ruin your life for a Mage who could never love you the way you deserve. Just go on with—"

Tarek yanked the phone from my hand. It was my last chance to give Logan peace of mind. I refused to have my death haunting him his whole life, and maybe it would settle his conscience if he thought that he'd never mattered to me.

But he did.

Logan meant *everything*.

I choked when Tarek's knee pressed into my neck. "You're a disgrace to our kind, Cross. You'll *never* know the emptiness of losing your true soul mate. I have lived my *entire life* knowing I will never have my true mate because she chose a man who could not guard her life. It makes you half a man, and it's a gift I want to give to you." His stony eyes flicked to mine and I gasped for air as his knee sank against my windpipe. "Every female you dare to love for the rest of your life will die by my hand, starting tonight."

My eyes widened.

"Know this, Cross. Before I take this female's life, I'm going to take her body. I will be baptized in her blood and born a new man. I have waited a long time for my revenge. Eventually, I'll find the one who matters to you. Goodbye, Cross. I hope you enjoy what you're about to hear."

Tarek set the phone down on the end table. I punched him in the groin and leapt up, running for the door. He grabbed my ankle and I flew over the edge of the coffee table, smashing one of the legs.

"Wooo! I love my females feisty!"

Laughter poured out of him like fifteen seconds of poison. He lost his grip on my ankle, so I scrambled for a shelf and lifted a gun. When I pulled the trigger, nothing happened. I cursed at myself, trying to figure out how to work the safety release. Tarek laughed at the show I was giving him, pouncing closer with each step.

"I wish you could see how your female fears me, Cross!" he yelled. "Don't worry, sweetie, I like to take my time with the chase. It satisfies the predator in me."

I ran for the door, but Tarek moved in front of me with his arms stretched wide. I spun around to the hall and he ran at Chitah speed to block me there as well. Every move I made, he blocked—like a chess match. No windows. No back door. No escape.

"Round and round she goes, where she stops nobody knows," he sang with a glimmer of fire in his eyes.

The room felt like a coffin and I broke out in a sweat.

"I feed off that scent," he said, lifting his nose to the air. "It's fucking magical."

"Why don't you take this necklace off me and we'll see what's what? I could take you on if you weren't such a chickenshit. You're a laughingstock, Tarek. They say you're a weak man for taking a Mage as a wife—couldn't even mate with a proper Chitah. Your revenge has earned you a soiled reputation and made you look like a fool."

"Shut up," he spat as I fed into his insecurities. Tarek had a habit of rubbing his chest when he was angry. The blood no longer smeared like it had before.

"Your illustrious career is nothing but chasing after leftovers. Ever heard the phrase 'get a life'? You fucking disgust me; look at you!"

My mouth took on a life of its own for lack of a better weapon. If I couldn't take him out, maybe I could get him riled enough that he'd make a stupid decision. Or perhaps kill me quickly in a moment of rage. Not that I wanted to die, but neither did I want to be tortured. Justus had taught me self-defense, but most of those moves relied on Mage energy.

Tarek swung his arm to slap me and when I bent out of the way, I tripped and fell to the ground. He flipped me onto my back and sat heavily on my stomach. I gasped, grunted, and hammered against his chest with my fists.

In a quick motion, he seized my wrist and sank his teeth into my flesh. I screamed from the pain, but his canines were still retracted.

"Let's see what all the fuss is about."

Before he could touch me, I scraped my nails down his chest and he shouted, prying my fingers away.

He tried to pull off my sweatshirt, but I locked my hands together to resist. Tarek pressed against the lump on my head with his fingertips until I made a shrill sound. Pain roared through my skull and I jerked his arms forward and began to roll, doing maneuvers Justus had taught me to throw off an opponent who had me pinned.

Justus would have been proud.

Tarek lost his balance and fell to the side. He grabbed a fistful of my shirt as I crawled in the opposite direction.

"Get off me!" I bent forward and twisted free from the shirt.

Tarek blocked my exit, so I grabbed a shotgun from the wall. If I couldn't shoot it, I was going to spear him with it.

Suddenly, the wall phone rang.

"Be right back," he said with a devilish grin. "Try to run for the door and let's see how far you get before I pluck out your left eye."

While he stalked off, I reached for the cell phone sitting on the end table. "Logan?" I whispered, "Hello?"

No one was there.

Tarek answered the house phone. "Hello?" His voice was bright and pleasant. "And who could have given you this number? Tell me you aren't friends with the Vampire who put his cock in your female." Tarek's boisterous laugh filled the room, "Priceless. You're a weaker man than I thought. Sorry, Cross, I'm a little busy right now," he said, glancing over his shoulder at me. When he saw the phone in my hand, his face turned to stone.

I showed him my middle finger as Christian answered my call. "Tarek, you worthless piece of—"

"No, it's Silver," I said in rushed words. "If Logan's on his way here, you need to stop him. Do you understand me? I hereby relinquish your duties as my guard and transfer you to Logan to protect him!"

"You can't do that," he argued. "Only Novis makes that call."

"Do it, Christian."

Tarek listened to both conversations. "By all means, Cross, come over." Tarek rubbed his finger against the stains on his chest. "Remember who you're talking to. I'm a Lord; keep that in mind... Really? I like the original plan much better. More for me... I warn you... Cross, you can't challenge to the death. She's not your kindred spirit!"

I was panting so hard my throat dried up. Tarek paced, angry and yet contemplative. "Katrina is dead. What would be the point? I have fucking honor!" He slammed the phone down and roared.

"What's going on?" I asked.

"Cross is challenging me," Tarek announced.

I covered my mouth, eyes wide. Tarek was double the muscle weight of Logan and already amped up from a kill.

Moments later, tires screeched out front and I fled to the door. Tarek shoved me down and quickly went out the front patio gate, locking it behind him. I rushed forward, gripping the bars and screaming for him to stop.

Stone's bloody remains lay motionless by the mailbox—barely visible through the early morning fog. The careless disregard for life sickened me. I would have liked to see that man retire and get the Mercedes he'd daydreamed about having.

The heavy humidity veiled the sun and I couldn't see beyond the street. Not that it would have mattered. Stone lived in a secluded area that guaranteed him privacy.

"Let him pass," Tarek ordered his guards.

Emerging from a cloud of dense fog was a tall man with fire in his eyes. Logan was exceptionally handsome, and I almost didn't recognize him at first with the short hair in disheveled chunks, longer on top and edgy. In the chilly morning with frost on the ground, all he wore was a pair of sweats and a black tank top. Not even a pair of shoes on his feet. He carried himself like a knight—a true man of honor.

I squeezed the life out of the iron bars with my grip. If I had to watch him die, it would break me in ways I could never comprehend. Logan's stunning eyes sought me through the mist and all I could do was shake my head as tears escaped.

"Let's end this," Logan declared. The closer he came from the dreamlike fog, the more the reality set in that I was about to lose him.

"Logan, don't do this," I begged. "Don't you dare risk your life for me; I denied you! Don't you get it?"

Tarek stood between us and Logan stepped to the side so he was within my sight.

"I said I would let you live your life, but I never once agreed to let it be taken. I love you, female. You are my kindred spirit," he said, beating his fist to his chest. "I promised I would never let you fall, and I meant it. I will always come for you. I will always love you, even if you deny me on your last breath."

"Which will be very soon," Tarek promised.

Logan's eyes cut away from me and fell on Tarek like hot, cindering flames. Everything I knew about sacrifice was about to change.

CHAPTER 27

TAREK SIDESTEPPED LOGAN WITH ALARMING speed, a behavior among Chitahs used to flaunt their abilities. Logan dropped his arms to his sides and bowed his head, suddenly moving so fast that he appeared behind Tarek, who pivoted in time to swing. Logan ducked and fell back. They circled each other like warriors, predators, enemies.

The cold iron bars burned my fingers as I screamed Logan's name. He glanced up and Tarek seized the opportunity to rattle him.

"You really want to die for a Mage? She's used. *Look* at her!"

Tarek talked a big game, but despite his impressive strength, it was obvious Logan intimidated him.

Logan's canines punched out and his murky black eyes looked startling against the crisp morning fog. His skin shimmered with a warm display of spotted patterns and I caught my breath. Within moments, the challenge began.

They fought in a blur of motion. Tarek threw Logan to the ground but shouted out in pain when Logan delivered a hard kick to his knee. They threw punches, lunged, and tore at each other's flesh with their fangs.

Minutes ticked by and I watched each heart-stopping moment.

There was so much blood on Tarek from Officer Stone I couldn't tell whose it was anymore. Chitah venom wasn't toxic to other Chitahs; their teeth were merely sharp instruments used to shred apart their victims with unconscionable savagery.

Two men, over a century old with a history as deep as the Nile, circled each other. Ready to fight. Ready to die. Both had gone primal, and only one would walk away.

Logan hammered Tarek in the face with his right fist and missed a final swing when Tarek ducked out of the way and punched him in the side. It was enough to send Logan to his knees, and without missing a beat, Tarek kicked him in the head so forcefully a spray of blood tainted the white fog.

It didn't stop there. Tarek continued kicking him in the face and chest until Logan no longer fought back.

My heart sank as his body lay motionless at Tarek's feet. All I could see was the top of his head and his broad shoulders.

I whispered secret words that no one could hear, words of adoration for the man I loved.

My beautiful man.

Tarek lifted a prideful chin before he dragged his eyes up to mine. He was in control of his animal, but Logan was not. "Watch him die!"

He peeled back his lips to move in for the kill when Logan suddenly sprang up and lunged at his throat like a wild animal. Tarek collapsed onto his back with Logan's face buried in his jugular.

Logan thrashed his head from side to side. Blood masked his face, making him unrecognizable. His roar penetrated the quiet dawn, a battle cry, and his entire body trembled as if it might come apart.

I had no idea up to that point what killed a Chitah. They possessed similar abilities to a Mage in that they could rejuvenate, but all Breeds had limitations. Maybe it was the blood loss, or the irreparable damage to the vein in his neck, but Tarek's body lay twitching as the last drops of life soaked into the earth. Still conscious, he watched Logan with a defiant expression.

Logan's eyes pulsed with life and retribution bled from his face. He'd made a vow to his mate that he wouldn't go after Tarek for raping her—a promise he kept even after her death.

The violence that had raged in his heart for all those years released as he tore open Tarek's throat.

"Logan!" Christian emerged from the street and tossed him a blade.

Logan bent forward, dagger in hand, and whispered something in Tarek's ear, but I was unable to read his bloody lips.

Just like a Mage, a Chitah could be killed by decapitation. When

I saw the blade, I turned away. I had told Logan that I never wanted him to kill a man because murder was wrong. What I was witnessing wasn't murder; it was justice. If Tarek lived, innocent blood would spill as more lives were cut down. He was untouchable as a Lord, and his time on this earth was done.

With my back to the violence, the sound of the gate door breaking caused me to jump as Christian tore it away with a few hard shakes.

"Are you hurt?" he asked, looking down at where I sat.

I shook my head at the broken concrete.

"Search him for a key; it'll be a small one," he shouted at Logan. "Let me see your face."

I turned and his fangs descended like angry switchblades. He bit into his wrist and I heard the sound his teeth made as they punched through the skin. But I denied his offering.

Logan removed his tank top, wiping his face clean.

"Did you find it?" Christian called out, holding my necklace between his fingers.

Logan strode forward, arms heavy at his sides. He tossed Christian a small key and with an audible click, the necklace fell to the concrete and released me from Tarek's magic. A prickling sensation swept over my body, like when the blood begins moving through a limb that has fallen asleep.

My guard turned to confront him. "You'll never appreciate what this Mage gave up for you. If you say one cross word, I'll break your face."

Logan wiped his mouth, averting his eyes from mine. "I will always come for this woman to protect her. But remember, Vampire, she did not choose me. I will say what I want, so careful who you aim your threats at."

"I didn't realize that girlfriends came with an expiration date. I merely planted a suggestion in your peanut head to find another woman, but it only took you a *week* to claim a new mate? That doesn't show much devotion on your part," Christian chastised.

"You *charmed* me?" Logan roared. "How dare you judge what I had no control over!" He took a hard breath through his nose and gave me a sideways glance. "I have given up my pride for your games. What has she given up?"

"Her freedom," Christian bit out. "Tarek threatened to put you in the ground if she didn't do exactly as he said. To the word, he ordered her to bed another man. I can tell you right now that she was not acting of her own free will. Tarek worked her like a puppet in order to have his revenge on you. When she thought you were daft enough to try to win her back, she cut your hair. I know what that means; I'm not a fool. It was the only way to cut the strings still attached and save your sorry arse. I've watched her endure all this pain and suffering so her loved ones would not, because he threatened them all. Her Ghuardian, your brothers, her friends; as long as she complied with his wishes, no harm would come to them. He just kept taking it one step further so that he would always have control over her."

Logan paled, taking a step back. The fire in his eyes dimmed, and a light switched on.

"After the engagement party, he tried to force himself on her."

Logan squeezed his eyes shut and turned his head away.

I could feel Christian's rage pumping through my veins and I hadn't even tasted his blood. "Let it go, Christian. It's over now. I'll take the blame for all this mess; I don't want Logan involved."

"The hell you will," Christian argued. "You have taken enough bullets, lass. I will not sit here and watch you bite another one."

"Is what he says true?" Logan watched me with a stony expression.

"What good is truth anymore?" I asked in a despondent tone, pushing myself up. "What's done is *done*. What kind of woman have I allowed myself to become because of Tarek? He's dead, but the damage is done. How can I ever look you in the eye again knowing what I did, even if I *was* forced into it?"

"Is it true?" His voice was a shout, and he moved toward me.

Christian wedged between us.

"I need to hear truth from your lips, Silver. I never sensed you were lying when you told me that you didn't want me."

"Because I *didn't*! If it meant watching you die, then I would never want you! Knowing you could have a normal life without me made it the easiest lie I've ever told."

He quickly exhaled. "So it's true," he whispered. The gold in his eyes vanished and beautiful markings rippled across his skin like a mirage. The coloring was heavier on his shoulders, arms, and flanks than on his torso.

Christian shoved me against the wall and caged himself in front to protect me.

"Christian," I whispered. "Let me go." His head turned just a fraction. "Back off, guard."

Reluctantly, he moved aside.

Logan stepped forward and wrapped his arms around my waist. I had forgotten how cold I was in my bra and jeans until I felt his warmth envelop me. The moment I knew that he still wanted me was when he brushed his nose against my neck, drawing in a deep breath, owning my scent.

"I'm sorry for—"

His hand fell across my mouth and he shook his head.

Logan's eyes were black because his switch had flipped. Yet somehow, his anger was under control. Enough that he allowed Christian to take my hand. Not long ago, Logan was a man who would snap because of jealousy. He swore one day he'd master his animal and gain control over his instincts. I doubted his word, and regret filled me when I caught his uncharacteristic reaction.

I had been so wrong.

"Do you love me less, Logan?"

His hands cupped my face as he unabashedly kissed the corners of my eyes, my cheeks, my mouth, and my forehead. Only one word fell from his lips, a single word spoken in his animal state that made my heart swell to epic proportions.

"More."

Chitahs could rarely speak when their switch was flipped; only a few Lords had acquired that kind of control and power.

"You have someone else now, Logan. It's too late."

He pressed his strong body against mine and I wept against his chest. Logan bent down and nuzzled my cheek in a single upward sweep—his eyes still obsidian black and vivid shades of honey and sand melted across his skin.

"I'm so sorry." I sorrowfully touched the ends of his short hair. Logan ignored my gesture.

"*My mate*," he growled. Logan collected me in his arms and I listened to the rhythmic pounding of his courageous heart. I hugged him tightly and yet it still wasn't close enough.

"Jaysus, get a room," Christian blurted out as he walked down the steps. "We can't call in cleaners on this one. It has to be reported." He stared absently at the mess that was Tarek. "I need a pint."

Logan dropped to his knees and held my legs as he nuzzled my stomach. "Forgive me," he said in broken words.

"For what?"

"You sacrificed your heart and I was blind to it. I couldn't see beyond my own pain to recognize yours. I should have known it; I should have scented it."

By the inflection in his voice, I knew his eyes were now gold.

"Don't do that, Logan. Don't make me out to be a martyr. I didn't sleep with Christian, but I was ready to. I've always had a choice and I took the one with the least risk involved. Christian had to charm you or you would have figured it out. Stand up."

Logan rose to his feet and I felt sterilized by his gaze. He didn't look at me like I was a woman who had betrayed him. He looked at me with love.

"Unless you have any objections, I'm taking my female home."

CHAPTER 28

A FTER WE ARRIVED AT HIS condo, Logan lent me his red Flash Gordon T-shirt with the lightning bolt in front while he took a shower and washed himself clean of Tarek's blood. I harnessed the morning sunlight to heal my wounds, although Logan took the liberty of grazing his tongue across a few scratches. He had put ice on his face and ribs, but said he would heal soon enough.

Then he placed me on his mattress and whispered, "Sleep, Little Bird."

Without curtains, the room was bathed in sunlight. I kept my jeans on and Logan grabbed a pair of clean white socks from his drawer and pulled them up to my knees.

Silent hours drifted by while I slept. In my dream, I remembered being in warm, crystal-blue waters. I was sitting in a shallow area with the sun on my shoulders, listening to the waves lap up on the shore. Just a little ways up the beach, Logan was sitting on the sand with his knees bent and his arms draped over them. He wore a thin white shirt and his jeans were rolled up at the ankle. A smile stretched across his face and he turned away to look at the ocean. Logan was not a figment of my imagination—he was dreamwalking. I'd once warned him to stay out of my head while I slept, but suddenly, I didn't mind. He respected my space and watched over me from a safe distance.

I wanted it to be real. No rules. No conflict. No politics. No prejudices. No death. Just the two of us, lying in a hammock, falling asleep in each other's arms as the clouds drifted quietly overhead.

When I awoke, Logan was standing in front of the curtainless window, watching the colors of sunset melt across the horizon. A light tap sounded at the door and Logan opened it, taking a tray from someone's hands. He set it beside me on the floor because his bed was nothing more than a wide mattress without a frame.

"Stay in bed," he insisted.

"Did I sleep all day?" I mumbled against a pillow.

Logan crawled into the bed and laid on my right side. He had changed into a pair of sweats and a white, formfitting undershirt. The cut emphasized the tight muscles in his arms and shoulders.

"My feet are hot."

He sat up and tossed my socks into a corner. "Do you want to remove these?" he asked, tugging my jeans.

"No."

His nose twitched and he took in two quick puffs of air. "I'm not sure of that scent."

"What do you mean?"

"The one you put out whenever I ask to remove your jeans. It's not fear, it's not... it's like a flavor I haven't tasted before and I need the name of it."

"Speaking of flavors, what did you bring me to eat?"

A mysterious grin crossed his expression and he rolled over. When he reappeared, an egg roll was between his fingers.

"Chinese," I said approvingly. My stomach growled and I sat up, propping the pillows behind my back as Logan set the tray on my lap. My appetite wasn't all there, so after a few bites of chicken stir-fry, I announced I was finished.

"You take good care of me, Logan. It was delicious."

He placed the tray on the floor and I scooted down, stretching my legs. The room seemed uncomfortably warm, so I swept my hair off my neck and pulled the sheet away.

Logan gave me the infamous Cross smile and waved a small sugared donut in his hand. My heart soared. It wasn't just a memory that we shared of the time we met, but hand-feeding was a sign of trust among Chitahs.

When I opened my mouth and took a small bite, he tossed the donut back on the plate and kissed away the sugar from my lips.

"Logan?"

"Yes?"

"If you have a new mate, you need to take what's best for you, not what you crave. I don't want to be your drug. Does that make sense?"

"I didn't know what I was saying, Silver. I had no idea," he said in somber words. "Charmed by a Vampire or not, I should have trusted my instincts. It will end tonight when I call to break it off."

"That seems a little cold."

He rubbed his eye with the palm of his hand. "She only coveted my position, not my heart. That was made clear when we spoke privately. I want you to know that I never bedded that female; it is not the courting custom." His eyes immediately lowered, heavy with guilt.

"Except with us," I said, stating the obvious. "It wasn't fair for me to push it that far when I wasn't ready to commit."

"It never felt right with her and now I know why. I'm not a man who will settle as long as my soul mate walks this earth. It will end tonight when I call to break the news."

"Do you actually believe that? Logan…"

His fingers fell over my lips. "I don't believe it. *I know it.* I swore I'd never enter your dreams without permission, but the night you cut my hair, I needed to know. I felt your grief, but it was confusing and you couldn't see me. You sat in a pile of white weeds of some kind with a disparaged look on your face."

"I don't remember that," I said, watching his eyes lower.

"I kissed your cheek and whispered in your ear that I'd always come for you if you needed me, Silver. I meant it."

"Can you ever trust me again?" I reached for the plate and took a fresh donut, holding it up. Logan caught my wrist and parted his lips, taking the entire pastry into his mouth along with two of my fingers, sucking every granule of sugar from them.

Logan had allowed me to feed him.

He trusted me.

"I'll eat a steady diet of whatever you feed me from your hand, Little Raven. I'll prove that I'm worthy of your trust, loyalty, and your love. Maybe it'll take decades, but I'm a patient man. Nothing has changed between us. You're still the same beautiful woman I watched sleeping in that cave the night I took you. You fed a stranger and welcomed him into your home. You fought bravely against me and aren't afraid to speak your mind."

"Logan," I softly breathed. The room darkened with only the beam of light from the hall slicing across the bed from the open door. "You have all these customs of courting and mating, and it's all so elaborate. We don't have the equivalent, but you know about our bonding ceremony?"

He gently nodded.

"The woman has the Creator's mark from her partner permanently inked on her."

Logan watched me pensively. "Are you denying my claim?"

"I did something and um… I can't take it back."

"You did what you had to do, Silver. You were forced into it," he said, softly stroking my hair.

"Not everything."

All expression fell from his face as his eyes flicked back and forth between my eyes and mouth. I rolled over and stood up. "Turn your head away, Logan."

From his seat on the bed, he looked over his shoulder as I began removing my jeans.

"It isn't fair for you to be in the dark, so I want to tell you everything." I stepped out of my pants and kicked them to the side. "I *never* liked Tarek. In the restaurant, he threw his scent all over me to confuse you and I played along. I said those things to hurt you, Logan. Things I can't take back, but I was afraid. It killed me to be so cruel; especially knowing those words would never be erased from your memory. Then Tarek announced his intention to marry me and things spiraled out of control."

Logan rubbed his mouth and averted his eyes. "I plotted to kill him in the beginning, Silver. Something I didn't tell you. Leo was the only one who kept me from carrying out the act; it's why I followed you. I planned to murder him and I didn't give a damn if that meant receiving a death sentence. Then I remembered the promise that I made to you—that I would be a better man than that." He closed his eyes. "I believed everything you said to me in the restaurant and when you cut off my hair… fuck, it *killed* me," he breathed in hurt words.

"Look at me, Logan."

He lifted his eyes to mine. I stood before him in nothing but a T-shirt and the truth.

"I don't know how you truly feel about me after all that's happened between us," I said, cupping his chin. "Or if enough time has passed for the gravity of this to sink in. You forgive me tonight, but who's to say a week from now you'll feel the same? I could be talking to another man and you'd remember what I did, or almost did. We can't erase what's been done."

"I trust you emphatically, Little Raven," he said in a resolute voice. But his angry words cut sharp and rose in volume. "Those who sacrifice for another among my kind are revered. That bastard tried to take your respect, your honor, and your modesty. He got his comings, and I will sleep soundly for the rest of my life knowing he died by my hands."

"For Katrina. That was a long time coming," I said.

Logan shook his head slowly. "For you. I had no thought in my head of Katrina when I challenged Tarek. I couldn't allow him to take *you*," he growled.

My heart fluttered. I knew Logan was devoted to a fault, but part of me suspected he was looking for an opportunity to avenge his mate. It didn't make sense that after everything that happened he would want to risk his life for me.

"You're always coming to my rescue. Someday, Logan Cross, I'm going to be the one to save your life."

He tilted his head and kissed the palm of my hand. "You already have."

"There's one thing Tarek couldn't take. He may have eventually broken me down in the coming years, but there was one thing he'd never have, Logan. My heart. Ask me why."

Logan's cheeks reddened. I'd never seen that coloring on him before and I knew it was because he didn't have a sense of what was about to come. "Why?" he asked nervously.

"Because it's already yours. It's *always* been yours, Logan."

I slowly lifted my shirt, revealing the cheetah paw prints—with claws—on my lower abdomen.

The look on his face was unreadable. His brows knitted together and awe filled his expression. I nervously watched as Logan brushed his fingers across my skin, as if he were trying to rub off the permanent marks with his initials in the center.

"Sealed with liquid fire," I confirmed.

The way he looked at me made my heart stutter. A thrumming vibrated deep within his chest.

Logan was purring.

"Giving you up made me realize how much I really wanted you. Maybe that's a selfish way to go about things, but I was always afraid that you'd eventually hurt me, or leave me. We can't escape life unscathed, and I tried so hard to protect myself from getting hurt that it only isolated me. If you still want to claim me, then I'm ready to tell you my answer," I said, brushing my hand apprehensively through his short hair. Logan's face pressed against my lower belly and his fingers lightly traced over the tattoos. "Maybe it's too late, maybe it's not the right one, but the answer is *yes*."

Logan pulled me onto his lap. I placed my tear-stained cheek against his shoulder and he lifted my chin with the crook of his finger.

"I will love you so sweetly," he whispered, drinking me in with his eyes. "I give you my word that I will care for you, protect you, love you, and die for you, my female. You may have doubts about my claim on you as a kindred spirit, but doubt no more. My eyes may not know all of you, but my heart does. I loved you before I was born, and I will love you long after I pass from this earth."

Logan's kiss fell upon my lips reverently, adoringly, and as far as I was concerned, could stay there forever. I turned away from the intensity of his gaze and Logan tethered his fingers around my chin, holding my face still.

"I still make you blush," he marveled in a soft breath, the corners of his mouth hooking into a smile.

"I'll blush for as long as you love me."

We talked for hours beneath the sheets. I wept in his arms without explanation, and he held me protectively close. I wanted that night to last forever before going back to my life. I wanted to carry that moment in my pocket and never let it go. I wanted to tell the world how much I loved Mr. Cross.

Logan would occasionally crawl down the length of my body, resting his head on my leg or stomach. Anywhere that would allow him to admire the tattoo. While we talked, he would kiss the paw prints and circle his finger around the edges. I had marked him as mine in the only way I knew how, since a Chitah did not have a Creator's mark. His brothers may have carried the same initials, but the tattoo was in a private place that only his eyes would see.

I told him I preferred his hair shorter, and that growing it long had never held any sway in my decision.

I was always his.

My days of courtship with Logan were coming to an end. I had accepted his claim officially. It was bittersweet knowing that it was the end of one relationship and the beginning of another. But a fiercely possessive feeling came over me like I had never known before.

Logan was *mine*.

CHAPTER 29

A DAM TUCKED HIMSELF AWAY IN the back corner of Northern Lights, a human bar located in the arts district. It had become his favorite hangout because of the relaxed atmosphere and stage performances. They promoted local talent with open mic night. The lights were always dim so that the bar and stage became the center of attention. It was a place Adam could sit back and sip his beer in peace.

It was a hell of a lot better than staying cooped up in the mansion; Novis only made public appearances when there was business to discuss.

Adam cupped his hand around the cigarette and lit up a smoke, blowing out a cloudy puff before snapping his lighter shut. He watched a group of men by the stage getting rowdy and whistling. Roxy Fox was on, and she usually brought the house down when she sang the number that ended with a few buttons popping free on her silk blouse. It wasn't really that kind of place, but she gave enough of a tease that the drunkards forgot they weren't in a strip club. Roxy had big brown curls that fell down her shoulders and she jutted her hips to the beat.

Adam's cell phone went off and he checked the message.

> Knox: Where are you, brother?
> Adam: Having a beer. What's up?
> Knox: Shit's going down. Get home and lay low.
> Adam: Call me.

"Ladies and gentlemen, put your hands together for a new act." The crowd applauded. "She's new to Northern Lights, and…

aww, come on, sweetheart. Don't be *shy*. Looks like we got ourselves a wallflower!"

"I'll pick that flower," a man exclaimed, followed by a few laughs.

The announcer squinted and looked in the back of the room as the crowd anxiously whistled and hollered.

Adam's phone rang and Knox blurted out, "Where the fuck are you?"

"Northern Lights. What the hell's going on?"

"You're in luck. We're right around the corner; Sunny wanted to check out a shop down here. I'll pick you up in five. Sit tight."

The line went dead and Adam furrowed his brow. He had his bike, but if Knox wanted to ride together, it meant that a conversation needed to happen. That's how Knox operated; he wasn't into phone tag.

"Honey, they won't bite," the man on stage said dramatically. The crowd was getting restless. Adam crushed his cigarette in the ashtray and stood up, placing a few bills beneath an empty bottle.

He lifted his leather jacket from the back of the chair and slid his arms inside, zipping up the front. It was a good look for him. Dark denims, a plain T-shirt, and lace-up boots. He was low maintenance and preferred casual, despite the wardrobe that Novis supplied.

Adam swiped the keys from the table and when he spun around, he crashed into someone crossing his path.

"Oh, no!" a young woman shouted. Her acoustic guitar hit the floor with a melodic sound and several people turned around but didn't move to help.

"Last chance," the guy on stage coaxed, tapping his mic. The crowd booed and hissed.

The woman knelt down and flipped over her guitar, tracing her fingers along the neck, searching for damage. Her honey-blond hair was long and wavy with a small braid that wrapped around the back and tucked in somewhere. It held her hair away from the left side of her face, but several locks on the right side swept across her eye. Adam smiled at her outfit—brown boots with a white dress. Not the fashion statement he usually saw from the women in Cognito.

"It's not broken." She exhaled in relief. "Just a scratch, but this baby's been through it all."

"I'm sorry," was all he could say. His body stiffened, waiting for her to lift her head and look up at him. Initial reactions were always the worst, but at least the humans got over it after a few stares.

But she just looked at his lace-ups. "Your boot has a long cut on the side," she said, rubbing her finger along the groove. "You should get new shoes."

Adam stared dumbly down at her. By the way she was crouched on the floor, it looked like she was hiding from someone. Her right hand continued to flip a red pick around in circles as she propped up her guitar, resting her forehead against the neck.

"Last chance to shake up the crowd," the stage voice called out.

She blew out a breath and sprang forward—running past him like a soldier marching through the crowd.

Adam's heart quickened as he admired the supreme way in which she threw her shoulders back and climbed on that stage. Her boots clicked on the wooden surface and a few men fell silent as she stood before them. She held the guitar upright and twirled it once by the neck.

The announcer looked her up and down before lifting a wooden stool and placing it in front of the microphone. The lights dimmed, leaving a spotlight that illuminated her wavy hair. "They're all yours, sugar."

Adam would have liked to hear her play.

But then a fist clutched his jacket and yanked him forward. It was Knox, dragging him through the building toward the front door.

"Get your ass moving," he ground out through his teeth. "I had to leave Sunny in the car."

Knox led the way with some of his wild black hair poking out from beneath his hat. They shouldered their way through the crowd that bottlenecked the hallway, but Knox was pretty much a bulldozer that cleared up that problem.

"Tell me what the hell is going on," Adam demanded, grabbing Knox by his coat.

Knox eased around and in quiet words said, "Tarek attacked Silver."

"That sonofabitch," Adam growled. "Is she okay?"

"Logan took him out, and you don't kill a fucking Lord. The Chitahs are out for blood. Our names have been floating around among his pride; Leo called and passed along the warning. He said to lay low until they sort this shit out."

"Is she okay?" Adam demanded again as they detoured out a side door that spilled into an alley.

"Leo's going to check it out."

"Where are they?"

"With all the ears around us? I'd rather not say, brother. It's just like old times, except now I got something worth living for, and that makes me dangerous. You can stay at our place in the spare bedroom and if they come for us, I got your back. Let's roll."

They crossed the parking lot in large strides, moving toward Knox's Jeep Commander. Sunny unbuckled her belt, getting ready to move into the back to let Adam ride shotgun. Her face looked distressed and Knox spun around unexpectedly. Without saying a word, he pulled a knife from a holster. "Something ain't right."

It sure as hell wasn't right. Adam could feel the surge in Mage energy and he sharpened his light, scanning the parking lot.

"Lock the doors!" Knox shouted at Sunny.

Adam's heart was a drum in a marching band. They stood back to back, just like old times. But Knox was at a disadvantage, being human.

"Remember that time in Mexico?" he said with a chuckle.

Adam's eyes were alert. "I said to never bring that up again. Feel me?"

Knox turned his head, scoping the parking lot. "Yeah, what the fuck ever. Stripping down to distract the opponent was the classiest thing I ever saw. God, you were so green."

"I was also drunk on a bottle of Cuervo."

"Well, well," a voice said from the right. A figure emerged from the dark shadows and he was a short man with thin hair and round glasses. "You must be Adam, Knox... and of course, the *lovely* Sunny." He glanced in her direction.

Knox stiffened, looking over Adam's shoulder as he kept his

back pressed tightly to prevent someone approaching from behind.

The man used his finger to push his glasses up, strolling along as if he didn't have a care in the world.

"Do I know you?" Adam asked.

"You probably should know the name of the man who's going to flip your world off its axis," he said with an apologetic voice. "I'm Nero."

"*Fucking hell*," Knox muttered.

Adam scraped him up and down with a single glance. Nero had an imperious demeanor, but his looks were anything but. He was nothing more than a lean scrap of a man with thinning hair, glasses, and a medallion around his neck. He had a sharp nose and looked more like a taxman than a mastermind.

"So you're the big cheese, huh?" Adam sniffed out a laugh, keeping his light as sharp as it could possibly get.

"Let me quash any notion that I have a personal interest in Silver," Nero said, rolling a toothpick around in his mouth. "Her light is very special, but she's caused me more than enough trouble. Tarek in a leadership role would have made me privy to inside information. That was a tremendous opportunity; do you know how hard it is to buy a good Chitah? Even Logan pissed on my doorstep," he said, scrunching his face. "But I had Tarek in my pocket. When you buy loyalty from a man like him, you have a stronger army." With each step, Nero made a point. "I had connections, access to private information, and my own enemy doing my dirty work. Chitahs can track, they're determined, ruthless, and are walking weapons to our kind with those revolting fangs."

"I hear golden retrievers are loyal," Adam mocked.

Nero's mouth twisted into an angry smile. "I was going to take her off Tarek's hands eventually. Her light is strong and I want that power, but this is the second time she's severed one of my connections. Merc was the only one I knew who could pull core light, and I had just acquired an Infuser. I plan to pull some of that savory light from my guests and infuse it to my own. Now Merc is gone and I have to find a replacement."

"Bummer," Adam said unapologetically, stealing glimpses of the parking lot. What Nero said was of no consequence; their situation *was*. What were the odds this man was alone? Looking at his size, Adam could take him down for sure. But that was contingent on any rare gifts he might have. This was a man with an agenda and Adam's senses were fully alert. A Mage couldn't use their basic powers against another Mage because it would only juice them up. Therefore, it was always hand-to-hand combat using whatever skills they possessed in fighting, and techniques in movement using their abilities.

Nero didn't look like much of a fighter.

"Yes, quite a... bummer. On top of that, I'm on the list of outlaws. All this because of that repugnant woman. Do you know *how* Tarek won her over?" Nero chuckled and stuffed his hands into the pockets of his beige slacks. "Quite clever, actually." He nodded a few times and turned on his heel. "*Quite.*"

Nero flashed away and Knox pressed against Adam's back. "Is he gone?"

"Yeah," Adam said skeptically. "Eyes alert."

They simultaneously walked toward the truck while keeping their backs to each other and their eyes on their surroundings. Laughter could be heard coming from the bar, and an angelic voice briefly floated on the wind like a haunting dream as the door opened and closed in the distance.

Their boots crunched on the pavement and Adam reached into the lining of his coat, pulling out a stunner—a dagger that could paralyze a Mage. Hopefully, it wouldn't have to be used. But he didn't have a good feeling about this. Nero wouldn't just unload that kind of information and walk off.

Adam sent a text to Novis that simply said:

Nrthn Lights. Trouble.

Probably misspelled because Adam didn't look down. They were still a good ways from Knox's Jeep and while he could flash to the car, Knox couldn't.

So they walked together. Slow and steady.

Adam saw a glimmer of a blade cutting through the air as a

Mage flashed at him from the left.

"Get low!" he shouted at Knox, ducking before the dagger made contact.

Knox engaged, sweeping out his leg and tripping up their attacker. The Mage rolled over as Knox tried to stomp on his wrist to release his grip on the dagger.

Adam briefly flicked his eyes around, but the man was alone.

The Mage hopped up, dusting off his bare arms. Adam's coat restricted his movements, but it offered protection against the cut of a blade.

"Cover me," Adam said, and Knox stepped back.

Adam sliced his blade in a series of patterns, but the Mage blocked the maneuver, throwing out a fist and clipping him in the jaw. He swiped the blade low at the Mage's belly, forcing him to hop back. They went into a series of expert moves that looked like something out of an action-packed espionage movie.

It wasn't Adam's first knife fight.

His blade sliced the Mage in the leg and he yelled out, flashing away before Adam could twist it in and take him down. It was times like these that being scarred worked to his advantage. The Mage eyed him apprehensively; uncertain what kind of man Adam was and how dirty he was willing to fight. Adam must have looked scary as hell with his black-handled dagger and fire in his eyes.

Knox stepped to the left and rushed the Mage, but the man flashed toward him unexpectedly. Adam's buddy had tactical skills in the bag. It's what he did for a living. The Mage may have been fast, but Knox could anticipate the move of an epileptic fly caught in a hurricane.

Knox dropped on one knee and stabbed the Mage in the back of his leg. The man shouted and jerked his leg so hard the knife tumbled on the concrete. Knox dropped low and kicked him in the knees from the side. The Mage folded like a piece of paper and hit the ground.

Lifting the infused dagger, Knox shoved it to the hilt in the attacker's thigh and clamped his hand firmly around his throat.

"What do you want to do with him, Razor?" he said in that

familiar voice, the one that declared he was willing to finish the job.

"Fuck it. Do him in; you need the knife!" Adam shouted as three men emerged from the shadows and closed in from different angles. Two against four—they had faced those odds before, just not with Breed.

Adam made an unexpected move that startled the Mage in the red coat.

He attacked.

Adam didn't play defense like they had expected. He flashed toward him and plunged his stunner into the Mage's chest, taking him down and finishing the job.

The second Mage wasn't armed and attacked from behind, kicking Adam in the back of his knees. He fell, flipped over, and immediately hopped to his feet. With a clean swipe, Adam sliced the man across the chest.

"Fuck!" the Mage growled, holding his hand across his heart. "You're going to pay for that." He had a full beard and the darkest eyes Adam had seen next to a Vampire or a serial killer.

Adam caught sight of Knox, who spat curses at a Mage with long dreadlocks. He gripped his dagger and stalked forward fearlessly.

Adam's heart hammered against his chest, his back ached, but adrenaline kept him focused and alert. The Mage circled around him, grimacing from the fresh blood pooling on his shirt. Adam swiped his blade again and the bearded Mage spun around and flashed behind him. This one was bigger and stronger than Adam, so his punches hurt like hell.

Especially the one that rammed against the side of his head.

Flashes of light filled Adam's vision and he was off-kilter, stumbling to his left as he sliced with his blade, keeping the Mage at bay. His attacker picked up on his disorientation and weaved left and right, making Adam dizzy.

Meanwhile, Knox was kicking ass and taking names across the lot.

That's when it happened.

The Mage came up from behind, and in a quick motion, grabbed Adam's wrist and plunged the dagger into his chest.

Adam had felt the power of a stunner before; Novis expected him to understand and experience all the weapons that could be used against him. It worked immediately like a numbing agent and all feeling evaporated as he hit the ground, landing on his left side.

"Piece of shit," the Mage muttered, kicking him in the back. Then he stooped down and patted Adam on the cheek. "I was given instructions not to kill you, although I'm having serious second thoughts at the moment. You're just supposed to watch; so I hope you enjoy the show."

Adam watched in horror as the bearded man stalked toward Knox, who was holding his own against the Mage with dreadlocks, getting in a few clean breaks with his fist. Somewhere along the line, Breed magic was put aside and these were just two men using their fists to solve problems.

But Adam's bearded attacker had a different agenda.

His heart sped up when the Mage flashed toward Knox's Jeep, pulling on the door handles. Adam couldn't yell out. He couldn't even feel his own heart, which he knew raced out of control.

Suddenly, the Mage smashed the window with his fist.

Sunny's eyes widened and she scrambled to the other side of the Jeep to escape. The door swung open and she stumbled out, running.

He flashed up from behind and grabbed Sunny's blond waves of hair, yanking her back so hard that she screamed and her purple scarf tumbled to the ground.

Adam used every ounce of will to move his hand—to somehow reach for the knife and pull it from his chest. He thought he felt his pinky finger move, but the magic was too strong. His stomach turned, fearing what he was about to witness.

"Take your hands off her!" Knox roared.

And then he transformed into a mountain of fury, striking the Mage he fought against with such precision you would have thought he was one of them.

A blood-curdling scream poured out of Sunny as the Mage threw her to the ground and prepared to juice her light.

Christ, Adam couldn't bear the thought. Memories of his sister's death came back, and now he was forced to watch helplessly as

Sunny was slain in front of him. She kicked her legs and the sound of her snow boots knocking against the concrete broke his heart.

The scumbag pinned her hands to the ground, struggling to remove her purple mittens. Sunny fought wildly, thrashing about and screaming as he straddled her. The wind picked up her scarf and it floated on the air, tangling around a light pole.

Knox's eyes were on Sunny but he wasn't able to get to her because of the Mage that circled around him. In a quick motion, he grabbed the dagger at his feet and threw it at his attacker. The blade plunged into his gut and he fell like a bag of concrete.

Leaving Knox unarmed.

Knox could have finished off the Mage to gain the advantage of a weapon, but he didn't have a second to spare. Sunny's body grew lax and her screams waned as the life drained from her.

Knox charged at them from the side.

The Mage rose to his feet as Sunny lay helpless on the ground. She was still alive, and while the attack was on all of them, a realization struck Adam. There was something so deliberate about this attack that he knew Sunny had been the target all along.

The Mage with the dark beard and dead eyes reached into his pocket and pulled out a gun.

A chilling roar shook the silence as Knox ran at them—his lips peeled back and the lines in his face carved deeper from the agony of seeing what was about to unfold. The Mage stood astride Sunny, slowly raising his arm until it was aimed at her chest. Knox had no time to knock him down without causing the gun to go off.

Adam would replay the scene in his mind for years to come, and wonder how something that happened so quickly seemed to take place in slow motion.

Knox threw himself on top of Sunny—the woman he cherished more than life itself. The woman he carried a ring in his pocket for. The one Knox looked at like she hung the moon and stars.

A flash of light sparked as the gun fired three times.

That night—after Logan fed me Chinese food—I slept for hours. Nightmares of Tarek continued to haunt me, and I'd wake up in a cold sweat with Logan at my side, lulling me back to sleep with his purr.

"Sleep, female," he said.

Around midnight, a tumultuous pounding coming from Logan's front door woke us up. The insistent knock made me want to crawl underneath the covers because I knew it meant trouble. Logan hopped out of bed, lifting his nose in the air to concentrate on the scent.

"Open up!" a man bellowed as the thundering sound of his fist continued to strike the door.

Logan looked over his shoulder. "It's Leo. Stay here or join me, but cover yourself up."

I wrapped a thin blanket around me and followed close behind. As he unlatched the door, two angry men flew in.

Leo's face was redder than the highlights in his hair. "You better talk, little brother. Word is out that Tarek is dead by your hand." He shouldered past him into the living room, pacing angrily in a circle.

"The rumor is true," Logan confirmed.

Levi patted him on the shoulder with a wide grin, flashing the tattoo on his inside forearm that read VERITAS.

Leo bared his teeth. "Tarek was a *Lord*. Do you realize what you've done? You cannot kill a Lord; the Pride is already seeking justice. They're all but lighting torches in the streets! I thought we talked about this?"

Logan pulled me to his side and his upper canines slowly descended. "Tarek Thorn intended to rape and murder my kindred spirit. He held her against her will, and every choice she made I was forced to accept. But it was *not* her choice to be assaulted, and I would not stand idly by so my female could be slaughtered at the hands of a lunatic."

Leo's voice softened. "Logan, you know it is impossible that she could be—"

"You are my brother, but do not ever… *ever* doubt me on this subject," he bit out harshly. "I challenged him as I had every right to, and he accepted that challenge."

His brothers circled the room and Leo pulled in deep breaths of air, tasting the truth of Logan's words on his tongue.

Levi slammed his fist into the wall and leaned against it, lowering his head as every muscle in his arms flexed. Curses tumbled out of his mouth, but they were merely whispers.

"I'll face the consequences," Logan said with bravery on his tongue.

"Logan," I whispered, stroking my fingers along his neck. His angered demeanor switched to one of adoration, and he hid his fangs behind closed lips. "Can they punish you for this? I want to know the worst-case scenario."

"Death," Leo confirmed somberly. He sat down in a rust-colored chair with his elbows on his knees. "If Logan is unable to prove his claim on you as kindred spirit, then he'll pay for his crime with his life."

"Oh, Logan. Why did you do this?"

I sat on the sofa and covered my face with the blanket. Levi sat beside me and wrapped his heavy arm around my shoulders.

"I swear, Leo, I tried to stop it," I said, lowering the blanket. "I didn't know he was going to call Logan and make him listen to it over the phone."

Leo snapped his head at Logan and his jaw clenched. "Is that true?"

Logan nodded. "Do you want me to describe my visceral reaction from hearing my female's screams at the hands of another male? I called her guard and he had the cop's phone number and address. I sincerely hope that neither of you ever have to endure the torment I suffered, thinking I would be listening to the last moments of her life." He raked his fingers through his messy hair. "I knew the consequences, and if I had it to do over again, I would have killed him *slower*."

Logan knelt before me and kissed my palm, placing it over his heart. I felt the sweet rhythm of his life beneath my fingertips, suddenly aware that his heart could stop beating because of Tarek.

"What if I prove I have Chitah blood?" I asked Leo.

"Even the human children we give up for adoption do not have enough Chitah DNA to make them a kindred spirit for a Chitah male."

"How do you *know* that?" I asked. "You dump your children off at a stranger's doorstep and never see them again. They never get a chance to mingle within your society or attend your Gatherings. They could very well be someone's soul mate. Didn't that ever occur to anyone?"

"It has," he added. "But what use would it be? They could never bear Chitah young and even if it were possible, they would be born human. Why would a male choose a female that would age and die before his eyes and have children that would grow up and do the same?"

"Love? Nothing lasts forever, Leo. Why do you focus so much on preservation of your own kind when it means denying someone happiness? No matter how brief. You know what I'm getting out of this conversation? That you don't approve of me because I'm not one of your kind. Logan's accepted me for who I am. Maybe he's my kindred spirit and maybe he's not, but does it matter? We love each other. Isn't that enough to justify him saving my life?"

"And if we can prove it?" Logan asked.

"If it can be proven, brother, then your challenge to the death was justified. Lord or not, no one can deny a Chitah's right to protect his life mate. They require evidence, and that's something you don't have."

His tone was heavy because Levi wasn't in the loop. Leo had inside information now that he worked for HALO. He knew that it meant going public with the genetic experimentation, something we'd kept secret because of the unpredictable upheaval that could occur. This became a choice to save either Logan or the Breed.

Logan stood up and leaned against the wall, uncharacteristically folding his arms. "I don't need proof that she has Chitah blood," he said, turning his gaze to me. "That kind of revelation would put us all in danger. They might lock you up and take you away from me," he said pensively. "I won't have that on my conscience."

"And I won't have your death on mine," I countered.

"God help us all," Leo breathed.

We looked up and he stared at his phone with a ghostly expression.

"What is it?" Logan asked, lowering his arms and stepping forward. The change in Leo's scent must have been alarming by their reaction.

Leo rubbed his short beard and lifted his sullen eyes. "Knox is dead."

CHAPTER 30

I couldn't breathe. By the time we reached Novis's front door, my chest was in spasms, sucking in air so quickly that I came close to hyperventilating. Logan drove and as soon as Adam opened the door, I fell into his arms.

"Is she hurt too?" I said in a high-pitched voice.

"Not that bad," he replied in broken words, stroking the back of my hair.

"Who did this?" I looked up and Adam's scarred face was stoic, as if the life had been drained from his eyes.

"Nero."

"What?" I gasped, adamantly shaking my head.

I backed away in disbelief, tears staining my cheeks. I suspected Tarek had given his guards orders to carry out his plan if anything ever happened to him. Nero was the furthest thing from my mind. Why the hell hadn't I continued searching for him? Why had I let everyone convince me the labs were more important? My eyes burned with guilt.

Logan held my shoulders from behind. My energy intensified and I had a sudden urge to throw it into someone. As I stepped away from Logan, faint blue particles of light dripped from my fingertips. My heart sliced in two as the image of Sunny and Knox holding hands flew into my mind.

"I'm going to kill him, I'm going to kill him," I chanted.

Adam caught my wrists and held my shaking hands. "Level it down, Silver. You can't see her like this."

"Were you able to heal her? Is it bad?"

Adam shook his head and let go of my hands. "My gift doesn't work on humans. I tried. I would have stopped it," he said in a pained breath. "The Mage thought he had put enough bullets in them and came over to talk to me. I was the fucking messenger," he bit out. "The witness. Novis showed up a few minutes later and took out the last Mage. As soon as he pulled the stunner from my chest, I rushed over to their side. I tried, dammit. Knox... that bastard was just too stubborn to come back," he said with glittering eyes. Adam blinked and looked down. Knox wasn't just his former partner, but his best friend.

"Are you okay?" I stepped out of Logan's grip and touched Adam's cheek. He flinched at first and then pressed his lips into a thin line. Adam would never understand that despite his imperfections, he was still the same Razor—unruly dark hair, dangerously sexy brows, and a smirk that could melt hearts. A man who once saved my life and showed me how to laugh again. Time was changing the both of us through our experiences. Our best friends were attacked that night.

Mine survived. His didn't.

"Novis is making burial arrangements." He struggled to keep his voice steady. Adam turned away, folding his arms. "She's upstairs if you want to see her."

He barely had to finish his sentence. Logan remained behind and I flew up the stairs. Uncertain of which room she was in, I opened all the doors. When I reached the last door at the end of the hall, I hesitated before going in.

Novis sat in a chair at the foot of the bed, leaning on his knees with his hands clasped together. When he looked over his shoulder, his mouth formed a grim line. It looked like he'd been running his hands through his hair so much that it all simply fell flat over his face. I'd never seen Novis this... emotional. Time had eroded the spark he had for life and he often appeared detached.

Until tonight.

"Close the door," he said in a soft voice. "There's a draft."

I wiped my runny nose on the sleeve of a sweater I'd borrowed from Logan. I just stood there, shaking my head at him in disbelief.

"Knox was brave." He sat back in the chair and stretched out his legs. "Not many men die for honor. By the time I got there, he was already gone. I believe one of the bullets pierced his lung and caused it to collapse and bleed out, but I'm not a doctor. He took three bullets for her. One of them ricocheted and hit her in the shoulder."

I glanced up and Sunny's left shoulder was in a sling.

"Is she sedated?"

"No," Novis replied. "She refused. *Adamantly* refused. We called in a Relic who patched her up and confirmed it wasn't life threatening. She'll have a scar, but the bullet went clean through."

I cupped my elbows and looked at her sleeping in the bed.

"You can sit with her for a while. I'll see to it she's not left alone. She shouldn't be," he said, rising from his chair and walking toward me. He stopped to my left and stood at my side. "Sunny watched the man that she loves die in her arms. When we found them, she was so weakened from the Mage having juiced her energy that she couldn't even wrap her arms around him. That's what pained her when we brought her back—that she couldn't hold him one last time."

I lost it.

Tears burned my eyes like acid and I bent over with my hands on my knees, sobbing. Novis closed the door behind me and silence filled the room as my tears spattered on the wood floor.

The pain was surreal, but I sucked it all in and blew out a few hard breaths. Guilt kept me from approaching the bed.

This was all because of me. *Damn* Nero. I hated him to the core of my being. I swore in that room that on my honor, I would kill him. Justus told me not to waste my life seeking revenge, but Nero had taken the life of someone I cared about while attempting to murder my best friend. Sunny was the nearest I had to a sister, and damn him if he thought I wouldn't avenge this senseless attack.

I crossed the room to the right side of the bed and sat on the edge. Sunny's face was different. It wasn't just her puffy eyes and red nose from crying herself into a deep sleep, but the carefree exuberance I once remembered had been extinguished. It was as if Knox took a piece of her heart with him.

Maybe it would help him reach his destination.

Leaning forward, I kissed her cheek and pressed mine against hers. What I nearly experienced with Logan, Sunny had lived through in a cruel twist of fate. My heart understood how broken she must feel—how lost.

"I love you," I whispered. "I'm here. I'm always here if you need me, Sunshine. Please don't hate me for what happened. You have my word I'm going to find Nero and kill him myself. He won't take another life; I won't let him." She roused a little and whimpered when I kissed her cheek again. Tears leaked from her eyes, and I couldn't imagine the pain she had endured without medication. Tenderly, my fingers brushed her wavy hair aside.

When I stood up, my eyes fell upon her body and I stood frozen in time.

Clutched tightly in Sunny's hands was Knox's black knit hat.

Logan didn't utter a word during the drive home. My emotions must have burned his nose, so he gave me the silence that I needed and dropped me off at my house.

It was very late, and the house was eerily quiet. I had so much pent up anger that I stood in the center of our training room, pulling every knife from the wall with my energy and throwing them against the opposite wall. It was enough to sedate my anger for a while.

The study possessed that wonderful smell of aged paper and leather bindings. No one was in there, and it's where Justus worked late some nights and fell asleep over the desk.

When I reached the end of the hall, Justus's door was open just a crack. The soft glow of candlelight remained still until a draft of air swirled in from behind me. Justus was lying on the bed, stomach down, with papers and photographs scattered everywhere. They were on the floor, the bed, a desk, and several opened boxes were lying about. Max stretched out on top of his back, so I quietly tiptoed to a chair, took a seat, and placed a stack of photographs in my lap.

They were the pictures Simon had taken of the lab, and it looked like he had hauled everything over here and they made his bedroom into a war room.

The documents were divided into separate areas of the room. The stacks by my feet were related to my case, the piles covering Justus were images of Page's apartment, vehicles, and other unfamiliar locations. I didn't recognize any of the names or medical terminology on the photographs I held, but a giant medical book was sitting on the sofa along with several notebooks and pens.

I stared at a photo of the fridge that stored all the blood. When I turned it sideways, the writing on the vials became legible. What caught my eye was that one of them wasn't marked the same as the others. After trying a few angles, I could read it and something jogged my memory.

It was just a series of numbers, but I *remembered* those numbers. That was *my* blood that Page had collected shortly after Tarek had attacked me. The numbers were the date she drew the blood, and the last letter was an S.

Why was this in the lab? Was Page involved with the experiments?

"Justus, wake up!" I shouted.

The cat went airborne and scrambled into the hallway, leaving a scratch on the back of Justus's arm. He spun around, sending an array of papers to the floor. One of his eyelids was still closed and he stared at me in startled confusion.

"Learner? Why didn't you…" He shook his head as if he was unclogging water from his ears, but he was really shaking himself out of sleep.

"Ghuardian, did you hear about Knox?"

He nodded, rubbing his chest sleepily. "I received a call not long after," he said regretfully. We both averted our eyes and sat quietly before I spoke again.

"I'm not going to marry Tarek. It was a lie. Logan had to save me and now he's in trouble."

Justus slid off the bed with his powerful legs and knelt before the sofa. "Are you hurt?" He scanned my body for injuries before his eyes met mine again.

I shook my head. "I heard what happened to Page and I want to help you find her. I need a distraction before I fall apart."

"Not until you tell me what happened."

"I lied to everyone." As I spoke, my fingers tightly weaved together. "Tarek blackmailed me to be with him. He threatened to kill everyone, including you. And Logan. Everyone," I whispered. "He made me do a lot of things I'll never get over."

Justus's face tightened and his large hands curled into hard fists.

"The night of our engagement party, I escaped with Christian, but we got separated. A cop helped me; just a regular human, but he was a decent man. Tarek tore out his throat in front of me," I said, covering my face guiltily.

"Why didn't you call? I would have come for you," he said. "I should have come for you anyway."

"You couldn't have known what was going on," I reassured him. "There wasn't any time and then Logan got dragged into it. He challenged Tarek to the death. Tarek's dead, Ghuardian. He's a Lord, and that's a serious crime."

Justus nodded gravely.

"I need to ask you something."

"Ask me anything, Learner."

I flipped the photo in front of his face. "Why was my blood in the lab?"

He snatched the picture and studied it. "I don't see what you mean."

"Look at that one," I said pointing my finger. "If you ever watched television, you might have seen a show called *Sesame Street*. There was a little song they used to sing called 'One of These Things Is Not Like the Other.'"

Justus gave me an annoyed glance but he turned the photo, squinting his eyes.

"Those numbers are a date. Does that date look familiar to you? I remember watching Page write it down. She put an S at the end for Silver. Wasn't this supposed to be for private use—for her to study? Why is it in *this* lab?"

"She swore she would not allow anyone else to see this, Learner. I believe her."

"If you trust her, then I trust your judgment."

Justus rose to his feet and Max strutted in, curling against his leg. I concealed my smile as Justus always pretended to hate my cat, and Max never came downstairs. Now here he was, curled up in

Justus's room.

"Where's Simon?"

"Where is your guard?"

"He's hanging out topside, keeping his distance. Simon?"

"He's here."

I shook my head. "I looked all over the house. He's not here."

A crease formed between his brows. "Are you sure? He went up to get food."

We both hurried upstairs and checked out the kitchen, which was empty. Justus opened the door to the pantry and chuckled.

"Here he is."

I peered around his shoulder into the walk-in food pantry. Simon was passed out on the floor—flat on his back—with an open plastic bag on his lap and his arm still inside it.

"Death by potato chip," I said. "What kind of warning do you think the Surgeon General would put on this?"

I smoothed my hand down Justus's arm. "I'll help you find her, Ghuardian," I promised. His shoulders lowered as if a weight had been lifted and it was the first time since the night of Merc's death that I'd seen him look so emotional.

On the floor, the bag crinkled as Simon pulled out his hand, rubbing his face to wake up. It smeared grease and tiny crumbs all over his cheeks and brown hair. I laughed when he wrinkled his nose.

"You are a national treasure, Simon."

"Miss me already, love? I hope you're back because you dropped the wanker."

"Tarek Thorn is dead," Justus said gravely.

Simon flashed his dimple at me and nodded. "Atta girl."

I laced up my boots to keep my feet warm. Justus called Novis and had a long discussion; it took some convincing that we had to raid the lab that evening. With everything going on, Novis had other things on his mind and gave us his permission.

An innocent life was at stake, and each passing moment could bring more danger to Page, wherever she was. She was connected to the lab somehow, and the two investigations merged into one.

I gave Justus the necklace Tarek had imprisoned me with, explaining the unique metal came from Nero. He left it in his bedroom beside a stack of photographs, and with Tarek's admission, we knew Nero was willing to sell it to anyone for the right price. Maybe HALO already knew this, but I wasn't privy to their investigations.

Justus blew past cars on the highway in his Aston Martin, using his energy to screw up any radar detectors, although we were going so fast I didn't think a trooper would see anything but a blur.

What we knew about the scientists wouldn't fill a thimble. Simon still hadn't discovered what Breed the third man was. He avoided following him because anything that would tip them off could result in the destruction of evidence.

We armed ourselves with stunners—mine strapped beneath my shirt. Winter jackets were left at home; Justus didn't need one anyhow, and fighting with a parka on wasn't on the list of top recommendations for Mage combat.

Justus emanated heat within the car and Simon complained. "Bloody hell, mate, turn that shit down. I believe your expensive little kitten comes with a heater, doesn't she?"

"Silver is cold."

Simon snapped his neck around. "Are you cold, Silver? Because if you are, you better get your arse up here in the front seat and change places with me before I incinerate."

I laughed and shook my head. "Turn it off, it's fine."

Justus tightened his grip on the wheel and the setting sun reflected on his gold ring, the one every member of HALO wore. Aside from their business card, it was the only identifier, which wouldn't be mixed up with a wedding band since it was on the opposite hand. I tightened the laces on my shoes, finding the repetitive task one that not only kept my mind distracted, but also prevented me from throwing up. I swear the wheels were lifting off the asphalt at every turn.

The car rolled up to the lab and we heaved up out of our seats. Justus and Simon flashed to the door and I simply ran at human speed. They turned and watched me before looking at each other.

"I'm out of practice," I muttered.

We had worked out a plan in the car of how this would go down. They needed me to get us inside—avoiding any commotion that might set our targets to destroying evidence or calling for backup.

I leaned against the door, concentrating my energy until the locks slid open. It was easier the second time around. Christian pulled up on his bike and parked it behind the Aston. I had to give him credit for spending the last hour on a vibrating motorcycle, trying to keep up with our car at speeds up to 150 miles per hour.

Justus turned the doorknob, gripping a large dagger in his right hand—one he kept mounted on the wall and never used. It was a frightening thing; slightly curved with a stunning black handle.

As before, the front office was empty. Justus stood motionless by the door to the lab while Simon quietly checked out the bathrooms to make sure they were empty. He was dressed in black from head to toe and dishing out sexy with a messy head of hair that only he could pull off.

Christian remained at my side, ears alert as he made hand motions to alert Justus how many men he heard in the room from the low murmur of talking. Two fingers went up.

Justus wore a sleeveless shirt and thin, black pants that allowed him the utmost flexibility. He used his hands to sense energy within the building. Simon inched beside him as they prepared to rush in. My heart galloped and I held my breath.

Everyone carried a weapon except for my guard. His weapons were his hands.

The two men who ran the day and early evening shift always left around this time. According to Simon, the mysterious third man (or woman) would arrive, concealed under a heavy winter coat with a hood. We were about to crash in on the two men.

The door flung open and Justus and Simon flashed in. There was a commotion of shouts and I followed quickly behind.

Justus transformed into a blur of muscle. I caught occasional glimpses of his sharp blade cutting through the air as he faced off with another Mage. Simon twirled his knife blade between his fingers as he stared at a silver-haired man sitting on a stool. He wore a green sweater and looked about as dangerous as a science teacher.

My eyes swam across the room toward a white curtain divider. I walked slowly to it as Christian kept his eye on Justus and the Mage.

Curling my fingers around the edge, I slowly pulled it along the track to the left when a hand clamped around my wrist and yanked me in. It was Slater, and I had just enough time to make out Page—unconscious—strapped to the examining table.

Justus still fought with the Mage and because of all the noise and shouting, nobody had heard Slater. Trays tipped over and instruments clanged on the floor. Slater's arm wrapped around mine. I wasn't charged up because after wearing the necklace for so long, I had lost the control I once possessed. It could be compared to your leg falling asleep—it takes time for it to wake up. Before I could react, a sharp prick of a needle slid into my neck.

Justus slammed the Mage against the wall and tried to stab him with the dagger when the Mage rolled to the right. He was too fast.

"That's enough, children," Slater interrupted.

Heads turned and everyone got the full picture. Slater standing behind me with his arm wrapped tightly around my body and his other holding a plunger to a needle buried halfway in my neck. It would only take a microsecond for him to inject me with whatever was in that needle, and that thought unnerved me.

"Let her go," Christian demanded.

"This is *my* house," Slater said in clipped words. "I call the shots, and you weren't invited."

Instruments went flying and the body of a large Mage slid across the floor with a knife stuck in his chest.

"Well, well, well," Slater began. "If it isn't Justus. Hardly saw you standing there. Don't even think about flashing because I can move my thumb faster than you can blink. If you want to know what's in here, I'll tell you. Chitah venom. And it's more than enough to kill."

Slater shoved the needle in harder to get a reaction from me. I reminded myself that he was only a Relic, and Relics were mortal.

"What do you want, Slater?" Justus looked like a mass of volatility, but he kept the anger in his voice leashed and remained in absolute control.

Simon never took his eyes off the older Mage, not even risking a glance in our direction, although I knew it was killing him not to see what was going on.

"I want you to remove the knife from my coworker on the floor and put it in your friend. Then we'll talk."

Justus walked to the Mage and lingered for a moment.

"Ghuardian, don't!" I winced as the needle went in deeper. *Screw him.* If Slater planned to inject me, then nothing I said was going to do anything but determine how much sooner that would be. "He'll do the same with you and then Christian," I warned. "Don't do it."

"Mouthy one you got here, Justus. No wonder you wanted someone to take her off your hands. I heard about that Chitah," he said with a short laugh. "Giving the bride away to her enemy? Fucking *hilarious*."

Justus bent over to remove the knife from the Mage. Before he could do it, I swung my heavy boot against Slater's shin as hard as I could. He yelled out and leaned forward, loosening his grip. I reached beneath my shirt for the dagger. When I stabbed him in the leg, a cold rush entered my neck.

We both dropped to the floor.

Christian dove forward and pulled out the needle.

He turned my neck and his fangs bit into the entry site. With hard pulls, Christian sucked out blood mixed with venom, spitting it all over Slater's face. Chaos ensued all around me. After his fifth attempt, I finally pushed him away.

"That's enough, Christian. As much as you like necking with me, you can stop."

I sat up and strangely felt okay. It wasn't the immediate reaction I'd previously experienced with pain, numbness, and blindness—just to name a few.

"I'm all right."

Justus dropped on his knees by my side while Christian sat heavily on Slater's chest. I pointed behind the curtain. "Page is in there." When I saw Justus wasn't listening, I reassured him. "I'm okay, Ghuardian. I promise. There wasn't any venom in there or I'd be dead by now. Go help Page."

He all but vanished. Behind the curtain, I heard soft whispers and the sound of straps unbuckling. "What are they pumping into her?" he shouted.

Christian bounced a little on Slater's chest, provoking an answer.

"Morphine," Slater grunted.

Blood trickled down my neck and I covered it with my hand, peering over my shoulder and watching Justus pull out the IV from Page's arm.

I glared at Christian as the blood smeared around. "You could have at least licked it."

He smirked darkly. "I hear that all too often."

"Ghuardian, take her home," I said. "We'll stay here and question them."

We had a lot of work to do, and it was fortunate we happened upon all three men at once. Christian intended to charm the truth from them and scrub their memories clean once we got all the information needed. Novis had no interest in the technology. His concern was preventing that knowledge from spreading because of the repercussions. Unfortunately, the memory scrubbing would be extensive and require a clean slate; God knows how many years their involvement dated back. End result: amnesia.

Justus carefully lifted Page from the table. Her hair was brushed back and she groggily moaned, lifting her heavy eyelids. They'd definitely drugged her with something. Her arm fell loose and he glanced briefly at her bare feet as he made his way out the door.

Christian stared at me, riddled with concern. "And how is the bite victim feeling these days?" He lifted the needle, squirting a few drops onto his tongue.

"I feel the same."

"Fecking hell, I thought it was a placebo. It's Chitah venom. When you were bit the last time, how long did it take before the symptoms came on?"

"Seconds. Are you sure it's not something else?"

Christian turned around and penetrated Slater with his obsidian eyes. "Better talk or I'll introduce you to my two best friends," he said harshly, holding up his fists. "Meet thunder and lightning. If you don't start talking, it's going to storm all over your face."

"She should be dead," Slater breathed, looking at me in disbelief.

"Are you okay, love?" Simon lifted the older Mage by the collar and gave me a worried look. Thankfully, the genitalia tatted on his forehead had completely faded, or else I might have lost it. "Do you feel off?"

He used his free hand to rake his tousled hair out of his eyes. Simon reminded me of someone who belonged in a rock band whenever his hair was messy, and especially when he wore his leathers. But mostly it was just a pair of dark jeans and a T-shirt with inappropriate writing or rips. Tonight his black shirt had an arrow pointing down that said *Joystick included.*

He lowered his chin and pointed at me while looking at Christian. "What did you do to treat her before? Do you remember all the steps involved?"

"Steps?" Christian asked with an arch of his brow. "We weren't doing the Charleston, you dolt."

"Christian," I warned.

Simon didn't trust Vamps and he sure as hell didn't like Christian's tone. They momentarily forgot the matter at hand and Simon didn't have his aviators on.

"Silver, hand me a pencil."

"Simon, put a cork in it."

"Got one on you? I'm not going to stand here and be called a dolt by a wanker," he argued, staring at my guard.

Christian sat on Slater with a bored expression on his face.

Simon forced the Mage he held by the collar to sit back down. "Was it just feeding her your blood and draining it out?"

"No," Christian replied, scratching his short beard. "The Relic first injected her with a concoction that drew the venom out. I bet arseface knows," he said, bouncing on Slater's chest, causing him to grunt in agony.

"Wait a minute, everyone," I interrupted, standing on my feet. "It doesn't burn, there's no discomfort, *nothing*."

"I'm sure your lady doctor will be relieved to hear that,"

Christian murmured.

"She was bit by a Chitah before?" Slater asked.

"Shut the fuck up, you," Christian demanded, bouncing on his chest as if he were a kid on one of those giant rubber balls. Slater was one breath away from passing out.

"She's probably immune," he grunted.

Christian rolled off him and pulled the knife out of his leg. Slater screamed and Christian held the blade to his throat, licking a drop of blood from the tip of his finger. "Mmm, tastes like uncertainty this evening. That always fires up my thirst to know more. Do share."

Slater pulled in deep breaths. "Like a vaccination or getting exposed to chicken pox. You aren't likely going to react to it again because you've built up immunity."

"Then why isn't every Mage in Cognito racing to his nearest Relic to get Chitah vaccine?" I said, narrowing my eyes at him.

"Because you have Chitah blood."

Everyone silenced.

"Prove it," I said.

CHAPTER 31

J USTUS WRAPPED PAGE IN A warm blanket and placed her on his spacious bed. The candle wicks were cut down and only a few lit, so the room carried only the softest glow of light. He assessed that Page hadn't suffered any physical injuries that were visible, other than a few bruises from the IV.

As she slept, Justus organized all the photographs and files and placed them into boxes. He stacked them in the corner and spent several minutes tidying the room until it met his standards. Everything in its place. He was a meticulous man—one who lived by routine and structure.

A glass of juice and a small bowl of fresh fruit sat on the solid end table beside the bed. It was frustrating to have healing energy he couldn't use on a mortal, to be forced to wait until her body replenished.

Two hours and fifteen minutes later, Page stretched like a cat, as if she were merely waking up from a good night's sleep. Relief filled him as he gazed upon her heart-shaped face. The sternness she often wore had softened—even her lips seemed fuller.

Her lashes fluttered as Justus sat beside her.

"Page, open your eyes," he said in a subdued voice.

He lightly touched her throat and she moaned, creating a vibration against the tip of his thumb. He immediately snapped his hand back and she slowly emerged from that place between dream and reality. Justus became a reservoir, drinking her in with his eyes and memorizing every angle of her face. He'd never paid attention to how long her lashes were.

Her coffee-brown eyes blinked open and he brushed his knuckles down her smooth cheek as gently as a breeze.

"There you are," he said in a low voice.

Before she etched a single worry line on her face, he continued speaking to her in a reassuring tone. "You're safe in my home. All of them, including Slater, have been detained. No further harm will come to you; I won't allow it. You were drugged and your body is weak. I'm going to take care of you the way you need to be cared for. When you are ready to leave, I will escort you home. You will have nothing from me short of protection."

"I'm thirsty," she replied in a sticky, cracked voice.

Justus swung out his arm, grabbing the juice from the table and placing the small glass in her hand. He cupped the back of her head as she tilted up and drank a few swallows. She gasped for breath and lowered her head onto the pillow.

"Better," she said.

"Did he hurt you?" As soon as the question he'd been wondering slipped past his tongue, Justus felt a knot of anger ball up in his stomach.

"I wasn't given food or water because it was all going in intravenously. They kept me sedated and gave me injections, but I don't think I'm hurt. I mean, I'm not missing a kidney or anything, am I?" Page looked down with a mix of humor and fright on her face.

"If I find but one scratch on you, I will break him to pieces. It is a despicable man who would lay a hand on a woman."

"Men and all that testosterone," she said with a sigh, avoiding his eyes.

It bothered him that she looked away and he touched her chin, turning her head to face him. Page blushed high in the cheek and it spread down her neck. It was becoming impossible for Justus to look away as he noticed her beautiful black lashes. The tiny mark at the corner of her eye that most women would have covered with makeup, but she didn't. The way she pulled in her upper lip, biting the tip. The faded marks on her earlobes that indicated she'd once pierced her ears but no longer fussed with jewelry. Then he spotted a tiny white scar on her hairline.

"How did you get this?" he asked, running his finger over the jagged line.

She looked upward. "Oh, I got that in the third grade. A boy named Tommy Farrow knocked me down. I think I hit it against the corner of the building, but it was so long ago."

"Always been a fighter, haven't you?"

"You have to be tough in our world."

He nodded in agreement.

She was beginning to sound more like her old self, and he liked that. Page sat up and his eyes fell to her hospital gown, a reminder of where she had been.

Justus opened a drawer and found a long, clean shirt. "You can wear this until we find you suitable clothing. I'll draw you a bath."

Silver had more bubble bath than he could tolerate, so Justus ran the hot water and added a lavender liquid. When he returned to the room, he helped Page out of the bed. She was unsteady on her feet but insisted he let her do this alone.

He waited in the hall for roughly an hour while she did what women do in the bathroom. When he heard her brushing her teeth, he dropped his head against the wall and thought about how odd it was that small things like that affected him. It was the sound of everyday life, of someone else sharing his space. These were the things he could imagine enjoying with a woman—the personal moments.

He decided to give Page the time she needed and walked down to the training room. It was his temple, and Justus spent twenty minutes practicing ancient fighting techniques mixed with martial arts.

"You're really good," Page said from the doorway.

He used the end of his shirt to wipe off his face and turned to look at her. His dark blue shirt stretched down to her knees.

"Do you know how to defend yourself?" he asked, remembering the videotape of a panicked woman running for her life. What good were locks if she didn't know how to protect herself?

Page shrugged. "I've never had to."

"Come here," he said.

Her brows angled into a comical slant. "Why?"

Nodding his head, he coaxed her with a wave of his arm. "Come here, I said."

She rubbed her nose and crossed the floor, stopping in front of him and putting her hands on her hips.

"Are you feeling better?" he asked.

"It'll take a little while before I'm one hundred percent, but I'm holding my own."

He could smell her hair; it was still wet at the ends and wild all around her face. She looked like a pixie with her liquid brown eyes and shapely mouth. Not a beauty in the way that most women were in today's time, but there was something fetching about her expression and unique features that held his attention. It reminded him of when he used to paint and how other artists would seek out the most beautiful landscapes, sunsets, or women. The paintings fell flat. Yet he had once painted the family of an aristocrat and the eldest daughter—who happened to be the least attractive—wound up becoming the most captivating face on his canvas. A lovely smile played in her eyes that never showed on her mouth. She held a classic beauty that was not favored during that time, and it was such a disappointment when the buyer refused to pay for it because his daughter outshone his own wife.

Justus reached out and wrapped his hands around Page's throat. "What do you do?"

She gripped his wrists and tried to pull his arms away.

"No, not like that. Drop your chin."

She did as he asked with each command.

"Good," he said. "Hunch your shoulders. That's right, Page. Good. Now take a small step back."

Page stepped back a little, half-smiling. "Are we dancing again?"

Justus was too upset to find it amusing that Slater was able to take her down in her own apartment. "Raise your left arm straight up and bring it down over my arms. Twist your body and neck to the right as you do it." She followed his orders and Justus lost his grip. "Now you can strike me in the face or kick me with your knee, but you must attack."

"Why can't I run?"

"Because I'll chase you. Throw me down and injure me and you buy time."

Page was hesitant at first, but he reminded her that he was a Mage and no injuries she inflicted upon him would matter. That hesitation kept her from delivering the move properly.

"Do it, Page!" he said angrily.

"I am!"

"Like you mean it. Pretend I'm coming after you."

She sighed audibly. "You're bossy, you know that?"

"You're weak," he dared, saying it under his breath as he reached for her neck.

The transformation in her expression was brutal. Page completed the moves and had Justus on the floor in three seconds. When he bent forward, she drove her knee into his chest and sent him to the mat.

"Oh God, I'm so sorry," she said, kneeling by his side. She rested her hands on his shoulders and then a cunning smile tugged the corners of her mouth when she realized he wasn't upset.

Justus was grinning, and he couldn't have been more proud than he was watching her rise to the challenge.

"You're something else, you know that?" Page caressed his cheek and he flinched.

"You don't like to be touched, do you? I'm sorry; I've overstepped my bounds." She sat back on her ankles and frowned.

It took most a while to notice his little nuances, but Page was a perceptive woman, always analyzing the situation.

He sat up, feeling vulnerable on his back.

It was a strange moment to think about Eleanor, the woman he'd loved from afar who was murdered years ago. He'd kept his distance so she wouldn't succumb to his charm. Only recently had he found out she was a Blocker—a Mage with a rare ability to block the gifts of others. Page had her own blocking mechanism that kept her from reacting to his energy the way other women did.

Since the night Merc revealed the truth about Eleanor, Justus realized he had wasted an opportunity he could never get back.

Walking into Page's empty apartment had reawakened a nightmare he couldn't live through again. But this time the feeling was stronger, and it made him question if what he had felt for

Eleanor was truly love or just the idea of something he'd never known for himself.

Justus leaned forward and kissed the tiny scar on her forehead.

"You really came for me," she said. "I'd hoped someone would find me, but I can't believe you came for me."

"I would have crossed a battlefield for you."

"Will you…"

He was so close that his nose touched her cheek. "Anything. Speak your mind."

"Will you kiss me?"

Justus dragged his lips slowly to meet hers and whispered across her mouth. "My lips are yours."

"Yes," she breathed.

That single word—not only the meaning itself, but the *way* she whispered it—seized him unexpectedly with desire.

Their lips touched warmly, tenderly. When he broke away, Page looked disappointed.

"Apologies," he said.

"No need. Now I know."

"Know what?"

"I wanted to see if I felt passion in your kiss."

"I feel passion every time I look at you, Page."

Without warning, he cupped her face and kissed her as a man who burned for a woman and wanted to discover her with his mouth. He could feel her hesitation at first. Justus didn't kiss women very often; sex had merely become an outlet. But a fire licked at him just as fervently as her tongue against his. The kiss was so deep their tongues made love.

He could have kissed her for lifetimes.

A tangle of emotions weaved through him: fear, lust, and something else wholly unfamiliar. It expanded within his chest with every passing second.

Sexual energy pulsed throughout his body, energy he'd always kept tethered with his sexual liaisons. A Mage could only touch another Mage during intercourse because if they released their energy into another Breed, it would injure their partner. He'd found ways around this by keeping his hands out of reach. However, accidents had happened, and Justus was enraged that he could hurt a woman who trusted him in the most intimate way. So for decades, he'd restrained all those desires. A woman could satisfy him, but it was a passionless affair.

But with Page, he couldn't control the energy and it spiraled out of control. God, her wet lips and the way she moved her tongue. The way she tasted, smelled, and how he wanted to know every curve of her body with his mouth.

"Wait," he said, breaking the kiss. They both were breathing heavily. "I don't want to hurt you."

"I kicked you in the chest and threw you down on a mat, and you think kissing is going to hurt me?" She chuckled and her laugh sounded like little wind chimes.

"Do I seem cold to you?" he finally asked.

She wiped a few wet hairs away from her eyes. "Why would you ask that? Brash, yes. But when you danced with me that night, you were anything but cold."

"A Thermal has that—"

"No," she said, lifting her hand to silence him. "That's not what I meant. A cold man would have left me out there on that floor to make a fool of myself. Or maybe he would have driven me home and taken advantage of my being drunk, only to leave me in the morning. You're anything but cold, Justus. I might say that you should consider toning down how you speak to people, but then I'd be a hypocrite if I did."

Justus rose to his feet and held his hand out. "Let me take you to bed."

"I'm not sleepy," she protested.

"Neither am I."

———◈———

CHAPTER 32

W E TIED THE MEN TO the tables using the restraints. Simon had a little too much fun scaring the big one with his knife. He did a trick where he could twirl the blade between his fingers, back and forth.

"How many other labs are there?" Christian asked Slater. There was no telling which of them knew more or less, but each man was going to have his turn with Christian.

"One that I know of," Slater replied in a monotone voice, completely entranced.

"Where?"

"The address is in the files," he said, nodding his head at a drawer.

I pulled it open, thumbing through the files until I nodded at Christian, removing a red folder marked "locations." Slater confirmed they had absorbed one of the other labs and acquired their paperwork.

"Simon, I think we're going to have to go through all the files," I grumbled. "We'll need Novis to help us move it out; there are way too many drawers here and it's not going to fit on Christian's bike."

A bike ride I dreaded. Justus had taken the car and Simon declared he was going to head over to a swanky bar up the road for a couple of drinks to take the edge off, leaving Christian to take me home.

Something with Simon was off, and I knew it had to do with Knox. That's why he was so anxious to get back on board, because Nero was involved. Simon may have given Knox a hard time, but deep down he liked the big guy. The vacant stare on his face mirrored my own as I occasionally lost focus, thinking about what hadn't quite sunk in yet.

Simon continued playing his game with the Mage, repeatedly stabbing the dagger into the table next to his head. The older Mage, who looked like a science teacher, remained quiet, hoping we would forget he was there.

The questioning went on for hours. The big Mage could only tell us about the women who were brought in. His responsibility had been maintaining the files, doing runs for the serums, and other odd jobs. His involvement was incriminating, but by no means was he the brains in this show. Whoever was in charge had the right idea in keeping the talent separated. Perhaps they were easier to control if only one person knew what was going on within each lab.

The older Mage tapped his finger against his leg, watching us with wide eyes. Simon guarded the biggest threat, but ever the strategist, the real person he was tormenting with his knife tricks wasn't the gopher, but the older man who was forced to watch.

Slater had been a recent addition to the gang. He didn't seem to possess the depth of knowledge one would expect in someone working on genetics. He had written a few papers that received some attention, and someone anonymously offered him a large sum of money to put his knowledge to use.

What Christian got from the big guy was that all the pregnancies yielded human children. The mothers were disposed of, and once they realized the children were not Breed, they would dump them off for someone to find. Even they couldn't bring themselves to murder a child.

It was a horrifying revelation, a fate that my mother was lucky to have escaped. They were looking for the next genetic leap and needed something special. They'd figured out how to manipulate sperm and eggs by altering the DNA. Half of what they were saying was over my head, but it sounded like they were trying all kinds of combinations based on the results of the other labs.

Slater confessed he had found my vial of blood in Page's possession and sampled my DNA to see if I might be a potential candidate for their experiments. To his surprise, he found that my blood was very similar to the infants born in their lab.

It took dedicated research to discover I was patient zero—the first baby born of these experiments. Now that I was a Mage, it excited him tremendously. Once he made the connection, he tried to locate my file, but the complete records didn't date back that far.

Some were missing.

Only one of their files had minimal information on my conception. It stated that Grady was an Infuser who was able to seal energy onto core light that would otherwise escape with time. I was told that not many Infusers come out because they're highly sought after. A Mage has no desire to become a commodity, so many keep their gifts a secret. Simon mentioned some of the Learners who discovered their gifts early and made them public were kidnapped and sold on the black market.

The egg had been fertilized and inseminated into the patient. Grady had concentrated a small amount of energy into the womb and then used his abilities as an Infuser. The idea was to strengthen the uterus and the egg so that the woman would be able to carry a Breed child. We had theorized it to death, but that explained the unusual buildup of static I always carried when I was human. Grady performed this same act several other times, and those were the only children who ended up on Samil's list. He wasn't interested in all the test-tube babies, only the ones whose lives began with an infusion of Mage energy.

"Why did they want my mother?" I asked the older Mage.

He kept his gaze on Christian while speaking in a monotone voice. "She was the human child of a Chitah."

I gasped and Simon spit out a curse.

"That can't be!" My hands trembled. I couldn't believe it! I would have never imagined that my own mother's life had begun in *this* world—that she was the child of a Chitah.

"They are usually impossible to locate, but yours had a Chitah mother who tried to claim her when she was an infant, so her identity was known. There's something in their DNA that increases the odds of carrying a Breed child to full term, so we discovered. We had no luck in the beginning with Breed females carrying; their body would reject any fertilized egg of another Breed."

"My mother is a Chitah?"

"Human. Just born of a Chitah. But she shares their blood, even if she is not a Chitah. They live ordinary mortal lives and will never share the same characteristic traits of a Chitah, but there is a magic in them nevertheless."

I sat down on a metal stool with my mouth agape. My mother was a human child of a Chitah. Grady was torn about following through with it, but had finally buckled under the influence of money. He agreed to help as an Infuser on the condition that he'd no longer have to retrieve any of the women.

"And what of the spermtabulous cocktail?" Christian pressed.

The older man stared blankly at him. "Our boss made sure that each of us only knew part of the puzzle. We did our job and kept confidentiality, even amongst ourselves."

"Who the hell is my father?" I screamed.

Christian leaned in and punched out his fangs.

The Mage continued staring into his eyes. "The egg belonged to a female Chitah. We think that's why it bonded so well in the early experiments, but we ran out of human-Chitah surrogates. Locating one of them who also happened to be of childbearing age became as easy as locating a goldfish in the Atlantic Ocean. They're given up anonymously, and we haven't had any success in recent years of tracking them down, so we moved on and tried different things. I don't know where the sperm came from."

I covered my mouth with my hand. "I'm a Chitah," I breathed. "Both my biological and surrogate mothers were Chitahs."

"Where is the man who knows about the sperm?" Christian asked in a cool and dangerous voice.

"Dead. Some knowledge died over the years, which is why we've had to try new things. Like vaccinations."

"Where is Silver's file?"

"Below the desk… by the door in the back."

Christian nodded for me to go look and I dug around until I found an old brown file with a coffee stain on it. I saw my mother's picture, her name, information about my birth and conception.

"It's here, Christian. I got it!" I said excitedly. I tucked the file beneath my shirt, inside my pants. "Are you two okay here? I need to go."

"Hell no, you're not going!" Christian snapped in almost unintelligible Irish accent. "You forget I'm your guard?"

So I waited it out for a grueling ten hours.

Christian and Simon extracted every slice of information they could get out of the men, including all their knowledge, how much of it was documented on paper, where those papers were, and if they knew anything that had not been documented. Christian got names of three other men involved, but no one knew the ringleader; he was a shadow. The criminals with money and intelligence operated like the Great and Powerful Oz, having other people do their dirty work and staying out of arm's reach. It reminded me of how Nero conducted business.

Justus led Page into his bedroom and closed the door. She leaned against it, and they stared at each other.

Even before he realized the Relic was immune to his charms, he had been drawn to her. She wasn't anything like the women he had been with before. She carried a subtle beauty and never flaunted it with provocative clothing or heavy makeup. He found himself attracted to her admirable qualities: intelligence, leadership skills, and how she handled difficult situations with great fortitude. He understood her personality in a way that few men would, and it's why he challenged her every step of the way.

When Page would visit with Silver, Justus stood quietly by the wall, noticing little details about her. Like how she sometimes tapped her nose while thinking, or whenever she was working something out in her head, she would twirl her finger in the air and look around. There was a brilliant light shining in her eyes that captivated him.

In his youth, Justus had been an artist. Life had excited him in much the same way as it did her, except his medium had been painting and hers was books. She absorbed knowledge the way a canvas absorbs paint. She reminded him of the man he once was. The man he never thought he could be again.

The air stilled between them and he dropped to his knees before her. Page smoothed her soft hands across his bristly head in a very slow manner. She was the first person he had allowed to touch him so intimately in a private setting. Not the heavy petting that went on in the clubs, but a touch that meant something as her eyes gazed directly into his.

He ran his hands up her naked thighs and slowly dragged his fingers beneath her long shirt. The smooth hush of skin filled the silence of the room and her head fell against the door as her eyes closed. It was the most erotic visual Justus had ever seen, and he suddenly had an urge to paint it. His rough hands journeyed higher up her smooth thighs until he reached the feminine curve of her hips. Justus had never experienced such a lack of control with his energy. He immediately let go and placed his hands on his lap.

"I'll hurt you," he warned.

"Then don't touch me."

His cobalt eyes sharply looked up at her. "That would be an impossibility."

She stepped around him to the bed. "Then maybe it isn't meant to be. Maybe what they say about dating outside your Breed is right."

Something caught his eye and Justus stood up. He lifted the object from the dresser and latched it around his neck with a click.

"Oh, that's darling," she said with a flurry of giggles.

Silver's necklace that suppressed energy hung around his neck, and Justus smiled at her like a cat that was about to eat the canary.

When her cheeks pinkened, he frowned. "Have I offended you?"

"Can I see you without your shirt on?" The palms of her hands turned red and she wrung them together as if trying to hide the fact that she blushed all over her body.

His heart unexpectedly beat faster. Page was about to appraise him, and while Justus was proud of his physique, he suddenly became nervous as hell. She was not under a Charmer's spell.

Page could reject him.

"Never mind," she said dismissively, clasping her delicate fingers together.

Without hesitation, he peeled off his shirt and dropped it on the floor. Over the course of the past month, the physical conditioning in his training room had strengthened his muscles. His abs were a force to be reckoned with.

He could almost feel the heat from her eyes sliding up his abs, broad torso, and then along the muscles in his arms. She wasn't looking at him with Relic eyes, but the eyes of a woman. Her blush slowly faded and he stepped forward within reach.

"Turn around?" she asked.

"Do I frighten you?"

"The only thing that frightens me is the fact you're into jewelry."

He was already concerned about what she thought of his tribal tattoo on his right arm that snaked around from his elbow to shoulder, but what would she think about the sun on his back? Justus turned around and heard her gasp.

He instinctively jumped when her finger touched the tattoo, tracing along the lines. "What does it mean?"

"It's who I am. The sun, the energy, it represents me as a Thermal Mage," he said over his shoulder, proudly. He had personally designed the tattoo of the sun with small bolts of lightning coming out. Justus had wanted a positive symbol and not a memory of something tragic as so many men had acquired. He got it when he first became a Mage and discovered what his abilities were.

When he twisted around to face her, she grabbed his right arm and slid her fingers along the dark marks of his tribal tattoo.

"And this?"

"It's personal to me," was all he could say.

Her hand roamed down his forearm and she curled her fingers around his. Justus's heart quickened because no woman had ever held his hand that way before. She used her other one to caress the back and looked up expectantly.

"Please share your life with me. I'm not asking because I'm a Relic; I'm asking because it's who you are. That's who I want to know all about."

He sat to her left, holding up his arm and using his finger as a pointer. "I designed it three hundred years ago after years of travel. That was when I learned who I was and the kind of man I wanted to be." He touched a jagged line. "This one is for courage, this one is for honor."

She lifted her finger and traced over the thick lines, learning every groove of who Justus was.

"This one is for perseverance, this one is for loyalty, and this one is for sacrifice."

"Where's love?" Page circled her hands around his bicep. "It's beautiful," she whispered.

Justus hadn't marked himself in over three hundred years, and suddenly he wanted to put another line in the pattern.

"I find it fascinating that many of you go through the irreversible process of liquid fire." Page let go and placed her hands on her lap again.

"What do you sleep in?" he suddenly asked.

Justus had bought Silver many outfits she had never worn. She would have something suitable for Page.

"Don't laugh," she quickly said. "I have this satin gown that's my favorite. It's the color of your eyes. The collar has a lacy little thing going on, but it falls to my knees. I don't dress in all that lingerie most women wear." She rambled on as if this were an ordinary conversation. It made him smile as she continued. "Although I do have this one baby-doll gown, but it's not practical at all because after a few hours of tossing around in the bed, it always winds up over my head. What about you?"

"I don't wear gowns," he said.

Page laughed melodically and straightened her legs. "Seriously."

He shrugged. "Sweats or silk shorts with a robe. I dress appropriately so I don't make my Learner uncomfortable in my presence."

"I know what you mean. I dress practical because it matters how I present myself to clients. I don't need to show off legs when that's not what I'm being hired for."

Nothing was sexier to Justus than a modest woman.

"There's fruit if you're hungry," he offered. "Or I can prepare something more suitable in the kitchen. I'm not the best cook," he warned, knowing she might be better off with the fruit.

Page crawled across the bed and fell on her back, fluffing a pillow. He glanced over his shoulder and she gave him a radiant smile. The kind that brightened her brown eyes, and then she tilted her head and a lock of hair swooped across her face.

"I lied, Justus. I think I could get used to someone taking care of me if this is what it's all about," she said jokingly. "What you have here is fine."

Justus walked around the bed and sat beside her, taking a pear from the bowl and slicing it with a knife he kept in the drawer. He handed it to her and she nibbled on it as he cut another wedge.

"So what's with the necklace?" Her eyes were brimming with curiosity, the kind he often saw when she was working out problems in her head.

"The Mage who kidnapped Silver several months ago purchased this metal on the black market. It can suppress many Breed gifts."

"Really?" Page went into serious mode as she reached up to touch it. "Have you had anyone take a look at it?"

"No. We don't want this knowledge in the wrong hands."

"I could analyze it. You can trust me."

His eyes dropped a little as he worked on the next slice of pear. "Why was a vial of Silver's blood in the lab we found you in?"

"It was?" She pinched the bridge of her nose. "It went missing and I thought I had misplaced it. I do that sometimes when I'm in a hurry and have been running on two hours' sleep. They had it? Slater was the last person I was around when it went missing, but I blew it off. I didn't see any reason why he would *want* it." The corners of her mouth anchored down. "Why? Why are you asking me, do you think I broke your trust as your Relic?"

Justus set the knife and pear on the table. "No. I thought you might know why *they* wanted it."

But he didn't reassure her enough. She was insulted, and Justus knew he had crossed a line in doubting her trust.

He tilted her chin upward and leaned in, lightly brushing his lips over hers. But it was nothing like before, because his kiss kindled into a slow burn and the next thing he knew, her hand slid across his muscular thigh.

He claimed her mouth with slow, soft strokes of his tongue, awakening every nerve in his body. She tasted like sweet pears. When her right leg crossed to the other side of him, he cursed under his breath.

Justus might have been a Thermal, but this woman was on fire.

CHAPTER 33

P AGE HAD NEVER BEEN SO swept away by a man before. Not once.

Justus had always rubbed her the wrong way, but she had gradually begun to see there was something of substance to him. Silver told her how Justus had stepped up as her Ghuardian and taken her under his wing. Page had known many a Mage, but that was not a characteristic common among their kind. Most would have juiced her, or just left her to fend for herself. Taking on a Learner was a lifelong commitment.

In the lab, all Page had thought about was dying. No one knew where she was and she didn't have the capacity to escape. Her only hope was to be saved by some miracle, and Justus was the only man she could think of who could do it. HALO had the connections and wherewithal to launch an investigation. They had a reputation for it, and she respected that. But why would he waste his time searching for a Relic?

Page had lost all hope.

Until she opened her eyes, and there he was.

Justus chiseled at the wall she'd built up over the years. It wasn't his physical appearance, or even the fact he'd cared for her while she was sick with the flu. Although that earned major brownie points in her book.

It was the way he *looked* at her. He soaked her in, drank her up, and thirsted for more. Page had walls up like most people, but behind them, she was just a woman who wanted a worthwhile man to love her for who she was. Analytical, workaholic, sensible, quirky, and sometimes she liked to eat peanut butter out of the jar with her fingers. She also wanted a man who didn't size her up like a baby farm and toss her to the side when he found out she couldn't reproduce.

The ambient glow of candlelight flickered against the tan walls. His bedroom was a stark contrast to the kind of man she thought him to be. It was simple and rustic. Not a single lamp or expensive painting. Just a grand bed with dark sheets, dresser, table, leather sofa, and a small writing table with a chair. What really made it romantic were all the candles and candelabras. The only time she ever lit a candle was while taking a bubble bath.

Beneath the layers of arrogance was a passionate man. Not just in a sexual way, but the tenderness with which he brushed his nose along her cheek and kissed the tip of her chin. She could still taste the sweet pear on her lips and wondered if he could too.

When she wrapped her long leg around him, his hard muscles began to shake. She wore nothing beneath that T-shirt, and he knew it.

Page had never been to second base with a guy—whatever that was. The most experience she had was a few serious kisses just after college, but there had never been any time for dating. Work was too demanding.

Yet here she was, in a bedroom with a Mage, and *she* couldn't stop touching *him*. His bare shoulders were strong and intimidating, and Page lightly squeezed them as if he might vanish. She trailed her hands down to his pecs and then the lines of his abs, which tightened as her fingers stroked along the grooves.

His body was something to admire. But it didn't hold a candle to the way that man delivered a kiss.

A wet, rapturous tongue circled and the feeling of his mouth against hers was so sexual that she found herself clawing at his sides. Her body buzzed with unfamiliar sensations and Justus used his skilled hands, rubbing her thigh in methodical motions with a sweet degree of restraint.

He was going easy with her.

It wouldn't have come as a surprise if he was the sort of man who would throw her to the mattress and rip off her panties. But instead, he held her with reverence.

If the necklace did what he said it would, why was he so careful?

It was as if he'd never allowed himself to enjoy a woman.

Page rubbed her leg against his side, feeling a tiny vibration as he groaned against her mouth. He pulled away and hissed through his teeth.

"Don't stop, Justus. *Please*," she begged.

Afraid of losing the moment forever, she grabbed the ends of her shirt and pulled it over her head.

Page felt awkwardly exposed.

She knew nothing of how to behave in the bedroom and her lack of skills must have been glaring. Maybe he didn't want a woman to behave so forward and desperate.

She was wrong.

He looked like he needed CPR. His gaze remained locked on her eyes, and *only* her eyes. But flickers of light sparkled in his irises like a glimmering ocean.

"You're so beautiful I can't even look at you," he said.

The air chilled and her nipples hardened. He blinked several times and it didn't look like he had taken a breath.

"Why don't you want to touch me?"

His lips parted, but his teeth were clamped together. "This is not easy for me, Page. I was once a man worthy of a woman like you, but no more."

She smirked and it turned into a chuckle. "That's really ironic. I'm not good enough for the Relics, and I'm too good for the Mage." She sighed. "I'm better suited for science than love."

Then it happened. She didn't even see his arm move but felt his warm hand cup her breast and his thumb roll over her nipple. Page gasped and lowered her head. His touch affected her entire body.

"Lie on your back," he commanded in a soft voice.

Justus stretched his heavy body on top of her and delicious heat covered her from neck to thigh. He leaned on his left elbow, rolling to his side while stimulating every inch of her skin with his right hand. Justus was more attentive than she could have imagined.

His fingers admired the softness of her breast, the curve of her waist, and the dip in her navel. He took his gentle time, stroking her belly with his knuckles and memorizing the length of her legs with his fingertips. Justus eased himself between her legs and licked the curve of her breast. "I haven't been able to touch a woman this way in a long time," he said in a low voice.

"I thought you had women all the time? You don't touch them?"

"I can only touch another Mage, but I prefer to not be with my own kind. I don't want to let myself feel more than…" He dropped his head on her stomach. "It's easier with humans. I keep my energy suppressed; it's the only way that I can be with a woman."

"If it's not gratifying, then why *wouldn't* you be with a Mage? You could experience this without any worry about hurting the other person, and you could feel everything."

"I never wanted to feel for them because their feelings for *me* were false."

The Charmer was afraid to love.

She curled her hands beneath his jaw, pulling his face up to meet hers. "Mine are not false. You make me angry, Justus. Sometimes I just want to scream because you infuriate me with the things you say and do. But you also make me laugh and feel like a woman. I mean, you sat on the bed slicing pears for me. *Who* does that? I'm with you now because I want you, and this means a lot to me. More than you could imagine. I want you to be my first. I want to be swept up in the romance for once. I'm scared as hell, but I don't want this to end."

"I'm not an honorable man. I've been with many women."

"Good," she said in clipped words. "I wouldn't want an inexperienced man." His eyes flashed up at her response and she grinned. "It's not the man you were that attracts me; it's the man you *are*." She felt the bristles of his shaved hair beneath her sensitive fingertips. "You're the first who's ever seen me naked, aside from the doctors. There were opportunities, but it wasn't right. I want this." Her voice fell to a whisper.

It was harder than she thought to be emotionally intimate with a man. But for reasons she couldn't explain, she wanted to open up to him.

"You may regret this."

"I don't want to marry you, Justus. Maybe all there is between us is physical attraction, but the biggest regret in life is when you don't take chances. I have issues, and clearly, you have issues of your own. But you've been fixing my sink and changing my locks for weeks. Why?"

His chin rested on her stomach as he looked up at her. His whiskers scraped against her skin, but it felt strangely wonderful. He was hiding something, because pain glittered in his eyes. Why did he try so hard to protect her? It made her want to know more about what had happened to break such a strong man.

"Another time," she said and then smiled. "Is this what it's like?"

His brows pushed together and her thumb ran across the vertical crease between them.

"What I mean is, when you're with a woman, do you lie around talking to each other this way? I kind of like it."

"You're the first woman I've brought into my bed."

Her fingers stroked the grooves of his chiseled cheekbones and his eyes hooded. "I'm glad that it's not just *my* first time," she said in a breath. Page summoned all the courage she could to ask the next question, one that would give her the answer that all the kissing and pushing away wouldn't. She already felt the blush rising in her body. "Will you make love to me?"

He lifted his head and rested on his forearms. "I would be honored, and I will make this as easy for you as I can," he said, rising to meet her gaze. "It will hurt, but only this once."

Page had gone to medical school; she was no fool. "I broke my hymen when I was fifteen while riding on a horse," she blurted out. "It happens. There shouldn't be much tearing or discomfort if I just relax during the process."

His lip twitched. "That's all very clinical, Page."

She trembled, having second thoughts. Justus slid off the bed and turned around to face her.

"I want you to see me before you decide if this is what you want to do," he said in his baritone voice. It wasn't too deep, but it was just the right pitch for a man, one that commanded attention and made a woman's legs quiver.

Page sucked in a sharp breath and held it when he suddenly

pulled his track pants down, kicking them to the side. His thighs were muscular; she had only seen them through pants but could now stare at them in admiration. He must do squats or lift weights, because they were perfectly proportioned. He stood before her in nothing but a pair of silk boxers and an expensive watch, which he was removing and placing on the end of the dresser.

Her heart raced in anticipation.

When his thumbs tucked into the waistband of his boxers, he hesitated. His eyes lowered as he slowly pulled down his shorts.

There was Justus, in *all* his glory.

He stood with his fists clenched; his head tilted to one side and he looked like one of those Greek statues. Page was a healer, a doctor, had *seen* men. She had even seen aroused men suffering from medical conditions, but no one matched the beauty of Justus. He was a thick and powerful specimen of a man. The sight of him was magnificent, from the dark tribal tattoo wrapped around his muscular arm to his angled jaw and warrior face. Everything about him was as a man should be, and she slowly grasped why he thought it important that she accept him.

She felt a flush rise all over her skin and her left leg fell aside, giving him the visual cue he needed that she wanted him.

Justus crawled on top of her and loved her with his mouth. His tongue laved in places that made her cry out. Slowly, tugging one nipple and then the other before he journeyed down to discover every conceivable breaking point on her body to mold beneath his hands and taste with his lips.

"How much money do you make?" she asked, staring at a dresser full of designer watches.

He lifted his head and liquefied her with his gaze. "I make six figures, but the only figure I want is this one," he said, sliding his hand down her hips. The necklace contained his power, and yet something was completely unleashed. "Do you trust me?" he asked in a rough, sexy voice against her mouth. God, his words alone could be foreplay and desire licked over her body.

"Yes."

She felt something hot and hard press against her core and she shivered as he began stroking himself against her. Justus eased her legs together and placed his shaft between them. She was wet, and he glided in faster movements with his hips rising and falling as she clung to him.

How could something like this be painful? Maybe if she still had her hymen in place. *Oh God*, she thought, embarrassed by her own scientific evaluation of her first time.

Justus worked her up to a frenzy and she forgot about being nervous. He kept his legs on the outside of hers so that she was unable to open them wider than a small gap.

Page was panting and feeling a rush all over her, a tightening between her legs that was spiraling out of control. The sensation roared through her, spreading across her legs as the tingling became stronger. The instinct to open her legs to him also became stronger.

"Let go, Page," he whispered. "Let it go and give yourself to me."

When she reached the edge of climax, he stopped and used his knee to move her legs apart. As Justus eased the blunt head in, he kissed her so deeply that she felt his tongue in a way that she hadn't before. It was as if he were inside her in every conceivable way. She began to writhe and work her body against his in a hungry fashion, a fresh dew of sweat glistening across her body.

He growled with each twist of her hips.

"Easy," he said, caressing her thigh. "Slow down and let me take care of you."

He sucked on her lower lip and when she wrapped her legs around his hips, he cursed. Justus whispered an apology against her mouth as he slid down, sucking on her breast and sending a lightning bolt of ecstasy straight down between her legs. He gently squeezed and rolled his tongue in such a fashion that each flick made her lose control a little bit more.

God, he knew all the right ways to touch her. He covered her with his body and her breasts molded against his chest. Page turned her hips in small circles, feeling a primal urge take over as he slid further in. His breathing grew loud and he placed the flat of his hand on her thigh.

"Stop. It's too much, Page. *Slowly*."

"Maybe I don't want it slow," she objected.

His brow quirked. "You are the most stubborn woman I have ever met."

"And you're the most arrogant man I've ever met."

His Thermal abilities might have been suppressed, but she certainly felt the temperature rising. He was partially inside her, so Page squeezed her core muscles hard enough that he jerked and dropped his head onto her shoulder.

Page continued with her Kegel exercises, something she knew all about being in the medical profession. Maybe her book smarts would come to good use, after all.

Justus was losing what little control he had, and while attempting to kiss her, his mouth slid to the side and he panted heavily against her cheek.

"Let me see your hands," he whispered.

Uncertain of why, she lifted her arms until her hands were on the pillow—palms up. Justus locked their fingers together. She had never felt more connected with a man than with that single gesture.

With his eyes fixed on hers, Justus slid in deeper. There was resistance and she gasped, feeling how totally alien it was to have a man inside her. He rocked his hips patiently, sliding in inch by inch. She winced at the unfamiliar discomfort, almost pushing him away at first.

"Do you want me to stop?" he asked in a serious voice.

This was it. The moment. Page shook her head and a flutter of fear tickled her belly.

Justus relaxed her by sliding his tongue into her mouth and kissing her so salaciously that every muscle in her body turned to jelly. She was so lost in the kiss that she didn't notice the moment when his pelvis was flush against her own.

The worst was over.

A single tear streamed down her cheek at the loss of her innocence. He let go of her left hand and smeared it away with his thumb. "*Pleure pas, mon ange,*" he whispered, kissing her wet eyelashes. "You are so beautiful, Page. I wish I could give you the right words. Is this okay?"

"This is better than okay, Justus." She smiled, realizing that her apprehension and anxiety were responsible for making it uncomfortable.

"I like it when you say my name," he said. "I don't want you to call me De Gradi anymore."

She reached up and pulled his face close to hers, kissing his cheeks, his eyes, and then around his mouth. He reacted coldly to her touch, as if no woman had ever touched him before.

"We should stop," he said.

Her mouth grazed against his ear and she whispered, "Don't stop. I want to feel *everything*. I want to feel every part of wherever you're planning to take me. Please, *don't ever stop*."

He slid out all the way to the tip and she sagged, thinking it was over. She'd blown it.

In one long, slow stroke, he glided back in. Then he did it again, and again, and again.

"More," she panted.

He took it easy with her at first, but soon, Page gave into the wild and intimate nature of the act. She crashed into him so hard she almost laughed at the idea they both might wind up in the emergency room.

What sent her over the edge was how he continued using his hands to touch her. He would prop up on his elbow while the other hand stroked the length of her body, twisting her nipple, pulling up her thigh, gripping her knee and raising it higher—all while he made love to her.

His blue eyes alone could have brought her to orgasm.

"Turn over," he said.

"Why?"

His mouth quirked. "Are you starting a fight with me, Page? I want you to lie on your stomach."

She did as he asked, once again feeling a new, unfamiliar wave of exposure to a man as his hands caressed her shoulders, thighs, and then cupped her backside.

"This is going to feel different," he said in a broken voice.

He widened her legs and she gasped when he filled her up again.

Simply changing positions brought a new experience, and it was deeper. Justus slid his right hand between her body and the sheets, cupping her sex and stimulating her as his hips thrust against her.

"Oh God!" she cried out, gripping the pillow and tossing it aside. Her fingers clutched the edge of the mattress and her nails dug in.

He kissed the back of her neck and circled his fingers in such a rhythm that Page was feeling the swell of her oncoming orgasm, something she hadn't expected for her first time.

His mouth grazed over her ear as he kept a steady rhythm. "I won't stop until I feel you shaking beneath me." He pushed himself deeper and she moaned as he circled his fingers maddeningly. "I could touch you like this for the rest of my life."

"More," she said, feeling completely uninhibited and gripping the sheets.

"Relax," he said. "I can feel it coming." His fingers slowed down and when he placed his mouth on the back of her neck and sucked on her skin, Page's muscles tensed. She was close and he sensed it.

"That's it," he said. "Open your legs for me… wider… yes, Page. *Wider*. Now relax and let me take care of you."

She cried out again, gasping as his finger stroked her in wild rhythm, sending bursts of pleasure through her body. Hearing his breath out of control turned her on more than anything, and it was with sudden surprise when she realized that her first time with a man would be everything she could have imagined.

When he ran his tongue along her shoulder and pinched her nipple with his other hand, Page found her release and cried out.

His lovemaking reached a fever pitch and when her body melted against the sheet and she whispered, "Oh… *Justus*," he climaxed, shouting out her name.

The candles finally stilled in the aftermath, allowing her a moment to catch her breath and calm her racing heart.

Justus kissed her shoulders and collapsed beside her. She turned so they faced each other. A lazy grin slid up his face and he pulled her leg over his hip and wrapped his arms around her. It didn't seem possible to feel so connected to someone she knew so little about.

Exactly how long do you have to know a man to feel *found* in his arms? A decade? A month? One night? He knew nothing about her dreams and aspirations.

But his mouth had known her a lifetime. Each kiss tenderly touched her skin from the shoulders to the crook of her neck.

"You seem more different than I do," she said with a relaxed smile, touching the silver chain.

He cupped her cheek and stroked her damp hair away from her face, carefully threading each strand into its rightful place. His eyes followed the arch of her brow and studied the contour of her mouth. It was as if ten years had been shaved off his features.

"Well? What do you have to say for yourself?" she asked impatiently. "Your silence makes me nervous."

Page rested her head on his bicep and he stroked his hand through her hair, brushing his fingers down the slope of her neck. "Do you mind if I watch you sleep?" he asked.

"Maybe I'm not tired."

"Mind if I make you tired?" Page shivered and Justus reactively pulled her closer. "I'll draw you another bath if you need one to relax. I can warm you more easily if I remove the necklace."

"No," she said quickly. "I like this much better. Let's just stay this way for a while." She feared that if he removed it, the moment would end. There would be no need for him to hold her and keep her warm in the chilly room.

Justus buried his face in her neck and she barely heard his whisper, so low it wasn't meant for her to hear. Page didn't understand French, but she enjoyed listening to him speak in his native tongue.

Not long after, Justus seduced her again. Only this time, the level of desire was so intense the two of them could have set the bed on fire.

Eventually, she fell asleep in his arms and for the first time, he watched a woman sleep.

CHAPTER 34

A FTER CHRISTIAN AND SIMON SQUEEZED information from the scientists like juice from an orange, the memory scrubbing began. Novis sent in two of his most trusted assistants to help move the files and information as well as give us a lift. They asked no questions and loaded everything into a delivery truck. I was relieved because I wouldn't have to freeze my ass off on the back of Christian's deathmobile.

I sat in the back of the delivery truck, looking through some of the files with the help of a dimly lit bulb.

"Where are they getting all the sperm and eggs from?" I muttered.

Simon sat with his knees pulled up and arms draped over them. "Black market would be a good guess, but most likely they had one supplier."

"One?"

He started rolling his tongue across his bottom teeth, looking up in thought. "I read a lot, Silver. Did you know when you're born you have about a million eggs? You lose them during your lifetime. If they found a female Chitah and harvested her eggs, they wouldn't have to worry about finding new donors for each experiment. Less chances of them getting caught."

"So we all have the same parents?"

"I don't know about the sperm. Sounds like they found a fertile egg, so maybe the sperm wasn't as important. I'd be willing to wager they tried different Breeds. These blokes weren't in charge of that part. Shouldn't be difficult to get sperm from a man," he said with a snort. "Look at how humans line up at those sperm banks. Imagine! A bank of sperm. They go in, make a deposit, and someone else makes a withdrawal."

"But who is my father?"

"Come away from those boxes, love." He motioned for me to sit and I dropped a file and crawled over beside him. Simon draped his arm around my shoulders and lightly tapped his head against mine. "Mutant or not, you're still the bee's knees."

My chest rocked with laughter and he tousled my hair with his hand.

"I can't believe Knox is gone," I blurted out.

Simon pulled away and stood up, one hand on his lower back and the other leaning against the interior wall of the truck. "That's the hardest part about immortality, Silver. Getting attached. You wonder why some of the older Breeds are distant and cold, but have you given it thought? Imagine living centuries of losing people you care about. Maybe it's better to not get too close to anyone."

I got up and stood behind Simon, wrapping my arms around his waist. We didn't say anything else on the matter. Everyone felt the loss, especially knowing how much potential Knox had with working for HALO. He was cut down in his prime, and now Sunny was left alone to pick up the pieces.

Deep down, I worried how I might cope if the same ever happened to me. I'd officially accepted Logan, and that meant taking the chance I might lose him someday.

Nothing lasts forever.

The truck dropped us off at my house and Simon unloaded the boxes he wanted to keep. The men took the rest back to Novis, who would secure the information. The living room was warm and inviting with soft lighting from candles and the faux fireplace. Justus wasn't into electricity within the home much, but in the new house, he'd always kept his candle obsession within his own bedroom and the dining room. I was a little taken aback by the ambiance and particularly the smell of brisket in the air.

Justus strode into the room wearing only a pair of silk boxers and my silver necklace.

Simon's eyebrows shot up, his jaw hit the floor, and he went into silent laughter with his hands over his knees.

"Subtle," I said, pointing at his jewelry.

I'd had very few glimpses of Justus when his guard was down. If it wasn't the ego from the flocks of women who adored him, it was his quiet side that got in the way of me seeing who the real Justus was. Now he stood before me as a gentle man. He laughed and showed no sign of embarrassment—not even a scowl. I'd never seen him walking around in his underwear in all the time I'd known him. Frankly, I was a little mortified.

"Did Page go home?"

He moved past us into the kitchen and lifted a tall glass from the cabinet. "She's asleep."

"I just bet she is." Simon snickered. "All tuckered out?"

"Do you have a problem?" Justus asked with a raised eyebrow, leaning casually against the counter. He crossed his feet, and his relaxed posture almost sent a wallop of laughter out of my mouth as I turned my back to him.

Simon winked at me and walked by with a serious face. "Do you mind slipping into something a little less… dramatic? There are Learners present," he said, clucking his tongue.

"Jealous? Maybe we should hug it out," Justus teased.

I barked out a laugh. They often shared banter as old friends do, but this was over the top.

Simon folded his arms. "No, I'm afraid I can't bring myself to do it, Justus. You're all… *dewy*."

That was my cue to leave. "I'm just going to pretend that someone gave you two a hallucinogenic and this will all go away. I'll be downstairs; I need to give Logan a call."

I headed down the hall as Simon's hyena laugh echoed through the house.

It may have been chilly, but I had dressed for winter in a tightly zipped-up hoodie, fingerless mittens, and my black furry boots, which were becoming my current fashion statement.

The bell jingled when I opened the door, and the smell of

Chinese food wafted from the entrance room. Novis sat in a corner booth next to one of those cheap pictures you see at the mall that light up a moving waterfall. I made my way to the buffet and filled up my plate, taking the seat in front of him. He didn't look impressed with the lemon chicken.

"This is different." I folded the mitten attachments away from my fingers, securing them on the back of the glove with the tiny button.

"Cool gloves."

"Simon got me into these, except mine are less… leathery." I could keep my hands warm and still use the chopsticks. "Ever been here before?"

He shook his head. "I'm having second thoughts, but some of it seems edible."

"I have something serious to discuss with you."

He lifted his plastic cup and sipped on his tea. "I'm ears and all."

I didn't even bother to correct him. "I'm seeking your advice, or maybe just giving you a heads up." My chopsticks tapped on the plate as he watched me in absolute silence, fingers laced together.

A little girl with brown ringlets all over her head ran up to our table and held out her hand. A miniature Barbie was in it with hair sticking out in every direction. She was just a toddler and smiled at Novis. He leaned over and looked her in the eye, smiling back. He had such an agreeable young face with piercing eyes and black hair. He patted her on the head and she giggled, spinning on her heel and darting off to another table. Her mother followed close behind, snapping her fingers impatiently.

"Logan is in a lot of trouble. I'm not sure how much has been circulated, but you know what happened with Tarek. That could mean a death sentence for him. I won't allow it, Novis. We have testimonial evidence from the scientist that my mother was a Chitah, and it might be enough for me to keep him safe. The only way he could be absolved of the crime is if he can prove that I'm his kindred spirit."

"You realize the repercussions of your actions? You may save one life, but at the expense of how many more?"

"How long do you think this can remain a secret? The knowledge is already out there and we have no idea how many other people know about it. Could be a dozen, but it could be hundreds. Can we spend the rest of our lives chasing down something we'll never have a full grasp on? If it leaks out eventually, then what was the point of this?"

His arm almost knocked the tea over and he quickly grabbed it, setting it beside the napkin holder. "What if you're wrong, Silver? What if we *can* stop this? If you expose it, then we have lost the opportunity."

Novis ran his finger over his bottom lip.

"What if? What if? Isn't that what hindsight is for? To tell us what we *should have* done? But we live in the present and can't possibly know all the outcomes of our actions. What if we expose the truth and people collaborate to protect the Breed and take these men out? What if it has no impact one way or the other? What if a new race is created? Life goes on, Novis, or it doesn't. But we can't control life; we're not gods."

"True, but if you knew that crossing the street in a busy intersection would cause a car to crash, would you still do it?"

"It depends. Am I going into the street to save someone from getting hit by the car?"

Novis watched me carefully with amusement on his face and wisdom in his ancient eyes. "Heard of the butterfly effect?"

"Don't even go there, because I can one-up you on that. Back to your scenario. What if I *didn't* rush into traffic and I let that person die? As a result, all civilization ends fifty years from now because of that one event. It could go either way. We can only follow our instinct, but there's no way to see the domino effect of our actions."

Depressed, I dropped my chopsticks and stared at my plate. It was hard to eat Chinese food with another man, because it had become a "Logan and me" thing.

"Silver, I am your employer, not your warden. I cannot stop you from whatever you intend to do. Just be prepared for any consequences to your actions. You may not see them now, but they will come."

"All actions have consequences, Novis. That can't be helped."

"I'm sorry that you must make such choices."

"Not your fault."

"Of course it's not," he mused. "We've all been faced with difficult decisions in our lifetime, but I'm pleased that you've uncovered the truth. It must come as a relief to finally know who you are."

I removed my gloves and set them on the table. "I don't know everything about who I am. My mother isn't my real mother—just a surrogate who carried a fertilized egg. All this time, my mom was a Chitah human child. My real mother I may never know, and there's still a big question mark over who my father is. Jesus, what if I'm related to Logan?"

Novis literally fell back laughing, slapping his hand on the table and drawing a few inquisitive eyes. His laugh was animated and completely unexpected.

"It's not funny," I murmured.

He sipped his drink and snorted out a little tea. "Let me assure you that you are not related to Logan Cross. I am a very old Mage, and I know a lot about many different Breeds. Chitahs know their own blood; there's a connection between them that can't be explained. Logan would never be able to bed a woman that gave him a... sister vibe. It goes against everything in his nature." Novis snorted out a few more laughs. "I do apologize; I didn't mean to make light of this. Logan is not your relation. The same way a Chitah knows their soul mate is similar to the way they know their siblings. You could split apart twins at birth, put them in a crowded room full of people, and not only would they find each other but they would know they were related. I've personally witnessed this myself. A young Chitah once grew curious about his human son after the baby was given up for adoption. He'd never seen the child since birth, but after a long search, he located the school the boy went to and somehow managed to nose him out."

"Good to know."

Meanwhile, my inner self threw her head down on the table and sighed in relief. Then I wondered about Logan's human sister, Sadie, and if he'd ever try to find her.

Novis dipped his finger in a puddle of sauce and his expression soured when he tasted it. "Whatever path you choose, Silver, you will have my support."

"It feels like no matter what choice I make, I'm going to betray someone." I leaned back in my seat with a huff. "I think I need some rose-colored glasses for Christmas."

Novis laughed cheerfully and stole a piece of beef from my plate. "I can arrange for that."

I scraped my fingers through my hair and rested my elbows on the table. "How's Sunny? Did she wake up yet?"

Novis nodded and pulled in his lips to lick them. "She's damaged from this tragedy. This is why I once warned you about growing attached to things that die so quickly."

"I'll love my friend, whether she dies tomorrow, or a thousand years from now. We've already had this discussion and if you can't see how precious life is, then what have you really learned through immortality? I want to see her."

"That can be arranged. She needs someone to speak to her."

"Why haven't you?"

He straightened his shoulders and looked uncomfortable with the topic... and quite familiar with it at the same time.

"You can't give consoling words to a woman who has watched her lover die in her arms." His eyes looked down and a glimmer of emotion sparked in his face before disappearing. "Let's enjoy what we can salvage of this dinner, shall we? Too much discussion of serious matters; let's not fill personal time with woes. So often, people will pollute table conversations with words that spoil the taste of food and drink. I've learned in my life that there is always time for both. I have given you my answer. Now tell me more about *Page*," he said with a curious quirk of his brow.

The thing about Relics is that they aren't just a plethora of information—they're a sponge. Particularly with any knowledge related to the Breed. Each generation not only inherits the knowledge from their ancestors, but has an opportunity to build upon this to pass along to their own children.

While Christian had performed a complete memory scrub, no one knew if Slater's would be permanent. Maybe he'd never regain his memory, but the knowledge was potentially hard-coded to his genetic memory, so he would be carefully monitored. It didn't occur to us until we were sitting at the table discussing it with Page, who was now fully involved through no fault of her own. She insisted that no physical harm come to him, and on Justus's word, that would be so.

I lent her some clothes, uncertain if I should ask how permanent the situation was between her and Justus. I'd never seen him bring a woman home before, and now I was wondering if I would be forced to sleep upstairs if she moved in. Just the idea that I might overhear Justus in the throes of ecstasy made me crash on the sofa the next evening.

The wall monitors were set up to display a starlit night, and I was curled up on the sofa in the dark room, stargazing.

"I haven't forced you to sleep up here, have I?"

Page walked into the room, wrapped in a dark green blanket.

"No. I'm having a little insomnia," I said, watching a shooting star blaze across the screen. "A lot going on in my head."

"Do you mind?" she asked, pointing at the spot beside me. I shrugged and she sat down, throwing the blanket around both of us. Page tucked the edge around my legs. "There. Snug as a bug in a rug."

The indentations in her nose were more pronounced; she must have been recently reading. She absently rubbed them and yawned.

Max sauntered into the room and collapsed on the rug before us—stretching out his beautiful black body and licking his front paw. He had adapted nicely to his new home and had already claimed a few spots in the house as his. Justus scolded him whenever he caught him licking the monitors on the lower end of the wall, but Max had always been a window-licker.

Page sat to my right with her legs curled up. "He's lucky, you know. To have you in his life. You do so much for him and I hope he realizes it."

"Thanks. Why does everything have to be so damn hard? Now that I know what I want in my life, it could be taken away from me."

Page touched the ends of her brown hair and smiled wistfully as she recited a few lines:

"Doubt thou the stars are fire,
Doubt that the sun doth move,
Doubt truth to be a liar,
But never doubt I love."

She tucked her hair behind her ear, watching another shooting star blaze across the screen.

"What is that?"

"Shakespeare," she said with a light chuckle. "I've always loved that verse."

"Why did Slater take you?"

The shine in her eyes wore away. "He was trying to impregnate me. All that crap they've been doing over the years, and he thought he had some kind of epiphany. He primed me up with injections and I struggled so much that they doped me up. Slater was infuriated, and through my foggy state of consciousness, I overheard him telling them it wouldn't work as long as they kept giving me morphine. The older guy wanted to get rid of me, but Slater was determined to prove his idea would work. I think he was planning on kidnapping me from the facility and taking me on his own to finish up his experiment. I don't remember much; I was out of it most of the time."

"I'm glad we found you when we did."

"Me too. Justus told me how you spotted the vial in the photograph. Most people don't pay attention to things like that."

"Luck."

"You're smarter than you give yourself credit for, Silver. I think it's time you own up to it."

"Well, in that case, I totally rocked at saving the day with my extraordinary talents of perception." I laughed and Page tilted her head back. "How serious are you and Justus? I don't mean to pry, I'm just—"

"You have every right to know. You're his Learner and I can see how protective you are of him."

"I definitely have to keep my eye on him sometimes. Doesn't he drive you crazy though? I don't see how you can tolerate the way he speaks so…"

"I keep him in check. We balance out each other's temperaments. I can be equally headstrong, and I think we both already know the woman is always right."

"You've worked your magic on him, that's for sure. I've never seen him so agreeable."

She curled her body toward mine with her knees pulled up in the same fashion and her voice fell to a whisper. "I've never fallen for anyone, and I never thought it could happen so fast."

I thought of Sunny and a tear slid down my nose. "It didn't work that way with Logan and me, but Sunny and Knox had that kind of connection. She said she just knew it from the beginning."

"Don't *ever* repeat this, Silver. Just between us, I think I love him. God help me, I don't know why, but that's how I feel about Justus. Please don't tell him; he'll think I'm crazy since we barely know each other, and maybe it's too premature for me to be saying things like that. Plus, I don't think that's where he wants to be with a woman, and I get it. A Mage doesn't settle very often and then there's him being a Charmer and me always being outshined by some woman. I'm not up for that kind of competition. I just want to live in the moment for a little while and enjoy what we have before it ends."

I wiped away a tear and attempted to smile. I didn't know if Justus felt the same way about Page as she did him, but a part of me hoped so. Especially knowing the kind of women he had reduced himself to being with because deep down, he never felt worthy of anyone who would want to know him on a deeper level. Charmer or not, Justus never gave it a chance.

Her eyes filled with compassion and she touched my arm. "It'll work out between you and Logan. You two deserve to be happy and don't let anyone try to take that away."

"What are you two doing in here?" a voice bellowed from the dark hall. Max meowed at him and continued licking his paws.

Page countered his remark. "The ladies are waiting for a knight in shining armor to bring on the ice cream."

In the distance, we heard the sound of a drawer opening and Page giggled, leaning in to whisper, "No matter what happens, Silver, I promise I'll be here if you need to talk. You got it? Not just as your Relic, but as a friend. There's no need for Justus to continue paying me for my services; you've paid me back more than enough by saving my life."

Justus flashed into the room with a large gallon of ice cream and two spoons. Big spoons. I almost doubled over with laughter. He handed me the carton and took her hands.

"Let me warm them," he murmured, cupping one of her hands within his and blowing a heated breath. It was a sweet gesture because he couldn't use his Thermal abilities with the necklace on, and it was such a private moment that I looked away.

"My hero," Page breathed. Justus unabashedly kissed her upside down on the lips and I thought about how much she had opened him up in ways I never could. "Now go back to bed and leave us girls to our vices."

Justus grunted a complaint but gave her one more kiss and left us alone to tear up the rocky road.

CHAPTER 35

"WHAT THE HELL ARE YOU doing?" Leo scowled. My seat suddenly reclined all the way back until I was lying down in the car.

Christian replied from the back seat. "I'd say I was getting the lady horizontal, wouldn't you?"

"What's the point of this?" I asked, staring at the roof of the car.

"I'd rather you not have your head poking out of the window like it's target practice just yet. There are a lot of nut cases out there and if anyone got wind of this from Tarek's Pride, they might do something stupid, or at least try it."

"That's Christian, always thinking ahead," I mused. "I don't think they'd hurt a female, would they, Leo?"

He merely flicked a glance at me and kept quiet.

Christian scanned outside the windows. The streets were dark and empty as we rolled up to a desolate building that looked like a warehouse. I leaned up to get a better look and Christian shoved me back down by my forehead. I had expected to be going to a mansion or something more ostentatious than a brick building in the hood.

"We're here," Leo announced.

"I'll get out first," Christian murmured. "Stay down for a minute until I knock on the glass."

Both men hopped outside while I stared at the roof. I wondered if Leo realized he had a small stain up there that looked like mustard.

The door clicked open and Christian unlatched my seatbelt. "It's just a short walk to the door. Stay close to me."

I leaned up and my leather coat made noise. "Seriously, Christian. You're taking this a little—"

The loud crack of a gunshot cut off my words. Christian threw himself over me and I listened to a struggle. My heart pounded against his chest.

"Got him!" an unfamiliar voice yelled from a distance.

Christian lifted his head and I saw a hint of a smile behind those scruffy whiskers. "Are you still going to argue with me, lass? Like I said before, there are some demented people that are itching for a little payback."

"I can't die from a gunshot."

His breath heated my face. "I don't care if they throw a fecking water balloon at you. I'm going to protect your life, and that's final. So quit your whining. I swear, you haven't changed a bit since we first met," he rambled on as he heaved me out of the car. "You rabbit on as if you know something about our world and you're only a little tadpole. You must think I'm a big numpty. *Of course* I know a gunshot won't kill you, but it can knock you down long enough that you wouldn't be able to escape and I would be too distracted to fight. Plus, I'd have to explain to your Ghuardian why you look like a donut with a hole in the middle."

"Okay, Christian. Point taken. Let's get inside already."

Without telling Logan, I had asked Leo to take me to their Overlord—the man who ruled over all the Lords. The idea of a manhunt with a bunch of Chitahs tracking us down gave me waking nightmares. Leo mentioned that Logan might be detained for questioning until they reviewed all the facts, due to it being such a serious charge. Unlike human laws, being arrested among the Breed meant there was sufficient evidence to impose a sentence. I wasn't familiar with Chitah laws, but I didn't think they would be much different.

Leo pulled off his winter hat and the streetlamp caught the red highlights in his short hair as he brushed his hands over the back of it. It was a Ewan McGregor color from some of the old movies I'd seen—reddish with blond mixed in. I wasn't sure why he had never challenged for the position of Lord in his Pride, but perhaps his time would one day come. He tucked the hat in his back pocket and unzipped his coat.

Six guards surrounded us and led us inside to a set of heavy double doors. Two reached forward and opened them, and my nerves bunched up in my stomach when before us was one serious-looking gentleman sitting behind a long desk with three men to his right. He wore all black, looked like he could have been six foot ten, his nose was strong and sculpted like a Roman, and his eyes were not the typical amber color. They were a brilliant citrine and sent a flurry of goose bumps all over my arms when he glanced up at me. He had hair the color of soot, and not one feature on his face changed as we approached.

Leo bowed submissively. "Sire."

I drew in a swift intake of breath when the doors slammed behind us and all six guards lined up against the wall.

"Leo Cross." The Overlord greeted him in a textured voice. "You may sit."

Leo took the empty chair on my right, leaving Christian and me standing in the middle of the room with no more available seats.

"Mage, come forward and let me have a closer look at you. Vampire, stay back. No harm will come to her in my presence and on this, you have my word."

I released my breath and took a few steps forward. I felt a little undignified standing there in a pair of black boots and a leather jacket when every man at that table was dressed in his finest attire. The Overlord slowly lifted a long finger, signaling I could come no closer. Nervously, I bowed, not knowing the custom.

He lifted an indifferent brow. "Logan Cross may be guilty on charges of murder. It is a serious offense to attack a Lord, and here we have one who was slain. The investigation is under way, but it has been brought to my attention you wish to speak on behalf of Logan Cross. If we bring him in, everyone involved will be questioned. My best men are determining the facts that occurred on the evening prior to the incident through questioning. I have also been made aware that you and Logan Cross have a… relationship." His brow slid up and he leaned back in his chair, never once removing his eyes from mine. I couldn't look at him directly, so I kept my focus on his hands, which were still on the table. "I'm sure you are aware this is frowned upon by our Breed, but it is not by any means illegal. You have the right to speak for or against him, as you wish, but you do not possess any rights as a mate."

"Sir, I love him." I paused and let those words settle in, but they seemed to have no sway one way or the other. "You may remember me on the night of the party, because it was an engagement celebration between me and Tarek. Not a mutual one. Tarek blackmailed me by threatening the lives of everyone I loved." I licked my lips and pulled in a breath, because I was finding it more difficult to breathe. "The night of the party, he held me against my will. Tarek had a history with Logan, and everything he did was for personal vengeance. When Logan brought a woman to the event, it threw Tarek into a rage. That's when I realized he was going to keep taking this one step further until he ruined Logan."

I caught Leo turning his head to look at me from his chair and saw his hands tighten into fists.

"Christian, my guard, charmed Logan into choosing a Chitah mate. We'd hoped that Tarek would release me if he saw his plans fall through. I counted on this, even knowing I would be giving up a life with Logan. But Tarek had also planned for me to work as a spy for the Mageri. I had to get away from him or he would have blackmailed me for the rest of my life."

Slander without evidence was a serious offense. There was no proof of the conversations exchanged between us, but then an idea came to mind.

"If you want to question me using a Vampire to pull the truth, I just want you to know I'm willing."

He smiled a little and tilted his head. "I can scent truth better than any man in this room."

That was a relief. "He would have tarnished the reputation of your leadership if he had remained in power."

"And no one knew of this?" the Overlord asked, fingers still interlocked on the table.

"Only Christian, but that could hardly be helped. I was to tell no one about the threat. Later that evening, I escaped with Christian and we were separated. I tried to get myself arrested by the human police so they would lock me up and I'd be safe from Tarek's reach.

The cop thought I was a battered woman and took me to his home to keep me safe until I found a place to go." This part of the story piqued his interest and the Overlord leaned forward. "Tarek showed up and murdered him in cold blood."

"Tarek murdered the human?" the Overlord asked in surprise. One of the elders to his right got up and stood beside me, taking short puffs of air.

"I can confirm she speaks the truth."

I stepped closer to Christian because someone smelling the truth out of me gave me the creeps.

"The cop was a decent man. He didn't deserve to die the way he did, execution style." I bit down on my quivering lip as the sounds of his death filled my head. "Tarek ripped him apart for the key he'd swallowed to keep me safe inside his house. Then Logan was forced to listen over the phone as Tarek threatened to kill me, and Logan challenged him. That's what happened."

"We are aware of some of the details you've pointed out from tracing phone calls and hiring a Sensor to investigate the crime scene. But we were not aware that Tarek had killed the human."

My eyes narrowed. "You thought Logan did it?"

The Overlord shrugged. "It's not customary to play witness to something you did not personally see. Logan has a black mark on his record and Tarek does not."

Their laws infuriated me. "Why not question Logan? Surely that would clear up this matter and he'd tell you the truth."

His brow arched. "Would he?"

"Would it matter? You could scent it out of him."

The Overlord didn't care for my tone by the way his cheek twitched. "We could scent the truth or a lie, but that would not tell us what the truth actually *is*. I am familiar with Logan Cross and his reputation."

"Hire a Vampire"

"It's not our custom," he countered. Then he blinked away a flicker of amusement and glanced at the men to his left.

"I realize the Pride is suffering a loss, but it would be generous to set up a donation to a battered women's shelter in the name of the fallen officer. He saved me and took me into his home. Stone held the key that would have saved his life, but he chose to protect me and died as a result. That's pretty damn noble and I think deserves to be recognized. I didn't know the guy, but everything I'll ever need to know about him I learned in the last five minutes of his life."

"The murder of human law enforcement is a serious offense, punishable by death. Even as Lord, Tarek would not have been above the law if this were proven." The Overlord rested his arms over the table and turned to the elders. "Unfortunately, this crime does not justify the death of a Lord at the hands of a lower-ranked Chitah." They nodded in agreement and he looked up. I didn't see sympathy or malice. He was simply a man carrying out the laws. "We will take all you have said into consideration, but in the meantime, we must make arrangements about setting a new challenge with their Pride."

"Wait," I said as the Overlord began to rise from his seat.

"Yes?" he asked with curious interest.

"Is that it? Nothing I've said will convince you that Logan is innocent?"

His long fingers splayed out across the desk before him and he leaned forward just a little bit. "If it were that easy, then no man would be punished. We must abide by the laws, and the investigation will continue. As I've just stated, your testimony will be taken into consideration."

I took a single step forward as I reached beneath my shirt and pulled out a slip of paper. The guards rushed over and grabbed my arms. Christian moved toward the guards with a rock-solid pace.

"Wait," the Overlord barked out. "Release her."

Hands slowly peeled away from my arms and Christian shoved one of the men down.

"I wanted you to see this." I handed him the folded-up paper and he carefully opened it. He licked the tip of his finger and touched the corner to see if there was a second page. His eyes briefly flicked up to mine and I nodded. The Overlord turned his attention to the elders and guards.

"I want everyone to leave this room. Guards, on my command, leave. The only person I'm requesting to stay is Silver."

"Sire," one of the elders argued.

He snapped a hot gaze at him and the man lowered his head, following the others out the door. The Overlord stepped around his desk and sat on it, looking as tall as the Empire State Building.

"Is this public knowledge?"

"No. That's only part of what's been going on with the experiments."

"Logan will not be admonished of his crime based on unrelated evidence. Why bring this forward?"

"Because…"

"Yes?" he pressed.

Now or never. "I was part of those experiments. My mother was a Chitah."

He blinked rapidly and glanced at the paper again. "It does not state this here."

"And it won't. I have no written evidence, only the confession of one of the scientists involved, and we scrubbed his memory. The reason I'm telling you all this is because Logan has put claim on me as his kindred spirit."

"Impossible."

"So I thought. You'll scent the truth on him if you ask. I can't explain it; I only know that it must have something to do with my birth parents. If we're kindred spirits, then his challenge would be justified."

"Speculation is not fact, therefore I cannot consider this."

"Not just that," I interrupted. I looked at the Overlord pleadingly. "Interbreed mating is not recognized by any law, but I want you to see that if I'm part Chitah, then I have as much right to claim him as he does me. Should we officially marry—or mate—I want it to be legal."

He folded the paper and handed it back to me. "Do not share this information with anyone if you value your life. Continue your investigation carefully, young Mage."

"So there's nothing I can say here that would make a difference?"

"Self-sacrifice is held in the highest regard among Chitahs, and you are an exemplary Mage who has protected many lives with your actions. You've shown compassion for the officer who was slain. I will see that a substantial donation is given to the appropriate charity in his name."

The Overlord walked around the desk and solemnly sat in his chair. "I cannot guarantee your safety, but I will speak to the Youngblood Pride and try to compensate for their loss. Do not think what you've shared tonight was in vain, but also understand that in many regards, my hands are tied. If you can provide sufficient evidence of your claim, then I may be able to grant a pardon, should our investigation not turn in his favor." He tapped his finger on his chin and looked me over. "I daresay it is a most curious pairing. It is obvious by the manner in which you speak of him and the fire in your eyes that you love him. It's a look I am very familiar with," he said with a smile. "You are free to leave."

And that was it.

He seemed like a generous and fair man, even though I'd made no headway in getting Logan off the hook. Leo thought my words might help Logan's case, and I knew he'd do anything to help his brother. I turned to leave and the Overlord spoke once more.

"I cannot make a formal statement on this tragedy until tomorrow, but I will place six of my guards with you for a twenty-four-hour period," he said, lacing his fingers together and keeping his eyes on me. "It's all that I can offer. They are out for blood and I cannot stop them until I have reviewed the case in detail and made an official statement on the crime. For your protection, I will announce that anyone who seeks vengeance before a decision is made will be acting against my direct orders."

Leo drove me to Logan's condo and the guards followed in front and behind. I didn't want them split up between Logan and me, so I thought it would be better if we stayed together for the night. I thought about hiding out in his cave, but Chitahs were excellent trackers and a cave would offer no protection.

Christian hooked his arm around my waist and rushed me

Dannika Dark

inside the building, choosing the stairwell instead of the elevator.

When Logan opened the door, I was surprised to find Levi was there, along with someone I'd never met before. His hair was onyx-colored and short, but those bright Chitah eyes were unmistakable. His features were familiar and masculine, and his build was somewhere in the middle of Levi and Logan. Logan was svelte with rock-solid muscle and strength, while Levi was thicker all around and strong.

"Silver, I'd like you to meet my youngest brother, Lucian."

Lucian made no gesture to shake my hand, as that was a human custom. He merely nodded once and kept his position by the wall with his arms folded. I tried not to notice his black hair, because it was not a common feature among Chitahs. Bright eyes and hair color were favored.

Levi twirled me in a small circle. "Hey, honey. Looking beautiful. Did you cut your hair?" He brushed his hands through it and then scratched his bristly jaw. "Yeah, I like it," he said in a deep voice.

Christian closed the door behind me and tucked his hands in his trench-coat pockets. We stood next to the open kitchen and Logan placed the flat of his hand against my back.

"What are you guys doing here?"

"We're here to protect you and Logan," Levi said, glancing over at Logan.

"It's not necessary," I insisted. "You shouldn't put yourselves in harm's way. We have guards assigned by the Overlord."

"For twenty-four hours," Christian reminded me. "After that, you're a sitting duck. Quack quack."

"Maybe someone needs to invent Chitah radio or something. Spread the word, why don't you!"

Christian rolled his eyes dramatically.

Lucian made a quiet suggestion, pointing at the sink cabinet. Leo patted him on the back and pulled out a few boxes of tin foil and they left the room.

"I really don't like that all your brothers are here," I said to Logan. If he was a target, then anyone near him was too. He kissed my temple and went into the hallway to speak with Leo.

"Honey, you couldn't get us out of here with a five-alarm fire, so just sit down and enjoy the Levi specialty." He put a saucepan on the stove and opened a canister of cocoa. I smirked and walked to the doorway when he suddenly rushed in front of me. "Sit down; let the men do their thing in there."

I sat in the chair, reaching around to braid my hair into a loose knot to get it out of my face. "So Levi, how many boyfriends you got these days?"

Levi's laugh was full of body and sin. Tough as nails but deep down, the biggest sweetheart. "You truly flatter me. The last one decided he wanted to be with one of his own kind. Shifters are like that."

"The guy at the club?"

He grunted a yes.

"Maybe you need to quit trying to meet your true love in a bar, ever think of that? Go to a library or something."

A boisterous laugh filled the room and he tore open a bag of marshmallows with his teeth, dumping them on the kitchen island in a giant pile. Levi grabbed a fistful and stuffed them into his mouth. "You slay me. I wouldn't know what the hell to do with a boy who had a head on his shoulders."

"Maybe the reason why you haven't found the right one is because you have an idea of what's right for you. Sometimes it doesn't always work out the way you think it will, you know?"

"That's getting a little too deep for me."

"That's what she said."

Levi hurled a handful of marshmallows at my tacky "Simon" humor. He finally poured our drinks and we sat awhile, sharing conversation.

Leo and Lucian went into the hidden control room, which was a neighboring apartment that had been converted into something out of an espionage movie. From there, they'd be able to keep watch on the building via the surveillance cameras.

Logan filled the open doorway. "You can come on out, Silver."

"Maybe I'm having too much fun in here with your brother. He's feeding me marshmallows."

"Are you trying to make me jealous?" Logan strode in, wearing his ashen sweatpants and no shirt. If the marshmallows on the table didn't melt by how sexy he looked, they should have. He stuffed a large one into his mouth and leaned against the counter, feeding me small bites.

"Why don't you two get a room," Levi groaned.

I flicked one off the table and it bounced off Levi's head and into his cup. That had us rolling for a good five minutes before I finally got up and followed Logan into the other room.

"Wow, you guys were busy," I remarked, staring at the windows in the living room.

The Cross brothers had covered them with tin foil from top to bottom. Logan didn't own drapes or blinds because he liked the scenic view of the street and said he had nothing to hide. Except for his secret room, of course.

Christian insisted that regardless of their extra measures, I avoid standing near the windows. He sat on the sofa and flipped through a magazine as Logan took my hand to lead me to his bedroom.

Levi sank into one of the chairs and crossed an ankle over his knee. "You two behave in there."

He winked, and I winked back.

CHAPTER 36

"I THINK YOUR BROTHER'S TRYING TO poison me," I groaned, rolling over on Logan's wide mattress. The foil created a blackout, so he lit a small candle and placed it beside the bed.

"I ate too many marshmallows," I murmured into the pillow. The Levi specialty was nothing but a concoction of sugar with a splash of rum. As a Mage, I had the ability to heal, but we were not immune to stomach upset.

"Let me rub your belly. Roll over, *my mate*."

I smiled against the pillow at his choice of words. Obediently, I turned to my back and Logan carefully unfastened my jeans.

"Hey, wait a minute. You just wanna get frisky."

"Scout's honor."

How I loved the way that he looked at me. Logan was a different man without the long tangles of hair in front of his face, but I always did like it when he pulled his hair back. It allowed me to see the carved features in his jaw, his strong nose, deep-set eyes, heavy brow, and crisp eyes. Not to mention the infamous Cross smile—wide and wonderful.

He tugged the jeans to my hips and softly caressed my lower belly with his large hand. Of course, what I really caught on to was that Logan just wanted to get my jeans low enough so that he could lie there and stare at my tattoo again. He was so damn proud of those paw prints that I think he might have been just as happy if I had gotten them on my forehead.

He smiled up at me and I stroked his choppy hair.

It was time to confess. "My mother was a Chitah human child, and the egg she carried was from a Chitah."

Logan didn't catapult off the bed like I had expected. He circled his tongue around the edge of the tattoo and gently kissed it.

"They weren't able to find out anything about my father, but I guess that's the proof you were looking for."

Logan slid up the length of my body until we were nose to nose. "It matters not."

"I thought you wanted to know so you could prove your kindred theory."

"At one time, I did. But I don't care what you are, Silver. I only care *who* you are."

"Maybe you should hear the full story. My mother was a Chitah-human surrogate. The egg belonged to a Chitah and the sperm is unknown. Grady was an Infuser and used his energy to protect the fetus; maybe that's why I've always had a little Mage light in me."

Logan kissed the corners of my mouth with his soft lips and all down my jaw and chin. "You may hate the genetic experimentation, but I sure as hell don't hate the results. It brought you into this world—into my life."

Never could I have imagined such a man existed who could love so unconditionally. My lips pressed against his bristly cheek and I whispered in a gentle breath, "I love you." It was the first time I'd said the words aloud, but love never needs to be confirmed through words.

Logan eased down the length of my body, dragging his lips across the flat of my stomach. His whiskers tickled my fingers as I caressed his jaw. "You going for the full beard?"

"You don't like?" he muttered through his continued kisses.

"Well, it's a little softer than the five-o'clock shadow, I'll give you that. Maybe now I won't have sandpaper marks all over my face after we make out." Logan nipped me again and I squealed as he sat up. "I prefer it when you're smooth," I admitted, locking my fingers behind my head.

"Then my female will get what she wants," he said matter-of-factly.

"Have you heard about Justus? I think he's finally found himself a woman."

"Did he now?" Logan reached down and unlaced my boots.

"Jiminy. Since when did you start dressing paramilitary?"

"Since I started getting serious about you?"

He pulled at the boot and my foot slid out. His fingers worked the lace on the second boot and he glanced over his shoulder. "Silver, I want you to keep Christian as your protector. He has proven himself a loyal guard. I owe him for that, even if I don't forgive him for putting his hands on your body and despite the fact I'd love nothing more than to tie him to the front end of my car."

"Christian, I feel the same way," I said in a passive voice. "But tune your ears out of the rest of our conversation, please."

Logan tried to pull off my socks and I flattened my feet on the mattress.

"My feet are cold."

He stretched out beside me. "Your jeans are staying on in case something happens; I don't want you running into the streets of Cognito half-dressed."

"It's not like I'll freeze to death," I said, kissing his arm that was folded beneath his head.

Logan rubbed his nose against mine. "No, but your body is not to be shared with any man."

"I guess that means I won't be wearing a bikini to the beach this summer."

A burst of laughter sounded in the other room and I narrowed my eyes. "Christian," I hissed. "So help me, exit from this conversation *now*."

Logan wedged his right leg between mine and we locked together like twisted pretzels. "What do you know of Chitah customs?"

"Not much. Why?"

"If it's your heritage, don't you think it's time you start learning about it?"

"True." I stared at the shadows dancing on the foiled windows from the candlelight. "Tell me it's nothing like all those Mage books that Justus keeps in his study, is it? If so, I'll take the *CliffsNotes* version."

Logan ran his hand along my arm and I wrapped mine around his side. Then all of a sudden, my stomach made a horrendous noise—like a troll growling from underneath the bridge it's guarding.

"Jeez, girl." Logan laughed and tucked his hand beneath my shirt to rest on my side. "What's going on in there?"

"A revolution."

He gently stroked my belly in small circles and I relaxed. I don't think it was doing anything to cure me, but it felt good. Not just having Logan's hands on me, but knowing I could always count on him. After everything that had happened, he could have left me. Never did I imagine that I would have him back in my arms, and never did it mean as much as it did now.

"Tell me how I can ease your discomfort. I will be most displeased if you respond with a joke," he said in his bedroom voice. The sexy, relaxed one that was reserved only for me.

"I want you to take me out to the movies and buy me some popcorn. I want you to put your arm around me and share my soda, because I haven't done anything normal in a really long time. I want to do stuff like that with you. I want to go to a bookstore and sit at a table, drinking a cup of coffee and arguing about what to buy. I'd love to go through a car wash with you, or go to the fair. It's been a while since we've had a real date."

"As you wish, my sweet. What do you like?"

"What do you mean? What kind of movies do I like?"

He rolled on top of me and watched me with unblinking, animalistic eyes. "What is it that I do that pleases you?"

"Oh." I grinned shyly. I thought about it for a minute.

We were about to have pillow talk, and I really liked our pillow talk. Logan didn't want to know what movie I wanted to see, nor was he asking about my favorite sexual position. He wanted to know the simple things he did that made me love him.

"I like it when you rub my legs."

He immediately rose to the challenge and took my leg in his arms, giving me a deep massage, probably the best I'd ever had.

Hands down.

Ever.

His fingers rubbed firmly into my thigh and all kinds of nerves were firing up. Naturally, he sensed it with a sniff of his nose. I didn't mind so much that he could read my emotions; it's who he was.

"I want to discover the things you like, Silver, and do them over and over."

"Maybe I should have said something else then," I joked, relaxing and watching the candlelight shimmering against his skin. "Logan, that necklace Tarek made me wear…"

"What about it?"

"Justus had it on the other night."

"You don't say." He smiled, working his fingers above my knee.

His nonchalant reaction irritated me. "Justus wore it so he could be with Page. It suppressed his light so he wouldn't hurt her, and he could touch her."

Logan considered this and switched legs. "Your point?"

"Well, I'm just saying that I could wear it when we're together."

"Absolutely not."

I propped up on my elbows, rattled by his answer. "Why, just because Tarek gave it to me? It doesn't matter where we got it because now it's ours."

Logan stopped the leg massage and gave me his serious voice. "That has nothing to do with it. Remember when I told you I would have you just as you are? I meant it. Every word."

"Yeah, but you need to be sensible about this. If it means that I can touch you when we're together, that I can be *normal*…"

"Ask me why I love you," he quickly said, caging me with his arms.

My heart stammered and he leaned in close with a piercing gaze. A serious one that made me slide down off my elbows and cross my arms over my chest. I was still wearing a shirt, but I felt strangely exposed with his glare. Not in the sense of nudity, but my heart being open to him like a book.

"Ask me," he demanded.

"Why?" The question I'd always wanted to ask but was too afraid to. Exactly why would a man like Logan Cross love a young Mage?

He scraped his teeth over his bottom lip before answering. "Because we *have* challenges, and we're *not* perfect. I love that with you—I have to try. That it's not effortless to keep you as much as it is to love you. You're remarkably selfless and headstrong like me. I received the same scolding remarks as you when I was younger and thought I knew it all. Don't change that about you, because it's what I love. The fire keeps you alive. I love that we can both screw up and find a way to work around it. I love you, Silver, because you are a creature of light. Do you think I would want to suppress that light to satisfy my own needs? I can sate you, female, without you having to touch me. If you wore that necklace, it would be an admission that I cannot accept you for what you are. That has nothing to do with pride; it's principle. I love you because of that very look you have on your face right now as I'm telling you all this," he said, stroking my cheek with his finger. Then his voice softened around the edges as his breath warmed my cheek. "I love that you were brave enough to cut my hair, Little Raven."

He struck a nerve and I teared up. Logan wiped that tear away—melting on top of me like a blanket and tasting the corners of my mouth.

"It proved how much you love me," he whispered. "Now forget the damn necklace."

"Yeah, but Justus—"

He kissed my chin and sat up again, placing my legs in his lap. "Your Ghuardian must wear it to protect his *mortal* female. I am not mortal. All you can do with that power of yours is charge me up like a battery. Now let this be the last time we discuss you wearing that damn necklace." I melted a little, and not just because he was rubbing my upper thigh, but because I didn't deserve a man like him. "I would have you no other way, because it is who you are, Silver. If you ever lost your ability, then I would still want you. If you grew fangs, then I would *still* want you."

"And if I grew a tail?"

"Well, that just might be fun," he purred.

Tingles surfaced throughout my body as his expert fingers continued massaging me. I heard deep huffs of breath as he watched me with hooded eyes. My scent was slowly doing him in, but with restrained conviction, he continued rubbing my legs until minutes later, I was completely satisfied.

"I need a cigarette," I said, stretching out my arms.

"I need a bag of ice," Logan replied. He fell on his back and I stared at the shiny foil on the window, flickering in the candlelight. My Mage gift told me it was 10:23 p.m.

It was going to be a long night; not that I minded a long night in Logan's arms.

Two hours later, I woke up with Logan draped over my stomach. It was typical for a Chitah to offer his warmth to another, but it was hard to get used to. My previous boyfriends usually slept with their back to me, if not falling asleep watching TV on the sofa.

Logan was fast asleep and I was dying for a drink.

"Oh, for the love of God," I whispered.

Usually he was a light sleeper. But for some reason, whenever he was lying on top of me, he not only became immovable, but he could sleep through a bomb dropping on the house.

Very convenient.

"Christian, can you have Levi bring me a glass of water?" I whispered.

I tried licking my lips but they were dry. A moment later, the door quietly opened and Levi came in, shutting it behind him. He gave a thumbs-up and I shrank in embarrassment.

Levi knelt down and let me take a few sips before setting the glass beside the bed.

"He really loves you." Levi looked over at Logan who was fast asleep across my hips. "He loved Katrina, but don't ever compare yourself to her. You're two different women who loved the same man, but in a way, you love a different man than she did." Levi spoke in a quiet voice as he sat on the floor with his right leg bent at the knee. "We know everything that happened between you and Tarck, and let me tell you right now that I would put your ass on a fucking pedestal if you were mine."

I reached out and held his forearm, sliding my thumb across the inked letters that spelled "truth" in Latin. "Why did you get this?"

"I was young and tired of hiding who I was from the people I loved. It was a secret for a long-ass time. Chalk up the tat to the rebellious nature of youth, but it serves as a reminder of who I am: a proud Chitah. It's also a vow that I'd always honor the truth and be true to myself. They didn't accept me with open arms in the beginning. It took a while for them to wrap their heads around the fact I wasn't going to carry on the Cross legacy."

Logan grunted sleepily and buried his face in my stomach, his fingers clawing at my hip. He released a long breath and I looked at Levi, who ruffled up his short hair.

"What changed their minds?" I asked.

"Someone tried to kill me. When I first started dating, I hit on a guy in a bar and didn't know he was straight until halfway through our conversation. By then, he'd figured out what my game was. It was humiliating, so I did my usual walk of shame out the back door and told Logan and Leo I'd meet up with them later. The guy followed me out—he was also a Chitah. Before I could turn around, he put a knife in my back and I tried to fight him. Got my ass kicked pretty good because of the knife, and Leo came out the back door when the guy was shoving his boot in my stomach for the umpteenth time. Instinct kicked in, and from that night on, my brothers had my back."

I touched his cheek and then looked at Logan. "I envy that kind of devotion. I don't have a family. Guess it was never in the cards for me. I always wanted a sibling, and Sunny counts in a way. You guys are really lucky to have each other."

"You have us," he said loudly and rose up from the floor, kicking off his shoes.

Levi suddenly crawled over the bed and plopped down on his right side, pulling my feet against his chest. It was hard to deny him the right to show affection in the Chitah way as I stared at the smile spreading across that tough face of his.

We were a tangled mess of bodies, and I'd never felt so loved in all my life. Logan lifted his head and for a split second, I prepared for a yelling match when he saw Levi lying in bed with us, holding my feet.

Instead, he smiled cozily and nestled his face in the soft pocket of my belly.

I reached for the water and noticed something on the floor.
A knife.

Logan's hand dangled off the bed just an inch or two above it. It wasn't my knife, because going to see the Overlord armed wouldn't have been well received. At first, I wondered why Logan would have placed a knife by the bed. A Chitah's speed and bite against other Breeds were weapons unto themselves. But then it occurred to me that if anyone were going to exact revenge on us, it would be a Chitah. A knife would not only bring him down, but also finish him off.

A snore vibrated at my feet and I realized our sleeping arrangement wasn't going to work out. A manwich to save my life was one thing, but this was Cross brothers' salad dressing.

The door slammed against the wall and Leo burst into the room.
"Get up!" he shouted.

Levi was on his feet in a heartbeat, but Logan didn't move an inch from covering me like a shield. Except now I noticed he was gripping the knife.

"We spotted movement outside and two of the guards are missing."

"Maybe they had to pee?" I suggested.

Leo tore out of the room and Levi turned to me. "Don't worry, honey. I still adore your terrible jokes."

I pushed Logan away and sat up, noticing my pants were still unzipped. While I secured the button, Christian strode into the room. He approached the window and stood very still, lowering his eyes to the floor.

"You hear anything?" Logan asked.

Christian raised a hand. "Your fecking voice?" he said pointedly. After a few seconds, he decided to be helpful. "Footsteps running. A dog barking. It's too far down for me to pick up through a windowpane. Silver, go to the toilet and lock the door."

"If there were a *fire,* I would be trapped. I don't particularly want to die on the toilet."

"Always the last word," he grumbled, poking a tiny hole in the foil and peering outside.

"Logan, where are my shoes?"

He twisted his back to look around when suddenly a cacophony of voices shouted out from the living room. Logan rushed out and Christian closed the door, pressing his back against it.

I jumped out of the bed and pulled at the knob. "Let me out of here!"

"Over my rotting corpse."

There was an explosion of noise in the other room—a struggle between men fighting and spitting out curses. Bodies crashed against the wall and glass shattered. My heart stopped in my chest as I thought about Logan getting hurt.

The bedroom window smashed in and glass flew everywhere. A cold blast of wind circulated within the room and a Chitah descended upon me with impeccable speed. He bared his fangs and threw me on the floor.

"You must be the Mage," he hissed.

It all happened so fast.

I charged up my light and the second he fell on top of my body and sank his teeth into my neck, I wrapped my legs around him and gave him an electrical bear hug.

Christian gave me a crooked smile. "You got everything under control, or do you think you need to go to the toilet? I wouldn't want there to be a *fire*."

"Dammit, Christian, get him off me!"

The Chitah flailed about and his teeth tore at my throat. Christian reached down, pried open his jaws to release his grip, and then threw him across the room. The Chitah went into convulsions and finally fell still.

"I thought you were supposed to guard me," I grumbled, wiping my sleeves angrily.

He snorted. "My job is to protect your life, not to kill spiders like that one. You're a capable woman, and maybe I like watching you roll around with other men."

"You're a pig."

"What's going on out there?" Christian shouted at the door.

"Four Chitahs. One contained, three left," I heard Logan

yell out.

Christian held me back and I smacked at his arm.

"You're my guard, Christian, not my boss. So if I'm going to run out there, guns blazing, you're going to guard me. Got it?"

His hands fell across the curve where my neck met my shoulders, and I could see that he was biting his tongue from saying something vulgar. Christian got it, but he wasn't happy with it. He stepped aside and I flew into the hallway, soaking in the visual.

Levi and another Chitah were on the living room floor, fingers wrapped around each other's throats in a chokehold. To the right near the kitchen, Leo and a Chitah in black were throwing punches. Logan held a third Chitah against the wall with his forearm and the man struck him in the head with brass knuckles. Logan grew disoriented for a moment, and the energy swelled in the air like snaps of electricity.

The moment I saw Logan in danger, all reflexes kicked into action. I flashed forward, knocking the Chitah away and diving out of his grasp. Before Logan could right himself, the Chitah rushed me and I ducked, sweeping out my leg and tripping him. As he fell to the floor, I kicked him in the groin like I was stomping the yard. That's when Christian stepped in and knocked him out with brute strength.

Logan and Leo cornered the Chitah in black near the front door and my attention went to Levi, who was on his back.

I casually walked over and tapped the Chitah on the shoulder. The gesture confused both of them and he twisted his neck around to look up at me.

"Excuse me, but you need to get your hands off my brother." I couldn't throw my energy into him since he was on top of Levi, so I touched his neck and gave him a jolt.

It was enough for him to lose his grip. Before I could charge up again, he lunged and sank his fangs into my neck. Levi roared like I had never heard him before and threw the Chitah against the wall.

Levi pulled me into his arms screaming, "She's been bit. Four, no… fuck! There's eight!"

"Levi, I can't breathe," I wheezed as he rocked me back and forth.

Christian could have easily taken out each Chitah, but that would have distracted his attention from guarding me. He wandered down the hall, scoping out the bedroom where the window was broken in. I also felt a little honor system going on with him allowing each man to have his own fight.

Leo and Logan were in full swing with the Chitah in the hall, but when Logan heard Levi screaming, he rushed to my side.

"*Silver,*" he said urgently.

In the background, Leo shoved the attacker's head against the wall and knocked him out.

"Let me go, Levi, or so help me I'm going to put a thousand volts into you," I complained.

"I'd do what she says," Christian said, tearing a wrapper off a flat red sucker and popping it into his mouth. "Or maybe as another torture technique, she'll sing you a song. I have to admit that my Vampire hearing is a curse; have you ever had to endure her singing those shower songs? *Jaysus.*"

"Shut up, Vampire!" Leo bellowed, pacing across the room to study the scene.

Levi finally loosened his grip and I crawled away from him. "Give a girl some space, will ya?" I rubbed at my neck, smearing away some of the blood.

Logan's face was as white as a ghost—as if he were in the midst of reliving the memory of my first bite. "You're—"

"I'm *okay,*" I said with a look of reassurance. "I'm immune. When we raided the lab, Slater injected me with Chitah venom. Probably a whole lot more than what you put out in a bite, but I didn't have any kind of adverse reaction. Page thinks that I have antibodies or something, like when you get vaccinated. She thinks my genetics play a factor."

Logan looked at my face with awe and bewilderment. "Impossible," he breathed.

"Believe it," Christian replied from his comfortable spot on the end of the sofa.

"You know, Christian, if I didn't know better, I'd think you were beginning to enjoy watching me get bit."

He twirled the candy around in his mouth. "Someone needs to call your people and collect the dirty laundry on the floor," he muttered, kicking one of the bodies at his feet.

Logan ignored him. "There *is* no immunity. Have you ever heard of anything like this, Leo?"

Leo shook his head and crossed his thick arms. "Then again, you picked a pretty unique girlfriend. I wouldn't put anything past Silver, including figuring a way out of her own death."

I sniffed out a laugh as Levi rose to his feet and looked like he wanted to vomit. He was green and sweating profusely. "I'll check on Lucian and make sure he didn't have a heart attack in there. Did we get it on video?"

"Yeah, brother," Leo replied. "We started recording when we set up the room; it was Lucian's idea to keep it running constantly. Sometimes things are missed in those first crucial seconds and these men will pay for attacking the Overlord's guards. All of you sit tight while I check out the hall. Levi, call for a pickup," he added, nodding at the pile of bodies. "I'll see how many guards are left outside. I don't think the Overlord will bump up security; we've already been granted six guards who *should* be watching *him*. The windows are broken, so we're going to spend the rest of the night in your control room, Logan. I don't like the exposure."

Levi opened the coat closet in the hall and went inside the control room while Leo slipped into his jacket and headed out the door.

"Slater thinks because I'm half Chitah that the initial exposure activated the same antibodies that you guys have naturally." I touched my fingers to my neck, wondering if the new bites would scar. I slipped my arms around Logan's waist and tilted my head to the side, smiling wickedly. "Will you heal me, my love? With your *tongue*."

He growled, going primal as his eyes rolled black and his bare chest flashed with magnificent spotted patterns.

Christian released a sigh and pushed off the couch. "Well, that's my cue," he murmured in a deep voice, dragging one of the bodies into the hallway while crunching on his sucker.

Logan's warm tongue glided across the puncture wounds and he released his scent, the smell wild and dangerous like an oncoming storm. It was a subtle, natural cologne that sifted from his pores—just enough that I wrapped my arms even tighter around him, hopping on my left leg.

He immediately dropped his gaze. "What's wrong with your foot?"

"Glass. No biggie," I assured him.

Logan bent over and gripped my ankle, looking at the sole of my foot. I didn't see any blood, but I also didn't like the look on his face. He wrapped his arms around my lower back and lifted me up, walking a few steps until he set me down on the couch. He slowly pulled my sock off and examined the cut. By this time, the bright amber had returned in his eyes.

I had a knee-jerk reaction when his finger lightly brushed over it. Logan snatched my ankle and in a swift movement plucked the glass free.

I hissed through my teeth and he immediately put his mouth around my foot and rolled his tongue over my cut. I shuddered as it went from instant pain to something else entirely. The healing agent in a Chitah's saliva worked immediately, sealing the cut and ending the pain.

Logan crawled up my body and ran his tongue over my neck—licking and sucking until I was writhing beneath him. My hands ran across his bare back, and his whiskers tickled my neck in the most delicious way. He growled, and I knew it was because I had accepted him as a Chitah. Who he was and what he could do.

Then he slid his hand secretively between my legs so the cameras couldn't see. "Anywhere else you're in need of my tongue, Little Raven?"

CHAPTER 37

J USTUS RECEIVED A CALL FROM Logan early that morning,
detailing the attack and stating they had everything under
control. He had anticipated this kind of retaliation might occur
and was relieved to know Silver was safe.

Page had reviewed every file in detail, focusing on the medical
information he and Simon didn't understand. She worked tirelessly,
refusing to sleep or eat. She was the kind of woman who let her
own needs take a backseat, and the signs of fatigue were starting to
settle in.

When he walked in the study, she was asleep across the desk,
papers scattered in front of her. Justus removed her glasses and she
roused from her dreamy state with a complaining moan.

"This is enough," he said.

"Just one more hour," she groaned, putting the glasses back on.

"No. These papers are not going anywhere. Now come with me."

She stood up and put her hand on the desk. "*God.*"

"What is it?" He may have been half-asleep before, but he was
wide-awake when her color paled.

"You're right; I need to take a break. I'm not feeling well."

Justus locked his arm around her side and walked her to the door.
"Stop pushing yourself so hard. If helping us means jeopardizing
your health, then I will not have it. You are mortal."

"Thanks for the reminder." She tried to sound humored, but
the closer they got to the door, the more she felt like a caged animal
about to bolt.

"Let go," she gasped and ran out of the room.

Justus found her over the toilet bowl. He flipped the phone out
of his pocket and stepped into the hall to give her privacy.

"Novis, I will be in your debt if you can assist with a favor. Page La Croix has fallen ill. Is there anyone you trust enough to bring to my secure location? … No, I didn't call a Relic to look at her when we found her. She slept off the drugs… She didn't know. Injections of some kind. There were no symptoms, just fatigue. I need someone who can come on short notice, and let them know she recently recovered from the flu and her immune system was low… Because I trust her word… You have my gratitude."

Justus paced outside the door, rubbing his jaw and wondering why he hadn't gotten her medical attention in the first place. He knew little about drug withdrawals and the effects they had on the body. Would she become addicted to the morphine? Maybe the bug she had was coming back. And then an ugly seed planted in his thoughts. What if this were more than a virus, but a terminal illness? He knew of things like cancer and organs failing. He wrung his hands together, noticing that it grew quiet in the bathroom. What if they gave her a medication that if she didn't continue with the injections, she would deteriorate?

Too many *what ifs*.

Justus shoved his phone in his back pocket and knocked on the half-closed door. "Is there something you need?"

"Give me just a minute."

"Page, I'm coming in."

He swung the door open and she quickly closed the lid. This time around, Justus knew what to do. He ran a towel under the cool water while Page wiped tears from her eyes.

"How do you feel?"

"Dizzy. It's either the flu again, or the drugs coming out of my system. The only way to know is to do a few blood tests, but my equipment is at home. I've never had drug withdrawals, but I know the symptoms peak up to three days after quitting."

"A Relic is on the way to examine you. I should have summoned one upon your return." He dropped to one knee beside her. "Here," he offered, holding the cool cloth against her forehead.

Justus touched her shoulder, coaxing her to turn around and scoot in front of him as he took a seat against the cabinet. "Lean back."

Page moved around and relaxed against his chest. He held the towel over her forehead and touched her hand with the other.

With all the women he had been with, in every kind of situation, nothing had ever felt as intimate as sitting on the bathroom floor comforting this mortal. She turned her head to the side, drawing in a shaky breath and letting it go. He brushed her brown hair away from her eyes, never more aware of her mortality.

Of all women to become attached to, he'd chosen one who would die.

"I'll see that you're taken care of, *mon ange*. The Relic will know what to do."

"I'm just tired, Justus. I haven't slept, nor have I eaten much of anything. My body is just weak and I need to take it easy."

"Good to hear you admit that for once."

"Don't press your luck," she said with a soft chuckle. "I admit to nothing."

Justus stood up and bent forward, lifting her into his arms. She was light as a feather, which troubled him, and he carried her into his bedroom.

"I really hate all the fuss. I'm—"

"If you say you're fine one more time, I'm going to throw you outside in the snow."

Page suddenly laughed at his dry humor and curled up on the bed as he pulled a thin sheet over her. It wasn't enough. Justus had no need of such things, but they kept a stack of blankets in the closet for Silver. He selected two of the thickest ones and draped them over her body.

By the time he finished tucking them around her, she had fallen asleep.

He extinguished a few candles and placed a small wastebasket beside the bed. Justus quietly closed the door and stood in the hallway for what seemed like an eternity until the visual alarms went off, absent of sound. A flicker of red lights illuminated the main rooms.

He disabled the alarms and went outside to meet the Relic. Simon escorted an older woman down the road who was yelling at him the entire way. A blindfold covered her eyes and whenever he'd try to take her elbow to keep her from falling, she would clobber him with her oversized black bag.

"Bloody *hell*." Simon exclaimed as she hit him in the shoulder. "Do I look like I want to shag you?"

"I don't see what the big secret could possibly be," she complained in a shrill voice. "Dragging me into the woods with a blindfold, like some kind of hostage. Be sure to tie my arms up before surgery." She turned her head toward Justus. "I sense someone present is a Charmer."

Simon rolled his eyes at Justus. "Novis gave me a ring to drive her over. What's going on out here?"

"Page is ill."

They walked inside and once downstairs, Simon removed her blindfold.

"Are you the patient?" She barked at Justus, scraping him with a womanly glare from head to toe. Her voice had a slight southern drawl but was loud with a sharp tone.

"No, I am not."

"Well, what are you standing around for? Take me to the one who needs my help and get out of my way."

She stood at a proud five foot three with short white hair and heavy glasses on her nose. The sort of woman you envisioned as the one the Big Bad Wolf had eaten. Justus grew skeptical that she could even see her own reflection.

The Relic stepped into the room. After one glance, she spun around and cut them off at the door. "Men, stay outside. When I'm done, I'll summon you. But during the examination, neither of you will set one foot in this room nor disturb me. I have a low tolerance for pestering. Do you understand, Mage?"

Justus nodded as she slammed the door in his face.

Simon merely leaned against the wall with his arms folded. "If I ever need a Relic, Justus, and *that* woman is called, you have my full permission to bury me in cement."

"Lucian, are the guards still outside?" Leo kept his voice just above a whisper.

I lay on a mattress half-asleep in the safety of the control room, secretly listening as I peeked through my eyelashes. After ending a call with Justus, Logan stood in the middle of the room, folding a stick of mint gum and placing it on his tongue.

Lucian glanced over his shoulder from a leather office chair. "Yeah, the guards are still milling about. The Overlord sent two replacements and these guys are much bigger. They're scaring the shit out of the residents leaving the building," he said with a laugh. "Do you want to view the tapes again before we make a backup?"

"Not necessary," Logan murmured. "Keep your voices down; Silver is still asleep."

"Why didn't you bring a mattress in here for *me*?" he teased.

"You're the smart one, Lucian. Can you not figure it out?"

Leo crossed his arms and all I could see was his back. "Where's the Vampire?"

Lucian glanced over the monitors. "There. You can see the edge of his coat outside the doors. He hasn't moved in hours. Literally."

"Lucian," Logan warned. "Keep *quiet*."

"I'm going to go make a call, see if the Overlord has made any public statements," Leo whispered as he left the room.

Lucian spun around in his chair, looking at me like a bug beneath a microscope. I blinked my eye shut, although my hair obscured most of my face so they wouldn't be able to tell I was eavesdropping. Lucian spoke his mind and didn't seem to have a firm grasp on tact. I could see why Logan worried about that getting him into trouble. He saw life from a practical standpoint, not an emotional one, so he often made inappropriate remarks.

"So, she's the one, huh?"

"Never doubt it, brother," Logan said softly.

"Yeah, but she's a *Mage*."

Logan's voice rose to a low growl. "You're young, Lucian, and full of questions. But tread carefully when you speak of my mate."

"I'm only saying we've never been on good terms with her kind. You have no idea what you're getting into and what kind of trouble this will bring. And what if a female Chitah comes along who—"

"First of all," Logan interrupted, making an effort to lower his voice. "It's time for a change. True, a Mage has always been our mortal enemy. But what good can come of holding these prejudices decade after decade? We hang on to them as if they mean something. They don't, Lucian. You're a smart guy, but life is more complicated than facts and figures. And secondly, *no* Chitah female can hold a candle to that beautiful creature stretched across my bed. She's the most extraordinary woman I've ever known, and someday, Lucian, she'll be your sister."

My heart soared. Logan didn't know I was listening, so it meant a lot to hear him say those things about me.

"Will you two keep it down," Levi complained. "People are trying to sleep."

That's when I noticed Levi was in the bed *with* me. My legs were bent at the knee and my feet were on his warm, bare chest. Levi made a snoring sound and nuzzled his face into the sheet.

My God, I loved the guy, but I was starting to think that maybe I was spending more time in bed with Levi than the man I was sleeping with.

A few quiet moments passed as I listened to the squeaky sound coming from Lucian's chair as he spun in a semicircle.

"Do you think more will come after you?" Lucian whispered.

"Not if the Overlord keeps his word. There will always be enemies in life, and sometimes you can be your own worst enemy. The life I once lived was fueled with pain and hate. If I can give you two pieces of advice, it would be to not live in fear or anger, and to find the love of a good woman who accepts you for your faults, and because of her, you aspire to be a noble man who is worthy of love."

"Why didn't you tell me that *years* ago, Logan?" Levi chuckled softly. "Might have saved me from hooking up with the wrong person." Levi's hand curled around a cold spot on my feet.

"Looks to me like you've already found someone, Levi." Lucian laughed darkly. "Better be careful, Logan might get jealous and tear out your throat like he did to Tarek."

"If I were straight, he might have something to worry about. I don't give a shit about race and public opinion. As it stands, I have no choice about the matter."

"Sure you do."

"No, Lucian," Logan said disapprovingly. "When it comes to the heart, there is no choice. It's like surfers catching the perfect wave. That's when you know you found the one; all you can do is ride the current and follow its flow. You have no choice about the direction, you only know with absolute certainty that you're caught in it."

"He'll figure it out one day, Lo. Just wait till he has a little chest hair on him. Maybe you need to get your nose out of those books, boy, and see about a girl."

"I see plenty of women," Lucian retorted. "And for your information, Mr. Wooly Mammoth, most women don't want to feel all that shit on a guy's chest."

"Thank God I don't date most women," Levi said.

I sneezed into the pillow and rubbed my nose. "Do you guys ever stop talking?"

The mattress depressed beside me and a hand gently stroked my leg. "Did you sleep well?" Logan asked.

"I slept a little bit," I said, clearing my throat and rolling on my back. "How long are we going to be in here for?" I stretched and Levi rolled on his side, facing the wall.

"How about forever?" Logan whispered.

"Levi snores, so I'm going to have to decline your proposition."

"I hope that's the only proposition of mine you decline, my sweet." Logan purred as he leaned over me. I pinched his earlobe and he stole a quick, minty kiss. His hand dipped below my jeans and a deep growl vibrated against my chest as his fingers clawed in the spot of my tattoo. I gave him a secretive smirk, as no one else knew about my tattoo aside from Christian and Finn, who were both sworn to secrecy.

"Leo's on his way back in," Lucian said, touching a monitor with his finger. A second later, the door to our secret room clicked open. Leo sat down on the sofa with a grim expression.

"It's done. The Overlord has made an official statement."

"What was said?" Levi sat up and rubbed his eye with the palm of his hand.

"The truth. Well, most of it. He emphasized the heroic deeds of the cop, and that will draw a huge sympathy vote. Not many people liked Tarek, and Chitahs hold self-sacrifice in great regard, even if he was only a human. I made a few calls, and there's already talk about generating a fund to donate money in his honor. Looks like something good might come of this, after all. The Overlord has privately spoken with Tarek's family, and my only guess is he's offering a settlement for their loss. The question will be if they take it or choose to pursue justice. They are continuing their investigation and haven't closed the case. The statement was just a formality."

Logan cleared his throat and sat up straight. "What are they doing with his position?"

Leo stretched his heavy legs and crossed one ankle over the other. "I can't even remember a time in history where a Lord was assassinated. Sorry, I didn't mean it that way, Logan. There'll be an open challenge, but none of his brothers want it."

"You're kidding me?" Levi marveled. "Jesus, they'll never have that opportunity again, and that speaks *volumes* about the kind of men they are."

"True, but not everyone is a born leader," Leo pointed out. "I don't think I could picture Tobias as Lord, could you?"

Lucian snorted and spun his chair around in circles. "Remember the party twenty years ago when Tobias put dishwashing suds in the fountain?"

"He's got to be at least a hundred years old and that shit never gets old for him," Levi remarked. "At least he'd bring a sense of humor to the Youngblood Pride."

"So his family isn't seeking retaliation?" I wondered aloud.

Logan rubbed his eye with the palm of his hand. "They disowned him years ago, so for them, this is probably closure."

It had slipped my mind that Tarek's brothers cut him off from the family when they found out he had raped his kindred spirit. I wondered why they allowed him to challenge for the position, but maybe they were concerned that it would shame the family if his dark past were made public. Or what if they had gained a newfound respect for him? The thought was unnerving. Time changes people, and sometimes not in a good way.

Leo scratched at his short beard. "The Overlord's word is good. Anyone who defies him and acts out in violence will be shunned. Unlike some Breeds, we thrive on companionship. Family is extremely important to us, and unity."

"Leo?"

He dropped his glance to where we lay.

"Thanks for being here. All of you. For standing by Logan and protecting him. I know you'd do it anyway because you're his family. It just means more to me now than it ever did."

Leo stretched himself into a standing position, as a man might who had been sitting for a very long time. He slowly walked toward the door and briefly stopped, looking down at the two of us. I knew our relationship was met with the most resistance by Leo. "We're here for the both of you."

He opened the door and joined Christian in the apartment.

"Logan?"

He leaned in and swept a few locks of hair away from my face, watching me with his rapturous eyes. "Yes?"

"I need to see Sunny."

CHAPTER 38

I T WAS EARLY SUNRISE, AND we were all on edge from the previous night. Logan drove me to Novis's mansion, while Christian followed behind on his motorcycle. The closer we got, the more I wanted to break down and cry. I hoped that she wouldn't hate me for not staying with her the whole time. Sunny needed rest and time alone to grieve—this I knew—but it didn't make our reunion any easier.

Logan sensed my nervousness and kissed my hand as he pulled up to the front. Novis had instructed the guards to let us enter the grounds without stopping the car and performing a search of any kind.

The inside of the house chilled my arms, but I allowed Novis to remove my jacket and put it away. Logan said goodbye as we agreed Christian would drive me home.

"She's locked herself away, and not even Adam could get through to her." Novis hiked up his jeans and paused on the landing of the stairs. "I don't believe they had a close enough relationship that she was willing to listen to him."

"Listen?" Now I was agitated. "Listen to what? The man she loved was killed."

Novis pressed his lips tightly and clasped his hands together. It took a minute before he said anything. "Adam feels responsible for his death. He tried to offer an apology but she didn't accept it."

"Where does your concern lie?"

A small line formed between his brows. "My Learner is always priority."

"And Sunny?"

He shrugged lightly. "She is but a mortal and death is a fact of life."

I stormed past him. "I thought you had a family?" When I reached the top of the stairs, I turned around. Novis slowly walked up each step with contemplative thought.

"I don't know how to feel about a mortal, Silver. What hope can I offer one who is fragile like glass? I have vague memories of this life, and have distanced myself from humans for this very reason."

"We're not immortal, Novis. We're all going to die someday. She might outlive us all. How can you deny yourself love because you're afraid of losing it? How can you deny yourself friendship because you're afraid of it severing? There's a woman in there who needs to know life is going to get better, and that she'll have people she can depend on to get her through it. You won't give her this comfort because she's human. I'm not even sure you can give *anyone* comfort. Adam is more than a Learner; he's a son. He looks up to you and respects you, but none of it matters if you're cold and distant when it comes to his needs and feelings."

I was certain that my nerves were taking hold and that's why I was venting to an ancient immortal who just so happened to be my boss. Perhaps not the best move.

My fingers wrapped around the doorknob to Sunny's room and I left Novis in the hall, closing the door behind me. The bed was to my left and straight ahead, a lacey white curtain veiled the morning sun.

I crawled on top of the white quilt and wrapped my arms around Sunny, careful not to touch her bandaged arm.

"Thanks for coming," she said in a weak voice.

"Did I wake you?"

She threaded her fingers through her blond waves and moved to sit up. I propped a pillow behind her back and then we held hands. She looked tired, as if she had cried out every emotion left in her body. I took a deep breath, knowing we were about to have one of those conversations that you never forget.

"Did Novis tell you?"

I shook my head. "Tell me what?"

"We're not having a funeral. He suggested an honorable burial, but Knox didn't want that. He told me once that he wanted to be cremated and have his ashes scattered in the Atlantic Ocean. It's where he grew up as a boy." She reflected for a moment and gazed out the window. "We talked about stuff like that," she said as a tear rolled down her cheek.

My heart broke. In that moment, we didn't speak, but wept for the loss. I couldn't imagine how hollowed out she felt, but I could see it in her eyes.

Sunny wiped her wet cheeks with the back of her hand. "Adam tried to apologize, but it's not his fault. He was angry, but none of us could have done anything differently. We never saw it coming. Knox died saving my life, Silver. Did they tell you that?"

I shook my head, allowing her to continue.

Her blue eyes glittered with pain and love as her lip swelled up a little. "He leapt on top of me and took the bullets," she said in a shaky voice. "All for them."

"Who?"

She looked up and smiled sadly. "The babies."

I gasped and my heart did a number. "You're pregnant?"

Sunny nodded. "Six weeks. I went to a Relic and found out that we're having twins."

"You didn't tell me."

"I wanted to surprise everyone," she said in a broken voice.

We fell into an embrace and I cried against her shoulder.

She wiped her nose and sat back, grimacing at her arm. "Novis doesn't know, but it's why I didn't want any pain medication."

"Knox knew?"

"He was so excited," she said wistfully, shaking her head. "Since the night we found out, he sang songs. Oh my gosh, have you ever heard that man sing?" She laughed through tears and when her lip quivered, she took another calming breath.

Sunny was hanging on by a thread.

"When he was shot and lying on top of me, Knox told me that he loved me," she said, losing her voice as tears streamed from her eyes. "I could feel him all over me, but I couldn't hold him. I just wanted to touch his cheek and tell him how much I loved him."

"He knew." I leaned forward and wiped her tears away, letting her tell the story.

She licked her upper lip and took another deep breath. "After that, it was okay. I knew he was going to die and then he started singing to the babies. He just rested his hand on my belly and sang 'Hush Little Baby', except he switched the Momma line around to Daddy. His last breath was singing about the diamond ring."

Then her hand opened, one she had been holding in a tight fist the whole time. In the palm of her hand was a diamond ring.

"Isn't it beautiful?" she said, sniffing a few times. "It was in his pocket; they found it later. Knox was going to ask me to marry him… and I would have said yes."

"I'm so sorry," I said, lacking the right words to make any of this grievous pain go away.

She smiled through the tears. "Don't be. I'm not. I truly knew what it was to be loved hard. Knox was my future, and I can't imagine one without him. But I have to, because the babies need me now. He gave me something I'd never imagined possible: to be in a relationship and to want children. You know those things never mattered before, but he left me with a legacy of hope. Maybe I'll never have another man give me the kind of love and devotion that Knox did, but I'm okay with that. He changed me," she said, rubbing her belly. "He said that if we have a little girl, we should name her Zoë."

I held my breath. "Why would he choose that name?"

"I think he always felt bad you were forced into this new life. I still called you Zoë sometimes, and he knew how much our friendship meant. If we have a boy, I'm going to call him Knox."

"Wasn't that his last name?"

"The children will keep my last name. Do you think I'd name my baby Knox Knox?"

We both laughed so hard that it eased some of the tension.

"When are you going to have the ceremony?" I asked.

She gazed out the window and wiped her cheeks. "I don't know; when it's right, I guess. I need more time." Then her face distorted into one of devastation. "I wanted to grow old with him," she whispered in a soft voice. "And call him old man. Knox would have made a tremendous father. I don't want our babies growing up not knowing how wonderful he was." After a deep breath, she finally erased the silence. "Will you take the trip to the ocean with me when it's time?"

"You really have to ask me that? Sunny, I'd follow you to Hell if you needed me to. We'll all be there; Knox has a lot of people who care for him *and* you. I just don't want you to get too upset. I'm not sure how that would affect the pregnancy but—"

"Don't worry," she said, holding my hand, "I'm stronger than you think I am. Knox is still alive." She placed my hand on her stomach and smiled. "This is the hardest thing I've ever done, but he left me such a beautiful gift. He left me love and hope. I couldn't have had those things on my own, and I want these babies to know just how special he was. Knox was a one of a kind, and the love of my life. He gave up his life so that his children would live—so that I would live, and I owe it to him to keep on living."

"Move in with me, Sunny. We'll take care of you."

"No," she insisted. "I have to figure this out. Novis said I could stay here for a little while, but he doesn't know about my condition, so that may not last long."

"Are you keeping it a secret?"

"Not really. There just wasn't a moment that seemed right to bring it up." She grimaced and then slammed her eyes shut. "I don't know what to do, Silver. He just painted the baby room green. And it's the most hideous color." After she wiped her eyes, she looked toward the window again. "Living at home without Knox there… I just *can't*."

"You're better off here," I agreed. "There's too much trouble following me around these days."

She snorted. "I see nothing has changed."

"Actually, something has," I said, fidgeting with my hands. "I've accepted Logan's claim. I don't think we can legally get married or mated, but I've made the decision to make what we have permanent."

I cringed, uncertain if it was the right time to spring that kind of news on her.

Her right arm curved around me. "Hold on to him for as long as you can. Cherish every moment."

The Relic had ordered Sunny to remain in bed for a couple of days until her arm improved. She was encouraged to walk around the room and sit in the sunshine, but the stitches had to heal first. She stood by the window after we said our goodbyes, and I opened the door and stepped into the hall with Novis.

"How is she doing?" he said in a quiet voice. "She won't eat."

"She's getting through it," I whispered. "It's too soon to expect miracles. Why is Knox's hat in a Ziploc bag on the dresser?"

His mouth formed a grim line. "She said something about not wanting to lose his smell."

I sighed heavily. "You need to know something because I want to make sure she's taken care of properly. Sunny's pregnant."

He blanched, turning his wide eyes toward the bedroom.

"She's carrying Knox's twins, and I want her to have the best care while she's here. Don't make her eat anything or do anything that would hurt them. She needs to be treated by her own Relic; she mentioned seeing someone. Don't give her any medication unless it's—"

Before I could finish, Novis flashed into the room and caught Sunny. Her legs had weakened and she almost collapsed. He lifted her into his arms and placed her on the bed, handing her a glass of water from the bedside table. She took a slow sip and he adjusted the pillows behind her before returning to the hall.

He looked like a man who had just seen a train collision. As Novis shut the door, the light in his eyes pulsed as his lips peeled back. "I can't care for this human the way she needs to be."

"You will," I said. "She won't stay with me and she doesn't have any other place to go that's safe, considering all that's going on."

"What can I offer her?"

I touched his arm. "Compassion? I don't know how much of that you have left, but you once mentioned to me that you'd had a family of your own."

"They were murdered in front of me," he said in a flat voice. "That was my mortal life. I had three children slain by my enemy, and you do not want to know how victims in my time were sent to slaughter."

"So on some level, you can relate to her suffering?"

He acknowledged the truth with his eyes.

"Just talk to her, Novis. Share your story; empathize with her pain. She just needs someone to listen, not someone who wants her to bury her past and her love for that man. I can't stay, but keep a phone or laptop in her room so I can talk to her."

I left with all the hope in the world that he would offer her a shoulder to lean on. I couldn't be there for her every minute, but I'd be there for her for the rest of her life. I hoped that counted for something.

Christian had lent me his trench coat for the motorcycle ride. It didn't take long before we were home, and I was certain that somewhere along the stretch of highway, we had broken the sound barrier.

Logan had taken off to help his brothers clean his condo and replace the windows. There was talk about using laminated glass, although I had no idea what that was supposed to do. I jokingly suggested they install mirrored glass, like the kind that office buildings used. Especially since Logan enjoyed sleeping and walking around in the nude. Kidding aside, I reminded them that Logan's home wasn't a fort, and you couldn't keep a determined man out.

I ran inside, tossing my coat on the hook. Christian remained in the garage to work on his bike. As I skidded around the corner to take a hot shower, I bumped into Simon and nearly fell on my ass before he grabbed my shirt and almost ripped it off.

"Damn," he said. "You should buy cheaper fabric. That would have been spectacular. You put a fright into us, you know."

I tugged at his leather collar. "Another night out?"

He shrugged. "Can't a bloke accessorize?" A short grin spread across his face, flashing his dimple as I poked my finger in it. Simon shook his head as if I were being childish and put me into a headlock. I did a little maneuver and got out of it. He arched his brows, clearly impressed.

"You remember the truck that drove us home? Novis found out it never arrived at the location they were ordered to go to."

"He didn't mention anything," I said in bewilderment. "I was just there."

"Rang a few minutes ago. I wager I know who's behind it."

A heavy thought sank in: Nero now had access to the files. He would figure out that Samil was not a unique Creator—that it really had more to do with the names on the list he selected in addition to how we were created, which I'm sure he could have discovered from one of the people he kept. A Creator's light made our abilities stronger, or gave us rare gifts. In any case, Nero was in control of the game, and only God knows where it was going to lead.

"Does Justus know?"

He shook his head. "You should go downstairs. Page is here. Something about her being sick again, so he called a *Relic*. Lovely woman if you're thinking of having a lobotomy done."

I raced down the elevator lift and met Justus in the hallway. He was uncharacteristically sitting on the floor. I knelt in front of him. "Is everything okay?"

Justus had a worry line on his forehead that would have created a permanent wrinkle had he not been ageless.

"How long has the Relic been in there?"

"Hours. She's running tests."

"Well, it takes a while when they have to set up their equipment," I said. "It sounds like she's being thorough. Do you know if the blood and medicine were destroyed in the lab? We cleared out the files but left behind the equipment, and I don't know what's been going on lately."

"Novis had his people take care of that."

"Good."

"I should get used to my Learner being in the midst of World War Three," he said.

"Trouble goes, I follow."

The door pulled open and a little old woman emerged with her bag in hand, lingering in the doorway. She wore nude stockings that stopped short three inches from the hem of her brown dress. "It's a good thing she wasn't on that morphine longer than she was or at a higher dose, or that would have become a problem."

"I didn't notice any immediate signs of withdrawal," Justus said, standing up.

The Relic stepped through and closed the door behind her. "She's finally asleep, so I suggest you let her rest. You should be ashamed for letting her become so sleep deprived."

Justus paled at her punishing words and folded his arms, cursing beneath his breath. "Will she recover?"

"She needs sleep and food. My advice? Keep work away from her for a while; too much stress on the body is no good and will only lower the immune system and trigger a happy home for viruses to spring to life."

"Is that what she has?"

The Relic made a cackling sound that was similar to a crow. "I've checked her blood and everything looks normal. She was given sedatives along with unknown drugs and we'll have to see how they wear off, so I'll be visiting her again."

The Relic moved down the hall and Simon held a blindfold between his fingers. "I don't think the blindfold will be necessary, Mage. I have a fantastic sense of converting movement into a mental image. I should be able to find my way up."

Justus approached the Relic. "Is there any medicine I need to give her, outside of sleep and food?"

She glanced over her shoulder and wrinkled her wide nose. "I swear, you men are about as bright as a bottomless pit. She needs to get all the toxins out of her system, not *in*. My fee has been paid, so you owe me nothing, Charmer. I'll see myself out."

His blue eyes memorized every line in the floor as if it were a mathematical equation.

"What are you going to do?" I whispered.

He took a deep breath and erased all his worry lines. "Make her breakfast."

That he did.

Burnt toast and undercooked eggs, but Page ate every bite.

Not soon after, I heard them arguing in his bedroom and she

stormed out. Simon drove Page home and I briefly spoke with her before she left. Page didn't feel safe in her apartment anymore and was planning to move. I didn't ask what she'd fought with Justus about and why she was in such a hurry to leave, I simply let her know I was there if she needed to talk. Justus had an abrasive way about him, and I guess part of me knew it was only a matter of time before she realized he was not a perfect piece of furniture—that some assembly was required.

Some people just don't have the patience to invest that much time and effort when it comes to a relationship.

CHAPTER 39

L OGAN MADE GOOD ON HIS promise and took me out to see a movie three times that week. The women in the theater turned around several times to stare at him. I smiled privately and squeezed his hand, knowing he was mine.

I visited with Sunny twice and kept a laptop in my bedroom with instant messenger open so she could talk to me whenever she was feeling alone. She said it didn't seem right coming to stay with me because of the murder and mentioned she wanted to find out where her brother was. He traveled a lot and had fallen out of touch with her over the past year or so. I knew she needed Kane in her life now more than ever.

I decided to stick with my routine and went to Simon's house on Friday for game night. He talked me into a backgammon drinking game and before the night was through, I hid the dice and locked myself in his bedroom, threatening to dunk his leather pants in the bathtub if he didn't let me win. I had never been a sore loser until I met Simon. That man could make me completely insane. The following Friday, I brought Logan with me because Simon said I wasn't worthy competition. I pretended to be insulted and sulked on the sofa with my glass of wine while they tried to save the planet in some new video game.

Christian remained my guard, and there was no weirdness between us.

Beyond the usual.

On the odd occasion, I would remember what had happened between us and somehow he could always read my expression. He'd say something infuriating and get me into a verbal sparring match with him. I would crack Irish jokes while he would say that I had sprung from my mother's loins, mouth first.

Christian was a man who was destined to live alone.

Logan invited me out with his brothers for a bite to eat and a drink at the bar. It was a ritual of theirs, and it was a great feeling to be a part of it. Leo wasn't as rambunctious as his younger brothers were. He was a serious man with a warm personality, but I still got nervous in his presence. He just had that vibe, and it had something to do with the fact that he was the eldest. I hadn't met their father; he traveled a lot for work and dropped into town only now and again. I had a sense that he wouldn't be receptive of our relationship, but Logan never spoke a word about it.

Finn was growing increasingly self-assured. In the beginning, he had little control over his wolf and shifted in public without a second thought. He still had his moments, but not around humans. The Cross brothers were rubbing off on him in all the best ways. Except that Finn had picked up an annoying habit of belching, thanks to Levi.

He fit right in.

Lucian had only gone out with us once, but being the introvert in the family, that didn't come as a surprise.

Tonight I had been given an assignment by my boss. Maybe I *was* just an apprentice, but I enjoyed getting assignments other than a consultation for my opinion. I was a girl who needed to be a street cop, not a paper pusher.

So I hopped in the Silver Bullet—the name Christian had baptized my car with—and headed across town just after sunset.

Novis had given me the location to a human club and I immediately got butterflies going to an unfamiliar place by myself. Breed clubs were like a church, or Switzerland. In a human establishment, all bets were off. Sometimes juicers hung out there, looking for new Learners who still hadn't left their old life behind. Juicing was such a problem because Mage light was addictive, like a drug. I had to periodically flare and release my energy in small bursts in case another Mage was in the area. Christian stayed close behind as I made my way inside.

Novis hadn't told me the name of the man I was meeting up

with, nor had he told me what he looked like. He'd handed me an envelope, suggesting that I pay close attention to what the man said and did and trust my instincts. Well, it was all very James Bond, but I was *so* in.

As instructed, I sat at the bar wearing a red button-up blouse. I sized up the humans getting their happy hour on and decided to order a bottle of weak beer. I tore pieces off the label, making occasional checks on my surroundings.

"You should order a drink that has taste," a deep and magnificent voice said. I turned to the left and nearly tipped my bottle over.

Towering over me was the Chitah Overlord. He slipped his arm around my back and guided me to a vacant booth, which was amusing to watch him fit in. He had to angle his body to stretch out his legs beneath the table. Women stared at him like he was royalty; they couldn't help it. His coal-black hair and bright eyes were as magnetic as his height, and he had years of wisdom carved in the small lines on his face and brow. His guards spaced apart, taking positions at key points in the room.

"I wasn't expecting it to be you," I said. "Novis didn't mention who I was meeting."

He gave a hint of a smile and pulled a heavy black scarf away from his neck. His short hair had a slight wave to it that reminded me of a classic style I'd seen in old movies. It wasn't uncommon for a Chitah to go out in public wearing contacts or sunglasses so they wouldn't stand out. Logan often kept his gaze low to the ground. The Overlord did none of the above, and these days with special FX contacts, I didn't think most people would think twice about it. How remarkably easy it was for Chitahs to blend into the modern world compared to centuries past.

"If you did not expect me, then Novis kept his word. It is important that we keep our distance and not show public signs of association. It creates too much… speculation. When we do speak on matters of the utmost secrecy, we cannot afford to draw attention."

"Is that why we're in a human bar?"

He nodded very slowly.

"So how do you know there aren't any Vampires here listening?

You can't smell a Vampire."

"What a clever Mage, thinking outside the box. I always liked that expression. Colorful, isn't it?"

"Guess I never thought much about it. I always liked 'coloring outside the lines' myself."

He studied our busy surroundings and smiled enigmatically. The Overlord didn't strike me as a man who got out much, and if he did, he sure didn't spend time lingering with the lower class. It made him wildly fascinating.

"You are uninjured from the attack? I hope my guards were of some protection," he ground out, seemingly annoyed.

"Yes, no injuries to speak of. It could have been a whole lot worse if they hadn't been there to buffer the attack. Thank you, your Lordship, um, Overlor—Sir."

He tucked his chin against his chest and laughed the way a man does to hide his amusement. "Sire is what I'm usually addressed as. But between you and me," he whispered, "I hate the formalities. Please, call me Quaid."

"Do you want a drink, Quaid?" That felt wrong. He was royalty and I was speaking to him like a regular person.

"I believe it is the male who orders the drink for the female," he pointed out.

"Did the female lose her voice?"

"No, but perhaps she lost her manners."

I tapped my fingers on the table. "What's so rude about being polite?"

Quaid stirred with laughter. "Now I know what the Chitah sees in the Mage."

I glanced at the bartender near our table and pointed at my bottle, holding two fingers in the air.

"He definitely bit off more than he can chew," I remarked as the waitress sauntered over with our refills.

"Mee-yow," she said, looking Quaid over. "Let me know if I can bring you a *big boy* drink. I'm Tina. Just yell out if you need anything, Stretch." She winked and Quaid looked offended by the casualness with which she openly hit on him. After setting our beers and a bowl of pretzels on the table, Tina shook a tail feather and disappeared.

"That was rude," I grumbled.

"How so?"

"She didn't even presume that I might be your girlfriend."

"Perhaps she did," he said as he lifted the bottle, staring at it.

"Go on, Quaid, live a little. It won't kill you, but it might put some hair on your chest."

He wiped the lip of the bottle and risked a careful sip, cringing at the bitter flavor. "Fascinating. You enjoy this?"

"Nope, but it passes the time."

Quaid studied the bowl of pretzels before he lifted one and tasted it with his tongue.

"Tell me you've seen a pretzel before? You're the Overlord. If I was in your position, I'd make sure my pantry was stocked full of ice cream, chocolate bars, and those horrible cheese and crackers with the little red stick." I snorted into my bottle of beer as if I were having a conversation with an old friend.

"I have staff to do the cooking, so there is no need for me to go out on such excursions. My food is carefully prepared by a personal chef."

"My chef's name is Boyardee." I snickered. Then I realized he didn't get the joke so it made it less funny. "In my humble opinion, I think you should go shopping one day and just throw a bunch of food in your cart and taste the world. I'm telling you, if all they serve you is lamb chops and roasted potatoes, you're really missing out on the little things."

"So I gather," he said, crunching on his pretzel and grabbing another. "Interesting. Stale bread seasoned with salt. So tell me, young Mage, what is it that you have for me?"

I reached inside my satchel and pulled out a manila envelope, sliding it to his side of the table. He rubbed his fingers together, knocking off a few salt granules before reviewing the contents. Several quiet moments passed as he read the paper, pulling pretzels to his mouth almost involuntarily. Finally, he leaned back and tapped his finger on the bottle, eyeing me.

A Chitah's gaze is terrifying; it's more than a gaze, it's a threat. If you dare to look deep enough, you can almost see the savage animal within, prowling patiently and waiting for you to rattle its cage. I lowered my eyes and felt my stomach do a somersault with a back handspring. My hands trembled as I peeled the label from my beer and when the bottle tipped over, I quickly grabbed it, only spilling a few drops. Maybe I had a record for spilling beer on laps, but this was one person I didn't want to end up on that long list of names.

"I thought a lot about what you said that night. You don't resemble a Chitah; how is it that you are half?"

I shrugged. "Kind of a long story on that," I stated, deciding not to go into the details. "I've never carried any physical characteristics of a Chitah, even in my human form."

"Ah, but you weren't so human, now were you?" His voice was thick and deep, leaving goose bumps across my arm.

"Guess not."

"Your employer does not bring me good news," he said, tucking the paper in the envelope. "The files were stolen?"

I sank into my chair.

"Extremists are difficult to control. This information tells me that there are Chitahs aiding in the experimentation, either willingly or not."

Aside from the Chitah DNA, someone had been supplying them with Chitah venom. Were they holding one prisoner and using him for their experiments? I couldn't imagine, as he would be difficult to contain and control. Especially since some Chitahs had the ability to dreamwalk. Quaid appeared to have more information in his hands than I knew about.

"I hope this doesn't bring too much trouble for you," I said. "I'm sure Novis has good reason for telling you whatever is in the note."

"You are correct. I do hate to cut our time short, but I must say that I have had a pleasant evening with you, Silver. It is not very often that I sit and converse with a Mage."

Taking that as my cue, I slid out of my seat. As I slung my purse over my shoulder, I caught a glimpse of the Overlord dumping the bowl of pretzels into his coat pocket. I turned my smile away to the crowd of drinkers, pretending to fumble for my keys.

"Do you have a driver?"

"No, I drove. Is there a message you want me to deliver to Novis?"

We moved toward the door and Quaid slipped his arm around my shoulder, guiding me through the crowd. Heads turned, watching a man who was at least a foot taller than me part the crowd like a superstar. His guards fell into place by the time we were outside, and he tipped his hand, signaling for them to stay back.

"Please tell Novis that his gesture in sharing information is one I will not forget. We have never been allies, but we have made progress with small steps to build trust between us. Regardless of what I have learned, it is not information that I can share publicly, therefore my hands remain tied when it comes to legal matters. Do drive safe, and my gratitude for the beer." He smiled warmly as his fingers fished in his pocket.

There was an awkward moment when I thought I was supposed to do something, so I bowed a little and said, "Sire."

Quaid spun around without a word and an army of men escorted him to his car.

Page nervously wrung her cold hands together as she sat in her car, staring down a paved walkway that led into the city park. She thought about how leaving Justus might have been the hardest thing she'd done, but it was the right thing to do. It would be unfair to drag him into her messy life. It wouldn't take long for a man like him to move on. It's not as if they were in a relationship, and he had every woman at his disposal.

The day after she had gone home, a delivery arrived at her doorstep. Justus had sent her a gold bracelet, and Page had to send it back without explanation. He shouldn't have spent so much on her. The most romantic thing he'd done was wipe her forehead when she was sick.

People just didn't click with her on a personal level because outside of work, she was a very private person. But at the end of the day, Page was just a girl who loved to curl up in her chair and enjoy watching the rain, working crossword puzzles, and dabbling a little at knitting. It was something her grandmother had done very well and Page tried to keep her spirit alive, even though she wasn't any good at it. She worked in a servitude position, and that was a humbling job to have. Her own needs were often put aside to help others. But what a great feeling it was at the end of the day to know she made a difference.

Justus seemed to get who she was, but they barely knew each other and this was for the best. It brought a small measure of comfort to have the memory of their time together. Maybe having a small piece of something wonderful is better than having it all, only to watch it crumble into a regretful ending.

The more time that he'd spent with her, the more she noticed him letting his guard down and revealing the compassionate man he truly was. In the end, they would have been incompatible. Better to not get attached to a man who would get bored with her and move on to the next woman.

Page had contacted Novis to request permission to have Slater's memory temporarily restored. It was regretful they had completed their questioning so soon without allowing her to provide any input.

"You realize the danger of this?" Christian asked from the passenger seat of her car.

"It shouldn't have been done so soon, Christian. Not without knowing the right things to ask. Are you sure it's okay for you to be here? Away from Silver, I mean."

"Novis has relieved me of my duties for one evening while she's in Logan's care." He arched his back around the seat to face her but she caught his black eyes drifting behind the car. "Consider me a loaner. Are you ready?"

Page nodded and they got out of the car, scaring a rabbit who hopped across the pathway and disappeared under a bush. The humidity created orange halos around the street lamps and they walked down a trail until they caught sight of a wooden bench with a man sitting on it. Her heart raced and Christian gripped her arm.

"The Mage assigned to keep an eye on Slater dropped him off, so we're alone."

"Mage?" she asked.

"The ones given a clean slate have to be watched. They tend to *wander*," he said, tapping a finger against his head. "Years ago, many committed suicide because of the gaps in their memory. Over the years, we've improved our techniques by implanting false memories so that they can go about living a regular routine. Slater thinks his name is Joseph and that he's been working in a coffee shop since he was nineteen."

Page tugged at her collar, saddened by the idea of it. As much as she despised Slater for what he'd done, scrubbing a Relic was a cruel punishment. She couldn't imagine having her memories and ancient knowledge erased. Then again, she wasn't so sure they could wipe him of that knowledge. It was hard-wired in their DNA and became as natural as breathing.

"We don't need protection?"

Christian made a disgusted sound and rolled his eyes. "He's only a Relic, no offense."

Page cupped her hand over her nose and blew a heated breath to warm it. Once they approached the bench, Slater looked up without a hint of recognition. "Are you lost?"

Christian bent down in front of him, pulling him into a hypnotic stare. The Vampire picked the combination to a mental lock and without so much as an audible click, the expression on Slater's face changed when Christian whispered a word.

Slater blinked and began looking around.

The Vampire wagged his finger. "Before you get any ideas of running, be reminded that you won't get far." He took his strong hand and clamped it over Slater's knee as a warning. Then he looked up and nodded at Page. "Go on now, let's get it over with."

Slater abruptly shouted, "What have you done to me? You can't do this; it's not right!"

"I need to talk to you," Page said in a lulling voice, moving into his line of vision.

"I got nothing to say to you, bitch." He flinched and recoiled from Christian, whose hand had tightened ever so slightly.

The icy wind licked the back of her neck and she shivered,

thinking she should have worn her scarf. "Slater, I need to know what the injections were that you gave to me."

He jerked back with a breathy laugh, staring up at her. "You know what I'd like to know? Why knowledge had to be wasted on someone like you, who doesn't even want to pass it on. You're a stupid woman."

"Some things just aren't meant to be, Slater. Not everything can go on forever—that's nature. You of all people should understand that, given your knowledge of extinct Breeds."

"Yeah, yeah, but we have the power to prevent that. Technology has opened doors. Why couldn't you see it my way? Our baby would have been exceptional, one that prophets talk about."

"Your ego disgusts me," she said, curling her lip into a snarl. "I'm not an incubator, but that's what you set out to make me, isn't it? Just something to grow your little science experiment in."

He leaned back with his arms draped across the back of the bench. "What did you bring me here for? To torment me with the truth that I'm going to live the rest of my life thinking I serve coffee for eight bucks an hour? Enlighten me, for the love of Christ."

"Why don't you enlighten me, and *tell me* what you injected me with?"

"Something those idiots hadn't thought of; they were so busy using humans as a Petri dish making cocktails that they didn't even comprehend they had some of the right techniques. All the right tools at their fingertips, but the formula was all wrong."

Page folded her arms, tucking her cold fingers beneath her pea coat. "So I was just a pawn for science?"

He scooted down in his seat. "Why not?" He gave her a relaxed smile and Page tightened her fists, sliding them inside her coat pockets. "We needed someone with genetics close to a human, but not quite. Why spend all that time looking for a Chitah human when we had a perfectly good Relic? You and I both know there's something different in our DNA, and yet we aren't like the rest of them. A human body can't nurture and develop a Breed embryo."

"What kind of mutant baby did you have in mind for me? A Sensor and Gemini? Or maybe a Vampire and a Chitah."

Slater snorted and rubbed his scruffy beard. "Only *ours*, Page. It was to be my baby. But all things would have been possible. Now we'll never know."

Her knees weakened. "I need to know what you put in the injections, Slater."

He leaned to the left and laughed wickedly. "I just bet you'd like to know, wouldn't you? That's the only trump card I have left in my hand, and I think I'll keep it. If you ever decide to take me out of my hell at Latte Lovers, then by all means, give me a call." He challenged her with a long, contemptuous stare.

Page sighed and touched Christian's shoulder. "I'm finished. He isn't going to talk. *Do it.*"

Christian looked up and cold terror spiked through her when he slumped over with a wooden stick poking out of his neck. Slater crouched over him for a second before he stood up and confronted Page with a malicious grin.

"Stupid Vampires—taking someone to a park with trees," he said, snatching her coat when she tried to turn away. "No, no, honey. You're not going anywhere. It's too late for that."

He yanked her against him and puckered his lips for a mocking kiss.

Page screamed.

CHAPTER 40

J USTUS HAD DECIDED TO SIT outside Page's apartment that
evening. He remained quiet in the shadows, keeping a close
watch for intruders.

When she had returned the gold bracelet, he felt the sharp sting
of rejection.

It wasn't enough.

He had a fortune at his disposal and it must have appeared that
he thought very little of her. It was so delicate—like Page—and
didn't cost very much. *Foolish gesture*, he thought. Emeralds would
have been better.

Justus knew something was afoot when Christian arrived
unexpectedly with Silver nowhere in sight. It was no secret between
the two of them that Justus was shadowing close behind. Christian
only acknowledged him once by a quick glance and then looked away.

They took off in Page's car and Justus tailed behind in his silver
Aston Martin. Page rushed through a red light and briefly lost him.
When he finally sped up, he had a hunch he knew where they had
gone. As he rolled into a parking space in the public park just a few
spaces away from her car, alarm ran up his spine. It was too late for
her to be wandering the streets, and it concerned him that she was
in need of a guard.

The hairs on his arms stood up when he tasted the energy buzz,
the way he often did in the club when emotions were ripe. He
somehow sensed Page in a way he couldn't explain; he didn't just feel
her, he gravitated toward her.

His heart stopped when he saw Slater shaking her as they
argued by a park bench beneath a canopy of trees. They were too
far out of range for him to hear what was said. All he saw was Slater

hurting Page.

With blinding speed, Justus flashed across the grounds and grabbed him by the throat. Slater let go of Page and she stumbled backward.

"Fuck you," Slater spat. When he reached out for Page, Justus tightened his grip.

That's when Justus saw the glimmer from his own dagger pulled out from beneath his shirt, and he felt the searing pain of skin separating as Slater swiped the blade across his chest. Blood immediately soaked through his shirt and Justus stepped back. Before he could react, the Relic drove the blade through his right shoulder, still holding on to the handle. Little did he know that it wasn't a stunner.

Slater's inexperience with knives showed. Hundreds of years of skilled practice had taught Justus how to disarm his enemy. Tonight that enemy would feel that cold steel in his body, pushed in to the hilt. He could have easily thrown his energy into Slater and ended it before it began. The level of power surging through Justus at that moment was so electric that he could have touched a power grid and taken out the lights in three states. But he leveled it down, stepping back and to the side until the blade slowly came out. In a quick motion, he snatched Slater's wrist, breaking it as he disarmed him.

Justus grabbed the knife and threw a hard fist into Slater's face. The Relic dropped like a bag of bricks. Justus fell to his knees and heard Page gasp; it distracted him for only a moment. He gripped the dagger with the sharp blade arrowing toward the Relic's heart as he pinned him down with his left arm across his throat. When Justus lifted his head, he saw Page backing up.

She shouldn't have to watch this. "Turn away," Justus said in cold words. "Go help Christian."

Slater was too unstable and couldn't be allowed to wander freely after another scrubbing. There was no guarantee it would work, and he had become a dangerous liability—one they couldn't bring to justice because of the risk. Justus was left with only one alternative.

When she turned her back to him, Justus plunged the blade into Slater's heart. In seconds, the man's life came to a staggering halt. He rose to his feet and looked down at the Relic indifferently. He held no remorse for a man who would inflict harm on a woman. Justus believed there was a moral code of honor, and that all men had an obligation to protect women and children.

Page knelt before Christian, who lay motionless on the concrete with a stick protruding from his neck and a pool of dark blood collecting beneath his head. She grimaced before pulling it out.

Christian rolled over, gasping and spitting out a mouthful of blood.

"Jaysus. I'd much rather get it in the chest any day. It's when they go for the neck—there should be a law against it," he coughed out, holding his throat. He stared at the blood on his hand and shook it angrily, wiping his fingers across his dark pants. "I should have been listening when his hands moved out of sight. The stick could have been sitting on top of the bench. Hell if I know."

Justus understood Christian's frustration—he himself had foolishly underestimated the man because he was a Relic. Only certain kinds of wood paralyzed a Vampire, and Christian hadn't considered his surroundings.

Page ran her fingers through her hair and he noticed the humidity had caused it to kink up at the ends. "I guess now we'll never know the secrets he kept in that head of his."

Justus stepped forward, his combat boots scraping along the concrete. He lowered his eyes and watched the way her hands trembled. "Would you rather he killed you?"

"Slater wouldn't have killed me; he was too polluted with the idea of impregnating me with his DNA so he could create a child with unparalleled knowledge."

Justus knelt down on one knee and tucked a strand of loose hair behind her ear. "Will you come home with me?" The moment the words left his lips, his chest constricted. He'd spent years caging his heart, and now it was on his sleeve.

She lifted her soft brown eyes to his and turned her beautiful mouth to the side. "It's over, Justus. I don't know that it ever really began, but this will never work out between us. I'm not the kind of woman that's good for you."

Christian slowly walked out of earshot, although for a Vampire, that would have to be the next state over. The illusion of privacy was merely a common courtesy.

"I care for you, Page. I want to see that you're looked after properly."

"Like one of your cars?" she suggested. "I'm not a possession. I know you think your heart is in the right place, but you'll regret it. We can't build a relationship out of one night. One beautiful night. I'll never forget you, Justus. The *real* you that you allowed me to see. I'll still be around for Silver, but I don't want you to be confused about how I feel. We can't see each other anymore."

"What has changed in you?" Never had Justus been denied by a woman; he had always been pursued, not the pursuer. Now it seemed there was nothing he could say to remedy what had happened between them, and he still wasn't sure what that was, but he had a good idea that the sex had everything to do with it. "What have I done to displease you?"

"Nothing, Justus. It's not you, it's me. And God, I hate that line, but it's true. You deserve to find a woman who will treat you right, someone who's also a Mage. We're just on different levels, and I'm mortal. Have you considered that in twenty years, I'm going to start getting grey hairs and arthritis? Don't even think about doing this to yourself. It's for the best, and it's a decision I've made that you can't change. If you really do care for me, then you'll let me go."

Two weeks later, I asked Sunny's permission to borrow Knox's ashes. They were kept safe in a beautiful brass urn. Knox wouldn't have wanted anything fussy or silver, plus he always liked to say he had big brass ones. Sunny hadn't come to terms with releasing his ashes just yet, but we knew the time would be coming soon enough. So it was suggested that we spend an evening with Knox, honoring his memory.

I placed the urn on the coffee table in our living room and we turned off the lights and lit up the hurricane lanterns, placing them around the seating area. Christian came up with the idea of an Irish sendoff, one where we would spend the evening drinking and sharing memories about Knox. He didn't know him very well but said it would bring peace to the living.

Justus sat with us for a little while, but he retired downstairs when Page arrived. He had a lot on his mind after finding out the documents in the truck had been stolen. Without him in the room, it was chilly, and I'd put on my slipper-socks. Page curled up with her oversized sweater pulled over her knees, and Simon tucked his hands in his leather jacket—the one with the teeth marks on the shoulder.

It was a somber occasion at first, but once we slammed down a few shots, the chatter began. Simon, who normally was the first to crack a Knox joke, was uncharacteristically quiet. He kept his face in the palm of his hand, studying the rim of his glass before each shot.

"I remember one night just after he quit smoking, we went to get some ice cream at that little store on Beacon Street," I said, laughter starting to bubble. "Knox disappeared and when Sunny went to look for him, she found him in the ladies' room."

"Aye, now there's an interesting place to be hanging around in," Christian said sarcastically, rolling his eyes to the ceiling.

I snorted and topped off my vodka. "He walked into the wrong bathroom; I guess he was in a hurry to light up. When Sunny swung the door open, he was standing on top of the toilet with a cigarette in his mouth, blowing the smoke in the vents. He was so startled that his foot slipped into the toilet and the automatic flusher went off." I laughed, tears streaming. "He had to walk home barefoot that day."

An hour later, the men drifted into the dining room and were on their fourth round of cards. Leo, Simon, and Logan were whooping and groaning, and I heard hands slapping down on the table as they continued knocking back drinks. I joined them for one round until Page brought out the deli sandwiches she had ordered. They went fast, and I devoured a ham and avocado before grabbing a bag of Doritos and heading back into the living room, leaving her to watch the men play cards. I'm not sure what game they were playing when I left, but each had a card stuck to his forehead.

Page didn't drink because she was driving and also on call for work, so she stuck to root beer, putting a dollop of ice cream in the glass to kick it up a notch. She'd taken over some of Slater's appointments and put in a request for a new partner to ease the burden. She wasn't confident that one would be assigned to her since they paired up Relics early on; anyone at this stage might be unstable or unqualified. Page was likely going to search for one herself or reduce her clientele. I knew something had happened between her and Justus, but I didn't bring it up because it seemed pretty mutual from the way they were both behaving.

I stumbled over the white flokati rug that Adam had given me for my birthday. He was the one who brought the ashes over, but he didn't join in the festivities in the other room. He sat quietly in the living room, staring at the urn while drinking his stout. Losing Knox was more personal to him than the rest of us because he was not just a friend but had watched it all go down. He had the same contemplative look a man might have standing on the edge of the world.

Adam was half-asleep on the sofa, lifting an eye to watch me.

"You drink like a fish," he murmured.

"You're one to talk, Shamu. How many kegs did you guzzle down?"

His glazed eyes slanted my way and he tossed a pillow at my head. My Adam was slowly returning, scars and all. They marked his jaw and lacerated his forehead and eye. Since that night, he always kept his jacket on or wore long sleeves. I knew the explosion had scarred him elsewhere, but I didn't know how to express to him that it didn't matter to me.

He ran his hand through his wavy dark hair and scratched his bristly chin before resting his fist against his cheek. "So, it's serious now with Logan?"

Adam watched me take a few swallows of beer and my voice softened. "I know you're thinking I'm rushing into this, but I can't begin to explain how I feel when I'm with him, Adam. He's not perfect, I'm not perfect, but together… we're perfect."

His finger traced along the scar on his right jaw, something I noticed that he did when thinking. "Just remember, if he breaks your heart, I'll kick his ass," he said, loud enough that I cringed.

"Keep it down, Adam."

"No, I *won't* keep it down," he replied, raising his voice to nearly a yell. "If he breaks your heart, I'll *kick his ass!*"

"As you should," Logan said, bringing enough swagger into the room to set my heart afire. "Come with me, Adam. Our man-to-man talk is long overdue."

"Wait a minute," I said. But Logan lifted his hand to silence me. He was as serious as a heart attack and I looked on nervously as Adam polished off his beer and accepted the challenge. As they moved toward the outside hall, Logan turned around and shot me a reassuring wink.

"You need to ease off that," Christian said, nodding at my drink as he slumped into a chair.

"I can drink you all under the table," I said with a hiccup.

He stared down his nose, looking as Vlad as a Vampire could with his short beard and apathetic eyes. "A drunken woman is not fetching."

"It's so much easier for you men in this world," I grumbled. "It's hard to relate to Mage women because most of them were brought on as sexual liaisons, not warriors. Most of them weren't even properly educated."

"Aye. And your Ghuardian has tried to remedy that by giving you all the best."

"For what? I haven't seen many independent women who weren't under the protection of a man or organization. Maybe Page is on the abrasive side, but she's more down to earth than some of the Loopty Loos I've run into."

"Well, you can piss and moan about it, or you could be the exception to the rule."

I rolled on my back, gripping the rug between my fingers. "I don't want to be an exception, Christian. I want it to be like this for all the women. I'd like more women to be created, and for there to be more balance in our race."

"Jaysus. The men would go wild over some of the modern lasses coming into your little society. Ever seen the girls in those clubs wearing the shorts that ride up over their arse?"

"And people like you are the reason why women were made into whores."

He frowned and looked up at the ceiling. I tried to keep our banter going because something had changed with Christian since the night of our blood sharing. He looked at me differently. Novis had shared his concern that he might not be fit to guard me because that kind of blood sharing sometimes created a personal bond not conducive to protecting me within the rules. He would become easily distracted. I didn't know much about Vampires, but I wondered if they felt a sense of entitlement to those who had ingested their blood.

"Is it true that your eyes silver?" Page curled up on the sofa, hugging a small pillow.

"Sometimes," I said. "Who told you?"

She smirked and pointed her thumb over her shoulder. "They're drunk in there. Loose lips and all that. Can you show me?"

Christian laughed enthusiastically. "I think I can help out with that."

"You can stuff it, Christian."

"Yes, I certainly *can*," he said suggestively.

I ignored the remark and glanced at Page. "The silvering only happens when I get angry or…"

"I believe *horny* is the word you're looking for," Christian responded matter-of-factly. He leaned in privately to Page. "Been there, done that."

I narrowed my eyes and decided to buy Christian a box of wooden stakes for Christmas. "Why do you ask?"

She rested her chin on her knee. "When it was mentioned, something clicked. It took me a minute to figure it out, but I'd have to see it for myself to know."

"See what?" Logan said in a deep voice, looking tall and delicious as he entered the room. He was wearing Knox's black hat, and his blond hair peeked out from the edges.

Adam came up behind him and I was relieved to see no black eyes on either of them. He looked satisfied and took a seat in a chair beside the faux fireplace, sitting with his legs wide apart.

Logan sat on the floor and wrapped his warm hands around my ankles.

"Page wants to see her eyes do that pinwheel thing," Christian answered.

A deep and guttural purr hummed from Logan's chest and I melted—it was one of my most favorite sounds that he made. There were different levels of purring and growling, and each had its own meaning. He had one particular purr that was reserved for me, because it was at such a low decibel that you could only hear it if you were next to him. He parted my knees very slowly and began to crawl over me.

"Not in front of a crowd!" I shouted. Laughs filled the room and Logan winked.

"I tried," he said with a wag of his brow. That dark gaze in his eye let me know he would have made out with me on top of the queen's dining table to prove his devotion.

Page picked a piece of lint from her black sweater. "I think I have an idea of what's in your genetic makeup if you ever want to show me."

I sat up quicker than a heartbeat. *Hell yes, I wanted to know.*

I grabbed a fistful of Logan's shirt and rose to my feet. "Give us a minute."

He stumbled behind me obediently, sliding his hands around my hips and dipping his fingers into my pants. I pulled Logan into the study and stood with my back against the wall.

Maybe it was the alcohol, maybe it was curiosity to know more about what I was, or maybe it was just Logan being so damn *sexy* in that tight black shirt.

He pressed his hard body against mine and I drew in a deep breath, smelling his wonderful scent. He pulled off the hat, revealing messy hair, and respectfully placed it on the arm of a chair.

Meanwhile, my hands were sliding around to grip his ass and he growled, pressing even closer to me as his mouth tasted the curve of my neck. "I'm afraid if you work me over, Little Raven, the good doctor will not be able to see what it is you want to show her."

"Why is that?" I breathed.

His tongue laved a sensitive part below my ear and kicked my heart into fourth gear. "Because I'm going to carry you to the bedroom and make love to you if you keep this up. Or maybe I'll just close the door and bend you over that chair."

He kissed his way up my neck and I touched his smooth jaw as his warm lips mashed against mine. Logan kissed me slow and sensually, curving his hand around the back of my neck and pushing the hard muscle of his tongue against mine. He kissed me that same way during sex.

The back of his hand stroked my stomach before moving higher. He circled his thumb over my bra and then took a detour, slowly heading south where he gave me a hard massage. I moaned against his mouth and wrapped my arms around his neck, keeping my hands at a distance.

It took all of fifteen seconds before he turned his head to the side and shouted, "Relic, come see."

And then his mouth was back on mine. "I don't think I can stop," he whispered against my lips. His chest vibrated like a motor and his breathing grew heavy.

Page walked in and looked startled.

Logan pressed the flat of his hands against the wall and lowered his head, looking at me like a six-and-a-half-foot predator. Somehow, he managed to pull himself away so that Page could lean in and get a closer look. I tried to straighten my shirt as I kept my attention on Logan's eyes; they dripped sex from every fleck of color that bled from them like honey.

Page suddenly obscured my view. Her finger pushed up my lid and she leaned in closer.

"Fascinating," she whispered. "I never imagined how beautiful it was."

Logan held my wrist as a reminder not to accidentally touch the Relic. I pinned them behind my back and allowed her to look at my eyes before the silvering disappeared.

She scratched the side of her nose and stepped back. "Has anyone ever told you that you were a…" Her lips formed a thin line and I knew what word was coming. She didn't finish because Logan was present.

"Logan, there's something I've kept from you," I said.

His heavy brow sank over his eyes. "What does that mean?"

I took a deep breath and met Page with a worried glance. "You're about to find out." I nodded at Page, because I did not intend to keep secrets from Logan anymore. Those days were over.

"There are different kinds of Uniques," she began. "Four that I know of. They were once called Elementals because their power was different from a normal Mage, and they're rare. But they *are* a Mage. No one understood their unique power, so they were feared and hunted. Part of my gift is learning the makeup of various Breeds: healing, treatments, abilities, limits, and believe me—I could go on in what we know. Some of us specialize in Breeds that are rare, or have gone extinct. Slater was one such Relic."

"I'm not following."

Page closed the door and lowered her voice. "My family used to consult with, treat, and assist Uniques. That was many generations ago. There were more in that time because they didn't hide who they were. Many were killed, kept captive in their younger years, or just disappeared. My theory is that they still exist and live in secret among us. I have never met one myself. Each possesses a unique ability that makes them easy to identify from a regular Mage."

I felt the energy dissipate and I held my hand across my racing heart. I'd never had anyone explain what a Unique was; all I knew was that my light was different. "Which one am I?"

She chewed on her bottom lip for a moment. "I'm not sure if they went by any kind of name during that time, I only know that my family referred to them as Shiners. They were the easiest to spot because of the silvering in their eyes," she said, pointing to my face. "Maybe that's why there are so few of you. Uniques can only be identified if someone witnesses their power or tastes their light. But Shiners would have been easy to spot. People feared those who were different."

I folded my arms. "They still do."

She smiled knowingly and Logan leaned on his right shoulder

beside me, clinging to her every word.

"I'd have to look through my ancestors' books to give you exact details, but Shiners had the ability to move metal. Can you do that?"

A shiver ran up my spine. "Yeah. Only if a Mage has touched it. Something about the energy left behind allows me to manipulate it. Just not all metals."

She began rolling up the sleeves of her oversized sweater and a small line appeared on her brow as she spoke. "If I tell you this, then you can't share it with anyone."

"I promise," I said.

"I mean it." Her brown eyes stared, unblinking. "I know you have a close relationship with Justus, and even Novis, but this stays between us. It could be dangerous."

I held Logan's hand and nodded. She flicked a glance to him and he said, "On my word." That was good enough coming from a Chitah.

Page blew out a shaky breath. "My family believed that you could make a Unique—specifically, a Shiner. They found a commonality between all of them, and that was that their Creator gave them their first spark during an electrical storm. Did that happen with you?"

I shook my head and that's when it hit me. "Do you know how I was conceived?"

"Yes. I looked through the files and your Ghuardian confided in me."

"The Mage light has been within me since conception. I was born during an electrical storm."

Her eyes went wide. "That must have triggered something in your DNA and when you were turned into a Mage, it switched it on. *Fascinating*," she breathed. "If Creators had this kind of knowledge, they could create an all-powerful Mage by simply hanging around during a thunderstorm. I'm not saying you are all-powerful, but that is the perception among your kind. Your light is significantly stronger than the average Mage, so you have the *potential* to become very powerful. I'd never be able to confirm this unless I met a Unique who was an ancient. You also have special abilities that others don't. There's all this talk about common and rare gifts, but honestly, they've documented every single one of them."

"So what does this mean? Are there others like me?"

She shook her head and stepped back. "I don't know. My family broke contact with Uniques three centuries ago. I have a few names, but they could have changed them since then. Did you know that you can hide the silvering in your eyes? The older ones learned how to do it and that's why I have hope that a few may still be around."

"What information do you need from your books that you don't already know?" Logan inquired skeptically.

Page lifted her eyes up to his. "What I know as a Relic is the equivalent of knowing what an orange tastes like, what it's made out of, and the nutritional contents. But I couldn't tell you what tree it was picked from, what name it's called in Mexico, or exactly what it looks like. Does that make sense?"

I glanced up at Logan. "Sometimes during a storm, I feel a deep ache in my bones."

"Uniques once congregated together, and I wonder if they still do," she said. "The only way to learn more about yourself is by connecting with others. The newer ones—if there are any—may not be aware of what they are or that others exist who are like them. Some of the older ones may not know much more than I do. There's just no way to tell. This is so exciting!"

"Is there anything else I can do besides moving around a tire iron?"

She stared at Knox's hat on the chair. "Shiners were able to wield lightning. I believe that's still the rumor that floats around these days, even though they thought it was something all Uniques could do. Some Uniques inherit the same gifts as their Creator, which in turn, made many of them Creators. But you don't seem to have this gift. Could Samil do anything else?"

"Simon thinks he was a mentalist. Sometimes I could hear him in my head, but I don't think I've ever done anything like that before. Surely I would have noticed."

She pinched her chin and looked up. "Sometimes abilities don't come to full potential for years, although you may have had a few episodes of it without knowing. Kind of like flickers from a lighter before the flame is actually lit. If you think back, you might make the connection. You should also be able to push your energy into metal, although I'm not sure what benefit that would be."

My mind went back to the day I'd found Finn chained up in the compound and how I felt my energy pour out through my hands as I swung that mallet. I'd thought about it on occasion after that, because I was certain that I didn't possess enough strength to have broken that chain. Samil's progeny was strong because of our DNA and how he created us, but he had no idea what he had made the day he put his first spark into me.

"Thanks for trusting me, Silver. I'll do a little research and let you know if I find anything different. I'd really like to see if there are other Uniques who are still alive because I think you could benefit from them." She offered a womanly smile and waved her hands together. "You may now resume your positions."

I sniffed out a laugh as she left the room. Despite the news, I felt at peace. Now everything was beginning to make sense, and it was exactly what I needed to get on with my life.

"Why did you not tell me?" Logan rubbed my arm and searched my eyes.

"Because I was afraid, Logan. My light is different—it's addictive. Consider me the gourmet version of a Mage. I have to be careful not to put my light into another Mage or they'll pick up on it. A juicer might not know what a Unique is, but once they taste my light, they'll want more. Just like Nero. There are those who would use me."

His body shifted and he tilted his head to the side. "What do you mean, *use you*?" My heart leapt into my throat as Logan pinned his arms on either side of me in a quick motion. "No one better even *think* about touching you!"

He roared so loud that Justus flew in the door.

Misinterpreting the situation, Justus slammed his light into Logan and sent him flying across the room. A small table knocked over and Logan stood up slowly with his arms at his sides, staring Justus down.

The old Logan would have flipped his switch, but now he had

managed to contain his impulsive behavior. His level of control still put me on edge.

Justus flicked his eyes back and forth between us. "What's going on?"

"I told him that I'm a Unique," I whispered.

Justus turned his attention to Logan and pointed his finger. "Break our trust and reveal this to anyone, Chitah, and I will not go easy on you by a mile."

"Ghuardian, let me talk to him alone."

"Worry not, Mage," Logan replied in a smooth voice. "To my grave I'll take it if that is what she wishes."

"And to your grave is where you'll be if you do not hold to that," Justus said as he looked me over and slowly walked out of the room.

I cautiously glanced up at Logan. "There's no one who can guide me through this. Only my Ghuardian. I'm not sure what I'm supposed to do with all this power, but going into the world alone frightens me. I've been on my own for a long time, and having to live with Justus has been difficult. Being independent in my old life meant being alone and doing things alone. Humans are in such a rush to leave the nest, only to give up their single life and get married. I used to think that was a bad thing—that you were giving up part of yourself. Now I get it. Independence isn't about solitude, it's about someone giving you freedom, trust, and protection. He's gotten better since I started working for Novis, but I'm not sure if I'm ready to leave Justus. I need friends and family in my life. I don't want to be alone."

He kissed my forehead and whispered softly.

"Logan, are you mad that I kept this from you?"

My Chitah nuzzled against the crook of my neck. "I adore you."

Logan moved his soft, wet kiss around my neck and then stepped back with his fingers tucked in the waistline of my jeans. He just couldn't keep his hands away from my tattoo. He finally let go and scraped his fingers through his hair—something I'd noticed him doing more often since I had cut it.

"Are you drunk, Mr. Cross?"

He covered his mouth with his fist, hiding a smile as he watched me with reverent eyes. I could tell by the glazed look in his eyes he was over the legal limit. "I'll be staying here for the night," he said decidedly. "Shall I go turn down the bed and put on my sleeping clothes?" Logan licked his lower lip and slid his eyes down my body.

"You don't wear clothes to bed."

"Precisely."

I got butterflies and smiled. "Can you send Justus in here? I need to talk with him privately."

Logan leaned forward and brushed his lips across mine. "As you wish. Don't keep me waiting, Little Raven. After I grab some sweets from your pantry, I'm going to hand-feed you in bed," he said intimately.

A man after my own heart.

"I bet you'd like that, wouldn't you?"

"Immensely."

Logan exited the room and a few moments later, Justus squeezed through the door and closed it. Laughter and loud talking echoed from the men in the other room. "You wish to speak with me?"

Justus was the only sober person in the house, aside from Page. His prominent tattoo glistened with sweat—an indication that he'd been working out. Nothing strenuous, probably just lifting weights.

I didn't get nervous around Justus very often, but I found myself struggling to find the right words. "I have something I want to tell you."

He tucked his hands beneath his biceps and widened his stance. "Speak."

But it was hard to look up into his sharp blue eyes. He could cut a person to the marrow with his stare, and I'm sure he could tell by my body language that I was about to reveal something that might upset him.

So I took a deep breath. "I've accepted Logan's claim. Do you know what that means?"

By the slide in his jaw, I knew he did.

"It means it's permanent. It means… I want to marry him."

His voice rose angrily as he tried to move toward the door.

"You're drunk, and what he did was coercion."

"No, wait," I said, grabbing his arm and blocking his exit. "This didn't just happen tonight. I was completely sober when we had the conversation, and to be honest, I made the decision when we were separated. That's when I knew."

"Has he given you a ring?"

"You know Chitah customs," I argued. "That's not how they do it. That's not how *we* do it either."

I waited anxiously for his reaction as he mulled it over. "You are young, Learner. And a woman."

"What is that supposed to mean?" I said in clipped words.

"It means you'll change your mind. Women can turn love on and off like a switch," he said with a clenched jaw, averting his eyes.

My hands fumbled with the button on my jeans and I pulled the zipper down. Justus's eyes widened and he snatched my wrists, trying to pull them away. "You're drunk, Silver. You don't want this."

I couldn't help it; I busted out laughing. "I'm not trying to seduce you, Ghuardian. There's something you should see so maybe you'll know how serious I am about this being permanent."

I pulled my jeans open far enough that he could make out one of the paw prints.

Then his eyes flashed up to mine. "Did you put liquid fire on that?"

My brows arched. "Guilty." I zipped up my jeans and held his wrist. "I know it's not easy for you to accept this because you're still my Ghuardian and you don't take a lot of what I say seriously. But please don't dismiss my feelings. I love him more than I ever thought that I could love someone, and we're going to face the firing squad of public opinion, but that's okay. I don't care."

"Logan is still a target," he said with a grim tone. "Retaliation will not be tolerated for the death of Tarek, but it can't be prevented. I've spoken with Leo and there's a possibility that Logan could be arrested. If that occurs, then the punishment for assassinating a Lord is death."

I bit my lip angrily. "He did *not* assassinate him. And I'll stand by him no matter what, even if I have to walk into the fire with him." I softened my tone and found the courage to address another important topic. "What happened between you and Page? I saw a change and… I thought you two were going to become an item."

His cheeks flamed and Justus looked away.

I knew right then and there Page had denied him. By the slant in his eyes, the waver in his voice, and the color of his face. My heart softened, as did my voice. "Don't give up," I said. "Logan never did. He once said something like 'anything worth having is worth chasing.' If you really care for her, then you'll wait. Prove to her you're the man that I know you are. Show her."

He drew in a slow and heavy breath. It was a sensitive topic, but something melted away in his expression.

"Once you marry, Silver, you're free. You no longer need a Ghuardian. That's law. It may not be legal, but it's as good as marriage in my eyes if you have a ceremony."

"Ghuardian, I don't mean that—"

"As you have accepted his claim, you no longer have to call me Ghuardian. You're in his care now."

My heart sank and a bittersweet feeling moved through me as my life was about to change course. New beginnings always meant an ending of something else. My eyes welled with tears—I hadn't realized how profound this moment would be once it finally arrived. I wasn't ready to call him Justus. I thought too highly of him. He would *always* be Ghuardian in my eyes.

A man who had mentored me, taught me the laws to live by, and showed me a stranger could influence my life in ways I'd never imagined. A man who'd opened his home and his heart to an obstinate young Mage with no family of her own.

"If I can't call you my Ghuardian, then what do I call you?"

Justus stepped forward and gently cradled my head with his strong hands. I nervously listened to the thumping of my heart as he leaned in and kissed my forehead, showing me affection in a way that he never had before. One of respect.

A gentle smile spread across his rough features, etching a deep line in his cheek. "If you will not call me by my given name, then I would be honored if you called me by another. It's an honorable name that I have never gone by, nor ever will as a Mage."

"What name is that?"

"Father."

Made in the USA
Lexington, KY
14 July 2014